BEASTS BEYOND THE WALL

ROBERT LOW

CANELO

First published in the United Kingdom in 2019 by Canelo

This edition published in the United Kingdom in 2020 by

Canelo Digital Publishing Limited
Third Floor, 20 Mortimer Street
London W1T 3JW
United Kingdom

A CIP catalogue record for this book is available from the British Library.

Print ISBN 978 1 78863 767 1
Ebook ISBN 978 1 78863 309 3

Printed and bound in Great Britain by Clays Ltd, Elcograf S.p.A.

Rome

In the tenth year of Lucius Septimius Severus Augustus, Father of His Country, Conqueror of Parthia in Arabia and Assyria, Pontifex Maximus

The man ran at Drust, screaming, fat wooden cudgel held high; behind him came others, yelling and shouting. One was laughing, but Drust paid him no more than an eye-blink.

He dropped a shoulder, moved slightly, slammed a fist into the belly of the screamer and then half spun while the air whoofed out of the man and he blundered on in staggering baby steps. He fell and clattered into big Pacuvius, who looked down at him with a mixture of disgust and astonishment, then smashed him with a downward hammer of fist.

'Get them. Get the fat man.'

Drust saw the one roaring this out, the same one who had been laughing. He wore a *bucco* mask, the grotesque features made more lurid in the mad leaping flames of discarded torches; the giant shadows capered on the walls.

Pacuvius started kicking the downed man, whose mask flew off – Pappus, the old fool, Drust saw. They were all *fabula attellana*, the characters of crude theatrical farce.

'On your right.'

Kag was blocking wild swings from another masked man. It was no great trouble, since the swings were *tiro*. Beyond Pacuvius, Tarquinus had been taken by surprise and was down, bleeding from the head while two more masked men rained cudgel blows on him. The torch-bearers had fled, the litter-carriers were wavering and the front of the litter had dipped where two of them were starting to drop it.

Drust spun to the new threat, blocked the blow, turned his wrist, moved his leg and sprawled the man on his back; the mask of Dossenus the Hunchback flew off and the wild-eyed youth shrieked as Drust raised the cudgel.

A boy. Barely into his teens. Drust hesitated, cudgel in the air; these were the night-stalkers, the well-born arseholes who ran the streets of Rome in the dark, terrorising the luckless. Probably he had done this before, the masks and the shrieks and the surprise being enough to send torch-boys and litter-carriers running.

'Six him,' Kag growled, coming up like a cold wind; his man-boy was down, writhing and clutching his groin.

'It's a child,' Drust said.

'Give him iron,' Kag called over his shoulder and headed for the Bucco. The boy on the ground scrabbled backwards, reached for his cudgel and started back to his feet. Drust cursed, shook his head and slammed two blows into the boy's kidneys. He arched and shrieked, fell down and started weeping.

He would piss blood for a month, Drust thought, and a flicker out of one eye made him half turn and block. Two more were headed for the litter; Bucco was trading blows with Kag while Pacuvius was trying to help Sophon; the *lanista* was hurt but the worst part of that was his pride as a trainer of gladiators. Quintus and Ugo were nowhere to be seen, the litter had been dropped, the bearers gone. It hadn't tilted and was still curtained, but the two who had rushed it were tearing them aside.

There was only Drust.

'Oi,' he called out and one turned. He had the face of Manducus the Glutton and was no boy. No *tiro* either – here was a cuckoo in the mix. When the other turned, growling from under Maccus the Clown, Drust knew he had a paired set of *ludus* fighters and they had training swords, twice as heavy as the real thing and heavier than cudgels; they would crack a skull open.

He managed four glissading parries against the pair before one slapped him in the ribs, making him reel and gasp. The other aimed for the head and there was no pull in the blow; it was an egg-breaker, designed to make sure Drust ended up as just a name marked with '6' – killed. Drust wasn't the best, even he acknowledged that – but he wasn't a *tiro* either; he managed to slip most of the blow, taking the main force on the top of his shoulder, which had the padding of his cloak.

His arm went numb and he lost the cudgel. He staggered back and weaved and dodged as the pair closed in.

There was a sudden joyous barking sound and Maccus the Clown turned in time to see Quintus roar out of a side alley, his grin big and wide as the Circus. Maccus had time to see it – the full, white-toothed force of it – then Quintus shoulder-slammed him to the ground and rammed the blunt end of the cudgel straight in the man's open-mouthed mask. Teeth and blood flew out with the screams and bloodied wood splinters.

'Get the leader,' a voice called from inside the litter. 'The Bucco.'

Drust turned. Quintus and the Glutton were dancing. The rest were down or crawling off.

'Get Bucco,' the voice called again and then Servilius Structus stuck his pig-angry face out of the torn curtains. 'Get him. Little fuck…'

Kag was down on one knee but blocking a rain of blows from Bucco. Drust arrived, trying not to wince at the pain in his ribs and hoping he could fight left-handed. Bucco backed off, pointing the cudgel at Kag and Drust; he was laughing.

'Ankle,' Kag said bitterly. Drust nodded, took a breath to see how badly it pained him and flexed the fingers of his fighting hand; the pin-sharp prickles told him feeling was returning.

'Get him,' urged the hog-voice from the litter and Drust cursed it, then followed the fleeing Bucco up the side alley of the Street of Sandal Makers.

They went up through the fetid, clogged alley, leaping half-seen objects, getting yelled at from windows. In the end, Bucco hit a dead end, leaped for the wall, missed and slithered down. Drust stopped, half bent and gasping. The Bucco gave a short laugh, more tense now, but he clearly fancied he had the upper hand and sprang forward. He is no older than the one I felled, Drust thought – but a cudgel is a cudgel.

He blocked it, felt the difference, heard the shunk of edge on wood. Watched the tip shear off his baton. Bucco snarled from under the mask and the naked steel gleamed.

'Not so cocky now, *damnatus*, eh?'

He knew a thing or two, Drust thought. Enough to call Drust a slave condemned to the arena. Enough to know Drust was not so cocky at all when faced with a bloody sharp *gladius* and was looking for a way out. There was a doorway, curtained with beaded strands, and Drust ducked into it. He heard Bucco stamp after him.

The room was small and grubby, the side door of a wine shop. There was a man in a leather apron shaking a sizzling pan over a stove; he looked up with astonishment as Drust came in. Beyond him and the amphora counter were a few crude tables whose patrons looked up from their dice game. Blue reek and rich cooking meat smells choked the air.

'Who the fuck are you?' demanded the cook.

'Dead man is who he is.'

Bucco came through the doorway and the cook yelped at the sight of the steel. Drust leaped the bar and the patrons scattered; they were Vigiles, he saw. Rome's night-watch. Saved…

Bucco rushed to the counter and started over it. Drust feinted running, darted back, grabbed the nearest pot and slammed it into Bucco's masked face. There was a gurgling shout as the man-boy went backwards towards the floor and the cook yelled again and backed away from the mayhem.

Drust leaped back over the counter, gasping and hurting and angry at this delinquent youth for putting him through all this. He swooped up the dropped sword and ripped off the boy's mask. To his surprise, the face grinned up at him. Young, sweat-sheened, wild curls of hair, the eyes glazed a little with pain above a white tunic. A fringe of pathetic beard fuzz – he was just old enough to wear a toga, yet his look was all sly and venal.

'*Missio*,' he said, holding up a finger and grinning at this, the gladiator's plea for mercy.

'*Recipere ferrum*,' Drust growled back – prepare to receive the iron. He meant it; the youth saw it and lost his grin.

'Ho,' he said. 'Just a bit of fun…'

'Get off your Imperator.'

The Vigile who growled it out was grim as old cliff and had his iron-tipped stave up like a spear. Drust stared, confused, and the boy grinned as the slow, sickening realisation spread on Drust's face.

Caracalla. The Hood. Marcus Aurelius Severus Antoninus Augustus, son of the Emperor and Emperor in his own right

– Drust remembered him on the day he had celebrated his elevation, standing with his arms wide, condemning Dog to kill his friend. He had been ten years old then and too far away for Drust to have recognised him now. A thought struck as the other Vigiles approached, starting to climb the counter and put a cordon around the youth.

'Well, I know who you are,' Drust declared. 'Do you know who I am?'

The boy looked puzzled. The Vigiles scowled.

'No,' the boy-Emperor said.

'Good,' Drust declared and slapped a hand down on the handle of the sizzling pan. Like a launching siege engine it catapulted into the air and everyone yelled as hot oil and terrible food rained on the Vigiles.

Drust booted the Emperor of Rome in the groin and fled.

Regio Tripolitania

Five years later

'Who'd have thought,' Kag said, as if there was still mystery left in it, 'water could make men mad.'

Drust thought most men had been mad long before they started fighting over water. They fought over who spoke more clearly to the gods. And land. And gold. Once, he knew, the Greeks had fought over a woman. Sometimes people fought for all these things at the same time and sometimes they fought for the entertainment of others.

They sat in front of the Golden Sweat, which is what the name translated to and made it sound like an emporium of extreme perversions, though it wasn't. It was what passed for a *taberna* here – the 'sweat' was the Latin translation of the local name for a brand of alcohol made from dates.

Kag perched on sacks just unloaded from the back of a cart. Drust sat next to him and both watched the crowds moving through the blood-haze of a dying day.

'I mean,' Kag said reflectively, 'look at them.'

They were motley, Drust had to admit. Billowing robes, white and brown, wrap-round rags, turbans, veils, straw hats, sandals and bare feet – there were all sorts here, every one a hopeful. They came with a handful of greed, a rickle of goats or dates or weave because there was the promise of riches to be made selling to the truly desperate, the ones with spade and mattock and the knowledge that there was an aquifer somewhere, waiting to be tapped. They would wander into the desert and dig until they died, looking for that clear, liquid gold.

'Mad,' Kag repeated. He also said that they should have gone home and were clearly madder than anyone, sitting out in a desert as the water table shrank, waiting for some patron of their patron to show up.

Not mad enough to go home, Drust thought. Not when a co-emperor nursed his sore balls and a deal of resentment for it. He hoped that Caracalla, his brother and the whole festering pack of them were all with pa, the Emperor Lucius Septimius Severus Augustus. That would mean they were far away in the north, at a place called Eboracum, so that old Severus could show his sons how empires are made by conquering the last little bit of this one.

Rome might be empty and the Empire ruled from some shithole in Britannia for now, Drust thought, but he was still not mad enough to go anywhere near the Palatine.

The day died and a dark shape shuffled around with a sibilant slap-slap of bare feet, lighting lamps. They sat in a room of planes and shadows, at a table pooled in wan light. The dark shape coalesced its shadows into an old man who brought olives then wraithed away while the heat died just a little.

Then the old man was back. 'He comes,' he said, and new shadows appeared; Drust felt rather than saw one behind another. In the soft glow, the old man presented a large bowl with a small flask in it and some cups – Kag and Drust exchanged glances; the cold came off the bowl and it sweated. It was full of crushed ice.

The old man poured while one of the shapes slid into a seat opposite. Drust tried to look at Kag, but his upper half – and that of the shape – was lost in the shadows, but Drust heard Kag grunt as the old man poured. They both tasted and tried to be nonchalant, but it was hard. It was nectar.

The old man slipped off into the shadows and Drust saw the shape in full when it leaned across into the light and became a man, which was a disappointment; Drust had half expected something Sybilline maybe with Medusa locks or eyes of fire. Instead he got a leathery face, darkened with heritage. It was hard to judge his height while he sat, but the man still had muscle which age hadn't turned stringy, though it was chewing on it. His face was ordinary, had no marks about it that hinted at destiny or greatness – save for the eyes, which held a controlled violence.

Servilius Structus had made much of Julius Yahya, given him a lion's fangs and roar, a tiger's claws, the omnipotent powers of some ancient hero. A creature spawned by gods, who owned great houses, with a calloused thumb that pressed on the rich and famous. Yet a slave. Not an ex, but still a slave to the Severan family here in Lepcis Magna, their home city. Birthplace of the Emperor.

Servilius Structus was a clever man – a fat, venal, vicious man who had worked up a little empire of his own operating out of the Roman slums of Subura. He traded in grain, sand for the *harena*, slaves, exotic beasts, exotic perversions and occasional pain; Drust and Kag and the others – his *Procuratores* – had been instruments of all that and so they knew his powers.

Yet Servilius Structus had put the name of Julius Yahya in his mouth as if it was the sweetest of poisons that he was forced to swallow. Emperors and generals hang on his every pronouncement, he said. The world is in his palm, he said – so it seemed to Drust just plain wrong that such a Hercules sat here, casting an actual shadow like a mortal. Showing mottled hands and smelling faintly of salt-sweat and expensive perfumed oils, and a strange tang Drust thought might be the smell of success or strength or fear. Or all of them.

Drust didn't look at Kag, though he knew he was thinking something the same. Servilius Structus had sent them all here, ostensibly to get them away from Rome, but there had been something in the way he had done it, in the way he had clearly not expected to see them again, which had made Drust uneasy even then.

Now he was wondering why this man, so rich, so powerful, had come such a long way and at such discomfort to meet with them, who had come at Servilius's request and in secret and at night. And what he had to do with Servilius Structus, who was clearly afraid of him.

Faced with such a mystery, Drust thought, what can you do? You can ask.

'What do you want from us?'

'My thanks for coming,' Julius Yahya said, which threw them both. Then he turned to the shadow of the old man and smiled. 'Abu – *sharbat* for me.'

The old man must have anticipated this, for the cold-sweated cup arrived quickly, the faint smell of it a moment of saliva-releasing joy. It was unreal, all this liquid, Drust thought. This place, lit by soft flickering light, with a bowl of crushed ice cooling them – unimaginable luxury in the middle of crushing poverty, like a heap of gold thrown on a dungheap.

'Thank you, Abu. Drusus, Kagiza – once again, thank you for your attendance here.'

It was his way, Drust realised. He tipped you off balance with this blandness, moved sideways like some snake wriggling for advantage. Julius Yahya turned to the shadow behind him.

'Do you wish wine?'

The man behind him moved only a hand, dark and elegant with economy, as if he was coiled and did not want to break the tension. Julius Yahya took the silent refusal as if he had known all along, turned back to look at Drust and Kag; he held up the cup, little runnels tracing the embossed maenads and grape bunches.

'Thirty years ago, it took 132 gallons of water to make a fat amphora of this,' he said. 'Today we've managed to half it. That wine you are drinking only took about 20 gallons to make and almost all of it was in the growing, not the final fermentation. You still need 5,000 gallons of water every day to grow a day's food for a family of four in countries like this, where the sand eats the water, this day or the next. Even with decent aqueducts and pipes.'

Drust said nothing, but Kag stirred in his chair, then saluted him with the cup.

'Thanks for the drink,' he said. 'Like the dole queues of Subura, I take the gossip with the bread.'

Julius Yahya did not show any annoyance – rather the opposite; he nodded soberly.

'I realise you believe it to be a lecture on the cost of water,' he said, 'and that you think you know all about such things already because it is a commodity to be traded and you and Drust here are part of the hard edge, watching the blood price being paid for successful trade day by day.'

He paused, sipped.

'You are wrong. You have no idea of the cost of anything. Not many people do, and if they think about it at all it is to complain about it. Of course, the Empire thrives on trade and relies on returns from investments.'

No one spoke into the silence that followed; it didn't last long.

'The greatest commodity of all is not grain, or gold,' he went on. 'Or even water in such a place as this. It is trust. The belief that people will honour their commitments. That's what fuels investments and trade, that's what provides profit.'

'So far,' Drust offered, 'this is not news. Any hand-spitting hawker in any city of the Empire knows this. Doesn't tell us what you want from us.'

'Patience, patience,' Julius Yahya said and smiled. Drust was starting not to like him now.

'I tell you this because, if you maintain the narrow field of view you have as regards trade, you may have reached the conclusion that it is immutable – that whatever happens, people will buy and sell.'

He sipped, pushed the cup away.

'It is not. Someone says "no", a simple statement, and the machine grinds to a halt like one of those magnificent water-lifters on the aqueducts with a stick thrown in the wheels. Like them, if the cogs grind to a halt, the effect spreads, terrible and destructive.'

He spread his hands. 'That's the battle I have,' he said, 'year in and year out, to manage, optimise and secure trust on behalf of my... patron. Trust can be assured, assurance comes in many forms and one of them is threat – that's where you come in.'

'I wondered about that,' Kag said. 'Where we came in.'

He had finished the wine and was sitting with a half-smile Drust knew well; it was a warning, that little grin.

'My patron owns an asset,' Julius Yahya went on. 'On this asset depends the assured trust of an entire people. This asset must be found and returned.'

Drust didn't look at Kag and hoped he'd stay quiet. He didn't.

'Patron,' he said, rolling the name round in his mouth like he had the crushed ice. 'You mean master.'

It slapped out on the table like a thrown turd; Drust felt the shadow at Julius Yahya's back shift a little in anticipation of something and tensed. Kag lounged and smiled. Julius Yahya, a slave with more spears at his disposal than a decent-sized country, looked at Kag, the freedman with a glazed clay cup and a smile. Their eyes locked like antlers.

'Patron or master,' Julius Yahya said slowly, 'the term is of no account to you. Neither does it matter who he is. It suffices that he has your patron in his fist and your patron holds you in his. So the world turns.'

Drust went chill from his neck to the base of his arse, tried not to look at Kag and failed. Kag felt it, turned slightly and shrugged.

If what Julius Yahya said was so, then whoever this powerful slave bowed to was a true arbiter of ruling. Servilius Structus bowed to few, and if he got down on his knees to this slave because of who this slave represented, then the power was tangible.

This city, Lepcis Magna, was the birthplace of the Emperor, Drust recalled. He felt the chill of the crushed ice bowl even more intensely than before, put that fact in the counting frame and tallied it up, sending it to Kag with his eyes. Kag nodded slightly.

Julius Yahya was satisfied with the impression he had made and held out one hand, the signal for the shadowed man behind him to step into the light. He wore a conservatively cut tunic, belted at the waist. His head was long and narrow, had strange-lobed ears and was bone white. He wore an amulet, which surprised Drust; he'd had the impression, from the mere presence of the shadow, that this was a man who did not fear or woo gods. In the unforgiving spotlight, all the planes and shadows were like rubbed ivory, the backs of his hands, when he handed a batch of wax tablets to his boss, were pale – but the palms were darker and, Drust saw, not soft at all.

Here was a man who couldn't take sun, not even for five minutes, Drust thought. He would blister and not tan or weather with it, but just scorch and die. He must feel like a turtle in the desert, waiting to be flipped by the sportive cruel – yet Drust did not think he would wait or allow such a thing. And in the shadows he would be deadly as a snake.

'Thank you, Verus,' Julius Yahya said and unfastened one of the tablets.

'The Brothers of the Sands,' he read and looked up with a nasty lip-twist of smile. 'How terribly colourful. Are you truly like brothers? I had heard gladiators had no friends and were allowed to make none.'

'When you are a slave,' Kag corrected flatly. 'Slaves have no friends.'

Julius Yahya did not blink or acknowledge this, simply sat with the tablet in his spatulate fingers and read.

'Six of you, I believe. Former gladiators, former slaves, employees of Servilius Structus in varying capacities.'

'Kagiza,' he said, and then looked up at Kag. 'Is that actually all the name you have? A slave name – it says here you are a freedman.'

He didn't wait for an answer, which was as well because Kag wasn't about to give one, just a cold, flat stare. He had a second name but thought that more of a slave chain than his real one. Julius Yahya went back to the tablet.

'From Thracia, in the south of that land. Father a citizen and Roman legionary in the 13th, died of fever together with your mother – a bad year, it seems. Taken as a criminal – stealing food, which is understandable but still a crime. Sentenced to the galleys or the arena. Lunchtime show.'

When Julius Yahya had started reading, Drust had thought this would be the sort of stuff Romans always recorded, the sort of stuff that was marked up as you fell into the torchlight of the State, but this was a different assessment entirely. This was the sort of stuff Servilius Structus knew, and he would have given it up only under duress or the lure of a lot of money. Or an obligation he could not refuse – Drust began to sweat and it was a cold trickle on his skin.

'Sentence commuted,' Julius Yahya said and stared thoughtfully across at Kag. 'Servilius Structus saw something in you and since you went to work with his stud horses as one of the *aurigatores*, I am assuming you impressed him. What was it?'

Kag didn't answer and Drust realised it was because he knew Julius Yahya already had the details and wasn't about to play the game. Julius Yahya showed no signs of disappointment – rather the opposite by his smile.

'Expert with horses, good with weapons. Sent to the *ludus*, fought fifteen times, won a dozen. Lost but let off on two – well, the *missus* is better than death, after all. Studied philosophy and learned to read, but only because your master hired you out to the House of Acilia to bodyguard young Marcus Acilius Glabrio, I believe.

'You had to make sure the young squit went to his lessons and stayed there. However, it is clear you learned more than he did.'

He looked up and smiled. 'Not much to do but learn, sitting there watching the boy waste his chance. The foundation of every state is the education of its youth.'

Drust reckoned someone famous had said that last part. Kag knew, as Julius Yahya had known he would; he nocked and shot back.

'Dogs and philosophers do the greatest good and get the least reward.'

'I am called a dog because I fawn on those who give me anything,' Julius Yahya intoned. 'I yelp at those who refuse and set my teeth at rascals.'

'In a rich man's house,' Kag said softly, 'there is no place to spit but in his face.'

Julius Yahya laughed easily, his teeth white in the dim. 'Diogenese of Sinope,' he explained to Drust, with the air of someone educating a child.

'You mistake me for someone who gives a fuck,' Drust answered.

For the first time Julius Yahya frowned.

'Drusus Servilius, known as Drust. One of the Caledonii, taken in a raid thirty years ago – a baby, clearly. Unusual to have lived long enough to be bought by Servilius Structus, so you are marked by the gods right there. Mother died when you were nine. You worked with the grain shipments of Servilius Structus and were placed in the *ludus* when you were old enough. Fought eight times – lost six, won two.'

He paused. 'Not of the first rank, nor even the second. Provincial arenas and touring groups. Forum fights, probably, in poor little towns with no amphitheatre. Nevertheless, you should be dead from a record like that. I am told you were let off each time because you acted well.'

People, Drust knew, had the wrong idea about gladiators, thought they all ended up dead unless they won. Since they cost a fortune to keep and train and fought maybe three or four times in a year, the only way they died was by accident, if the patron of the games paid to have the death – or if they put up a poor performance and lost.

Drust never put up a poor performance and fought only in provincial arenas, or even dusty forums where the games patrons were always town councillors who were anxious to spend as little money as possible and couldn't afford death. He acted a great heroic role in carefully staged fights and got away with it for four years.

He did not say any of it, simply shrugged. 'We are not all Spartacus.'

Julius Yahya paused. 'You saved the life of your *lanista* one night while escorting him through the streets of the City. Fought off a dozen thugs. Killed one with only a wooden cudgel.'

'If you hit the right spot,' Drust answered levelly, 'you can kill with a spoon. You shoot badly from your little tablet and have missed most of the marks. It wasn't me who killed him, nor was he a thug, but a fighter from another *ludus* hired for the assault. And it wasn't a dozen, only a handful. Wasn't the *lanista* either, it was Servilius Structus, who was the owner. The *lanista* is the trainer and ours was a fuckster called Sophon. I wouldn't have pissed on Sophon had he been burning.'

He remembered the grinning face of the boy-Emperor, his finger raised, his laughing call of '*missio*' a minute after he had been manically trying to kill Drust with a naked blade. Caracalla had known it was Servilius Structus, had included a couple of decent fighters in the mix to make sure the fat man suffered. The why of that remained a mystery, but there needed to be no reason for it other than a brat youth's overprivileged desire to hurt someone.

Servilius Structus had shrugged at all Drust's questions, though he was pale and sheened when he did it. Said it was an old affair and not to worry. Said it would be best, all the same, if Drust stayed out of Rome for a time.

It was a shock to Drust, almost as much as when the fat old man had pushed the *rudis* at him, wrapped up in his manumission. The sight of that simple, engraved wooden blade was a shock, like falling in an icy ocean, that left Drust gasping; in a moment, no more than an eye-blink, he had gone from slave to free man.

Freedom had been a bitter fruit, he remembered. A slave who fights in the *harena* has four meals a day, his accommodation paid for, his medical ailments tended and, if he is a gladiator, all the sex he can stand from whores provided by Servilius Structus to the perverted attentions of high-born who should know better.

The new freedman Drusus Servilius needed to provide all of that for himself, and the only way to do that was to continue working for Servilius Structus for the sort of money which guaranteed bonded slavery anyway. The only difference, Drust soon realised, was that he was out of the sandpit and trusted now to escort the more valuable trade cargo as far from Rome and the attentions of an annoyed boy-Emperor as possible. Chariots and horses and second-rate fighters to provincial *spectacula*; studs to Africa; grain and special white sand for the Flavian back to Rome – it took Drust and the others far out of the City for extended periods. When he came back, he and the others were called on to provide other services, involving pain and blood and pleading from the victim.

The other thing he learned as a free man was that ex-slaves are scum. He'd learned that long since about gladiators, who ranked one step below whores. Which was just about right, Drust thought. One makes a living by being stuck, the other gets life by avoiding it. Same coin, different sides. He had thought that leaving the life, becoming a freedman, would elevate him. It didn't; people knew, and hiding his branded hands in his tunic, even on the hottest days, simply marked him out more.

'Now you are head of these co-called Brothers of the Sands,' Julius Yahya went on, 'which includes our philosopher stable hand here. As Heraclitus says: "Day by day, what you choose, what you think and what you do is who you become."'

'Fuck you,' Kag answered amiably. Drust saw the man behind Julius Yahya seem to shrink a little, as if collecting all his tensile strength. He wanted to say something, lay a hand on Kag's arm, but did not move nor speak.

'We are *Pocuratores*, after the *procuratores dromii*,' Kag added.

There was a pause, then Julius Yahya chuckled and nodded. The *procuratores dromii* were the ones who moved out into the middle of chariot races, scooping up the wreckage, the spilled bodies, dragging out the dead and screaming, the broken horses, scattering fresh sand to soak up the blood and raking the rest smooth, all so the entertainment could go on. It was dangerous work, unsung and poorly paid – Servilius Structus had called them that for a joke. Amongst themselves, they were the Brothers of the Sands.

'Sibanus Servilius,' Julius Yahya went on. 'Strange name, but he is a Garamentes, a *mavro*. Your former master took him on as a charioteer – I see here he raced thirty-six times, won nineteen, came second twelve, unplaced the rest. He also seems to be a scout of some sort for your little group.'

Drust simply stared. *Mavro* – charred – was the what Romans sneeringly called anyone with too dark a skin, though that was muted these days, since the Emperor was more dark than fair and his sons only a little lighter. Sib was lithe and invisible in the night unless he smiled. He did not often smile –

and he was not Garamentes, but from somewhere even further south in the far deserts.

'A desert raider originally,' Julius Yahya confirmed and sighed. 'Throw a stone from here in any direction and you will hit half a dozen like him. It was by the saving grace of the gods that he was captured and swept into the arms of Servilius Structus, who seems to have an eye for talent. Otherwise he would have been one more wasted young life.'

'Now, of course,' Kag said quietly, 'he bleeds for the Empire.'

'The Empire saved his life,' Julius Yahya answered with no seeming malice. 'Swept him up when the garrison of Tingis would have crucified him – they don't have games there, as you know, so their entertainments are more crude and final.'

They did know. Same as they knew the others on his list. Manius Servilius, a man with the seeming benevolence of a priest of Ceres welcoming the faithful to a harvest festival, with his crinkle-eyed smile and even teeth, slightly yellowed from some Eastern concoction he chewed when he could get it.

He might shake you with one firm, strong hand, but the other would be spinning a *sicarii* dagger, that curved sliver of deadly Judean knife that was like a fang to the snake. He could move silently and kill with no scruple at all. He was a bad man to find looking at you down the length of a barbed arrow nocked in a drawn bow.

He was from somewhere in the desert, too, but Sib was wary of him, saw darkness and demons there; Manius did not care. He had ended up in the Ludus Ferrata, the Iron School of Servilius Structus – fought sixteen times and won them all, but he earned his freedom working with Drust on the less savoury tasks Servilius Structus had on offer.

Ugo was a short-coupled flaxen-haired expert with a long axe – from Germania according to the books, but he was really a Frisian. None of those names meant much to him or the tribe he came from and neither did the weapons he fought with on the sands – he'd been a big, armoured ring-fighter, the *hoplomachus* – but the axe was part of what he was. He was grizzled, venal and a chief in his own lands, or so he claimed. He could take orders, think for himself and was always coinless.

Quintus Servilius was made from bold strokes and unshaded colours, from his long legs through his lean body to his vagabond smile. He had been everywhere, done everything and had a sense of humour stropped by experience into a sharp edge that appreciated folly but extended a surprising gentleness to fools. He had fought as a *retarius*, with net and trident, a role that required speed and cunning and timing; he had been good at it for a dozen appearances in the provinces, but crowds hated the *retarius* for fighting almost naked, which was too Greek, and him in particular for not dying; the *retarius* wore an open-faced helmet and the crowd loved to see one killed, see his face as he died.

Drust remembered him in the street fiasco, coming out of the alley like a roaring wind. He had been laughing then, as he had on all the other occasions he had fought as a paired team with Supremus, the Gaul. When Supremus took the hook through his heels and was dragged off to be knocked kindly on the head to make sure he was truly dead, it was Quintus who claimed the body, made sure it was cleaned up to be properly buried. He had laid his knuckle-marked hand on it, having nothing else. He had been the only one who bothered.

All of this was known only to the Brothers and Servilius Structus and it bothered Drust that this Julius Yahya, a slave smelling faintly of cinnamon and roses, should know it too. It was as if they were stripped bare and on the selling block.

These were the *Procuratores*, the Brothers of the Sands, men who knew Drust and each other, bound by memories of sweating fear in the dim undercrofts of shabby amphitheatres, of frying goat in strange desert holy places, men who fought back to back and side by side. They had walked with the dead and been splashed with the commingled blood of them and cowards, total bastards and ugly souls of all stripes, colour and creed. Their ears had shared the last words of the dying and the gasp, however fake, of lusted love.

They had, one glorious year when they had been forced to travel with the Army, enjoyed the role of liberators, marching into villages and towns with the metalled men of the 3rd Augusta putting down some rag-robed rebellion that had no part of Servilius Structus, who only wanted his massive carts rolling safely to Rome. The Army all thought the carts held grain for the dole, but it turned out to be sand, fine white sand for the Flavian; Drust and the others had almost died for it.

They had let all the prisoners free in their liberated town, Drust recalled, stolen anything of worth not nailed down and handed the power to local leaders – then watched as they hanged all 'collaborators' from the lintels of their own homes, so that they looked like strange gourds.

They had watched people they knew die less than gloriously, people whose last words weren't to their emperor, or their country, but usually just 'Oh, fuck' or 'Don't let my ma know I shit myself'. Some they had killed, standing above them as they knelt, waiting for the iron as the crowd howled.

In the end, Drust thought, you started drawing back, which was the first sign. You drew back from everyone, as if putting some distance between you would make it easier, for them and you, when the time came. Even as freedmen. That was when you took the easier routes, the lesser cargoes where the only danger was likely to be kicking the arse of some frantic pilferer scrabbling away at a fast lick. Servilius Structus had known it as he knew everything about his properties. They were reaching the end, losing their edge.

Drust didn't want anything tougher than escorting carts and Julius Yahya saw it, like a good angler sensing the moment when he can tug the hook a little and snag a fish reluctant to take the bait. He held up that imperious hand again and a scroll was slipped into it. He unrolled it, turned it to face them and tipped it slightly so that it rolled at them, limping on the seal. It was white as a new lamb, the seal like a drop of fresh blood.

'That is a letter with the sort of power a legate would envy,' he said. 'It will get you through any barrier officials of the Empire might otherwise put up.'

Drust simply stared at it. Julius Yahya did the hand and scroll trick again, smiling.

'All you Servilians – what a strange brotherhood – are about to be made richer than gods. This is a contract. You each will sign it or make your mark. Completion of it will make you wealthy for five years. Or ludicrous spendthrifts for one.'

His smile grew stiff. 'Of course, money is of no use if you cannot own anything you can sit on.'

Drust caught his breath. Freedmen had power but there was more…

'You offer us citizenship?' he asked and Julius Yahya nodded, then Kag laughed and Yahya's head jerked; for a moment, the mask fell and showed the feral.

'You scorn citizenship?'

Kag shrugged. 'What does it profit me? Even a slave can sue in a court since the days of Nero – but those with money will bribe for their law. Make me a citizen and I can vote – if I can afford to travel all the way to the City, because it has to be done in person, on the day. I may become one of the *honestories* or one of the *humilores* – either way, it does not matter since whether I am elite or scum is no longer recognised in law. We are both the same – irrelevant, because we have no say in affairs of state. The emperor rules as he will.'

Julius Yahya stared and Drust almost wanted to shout his delight aloud at Kag's having struck him hard enough to render the man speechless. Drust didn't shout, but he squirmed; it was a prize to some, but becoming a citizen of Rome was not what it had once been.

'Better that than mere freedman,' Julius Yahya managed to answer, and he had to fight to control the hoarse bitterness in his voice. 'Or a slave.'

'You sit there as a slave,' Drust said, 'so it may seem glittering to you. Being a freedman was once such to us, but being a citizen never was – the money in this contract is the most of it. If, as you say, it makes us richer than gods, then, as a freedman already, I might even be able to purchase you.'

There was utter, compelling silence; the hate rolled off Julius Yahya like heat from a furnace.

Drust leaned forward and held up both hands, backs towards Julius Yahya. 'A slave is bought entire. Everything he is. Every waking moment and even his dreams if the owner wishes it. His every day of labour belongs to the owner and, for most, that life is harsh. When age claims strength, the slave is discarded and a new, younger one purchased.

'No matter what happens now, this mark stays unless we lose our hands,' he said. Julius Yahya looked at the knuckles and the ugly letters on each one – E.S.S.S. Drust saw him twitch slightly, a gesture of his right hand up to his left shoulder; there was where Julius Yahya had his own mark, discreet and easily hidden on a prized slave; Drust smiled.

'*Ego sum servus Servilius*,' he intoned. 'Every gladiator has these *stigmates* or something like them. We get them on our hands where they cannot be hidden, for we are slaves of the *harena* and doubly cursed in any society.'

He placed his hands on the table, palms down and looked at them. 'This is how a slave is made – not birth, not breeding, not Clotho or any of her sisters of the *Parcae*. Egyptian pine wood bark, one pound; corroded bronze, two ounces; gall, two ounces; vitriol, one ounce. Add pain and shame as you will. Mix well and sift, wash knuckles with leek juice, prick in the design with pointed needles until blood is drawn. Then rub in the ink.'

He locked eyes with the glitter of Julius Yahya's stare. 'But you know this. No matter how clever – like you, like Kag here – you can never truly hide what you are, can you? You just become valuable and more coin is invested in you than any middling merchant might spend on his children. Yet you are not free, though you can claim more of it than a fisherman throwing his nets at dawn, or a litter-bearer straining to carry the likes of Servilius Structus out of Subura. You can claim more of it than us freedmen, still marked with servility and sitting in front of you and having to follow the whim of that same Servilius Structus – and your patron if we make our mark on this document.'

He leaned back. 'A freedman makes his own way in the world. All that is required is to become valued, whether citizen or not. What need of citizenship when I still need to tuck my hands inside my tunic?'

'The philosophy of the New Man,' Julius Yahya growled.

'No one sprang fully formed from Jupiter's brow,' Kag fired back. 'We were all New Men once.'

'What next?' Julius Yahya said, outraged. 'Legions led by generals from the Germanies, with hair to their shoulders?'

'Rome ruled by a *mavro* African?' Kag suggested softly and Julius Yahya's head snapped up. He managed a smile, then pushed the scrolls towards them.

'Either way, it is life-changing.'

Drust stared and felt Kag look at him but did not dare look at him. Life-changing…

'I might add that your patron, Servilius Structus, also earns reward for your endeavour,' Julius Yahya went on.

'Oh, that's all right then,' Kag said, laconic and hoarse. No appeal from that quarter then, Drust thought. It was as Servilius had said when he had told them where to meet Julius Yahya – do as he says without quibble. Farewell. I do not expect we will meet again.

He had hired them out, Drust had thought at the time. Like stud horses past their prime. Now, he thought, it is we who are about to get fucked – we haven't been hired, we have been sold.

Julius Yahya perhaps saw what Drust was thinking and smiled.

'We must exercise ourselves in the things which bring happiness, since, if that be present, we have everything, and, if that be absent, all our actions are directed toward attaining it.'

Kag shrugged diffidently at that. 'If man's life is ever worth the living, it is when he has attained this vision of the soul of beauty. And once you have seen it, you will never be seduced again by the charm of gold, of dress, of comely boys, you will care nothing for the beauties that used to take your breath away.'

'*Aplaudo*,' Julius Yahya said with soft admiration and genuine delight. Drust was tired of them shooting some hairy philosopher at each other; it was always the innocent bystanders who got hit, he thought. Besides, he was being ignored, as if two lovers were in the room, and he did not care for that; there was too much at stake and too much unknown to play at that.

'Well, we will all become good, rich little citizens,' he said harshly. 'I'm happy with it. I am afraid to be happy. Each time I get happy something bad happens. I saw that on a wall in the Forum once.'

The noise was shocking and surprising in equal measure; even Julius Yahya was taken aback and everyone turned to look at where Verus, the silent, shadowed man, had laughed.

'What do we have to do for all this happiness?' demanded Drust into the silence that followed.

Chapter One

Britannia Inferior, six months later

Simple enough. Fetch back a woman and child captured by bandits. 'The Epidi,' Julius Yahya had added, rolling the words round as if it was a fine wine. 'They are all bandits. A certain woman must be returned; she has a child and will be made biddable by threat to it, so you should bring it too. A boy. Both are slaves – do not listen to anything to the contrary, for the mother will say anything, of course. You will bring them back to one Kalutis in Eboracum, which I believe is what passes for a city in Britannia Inferior – the whole Empire is now ruled from it until the Emperor is done with the skin-wearers. Verus will also be there and will take charge of the woman and child and pay you all. You are then advised to enjoy the sights of the Empire, anywhere but Rome.'

Bandits. What a fine word that was, Drust thought, summoning up a rough romantic lot, all swagger and bravado. The Epidi were far from that. They did not exist, of course, save as a name Romans had given to the Blue River People, the Stone Clan, the True People of the Black Bear and all the others, far up to the northern forests. Drust's people once, though they were worse than strangers now – he had been in his mother's arms when taken. He did not think this was why he had been chosen.

The Army was there already, suffering and tramping miserably round bogs and marshes and dark forests, trailing a snail slime of blood and bodies. Still, there were a lot of them and some brave and skilled men could surely be found for an enterprise like this, but it seemed the matter had to remain among as few people as possible.

'Then pay the ransom,' Kag had said. 'There is always the chance these bandits will honour it and release this woman alive. Political, was she? A chief's daughter held hostage to fortune?'

'The man who took her has dared to say "no" to ransom,' Julius Yahya had replied, which made Kag and Drust look at each other.

Love or politics then, Drust thought. Or both, and involving the purple-born of the Palatine. Either way he did not want it, did not like it, was afraid of it, as if some shadows from Dis had lurched out of the Underworld and snagged him, dragging him straight to the very place he did not want to be. He had left the proximity of the Palatine Hill, fled south to evade the vengeance of an imperial brat with sore balls – and here he was being bribed to march back there. It was a trap. Nothing would make him walk into it…

Julius Yahya had looked at him, the way you do when you have snagged your trout.

'The man who took this woman and child was called Colm. I believe you know him.'

Drust knew him. All the Brothers of the Sands knew him as Dog, but when Drust thought of him he saw a face twisted and raving, hands clawing at the air and held by chains. Begging Drust to come back to him, to come back and die for what he had condemned his woman to.

Drust didn't know his woman, but Dog had always had one somewhere, so it was no surprise. The surprise was what he had done for this one – joined Bulla, the bandit chief. Six hundred men ravaged up and down Italia while Severus was conquering new territories. It took the Senate two years to catch Bulla, but eventually offers of gold got the bandit chief betrayed and then the whole band fell apart. Dog, with his usual luck, had joined too late to profit and almost left it too late to escape.

Was the child she had Dog's, Drust wondered? If Dog had waited, Servilius Structus would have manumitted him, too. Instead, when he heard Dog was off with bandits he sent out his *Procuratores*.

'I don't want him dead,' he said, 'I just want him to wish he was.'

They spent a long time hunting him after Bulla's band fell apart and, in the end, had to trail back to the City, disgruntled and empty-handed. Yet Dog couldn't stay away from Rome, and when he came back, it was inevitable he'd be found; mercifully, there was no woman or child with him, because Ugo beat him until his piss bled, then they left him chained up in the cellar of one of the slums he was hiding in.

Dog begged and ranted about how they should just let him loose, that he had been punished enough; Drust heard later he was to meet this woman again and that she was depending on him, but he never would have made it anyway, since they broke his leg.

Drust thought about this a long time – then scratched his name on the contract and looked at Kag, who blew out his cheeks and did the same.

Neither of them could explain why, but all the others had made their marks when they learned that Dog was involved and yet none would admit that he was the prime reason; they pretended it was money, or the chance to be a citizen.

Drust stuffed it in the back of his mind, along with everything else he didn't want to think about, and filled the space with all the problems of shifting north as quietly as they could.

–

The boy saw them first, coming up west along the southern line of the Wall. Short Hairs, but they had the reek of Long Hairs and the same worn, nub-end look, save for their weapons. The boy had a corner of his cloak – a rough-weave affair, but still a cloak – up over his head against the rain and the bottom was shielding his find of sticks. Good sticks – straight and with no knots – make good mattock shafts, he thought.

He moved slowly but determinedly to find his da. Strangers were always worth a warning, even now when there were a lot more of them than the boy had ever known.

His da wasn't listening at first, too busy working out the best way to bottom-haft a mattock. Top-hafting was easier but made a bad mattock – a couple of dozen pulls would slide the metal collar off and the annoyed owner would bring it back. Since half the owners were the Army, it didn't do to sell them top-hafters.

Bottom-hafters were harder, of course. The mattock blade collar was already forged and so the shaft had to fit in it, which meant shaving a bit here and there, working it up the shaft until it bit hard enough to dig up wood. You could cut the spare off the top but it was a skill, judging the length and thickness of a good stave so you had a fair shaft of mattock…

'Strangers, da. New ones.'

'No old ones, son. All strangers is new.'

The boy was right, all the same. These were new strangers, for sure. There had been a few sights of late, now that the army was back – three emperors, too, if all the tales had it true. The north was in turmoil again and the rumour was that the three emperors – father and two sons – had moved beyond the Wall of Hadrianius back to the Northern Vallum. That had been built years before, then abandoned and unmanned for long enough for the Wall of Hadrianius to be refurbished – the boy's da remembered that as a young man working for his own da. Mattocks and pickaxes in big demand – the north-facing gates had been taken out as not needed and the Army lads now had to scramble to put everything back, dig out the ditches, replace the stakes.

Now it was all change again with the Emperor and his sons. The Wall of Hadrianius didn't know where it was – the chief of the tower's eight men had set them working to make it look like his part of the Wall was defended and ready but the Empire seemed to have washed on beyond it and he was scratching his head with confusion because he didn't know if his tower would even be needed now. Didn't know if he needed mattocks or hammers. Didn't know if he was on his arse or his elbow.

And there were strange sights. Men on little horses wearing the pelts of yellow, spotted beasts, carrying little throwing spears. They had hair like matted birds' nests hung about with silver and bone, but the strangest sight about them was that they were burned black as the forge charcoal. They came riding along the Wall from the west and spoke no language anyone but themselves understood, yet they were Army. They'd laughed when he'd seen their unshod horses and offered to shoe them for a price; they'd made it clear none of their mounts wore iron shoes nor ever would. They let the boy touch their skin to see if it smudged on his fingers, watered their dog-sized horses and rode on.

One of these latest strangers was burned the same way, which was what had reminded the forge-man. These latest weren't quite as strange, the boy's da thought, but more like to give you chills, way they looked at you. Cropped chins and cropped hair, Roman-style, but it was growing out while the flat, hard-eyed gaze was the same as those of the beasts beyond the Wall...

Drust led the way to the man and boy, knowing them for what they were. Scraping a living in the shadow of the Wall of Hadrianius, called Votadini or Brigantes by Romans who liked to label such things neatly even if they had no true idea of who these people were; if they still remembered it, the man and boy would know themselves as something different. The man worked a forge, made nails and tools, and the boy would follow him one day, living in the same round, thatched mud hut until he died on the same packed-earth floor.

The man's name was Ander, the boy Young Ander. Kag gave Drust a look and shook his head, smiling. Too poor to even afford names was what he didn't say aloud. Which was rich, Drust thought, coming from a man who used only one and that as short as he could make it.

'I need a shoe done,' Drust said once the greetings were over. 'Can you handle it?'

He spoke Local, that mix of bad Latin, worse Gaul and whatever the tribes spoke here, and saw Ander's eyes widen a little. The smith wiped his hands on a handful of wet leaves and nodded, looked at his staring son and half smiled apologetically.

'Wants to touch your burned man there,' he said in the same language. 'Stop gawping, lad,' he added to the boy.

Sib came out from under his leather hood, his face gleaming with rain slick and his teeth startlingly white. He reached out one hand, fingers splayed, as if to wipe his stain down the boy, who backed off. The boy stared, fascinated, at the fat, brown-pink callous of his palms. Sib laughed.

'You from around here?' Ander asked, fetching his tools. He nudged the boy to start the bellows going; the forge growled.

'North of here once,' Drust replied. Quintus brought up the mule, smiling his big shit-eating smile; Anders merely glanced at him, then Sib, then the others. He can see we are not all from round here or anywhere close, Drust thought.

'You with the Army?'

Drust shook his head. The man got to work, seeing he shouldn't push more, and Drust was pleased with that for it meant the man wasn't greedy. Knowledge was valuable in these parts and he had no doubt Ander would pass on what he knew, for favours mainly and to anyone.

'Makes you wonder,' Ugo growled, working a finger into his mouth in a vain attempt to dislodge some of his last meal. He spoke Latin but Drust knew Ander understood that well enough and he let Ugo know it with a slight movement and a warning flick of his eyes.

'What?' he demanded.

'This place. Why it's worth all the trouble?'

Sib laughed. 'Because emperors want it is all.'

'We are all slaves,' Ander said suddenly – in Latin – raking the flames until they turned yellow and blue. When he became aware of the stares, he looked up, half defiant, then shrugged.

'What? True. Even emperors. Held slave to wanting what they don't have.'

'You've got some Greek in you,' Manius declared, approaching in time to hear this. He was long and lean and good-looking in a hawk-like way, in the way a well-made knife was. Had to be treated the same way, too.

'What's Greek, da?' the boy asked, holding the mule's head for his da to measure shoe to hoof.

'Folk from far away,' Drust answered, 'who think too much about all sorts. Who commands in the tower?'

Ander bent and fitted while his son held the nose of the mule and soothed it. There was the smell of burning hair, a plume of reek.

'Tullius.'

'Good sort, is he? Friendly?'

Ander worked the shoe back into the coals and pumped until the flame turned blue-green.

'New,' he said eventually, having weighed the worth of the information and decided free was best with men such as these. 'Aulius went north with the army.'

Drust let him work, turning away to stare at the rain-darkened wall, the whisper of mirr and the faint shape of the tower. Behind him was a mile fort. Beyond the tower, exactly a mile, would be another. Beyond that the Wall leaped the river on a three-arched bridge.

Ander had confirmed what he had expected: the original Wall garrison had been scooped up by the emperors and pushed north, to the old Vallum and beyond it – old Severus wanted some last hoorah for his old age, though most of the talk was of how he thought the Army and his sons were idle and spoiled and needed some campaign discomfort to sort them out. Everyone else in the court, forced to move to this cold, wet place, thought he had been here too long.

So a new lot garrisoned the Wall of Hadrianius. Well, made no difference – Drust had a carefully wrapped answer to all officious questions.

The shoe went on in a hiss and another cloud of blue reek. Manius watched and the others milled and idled. Kag followed Drust's gaze to the Wall.

'Lot of trouble for a place like this,' he said. 'What's it got that everyone wants? Rain and a too-big sky, far as I can see. How is that worth dying for?'

Drust looked sideways at him and smiled. Ander had finished and the mule was lifting and stamping, favouring the new shoe.

'Who'd have thought,' Drust said pointedly, 'that water can drive men mad?'

Kag remembered and laughed. 'Pay the man,' he said, nodding to the smith.

Chapter Two

Tullius was tall and thin with an undershot jaw that pushed his bottom teeth over his top lip. Kag was sure the man suffered from dental aches and that that was what made him morose and miserable. 'If he was a horse,' he managed to whisper to Drust, 'I'd have put him down.'

Drust was sure teeth contributed, but he was also certain Tullius was on edge mainly because of the silent, sullen people clustered in the rain round his little tower. They were the families of legionaries uprooted and sent off north with the Army and also those of the men who replaced them. No doubt Tullius's own family was among them.

Tullius did not want more problems, so he scowled and used his fearsome face like a stick. It no doubt worked well on recruits, but it broke on the marble of Drust and the others. Tullius saw it and was made wary.

'Felix Tullius,' he said eventually. 'Decanus, 5th Gallica.'

A Decanus commanded eight men. The 5th Gallica was an auxiliary cohort which had been in the north for years – any Gauls left in it had long since lost accent or contact with the place they had been raised in.

'I have business north,' Drust said and Tullius snorted.

'You and half the world,' he answered. Yet he saw they were neatly cropped. He favoured a barbered beard himself, in the hope of hiding his affliction, but you might as well have tried to smuggle an elephant behind a hedge, as Sib said in his *mavro* tongue.

The laugh that followed, the language he did not understand and the general, casual air of being unimpressed made Tullius more uneasy still; he fell back on truculence.

'No one goes through without a permit,' he growled. Drust eyed the plodding trail of people north of the Wall, heading into the rain mist in search of their menfolk. He knew about half of them had permits, if that. He knew that Tullius was awash with livestock, small coin and the favours of women desperate to rejoin their husbands, where the shelter and food and coin was.

'The Emperor should never have let us marry,' Tullius growled. Drust had sympathy; since Severus had signed the decree, legionaries had formalised the informal – but that meant the Army now had to cater for wives and children; neat, traditional camps were now leprous with a barnacle cluster of huts to accommodate them. And they had to move with their menfolk.

'I have a permit,' Drust said and took Tullius by one arm, steering him to where there was shelter from the rain. It was an act so shocking, so singular, that Tullius was at first too stunned to resist and, by the time he thought of it, he was released and staring at a scroll. He did the only thing he could: he read it and Drust saw the flesh ruche on him when he saw the seal. He knew the feeling from the first time he had laid eyes on it too.

'North?' Tullius managed. 'To the Northern Vallum? Beyond it?'

'That's what it says.'

Tullius rolled the scroll and handed it back as if it burned. He wanted to ask what they were going to do and who they were but now did not dare. The scroll's seal and the revelations combined to push him beyond wariness; he found he was afraid, did not know why and was afraid of that too.

'There are beasts beyond the Wall,' he managed.

'No one up there is a friend,' Ugo called out, marshalling mules towards the tower gate.

'No. Really. Beasts. Strange, horrible creatures. Men are dying… the Army…'

Tullius stopped, clapped his lip shut so that his bottom teeth almost touched his nose. Drust knew the man was afraid he had said too much to people who had the ear of those in power, those who could use such a seal on a scroll.

They had all been hearing of the casualties all the way from Eboracum and even south of it. Hundreds. Thousands, since the emperors had tramped over the Northern Vallum to bring the Caledonii to heel. Thirty thousand at least, the rumours said; the Army was bleeding to death.

But now there was peace and the Army was trailing thankfully into winter quarters. The beasts beyond the Wall were sleeping sullenly again.

Drust watched Tullius, measuring him for what he knew now and what he might have known before. They'd come up through Gaul and Inferior and met with Kalutis, their contact in Eboracum. He was a *ptolemy* and Drust had wondered how he suffered the cold and damp, but the Egyptian didn't offer more than a shrug when asked.

He told them he had spread the word of their arrival far and wide, which made Drust stiffen.

'Hide in plain sight,' Kalutis said cheerfully. 'Six gladiators sent from a *ludus* in Rome all the way to give demonstrations – now no one will question your travelling about.'

'Do they have a fucking amphitheatre in this pest-ridden country?' Sib demanded.

'Isca Ausgusta,' Kalutis replied mildly. 'Calleva, Moridunum, Deva Victrix and here in Eboracum, to mention but a few. But you lads are more used to sparring in forums, so I hear.'

Quintus laughed at the Egyptian's barb, but Sib bridled and said: 'Fuck you.'

Kalutis had ignored it all, then told them to bring the woman and child back to him. Drust saw the truth in his face – the Egyptian had no idea who would call for them after that and made it clear that Drust and the others were done with the business after delivery.

It had worked out as Kalutis planned; they went from point to point and no one bothered much – but this was a long way past the lie of giving fighting entertainments and Drust watched Tullius closely and learned nothing. It was clear that news of the presence of gladiators all the way from Rome had not filtered this far north.

Tullius turned away and started shouting for men to clear the cluster of people away from the gate and make way. The displaced stood with blank stares and the detritus of their lives dripping in the rain while six men and eight mules splashed past them and out the northern gate.

In half an hour the tower was lost behind a fold of hill and the last of the plodding hopefuls with them vanished into darkening rain mist, heading up the eastern road with its handy, neatly placed marching camps and garrisons and road gangs. Drust called a halt and they made shelters and fire. After they had eaten, Sib and Ugo stood first watch while the others clustered round the spitting fire, shelter cloths looped round their heads.

'He speaks well,' Kag said.

Manius offered Drust one of his leaf-wraps, knowing it would never be accepted; he was chewing already and his teeth were either bloody with that or firelight. You could track Manius by the little pools of seeming blood which were his spit from such chewing; it came, harmlessly, from some crushed nut in the mix.

'Who does?' Drust demanded.

'Julius Yahya,' Quintus said and grinned. 'That's because he can speak philosopher, or so Drust tells me.'

'He speaks softly,' Drust interrupted, 'but I am sure the club he has is solid and large.'

'Verus-shaped,' Kag agreed. 'But you are right – a soft voice turneth away wrath, or so it is written.'

'Once wrath has his back to you,' Quintus answered, 'you stab the fucker in the neck.'

There was only silence on this truth of this and Drust, when he looked at Kag, knew he was going back over the details. Dog. A woman and her child.

'Is it his child, d'you think?' Kag asked, not for the first time, but that had all been talked to the bone before and no one was wiser.

'This mysterious patron really loves this woman, then,' Sib said. In the dark, his ebony face was all shining planes of firelight. He put another half-dried log on the fire and raised his head, nostrils flaring slightly as he smelled the fog.

'Strange,' Quintus said, grinning his wide, firelight-bloody smile, 'what a man will do for a woman.'

'In your case, what he will do to her,' Ugo corrected, then frowned. 'But it is strange. Who is this woman? The wife of a senator perhaps? Or the Caledonian king? Who is the boy – Dog's son, or just a bit of baggage he has to take to get the woman?'

'Money,' Quintus said laconically. 'It will be about money.'

Manius snorted, looking up from where he was softly, gently, whetting. Iron sharpens iron, in men and blades he would say if asked. Few asked, preferring to keep distance from a man putting a meaningful edge on a blade.

'It was not money. He has not asked for any and has fled back to his homeland.'

He paused and looked sideways at Drust. 'Your homeland, too. I am thinking this is why you were chosen by this Julius Yahya.'

'Then he chose badly. I was a child when taken from here. Dog is also from the dark north, but he is nothing to do with me. Whoever thought of it should have chosen someone else.'

'Whoever he is. Whoever chose Julius Yahya to choose us,' Sib said and Manius grunted and whetted his daggers.

'There is no mystery there,' Quintus said. No one answered him; no one wanted to voice it. No one wanted to think about the Palatine and the plots.

'This is not helping,' Ugo growled. 'It will be about loans. These Epidi owe money. An emperor is no different from Servilius Structus when all is said and done.'

'No matter who wants it, or what this woman and her kid have to do with it, the problem is simple and no different from others we have solved,' Quintus added. 'We have runaway slaves and we have to get them back. We go, we kick in the door, kill everything that is not her or the child and get them back. Then we take the reward and spend it.'

No one laughed. It was about as much tactics as they had ever used and always worked in the end.

But the nag of high-born plots was on everyone, especially Drust. He remembered that night in Rome, when he had kicked Marcus Aurelius Antoninus Caesar in the balls. Hard enough to make his eyes pop, he had said to Kag later, when they were alone and touching heads in the dark.

'Had they even dropped?' Kag had answered, the grin in his voice.

'On the floor of a wine shop, for sure.'

They had laughed, drunk with wine and having got away with thumping a brat emperor, but it was not so amusing now, Drust thought. Has he found me – us? Is this revenge? Yet The Hood had legions at his call – why would he need to be so convoluted?

'Kidnapping,' he said later in the quiet, head to head with Kag, who met his gaze briefly, shrugged and looked away.

'Not Dog's style,' Drust persisted. 'He steals a woman who may or may not belong to some purple-born. He takes her and a boy, presumably her son, all the way beyond the Empire, all the way back to a home he hasn't seen in...'

He stopped. Almost long as me, he suddenly realised. No one would know him there, same as no one will know me, nor I them. He had a momentary flash, of warmth and a smile, the touch of a hand on his face and her voice, sad with longing: 'Be safe'. His mother.

He looked at the ground, seeing nothing. Be safe. She had died when he was too young to know it properly and Servilius Structus knew more about it, though he had not said, and Drust, though he had burned to know, had dared not ask. In the end it had faded like the brand of his slavery; he looked at the backs of his hands, as if insight was inked there.

'Should have slit Dog's throat when you had the chance,' Manius said. Drust shrugged and Sib laughed with no mirth; they had all been there, so they knew why he had not. Drust still saw Dog's cruel little eyes, fever-bright with anger and...

desperation, the sweat-dried black spikes of his hair defying gravity and caked with his own blood.

'Better get some sleep,' Kag advised. 'It is almost light and as soon as it is, we're up.'

Ugo nodded and simply rolled into his big cloak. He slept with the innocence of a child – they all did, not because they were morally pure but simply because of the way they spent their lives. The gladiator way. There was no room in any of them for the stupidity of weighing one man's skill against another's on a bigot scale – it was measured on who lived and who died.

That's why no one had liked Dog, Drust remembered. He had always been too good at the business of fighting and killing and sneered at those he left behind in the provincial arenas as he and Calvinus the Gaul had become the pair to watch. All the way to the Flavian in Rome, where Drust had seen the price of such fame in the games to celebrate the elevation of Antoninus to the purple. Matched pairs, to fight *sine missione* – no possibility of reprieve to the loser.

It had been Dog and Calvinus, of course. The crowd loved them, bayed for them – and Antoninus, ten years old and already homicidal, but not yet The Hood of Rome's dark streets, had set them at each other in the end, despite the boos of the crowd. A marker, Drust thought, for how he was going to be.

Dog killed Calvinus and walked out while the slave dressed as Dis Pater, god of the Underworld, was still smacking the corpse with a hammer. He had a face on him, Drust saw, like weeping granite and one hand clutched the amulet he always wore – Sol Invictus – so that the rays of bronze needled blood between his fingers.

Servilius Structus had realised that something had broken inside Dog and had spoken to Drust about giving him the *rudis*, making him a trainer, but never quite got round to it, though it was said Dog had chosen a Roman name in expectation of his manumission.

Servilius Structus had put him with the *Procuratores*, but Dog had been too wayward for that and still a slave besides; it irritated him that everyone else was a freedman. He had never quite been one of the Brothers of the Sands and Drust had not been surprised when he turned rogue and bandit, only at the seeming reason for it. A woman? A son?

Maybe it was the same woman. Maybe another, but whoever it was she was the belonging of someone else, perhaps not any of the high-born but some speculator with clout and gold who wanted his slave or hostage back.

Perhaps Dog had thought to steal her and the boy for ransom, then realised what he had done and simply ran, all the way out of the Empire in the hope that would keep him safe. If he had to do that, Drust thought, feeling the chill of it, the patron had a powerful long reach.

If so, he reckoned both woman and boy were dead long since and they were on a fool's errand – but for a great deal of reward. It still made no sense he could see and he nagged himself with the wondering at some sort of revenge by The Hood. But the man was an emperor. He led the Army because his father was laid up in Eboracum. Here was a man who openly declared his hatred for his own brother, Geta. Who had drawn a sword at his father's back during a peace meeting with the tribes beyond the Wall – he had no need to be coy about revenge on the likes of the Brothers of the Sands, a band of sometime gladiators who had never been of the first rank when they had been in their prime.

Whatever happened, Drust had realised when Servilius Structus had said his farewell, this was the end of the *Procuratores*; he had an idea they all had realised that.

Drust lay back and listened to them breathe and stir. They were all the same, yet not the same – none of them fought in the same style in the *harena* and so were allowed to form friendships, since fighters of the same style were never matched one to the other; it was dangerous to make a friend you might have to kill one day.

Yet they shared the fear and the stink, jokingly called themselves the Brothers of the Sand in that fatalistic, wry way you do when Dis, ruler of the dark Underworld, walks at your elbow. Yet it had stuck, grown, become more. As a result, they lived with people, not beside them, and when they formed, they formed against all wind and tide, so that anyone who failed that test was never looked on the same.

These had looked on one another at one time, at the worst time, and they had made their decision for this time based on that. It was all you could do.

Drust smelled the wet-dog tang of himself, heard the mules shuffle and grunt. He wondered what he would do when they went their separate ways. He slid off into the little death of sleep.

–

In the morning, Drust spoke with Kag about Dog and the woman and child, gnawing it as if it was a morning meal while he fought with the mule pack lashings, crossing this rope, holding that one tense while Kag made some knots look easy and secured the packs.

'Euclid of Alexandria invented this,' Kag said, seeing Drust's scowl. 'Look – it is shaped like a diamond and if you get the angles right…'

They secured the pack, then Kag slapped the mule with satisfaction.

'What happened?' he asked. 'To Dog? After we broke stuff on him. I thought Servilius Structus would kill him or give him the *rudis* but he did neither.'

'I think Servilius Structus favoured the latter,' Drust said. 'But Dog was mad by then.'

'He did have some abnormal eye contact,' Kag admitted and they laughed.

'Abnormal eye contact,' Sib repeated, coming up in time to catch the conversation. 'Things you say, Kag – Dog was crazed as a basket of burning frogs. Should have been put down long before. They did it to Felix Spurius for less.'

Kag checked Sib's work, leaning back to put some serious tight on a rope. 'To be fair, Spurius did kill the woman.'

'Accident,' Sib said, cocking his head to one side a little. 'So I heard.'

'The boy he killed was an accident,' Kag corrected. 'The woman might have been – but since it came two days later, even Servilius Structus couldn't ignore it.'

Drust thought about it while they walked into the dawn light, aware now that they were completely alone in a rolling landscape of forest and scrub-covered hills. Beyond the Wall…

Felix Spurius had been the bastard by-blow of a tanner, taken in by Servilius Structus for no good reason Drust could see. But, then, none of the ones taken in had immediately discernible talents and only time told what they were and if they were useful. Servilius Structus had a weakness, a pride in his uncanny ability to spot special people with talents that could be nurtured in his service – but Felix Spurius turned out to be something darker, a *lusus naturae* with sinister tastes.

He had been sentry on the wagons coming up from Ostia with the Egyptian grain, bound for the Temple of Ceres to be distributed as dole. Servilius Structus had bribed his own wagons in with the State ones, an old trick. It was dark, because wheeled traffic was only permitted after sunset and the area round the temple was thronged with the desperate, bobbing shadows spattered by bloody torchlight.

The boy came out of the dark, Felix Spurius explained, and he thought he was coming at him with a knife, but it turned out to be a brass pot, his only possession. He was eight, maybe nine – hard to tell with the starving – and dying to be first in the queue. Literally. Picked the wrong one.

The Vigiles accepted it, Servilius Structus accepted it, but no one else did; the boy had sixteen wounds, which was a little overkill for self-defence. Two nights later the same thing happened to a woman trying to feed her destitute family. This time her nose had been cut off, real slow, real savoured.

The Vigiles arrived and the law served Felix Spurius up, babbling and screaming his innocence, to the equally starving animals at the lunchtime show at the Flavian Amphitheatre.

'Can't say Rome hasn't a sense of justice and humour,' Dog had said at the time, but he wasn't smiling by then. He'd watched his paired mate dragged off out across the same sand not long before while the ten-year-old boy who had ordered it nodded and smiled. In a week, Dog vanished to join Bulla and a month after that Drust and the others were sent to find him and show how long and determined was the arm of Servilius Structus.

Now that same Servilius Structus had felt such an arm, stronger and longer than his own. And so, Drust thought bitterly, we are served up. Well done is ill paid…

They led the mules out just before dawn and moved until it grew to full light, then stopped, unpacked and laired up for an hour or two, then moved on. Kag rode, but the others were used to feet and unused to riding.

'I won't get blisters on my soles,' Quintus said, grinning the white frets into his tan, 'but I surely will get them on my ass.'

They laughed at his bad pun, moved steadily, a line of men and mules twisting through the sullen green, where the devil witches swirled leaves up and raced gleefully across the land and the cold seeped in, despite the warm work they were doing.

Everyone was dressed the same – nondescript breeches, tunics, cloaks and the wrap-round hoods the locals wore against the cold. They had started to grow out their hair and suffered the itch of untended beards. Drust knew it wouldn't fool anyone into thinking they were locals and it wasn't meant to – but they carried no visible weapons and the most revealing things about them were the mules and the packs. Just one more band of ragged hopefuls – either lost haulers for the Army or adventurous traders.

They came upon the scarred trenches of fields which had been tended by the villagers before they fled. The round houses were cracked open like eggs, the roof thatch burned off and some of the beams collapsed to char; the stones were blackened and the ruins had all been abandoned long enough for weeds to have colonised the rafters. Raiders might have done it. Or the Army. It made little difference to those who had lived there.

The winter sun died like a trembling blood-egg. The men crouched in a broken hut whose walls would hide the firelight and ate hot for once, grain porridge with salted meat in it.

Afterwards, they buried all the remnants after they had shit on it; they did not want any other visitors seeing who had been there and the shit left a lingering smell of man that would keep the foxes from digging it up.

Drust went over the notes scraped in a tablet, squinting in the poor firelight, trying to work out distances and matching it to food and water. The mules took most of the food and, though they could forage, that meant wasting precious hours of daylight while the animals cropped and chewed. In the end, fodder would give out and not all of the mules would make it; Kag had tallied that in, so that on the return journey – with at least one mount for the lady and the boy – they would be lighter. The boy, they had been told, was six. Or eight. Old enough to ride if put to it, and he would need to be, for they would be moving fast, running for their lives.

The others listened closely, for everyone would have to know in case they got separated – or was the only survivor. They had been on many other trips and knew how things stood.

'What did Julius Yahya say about this contact?' Sib asked. He had asked before and been told but gnawed at the bone of it because he was an uneasy hound. Drust told him – there was a man, a tribal of sorts, called Flaccus in Roman lands but whose true name was Brigus. He was the one who kept Julius Yahya's patron informed of matters in the Land of Darkness far to the north and he was the one who knew where this woman and child lay. More to the point, he was the one who knew what she looked like and what her name was.

Sib sat, nodding and saying nothing. Quintus voiced it this time.

'Doesn't get better with the telling. No one knows what she looks like? Or her name? I hope we can trust him or we will be Greek-arsed.'

'I don't like informants,' Manius said in his soft-voiced way. 'Especially locals. Better to scout on our own.'

'I think he is a *frumentarius*,' Quintus offered, and there was silence for a time as everyone turned that over and over. It was likely, Drust thought – the *frumentarii* were part of the Army and yet no part of it, folk who went out searching for grain supplies in the area of operations. They had long since branched off into looking for everything else, too – the Army's spies.

'Two hundred armed men,' Drust pointed out. 'That's what Julius Yahya was told stand in our way. We need to know more about them before we make a move – and we will get one throw at it. Knowing is key – and all we have is this man, this Brigus. It's not that no-one else knows what she looks like or what she is called – it's that they don't want us knowing until we are there. Until it is too late for us to go asking questions.'

'Questions that would make us run from this,' Manius answered bitterly.

'No one runs from the amount of money on offer,' Quintus countered, grinning.

'If we fail, we are all marked as "6",' Kag pointed out. 'So let's get the dance of it sorted before we leap into the *harena*.'

There was no answer to the logic, which was colder than the night, so they wrapped up and sat close together for the warmth, trying to imagine a bigger fire. Two voles came out, attracted by the warmth of the firestones and popping out of holes almost in the embers; Drust watched Manius feed them little bits of hard cheese – these bold little pirates had grown used to fires and humans when this place had been full of talk and people and lives.

Drust felt Kag's heat as the man sidled closer, felt the breath on his ear.

'Who is this woman?' he asked. Another question asked many times on the journey, so that it had become a game. A stolen queen. A hostage princess. The best whore the world has ever seen. The Emperor's mistress… it went round and round and foundered, every time, on the rock of Dog.

What had Dog to do with her? Why had he stolen her and fled to the beasts beyond the Wall, as if that would keep him safe? What did he want for her? For the boy?

The talk flowed, soft and low, fired in short bursts so that Drust caught only the odd mumble of it like a distant wind: 'I prefer a straight blade…' 'I shot three…' 'who was that woman…? 'remember Paegniara?'

That last was Quintus, talking to Manius about a *mavro* they'd known who had been one of their desert informants. He was putting soothe out at Manius over this Brigus, but wrapping everyone else in it too, telling the story to people who already knew it but liked to hear it again anyway.

'Remember him, Sib? Best translator we had,' Quintus said. 'Always told it true…'

'Not like the others,' Sib admitted. 'Not like Juba.'

Everyone had known Juba at some time or other, the moon-faced translator who wore Roman tunic and military boots and really wanted to be in auxiliary armour, that ring-linked coat which marked you as Army. That and a longsword for fighting from horseback – all the toys. No one would give him it, all the same, because he was a rag-arse *mavro* and nothing to do with the Army and not one of the *Procuratores* either.

Juba wanted all that gear because he feared his own kind and what they might do to him, even though they weren't the enemy, just people in the path of their journey – or greedy raiders out of the desert looking for water. Always water.

The desert tribes bought and sold everything, especially information, so Drust and the others pounced on a few now and then as they moved about with their mules and goats and camels and herds of women and children. They were hawk-nosed and blank-faced, but the eyes followed you, Drust remembered, even when you couldn't see them; even other *mavro* were afraid of the deep desert tribes.

Juba feared them most of all. Called them 'goat-fuckers' in his broken Latin, a patois of so many dialects from the people he had worked with, spattered with bits of Army slang to add to his swagger. Even his name was false; it had belonged to some Numidian king.

Malik the camel-handler put Drust right on Juba the day he turned up to brokenly ask for permission to include some purchases of his own with their cargo; it was fair, for everyone had a little personal trade and it was right of him to ask rather than try and smuggle it. He was neat and polite but was always frowning when he listened to Juba beat on one of the desert tribesmen, with slaps and a harsh language.

'This one is rag-arse spy, for sure,' Juba would announce and Drust would ask him to ask the tribesman if he had seen any raiding parties. Then, one day, Drust turned and asked Malik.

'You heard Juba. What did he say?'

Malik made a little head-bobbing movement, a tribal gesture which was part apology, part negative. 'It is not for me to say, I think.'

'Is he translating truthfully?' Drust demanded, staring hard at him and holding up a copper chit that would allow him a certain weight of trade goods. Malik reached and took it, not in that snatching way that others did, like the voles taking crumbs from Manius, but slowly, between finger and thumb, showing he was unafraid and that this was not him accepting a bribe.

'He translated it more or less true, but he added threats you did not make. He always does, to show that he is beloved of the Romans and their Army. He said to the tribesmen that you instructed him to tell this worthless dog that he was to be blessed into your *pantheon* and from henceforth should call himself Unbeliever Redeemed by the Gods.'

That day, Drust kicked Juba out. Malik worked for them from then on and the others called him 'Paegniara', the name for the fake fighters who did comedy turns during the lunchtime shows in the *harena*. It was a scathe but meant kindly enough; they had foul names for everyone, including themselves and, after all, Malik was just another robe in bad sandals.

Yet it was he who revealed the true nature of Dog.

Chapter Three

'They are careless,' Sib said, hunkered down by the blackened ring of stones. 'I do not know this land well, so can't say who they are. Four, maybe five, with a pony or a mule. The leader wears Army boots. This is a week old.'

He sat back on his heels and wiped wet soot from his hands down his tunic, then looked up at the horizon, a gesture Drust knew was nothing to do with threat – he had seen him do it once or twice before and thought the scout had spotted the flicker of a reflection of sun on metal. Not that there was much sun, Drust said, and Sib, half ashamed of this tic, said it was nothing, that he had just been looking at the sky.

Quintus laughed, but gently, and Drust thought he knew what Sib meant; that great, free dome, stuttered with little dark clouds, washed grey and sodden. The wind that hissed out of it made the grass ripple and the forests growl like beasts.

Beasts beyond the Wall...

The commander at the Western Fort had muttered that after studying the scroll and the seal on it. That was after looking Drust up and down, then sideways at the others. He clearly did not know what to make of it, all these men who were trying to look like traders but handled weapons with easy familiarity – but he had other problems to deal with and he was only an *optio*.

The Western Fort was the last one at that end of the Northern Vallum. There was what had once been a good road leading to it, following the line of the river the locals called the Cleansing One, but that road wasn't on the line of march the Army had taken. They had gone up the east side and the road there had had all the work put in to make it less of an overgrown nightmare, the old forts refurbished into marching camps.

On this side, the road was weed-choked in most places and the forts, all wood and turf, showed a decade of neglect and pilfering; most looked like raddled harridans after a fight in the street.

The Western Fort housed most of the *Petriana*, auxiliaries of a mixed unit, horse and foot. They'd had a bad time of it during the summer and were glad to be in winter quarters. The *optio*, a short, squat Illyrian, was worried about supplies, fretting about losses and frantic about rumours of the Caledonii to the north having come out of their holes, winter or not, which would force everyone back into the field. He was equally afraid that the Maetae to the south would do the same and cut him off. He and his men had tramped into the mists of a place the maps marked as the 'Land of Darkness' and were glad to be out of it, even if where they were was only a little less bleak.

'Fucking beasts,' he kept muttering. He did not understand why Drust and the others were leaving the fort and heading out into the winter and the Land of Darkness. Nor why ex-gladiators should be here at all and this last he said with a lip that curled out all the disdain he and everyone else had for such fighters. The fact that they were ex-slaves only added to his dislike.

When it came to it, Drust had realised long since, we are gladiators – then, now and always. We belong in the *harena*, the sand. Not out here.

Manius voiced it, defiant and embarrassed at his own horizon-staring. 'This country is too much skyline. It goes on and on,' he said, 'until the world's candle burns out, like my life. You can travel on and on to it, but you never reach it – like my life. I tried to leave my life once, find another one in the world. But, well, you know...'

Drust knew. They all knew. They had sat in *tabernae* and listened and watched people, normal people, unchanged and unchanging it seemed. Bakers, dock workers, family men with children. Normal people, who loved their family and didn't kick their dogs, who honoured their household gods and treated their slaves well enough – and who went to every games at the Flavian or the Circus and howled for the blood of people like Drust.

They made gods out of us, Drust thought. There was Pacuvius, a bent-nosed, broken-eared thug Thracian, ugly as a burned boot, who had his name on the walls – *suspirium puellarum, Pacuvius Thraex*.

Yet the fathers of those swooning girls sat apart and made it clear they did not want to breathe the same air; the only people worse than us, Drust thought, were the female fighters, novelties with names like Achillia or Amazona who fought dwarves or the condemned – but old Severus had finally banned them from fighting.

Now all the odium fell on the play gladiators, the young and free who went into the *harena* to show off, or who voluntarily bonded themselves to a *scholae* because they needed the money. Even if you were the son of a senator you got curled lips at making yourself a slave – but once vainglorious *nobiles* such as these had been lauded and the act of leaping in to fight had been widespread, so much so that the Divine Claudius, in between drooling, had been forced to try and stop it.

Still, even emperors could not stop joining in now and then – Commodus had strutted round wearing a lion skin and thinking he looked like Heracles, when most people were outraged and scathing, saying he looked like a slave or a whore, or both. The actual fighters stayed tight-lipped on it, but everyone knew he had never won a single bout that hadn't been fixed.

Yet the women who adored Pacuvius were the same ones who declared their love for any heart-throb fighter. These *amorates* could lose their minds over them sometimes – tales abounded of senators' wives running off with bent-nosed growlers; the *Procuratores* shared those tales back and forth now round the fire, laughing at memories but no longer amazed at what folk were capable of.

These bakers and shoemakers, these butchers and wheelwrights and those who did nothing but live on State dole, drank and argued about fights and fighters knowledgeably, complained about techniques, about who had fought well or badly, about odds. They knew the price of a gladiator and nothing about the cost. Drust had once thought he could slip unseen into their midst, forget the world he had been in and embrace theirs. Until he found he had nothing in common with them – he had the wooden sword, but the ring barrier of the space he had occupied separated him from them forever.

Even though he wasn't of the top rank, Drust was an exotic perversion to the women there, so that walking off with a heavy-breasted daughter of the *nobiles* had been no chore. They took the front-row seats and howled and clutched themselves – even wet themselves – then came down to the festering underworld of reeking dim afterwards.

He had slipped into the wet of more than one and they had collected what they had really come for – the sweat off his balls, or the discharge from their love to mix into a potion to make husbands hard or wombs fertile. Once or twice Drust took an old, rusting dagger – they had a score or more for just such an event – and gave it to the woman, if she warranted it by skill or enthusiasm. Or paid solid coin.

A rusting dagger stained with the blood of a slain gladiator was used to part the hair of a rich bride on her wedding day, an old tradition that gave a wedding that final touch. Drust wondered if the proud husbands ever considered how the bride had gained such a prize.

The blood, of course, belonged to whatever beasts or *noxii* – the criminals – had been slain in the lunchtime show that day; the Ludus Ferrata of Servilius Structus seldom lost a man, and if they did would not sully his last by selling even the least part of him to some high-born whore.

For a week after he had the *rudis*, Drust had walked around with people who were unarmed, their lives filled with the ability to go anywhere without censure, to eat what they liked, to never see a heavy wooden practice sword or shield. To not know what it was like to wake in a pen, waiting for someone to unlock the door, to wonder if this was the day, the one where a slip, a stumble or the whim of some no-chin with more money than sense made it the last one.

On the last day of the week, Drust went back to Servilius Structus, who merely smiled knowingly out of the venal pouch of his face, nodded, bonded him with contract and money and made him leader of the *Procuratores.*

'Caledonii,' Quintus said, jerking Drust back to the present, the misted wet hills, the little circle of old black in a slight depression, where the red bloom of the fire would have been hidden. There was a rotten-tooth ruin of an old hut, smoke-blackened turf walls crumbled. 'That *optio* said the Caledonii were out. The beasts beyond the Wall.'

'Pony,' Manius said, uncoiling from studying the tracks. 'Or ass. A single one. They are no raiding party, they are scavengers looking for blown-out homes like this one. Or the dead of both sides, left behind. They were headed south and spotted us, I think. Took off east to try and avoid us.'

Kag squinted at the hoof marks. 'Not ass or mule. Pony. One of those tribal ones without shoes. Can live for a week on what grows here and a lick of tarn water.'

'Scouts,' he added. 'From them Caledonii.'

Sib grunted dissent.

'Scouts would have a pony each. Or none at all – you need to travel fast, not plod along dragging a laden mount. At least, they do everywhere else I have been. Drust – you know these people? Is that how they work here?'

Drust had been in his mother's arms when he'd been taken from here. He had told them that so often there was a groove worn in his tongue, but some things he knew, such as how the Caledonii were not one people but lots of little tribes: the Stone River Tribe, the Fox Clan, the People of the Wolf, the Skin-Marked. He did not know who these people were and that was all he knew – that and the language, though he was not sure how much of that he could remember from his mother's teachings.

'Scavengers,' Sib said, then rolled spit round and let it go, as expressive a gesture in wasted moisture as you could get from a man of the desert.

They all looked, one to the other, and did not need to voice it. Dog had been a scav, one of the worst they had seen – was he out there now, watching and waiting with his woman and child and 200 men?

Drust stared at the horizon you could never reach; somewhere beyond it, he thought, a handful of men slithered through the land, either scouting for some clan or other, or looting and stealing. He said as much, trying to shred the image of Dog.

'It does not matter,' Manius growled. 'They have seen six men and eight mules who are nothing to do with the people of the Caledonii. Scouts for Dog will ride to him at once with the news. Scavs will come on us, looking for profit.'

-

Scavengers. Out in the sun-drenched hills north of the City, silently cursing Dog for having driven them out here, Drust and the others had encountered scavs.

Drust and the others came out of the last raddled streets of some blackened village into fields of fig trees, half trampled by studded army boots. The Heavies, the iron-clad legionaries, had gone through here some time before, slamming it with fire and sword as if it was the barbarian hovels of the north and not the civilised farms and villas of Italia.

But when war got in the hand and head, nothing and no one was safe, as Ugo growled when they prowled up to it. Drust was just glad the Army was with them, in the shape of a Ses and a unit of Batavians, all nervously moving their horses through lands rumoured to be thick with the men of Bulla Felix.

No one knew much about Bulla Felix. Even the name simply meant 'Lucky Charm', the amulet you give as a birth-gift to new child of Rome. Folk who swore they knew said Bulla was honest and upright, cunning and unable to be caught. That he had 600 men only, same number as the Senate. That he never killed anyone if he could help it. A new Spartacus, they said. They also said he was dead.

'Let's hope that's true,' Quintus said fervently, but no one thought it likely.

The Sesquiplicaius was called Pacula and he had been running the remnants of his turmae up and down the Italian hills for weeks. He had half of the twenty-something men he'd started with, the others mostly sent back because their horses had foundered, or they'd become sick, or just malingered. They were a millaria, a big unit of Batavians, but soft after some time in Italia. The Decurion had sprained an ankle, the Duplicarius had been trampled by his own horse in the night camp, which left Ses Pacula in command. It was a weight too heavy for him and he was cracking under it.

His eyes were dim as he scooched over to Drust and the others and squatted, back to a gnarled fig tree in a parody of everyone else, who did the same with a friend, swaying until the weight of their bodies found a balance. They were in armour, stiff leather that didn't let you sit well and still spring up to fight, so pair-squatting like this took some of the weight off. Drust felt sorry for the Ses, the young-old man who had no one to lean against. His men didn't even call him Ses, just Pacula, and that lack of respect ate him.

He seemed to feel it that day, too, giving out with a short sigh and rubbing the rash at the side of his mouth, a strawberry-coloured affair of spreading oval that seemed to creep inexorably even as Drust looked, following the curve of his cheek.

He was a lonely person by inclination anyway, the Ses. He didn't socialise – certainly not with the ex-slave gladiators who had turned up on some crazed hunt for one of Bulla's band calling himself Dog – but it wasn't elitism, he just seemed not to be quite there, like a drifting cloud Drust felt only as a chill presence now and then.

He was chill now, telling Drust that his gladiators should push on up the furrows through the thick fig trees which might hide any number of desperate men. Bulla Felix was taken, or so rumour had it. Or dead. Or escaped. No matter the truth, his band was splintered and fleeing, but still dangerous and particularly in closed terrain where they could leap out on horsemen. The Ses suddenly looked at the smoke smudges from the burning buildings and frowned; there were faraway screams, shrill as bird calls.

'How long has that been going?' he asked.

'Couple of hours,' Kag said and the Ses nodded, looked nervous and passed a hand across his face, as if some cobweb had fallen on it.

'Not right,' he muttered. 'These are not bandits here. There will be trouble over it.'

He stopped, looked at Drust and blinked. 'Where was I?'

Then he lowered his head a little and shook it wearily. 'Fuck,' he added, levered himself up and shuffled back to where his men sat their horses, patiently waiting for the disdained gladiators to do their job for them.

The smudged smoke spilled out, seemed to sprout up from a hundred different sources and blacken the sky. They sorted out gear, got ready to move on and Paegniara came up.

There wasn't any need for him to be here; he had come back with them on the grain ships, which was better than leaving him behind to be picked off by the desert raiders, who hated him. Besides, the Procuratores liked him – he could easily have stayed in Rome with Servilius Structus, but he came out with them to hunt down Dog. Now his face was sheened with sweat and creased in a frown.

'Tell me who these are, please,' he said, and they loped after him, wary and watchful as cats. Four hundred yards away, in a square that passed for a forum in the village, lay a scattering of naked bodies. Six in all, looking strange, eldritch, until Drust realised they had no heads. He looked at Kag, who sent men left and right in a wary prowl of scouting.

'Are they the enemy here?' Paegniara asked. 'I know we hunt bandits and they are the same everywhere, but these are beheaded. I do not know the way of matters here and perhaps the Army does that

in their own lands – in my country it is what you do to hated people you have captured. Yet, if they are not the enemy, I am also puzzled. I had heard this bandit chieftain did not commit atrocities such as this.'

'Scavs,' said Kag grimly. 'The tribune in charge pays for heads of bandits brought in as proof they are dead. These are not Army.'

'This one is a woman,' Manius declared. Quintus grinned like a rictus and shrugged.

'This one is a child,' he pointed out, toeing the limp bloody little body with a gentle foot.

'These also can be bandits,' Sib pointed out and then spat sideways, 'to a tribune who does not care much.'

The Ses sighed when they told him, then did what he had to do and sent men to search. They finally found the heads, stacked in a neat pyramid near a fountain. In the drying foreheads, above the astonished, agonised blind stares and the blood raggles of the necks, were the crude carved letters, turning black in the heat and clearly put to mark who had taken them, so he could claim them later.

Cns.

Dog.

–

Drust ordered a camp made in the soot-blackened hovel. It was a bad place, with no defence to it at all. He sent Kag ahead on a mule, because he could ride best and he wasn't Sib, who could move like a silent snake. His task was simple – don't move like a silent snake. Look like a *tiro.* Track them and be careless, get spotted for it and then run, as if in panic.

'If they are scavs and not scouts for Dog, we need to know. Bring them to us if they are scavs,' Drust told him, 'else we'll be crawling all over these hills with them itching our backs until Dis floods.'

They made quick, expert preparations among mud-brick ruins, the roof fallen in and the old outbuildings sagging and leaning and sorry. It had never been a grand affair and was solitary, as if the folk who'd lived in it had chosen the joy of having no one to bother them. The price for it, Drust thought, was that you had no one to band with when blades came at you.

They hunkered down and waited. The rain sifted, fine as baby hair and doubly soaking as a result; there was almost no shelter in the ruined hovel.

'Dog and you come from the same place?' Ugo asked, squatting against Drust's back in that comfortable pair-bond that let them sit and keep off the wet ground.

'The Land of Darkness,' Drust said back over his shoulder and waved an encompassing arm. 'My mother told me I came from the Red Hawk Clan, up in the Village of the Narrows, under the shadow of Mount Malicious.'

Ugo grunted. 'Not friendly names, none of them. What about Dog?'

'From the Red Hills, far to the north,' Drust said, remembering what Dog had told him once. Remembering also the bitterness there.

'He was from the Blue Face People,' Drust added.

'His face is the same colour as everyone else's,' Ugo pointed out, then Drust felt his shoulders move in a shrug. 'Except when he gets angry. Then it turns the colour of a baby's slapped arse.'

The Blue Face People made stained skin marks on the faces of their warriors, tokens of deeds done, enemies killed, all of that. Dog's bitterness came from the fact that he had none – he was taken as a toddling boy in a raid by a rival tribe, the Black Wolf Clan, and then he and his mother sold on, ever further south, until he ended up in Inferior, then Superior and

Gaul and so on, right to Rome itself. That was what we had in common, Drust told them.

'That's what made him vicious,' Manius said, coming quietly up in time to hear this. 'Made him the fighter he was. A decent *crupellarius* who might have gone far if...'

He stopped. They remembered the 'if' being dragged off through the Dead Gate of the Flavian while the new Emperor Antoninus accepted the plaudits of the crowd. Ten years old and the same rank as his da, yet too young to wear a proper man's toga. He was older now...

'No one cares for the *crupellarius*,' Ugo growled. 'Wears too much iron. They liked Calvinus best.'

Dog had been a fighter they called 'the oven wearer' because of the amount of armour he had – so much that, if you weren't limber and strong, you couldn't get up if you fell. He carried a huge shield and a little *pugio* dagger, a ridiculous weapon for such an armoured man, but that was the jest in it – big man with a little weapon. It let the crowd hurl suitable insults.

Calvinus was a *dimaechaerus*, who wore nothing more than a loincloth, but had two longswords. Few fought in that role and only the best and fastest. He and Dog were meant to complement one another as a pairing, and when they went at it, fast and furious and meticulously rehearsed, they looked magnificent.

In a straight real fight, one against the other, it was no contest, and Calvinus had known that from the moment they'd turned to face one another, condemned by contract and the viciousness of a man-brat in purple. He had tried his best and, when it came to taking the iron, he had knelt submissively, looked up once and spoke to Dog, then bowed his head. No one knew what he'd said but Dog and he never told anyone.

'Time,' Sib said and Drust looked up to see Kag loping back in with a loose-kneed, ground-eating stride. He felt as if he had woken from a long nap, disoriented and unable to remember any of what had gone before he'd stopped talking. The world had continued uninterrupted while he left it.

Like death. The world would go on and the only difference would be that he wouldn't be in it. The first sign of cracking was the drawing away from people, from the world, Drust had long ago realised. You reconciled it with not wanting them to suffer when you inevitably got unlucky and died and, sometimes, half admitted that you didn't want to feel the same. Gladiators had no real friends in the *harena* and nothing they could not leave simply by shutting a door. Dog had learned that.

Yet, in the end, it was just the mind trying to scab over. Drust had thought himself gone from all that. Thought he could handle this little, last piece of it, just this once for the life-changing reward; now he was not so sure.

Manius had found a little snake, courtesy of the snorting mules, and cut it in half with a swift, economical slice of a long knife.

'Is it poisonous?' Sib asked, alarmed and looking round at where he squatted. Manius said all snakes were poisonous, which was a sensible approach. His people also believed you had to cut them in half and throw the halves far away on opposite sides, otherwise they would slither back and join up to make a whole, live snake again.

Ugo and Quintus were up in the rocks, hidden and saying nothing, while the rest went about the business of looking innocent, unarmed and carelessly foolish. 'An hour,' Kag said laconically, wiping sweat from his face and hunkering down under what shelter there was.

Sib held up a shell, squinting at it. He had dug it out while making the fire pit and was in wonder about it.

'Look,' he said, waving it. 'All this was a sea once. Or a lake. Water everywhere – just everywhere. Now look at it. This is how the world will end.'

'It's probably what they had in a stew,' Manius said, laughing. He spat his bloody concoction onto the fire pit. 'Brought from the sea, you arse.'

Sib scowled, knowing he was probably right but not wanting to let go the wonder he had felt with his idea. Besides, he said, he was sure it had come from inside a stone cracked in half by the heat of an old fire. Put there by Vulcan, perhaps. Or Jupiter Optimus Maximus.

They argued, soft as the rain, and Drust looked at them, these men he knew just well enough to trust. He studied the camp like it was a theatre. The ones on show were innocuous as Vestals, with sodden hats and hoods, baggy breeks and no sign of a weapon anywhere. They looked like big southerners, thinking to make their fortune with a little risk and a lot of luck, arrogant in that way such men are, full of the belief that they were superior to everything and everyone, even the gods. Thinking the Caledonii were subdued and looking to profit from it.

'How many?' Drust asked Kag.

'Five. One donkey,' he said, then looked at Manius, who laughed softly and spread his hands in acceptance of the win.

'One wearing Army boots,' Manius went on. 'He is not Army and never has been, all the same. They all have short throwing spears, but I think they will hide them, come up as friends to get close.'

'Fighters?' Ugo asked.

'From what I saw,' Kag said, rocking on his heels, 'the donkey is probably their best one. They can't throw better than a Greek girl.'

Drust gave him a look; he hadn't wanted him close enough to get javelins thrown at him, but Kag saw it and shrugged.

'I got them mad and following. They are not Dog's scouts after all.'

He levered himself up, wiped his hands down his front and grinned. 'Same old same old,' he said.

That's what it was. Drust could see it played out in his head like a rustic farce – the men would lead their donkey up, reassured that they were dealing with careless southerners who had no idea that staying secret was the only way of avoiding trouble.

They would see three men and a string of hobbled mules packed with equipment. There was no sign of the one they had followed, but if any of them had suspicions, greed would swamp them. The three men would rise up with surprise and some anxiety, all empty hands and uneasy smiles.

The one with Army boots would be a reasonable man, raising an arm in greeting and the others would be keeping their battered, scarred weapons hidden, but accessible. If they were truly what they claimed, they'd come up in single file, donkey-man last. If they planned murder and greed, they'd fan out and come up in a vee, so that every weapon could be deployed at once.

The one with boots, the status of a leader, would talk constantly, calling greetings, asking where they were bound, asking if they were scavenging, asking if they'd had any luck… until the moment he made the signal.

It would be a drop of a hand to one side or the other, as if weary. Or a drag across a rain-wet forehead, or the casual removal of his headgear. Something banal that would be full of moment.

The men came up with their donkey and there was mock surprise; one of them shouted and held up his hand in greeting; his voice piped like a bird, the words falling out dead and dull into the sullen air.

They came up and slowly fanned out.

Drust felt the familiar little ruche up his spine, the sick slide of stomach as they did that, the leader – the one with boots – at their head. His boots were battered leather *caligulae*, the symbol of his status above the barefooted or badly shoed and no doubt looted from some forgotten legionary rotting in the bracken. He had no seeming weapon at all, just the familiar mud-coloured tunic and bag trousers gathered at the ankles with worn bindings, a hooded short cloak, one end dangling across his front, on the arm that didn't wield a weapon in a fight. He had no hat and the dags of his hair dripped on his mad beard.

The others were the same, shuffling closer, the faces coloured by weather and fire reek and venality, but all of them with the same look in the eyes, whether their faces were thin or fat – even the donkey-hauler, who was no more than fifteen, had greed and cruelty etched in a round face whose camel-lashed dark eyes, like those of a girl, assessed them all at the low value they put on everyone.

The leader's eyes fretted up as he smiled the sweet milk of human kindness at Drust, who wondered what he saw. A man no taller than he, no more muscled, with no better clothing but decent sandals and sodden socks with no toes. A broad face with a broken nose, full-lipped and laced with a dark beard growing out from a neat Army-style crop. Hair likewise, slightly curling from under a broad-brimmed hat with rain running pearls round the rim. Eyes, Drust remembered from the last time he had seen himself in a mirror, that would give him away to the discerning. Slightly liquid, a little popped, with that fret at the corners which the sensible did not dismiss.

The man was not sensible. His voice was a high pitched and rasping lie of concern and warmth in Local, the trade tongue folk used here.

'Friends – good day to you in the name of Ogma and Scathach and all the gods. Well met. This is a dangerous place to be.'

'Good day to you also in the name of the gods,' Drust answered in the same language and there was a slight stir at that; they did not like such expertise, for it made them wonder what else these strangers were expert at. Yet they saw no weapons, only mules and laden packs and gear littered everywhere. Packs that reeked of riches.

'Why is it so dangerous?' Drust added and the leader smiled.

'There are bad people here. Look at your fine mules – the size of that one there, the big dun! If he could breed, you'd have giants off him. And all these packs – what have you got in them, friends? Gold? Silver, perhaps.'

'Fodder enough for those mules,' Drust replied easily. 'But for thirsty travellers in the name of no evil, something might be found to put warmth in the mouth this day.'

'Drops from your tap,' the leader said, and now his eyes were hardening. 'It won't empty any of those containers – but bad men will.' He raised his voice and tilted his head slightly, but his eyes never turned from Drust. 'We cannot let that happen, can we, my brothers?'

They all agreed and the teenager snickered.

'That's kind of you,' Drust answered and the leader grinned; he put one hand behind his back, as if to ease the strain in it.

'Weapon!'

Quintus called it a second before he popped up from behind one of the rocks and let loose the bow. Ugo, who had been standing like an ox waiting for the trace, suddenly changed as if throwing off a cloak. His foot moved and, as if by magic, a long-shafted axe was toe-flicked up out of the bracken where it had been hidden. It came up in a shower of diamond droplets and when it was waist height his big hands closed on it and he roared his way towards one of the astounded men.

The leader reeled with the shock of it. The arrow took him in the chest and bowled him backwards. Sib came screaming up over the rocks and the house walls, springing high with his curved little knife and gutted a russet-haired man before he could do much more than flap his hands.

Ugo whirled the axe in a mesmer of hissing circles, slammed the butt into the face of his target, booted him in the cods and then stood over him. He turned to Drust and grinned out of the thicket of his face.

'*Pugnare ad dignitum*,' he said, stating that he had fought the man to the point where he had raised as finger in submission. It irritated Drust that he did this, as if Drust was the *munerarius* of some spectacle who could order life or death for the man. The fighting was not all done, so he made the slice sign and Ugo stepped back from the struggling man.

'*Recipere ferrum*,' he intoned – prepare to take the iron. Drust did not wait to see if the man moaning on the ground would actually get on his knees and bare his neck; he strode forward with his own *pugio* and daggered the man in the throat.

'Find your fucking head,' he snarled at Ugo, 'and pull it out of your arsehole. This is no provincial contest here.'

Ugo looked like a slapped six-year-old, but he went looking for another kill, though it was too late; the shrieking was done and only the mules honked and brayed, tugging and frantic at the violence and the blood; the donkey bolted, dragging the teenager across the ground until the reins slipped off his wrist.

The blood-stink washed out. The others came down and Manius rose up, blew out through his nose and then went to the ragged, bloody shreds of what had once been bad men. He sliced every throat, just to be sure, while Drust watched the leader's Army boots tremble and kick him out of the world; most of the studs were missing on both and there was a hole in the left sole. It must have hurt, that boot, on every stone on the rugged path he took, but he would not give up on the symbol of his rank any more than he would have given up the dagger he had sheathed and hidden in the small of his back.

Kag went after the donkey and brought it in, soothing it with soft words and a hatful of precious grain. Ugo, trying to make up for his silliness, made a bloody fretwork of the boy's face, even though he was already dead.

The donkey's pack was stuffed with tunics and spearheads, belts and bundles of discarded Army gear, stained rust-red with old bloodstains. Drust recalled the stories from the forts; tens of thousands, they had said bitterly, killed by the beasts beyond the Wall. Somewhere out under that vast sky there were dead men festering to blue-black marble and stripped and forgotten. Men whose letters pleading for socks or a little money or telling how they had finally achieved relief from fatigues would be being read by mothers who did not know the writers were already dead.

Manius killed the donkey because Kag couldn't bring himself to do it; he hated harming horses or mules or any kin of them. They broke out two shovels and scooped out holes, burying all the men and the dead animal, but it was necessity not kindness. They buried all their gear, too, piled rocks on them to make it harder for the scavengers to scavenge the scavengers.

In time the wolves and foxes would dig them up and then the carrion birds would give away what had happened but they hoped to be long gone by then, unnoticed towards their meeting with the man called Brigus.

They moved out, the rock mounds losing shape and shadow in the growing dim, becoming lost amid the scree and at least spared the mockery of some sort of service to honour Ogma and Scathach and all the gods.

Chapter Four

Kag had rules he swore by. Sometimes he swore at them, too, and anyone who pointed out that he did not always abide by Kag's tenets. That's when he would give them number twenty-three: mockery and derision have their place. Usually under a big tomb on the Appian.

Amid other philosophical insights such as 'if you can see the whites of their eyes, somebody's done something wrong' and 'if the damage you do can be repaired, you didn't do enough damage', there was one he trotted out frequently and often.

'If you're leaving tracks, you're being followed,' he said, studying the sky and the hills. It was colder than before and the rain had a sleety feel to it; winter was settling on the Land of Darkness like a hen on eggs.

They'd had about eighteen hours without another encounter with bad men, which was better than Drust had thought and he said so. Mockery and derision looked up from round the fantasy of a campfire and then went back to talking and trying to pretend there were flames and heat. They talked about what they always talked about – what they knew and had shared in common, be it war or women. Mockery and derision was always woven into it; you couldn't separate it from the talk of men fuelled on unwatered wine and fear, for all Kag's tenet.

Time mellowed it. What drink and punishment you could take at twenty with steel stomach muscles made you sick up a dog ten years down the line, while all muscle became stringy – unless you went back to the world, where it became fat.

They talked about women and fighting, which is what they knew. Kag was obsessing about the enemy on their trail – he could feel them, he claimed. Sib, who had the sort of desert magic that probably let him feel them, was unconcerned, but wondering if this woman they chased was perhaps a fighter, one Dog had met in the *ludus*. He did not consider it likely, but fell to wondering why women became fighters, put themselves into the *spectacula*.

Quintus, his hair growing bushy and his smile bright out of the scrub of beard, put him right on it.

'I have known many of them,' he said, grinning knowingly. 'I worked with a dog-lady once, name of Patrocla. The lady, not the dog. It had a name but I never knew it. A right snarler – the dog, not the lady.'

'Where was that?' Sib wanted to know and Quintus frowned, thought hard, then shrugged.

'Dyrrachium,' he ventured. 'Or the Flavia Solva – can't remember. She and about twenty others formed a dog pack for the *ludus* of Tacferinas – you remember him? A *ptolemy* from around those pyramid tombs who shared our training grounds. It was a good idea, that dog pack. Fighting them was like eating soup with a knife. Nothing solid in it – the girls just unleashed the bloody dogs and it became chaos. They ran almost naked into the middle of it with knives – the crowds loved it.'

He shook his head. 'Should never have women in a world like ours. No wonder they call it *infamia*.'

'That's because you got beaten, seems to me,' Sib answered. 'So old Severus did you a favour by banning them.'

'That's where you'd be wrong,' Quintus answered without a smile. 'Never fought them. Never saw a woman who actually fought anything other than poor *noxii* armed with clubs, or stunted short-arses. Never fucked one of them neither. That's the attitude, see? Not fighters or friends, but women in a *ludus*. At some point, we'd all have made a move – in the name of all the gods, you remember how we were? Barley-fed, trained to fitness? Full of fighting fury and scared – and she's no different by then. We'd make a move and either get lucky or get rebuffed. Get lucky and everyone wants the same and then you don't have a female fighter, you have a pack whore. If she says no and someone actually listens without having to be stabbed, you have a resentment which leaves her out in the cold, on her own. If she says yes to one, we all hate them both and he gets like a ram in a field, seeing the least smile as a threat.'

'Gods above and below,' said Ugo, 'you thought about this, didn't you?'

Quintus nodded, the grin back, bright and wide. 'No place for women with the likes of us, not even as wives.'

'You knew one, then?' Kag said quietly and Quintus paused. Shrugged.

'Well enough. The dog-lady. The dog got killed and she was never the same. When Severus kicked the feet out from under fighting women, she got sold on and left with no word. Just as well.'

Drust remembered a female fighter in Scythopolis, a dusty shithole of a place which had brought in a band of women warriors, claiming they were the famed Amazons in an attempt to spice up an important *munus*. Good fighter, her cotton loin-cloth round one ankle, giving birth in the fetid dim. Birth, we called it, Drust remembered but it was practically an abortion. Born too early, the *medicus* said, brought on by the fear and the exertion, the potions taken too late to prevent such a thing and the others to boost speed, or for the promise of invulnerability.

It was a wonder she had found the privacy, never mind the man to do it with, the *medicus* said, elbow deep in her gore. How she had hidden it for so long was a bigger mystery than Mithras. Someone had tupped her when she was vulnerable and lost, Drust offered. Even then, the *medicus* said, the chances of it fruiting into a life couldn't have been worked out by a pantheon of gods and an abacus – and if it got this far…

It got no further, that life, despite the best efforts of everyone. It expired in a bloody slither of half-form on the floor of a grit-rubbled undercroft of a provincial area, where the dust greedily sucked up the juice of it. The *medicus* wasn't consoled by saving the woman.

'Mother,' he corrected bitterly. 'Of a child she never saw and never will. No career now either, because she's a slave and the owner will not be pleased. He'll sell her on. If she's lucky.'

Voided everything into the blown sand…

Drust blinked back, flushing with that old cold sweat. Ugo was telling anyone who would listen about the way to perfectly judge the height of a long-hafted axe. Manius was putting an edge on Ugo's axe blade, because he had seen the big German hack the donkey-boy and said it was more like watching a nailed club than a cutting implement.

'How are we faring?' Kag asked, the first time he had spoken that stop. Drust looked at the tablet of scratchings, squinting hard – he was not as good at the business as Kag and it was slow work for them both.

'On track,' he said.

And who knew what lay ahead – or what was behind, as Kag feared. Enemies all round like dog packs. Like eating soup with a knife.

Drust wondered what would happen if six men disappeared into the Land of Darkness, this sullen wasteland. Would Julius

Yahya search for them? Would his mysterious patron – or even Servilius Structus?

'Time,' Kag said, as if reading Drust's mind.

They moved eighteen-and-a-bit miles and would have made more save that a mule slipped, cracked a hoof open and had to be unloaded and then killed; Manius did it with a surprisingly gentle gesture, a swift and sure strike into one ear that hit something vital and dropped it with hardly a grunt.

They repacked and went on, reached the edge of a forest, one of those dark northern forests that chill you, Sib said, even when you stand at the edge. Ugo laughed; this was home to him. Two hours before night they went dipping down a valley to a place with a huge sculpture of swooping rocks looking vaguely like a pod of dolphins leaping across their path, all scalloped backs and wind-etched fins delicate even in granite. The wind was up and hissing; it had a bad winter in it, Ugo said, and no one scoffed.

Sib scouted out the best place to lay up, finding a deep hollow that had once been a riverbed, the stones still smoothed but by the sifting hiss of rain-wind. A twist of trees clung here, woody and gnarled as claws, and they arranged a shelter as best they could.

'Weather is coming,' Ugo said, sniffing the air, his beard pearled with wetness. Well, Drust thought, it didn't take a sage to work that one out, nor even a dark giant from the Germanies. Ugo wanted to go out and scout, but Drust said no. He had half an idea Ugo only wanted to go off into the deep dark of the forest and offer something to one of his many gods and wouldn't have minded it save for the danger. But Ugo was no scout and could not move quietly if he chose.

'We fight together, to the finger.'

Ugo nodded at the sense of it. The pack was everything and Ugo knew it; Drust watched him settle like a hound, circling once or twice, then curling into a spot. He remembered the day Ugo and he had met, had ended up closer than lovers.

It was the first time he had killed for Servilius Structus outside the *harena*, on a night when the City growled and roared like a beast. All the hauliers brought in their carts at night, forbidden during the hours of daylight, and the night workers thronged into the fetid, clogged streets and alleys. The *tabernae* opened to catch the trade, the Vigiles strutted to make it seem as if they kept order and the toga owners shuttled back and forth in litters, making sure their cargo was safe.

'Drusus Servilius,' Kag had said, grinning. 'Are you ready for this?'

Kag nudged him and Drust moved forward like a blind man. It seemed to him that the world was a whirl of noise and people whose faces were filled with black hollows where the mouth and eyes should be. Someone shrieked.

Clodius Flaminius was a big man with a shock of white hair and still with the muscles hauling carts and horses and cargo had given him in youth. He dropped off the cart while his sons worked the team out of the traces, tilting the pole up.

He was standing, looking up to where one of his crew was gathering up the reins to throw to the sons. Never saw Drust. Never saw the knife.

All the times he had practised this, been shown the heart in the throat, shown how to use the blade like the quick flick of an adder's tongue. The knife had gone deep into Clodius's neck – but it was a short blade, the better to keep hidden, and Drust had trembled at the last, as he had so many times under the tutelage of the tutting Greek; it missed the vital part, the heart in the throat that would have spilled blood like water from a burst pipe and dropped the carter like a puppet with cut strings.

Instead, Clodius had jerked away from it, clapped a hand and must have felt the hot flood of his own blood because Drust had watched his eyes widen in disbelief.

'From Servilius Structus,' he had said as he had been instructed. 'Taking his due for all you have skimmed.'

Clodius had staggered sideways. The man up on the cart gave a yelp and the sons shouted. Clodius should have hit the ground and died, but he didn't; he started to faint with the shock and slid reluctantly, fighting with all the carter's strength and grabbing Drust's hem as he did.

The pair of them had fallen. The horse team, unnerved by the noises and the blood smell, had milled and squealed; the frantic sons lost their grip on them and the reins looped round the raised trace and jerked it down.

It had crashed on Drust and Clodius – there was a moment, he remembered, when the world was blasted with pain and light. The cart, unbraked, had jerked as the horse tore the traces free, then it started to roll, iron-shod wheels grinding slowly.

Drust remembered it, the huge bulk of it crushing towards him like an avalanche. Clodius was on the ground, gasping, staring up at the night sky.

Someone came out of the dark shadows and Drust felt himself wrapped in iron bands, saw the cart move away from him then realised it was the other way around. The cart rolled on, one iron wheel crunched through Clodius's skull and his sons screeched. A man turned away, vomiting.

In an alley, Drust had been dumped on his arse in the wet. When he'd blinked back to pain and shapes, Kag had been grinning at him.

'Bit flashy, but it will do,' he had said, then clapped the dark shadow beside him on the shoulder.

'Thank the man,' he said. 'If it hadn't been for him you would have a head in two parts, like Clodius.'

Drust had looked blearily at the dark man, who shoved forward into the poor light. A big face, nose like a fat bag, a badly cropped beard just growing out from the raw scrape of a slave, a shock of wild hair wanting to be braids. A ham hand came out, the knuckles skin-marked like his own and took Drust's limp arm, hauling him up closer, to where the teeth and eyes beamed.

'Ugo,' the apparition had said.

Ugo and me have fought side by side since, Drust thought. Him and the others, sent out with Servilius Structus's stud horses and stud fighters for *spectacula* all over the Empire, especially Creta and Cyrene, Aegyptus, Numidia. There was something, Manius said, of the Punic about Servilius Structus, who bribed the State grain ship captains to take his horses and fighters out in their big empty vessels and allowed him cargo for his private grain on the way back. Or sand for the Flavian, which was more important and more expensive.

There had been others like Clodius Flaminius, people who made the mistake of thinking Servilius Structus was an ex-slave too fat to leave Subura save for the odd litter ride to the *ludus* to personally judge his livestock, or the annual visit to the Flavian dinner. We worked with him all out lives, Drust suddenly thought. Long years, each one another inch from the slave pens of the *ludus*.

Long enough, Drust thought, to trust these men as they did him. All of them were the same, curled like dogs, whimpering in their chilled sleep.

The long night slid away to a milk-fed dawn; the watches changed and cold chewed. They fed and watered the mules and sipped their own mouthfuls in a dark that ate stars, then went on, plodding over the brackened hills, avoiding the thick forests, hearing only their own muted talk and the harshing of crows.

At the end of one bad day under a sky gone to pewter tinged with russet, they reached the lee of a gaunt hill where the bones of the earth thrust up. The rocks spilled left and right for a long way, towering and grim and broken only by a cleft, as if cut by some giant axe.

'One of your gods,' Sib growled to Ugo when Kag offered that up. 'With your axe.'

'When did you start using that engine?' Manius demanded. 'I never knew you to fight with it in a *munus*. You were a *hoplomachus*.'

'You can take the warrior out of the Germanies,' Quintus said, and everyone laughed softly at the bit unsaid; Ugo acknowledged it with a flap of one hand.

There was unease, for all the quiet laughter. Drust knew they hadn't made as much distance as they should have and time was slipping away like sand; Kag was still watching the back trail and frowning. Everyone was still churning with the mystery that was Dog and the woman and child.

Sib looked at the strange mackerel sky and remarked on it. No one knew what it meant, save that it was no good like it was, so Drust had the packs staked to form a semicircular break against the curve of rocks, and while they did it the wind grew from hiss to moan and then started in to calling like the lost souls of children; they huddled in their fort, swathed in cloaks and trying to soothe the mules. They swaddled themselves to the eyes and still shivered.

'How long will it last?' Quintus called out to Ugo, who shrugged and shouted back, his words whipped away almost as they fell from his mouth.

'Three hours. Three days…'

More lost time. Drust did not say it, just saved himself for breathing the frozen air through the sieve of his veil. The wind was an untuned horn that drove freezing rain down their necks, rammed it between teeth onto tongues. It shrieked out a promise to blow forever, but it was gone to gasp and puff in an hour and they heaved up out of a crust of snow; a mule had torn free and run for it.

'Leave it,' Manius said, but Quintus put them straight.

'That's Tauratus,' he said meaningfully. It was named after the ugliest, most insolent and blood-crazed fighter who had ever disgraced a *munera*. The mule was the biggest and strongest and carried the pack with some of Quintus's strange-brew pots. It would not die easily in such a puff of storm, so Drust swore up a storm of his own, then sent Sib to track it, bring it back if he could and, if not, make sure it was dead and hidden, not lurching around looking for people to feed it, people who might see it for what it was.

They sorted out the mess, burying the discards of what they could no longer pack – they'd dumped fodder for the mules and food for themselves to accommodate Quintus's pack; no one quibbled.

Quintus looked at Drust, then at the cleft. 'If we come back this way,' he said, 'moving fast and with folk on our trail…'

Drust nodded. Quintus unpacked a box, cracked it open and revealed little pots, nested in straw like eggs. The others looked once or twice and moved away, trying not to show it; Quintus grinned his big wide grin and dandled a little pot in one hand.

'What?' he asked, spreading his hands. Then he flipped the pot from one to the other along the length of his arms; Drust held his breath and Kag made a sound in the back of his throat.

Quintus placed the pot carefully back in the box, then hefted it up and swaggered away towards the deep of the cleft. He was grinning and there no sweat on him.

There was on everyone else.

By the time he swaggered back, Sib was in. He was almost on them before they realised and he moved as if he did not want to push any destiny into the sluttish ground, as if making a mark was an affront to the gods.

Quintus came up and carefully placed the box down. Then he explained what he had done, so everyone would know what to avoid – and what to do if they were the only one left. By the time he had finished, Sib was taking water and making a face at the way it hurt his teeth. He soaked some of their hard bread and sucked on it.

'Dead?' Kag asked. Sib nodded.

'Fell or was blown over. Cracked a shin. I cut its throat and put as many stones on it as I could.'

'Did you bring my box?' Quintus demanded and Sib seared him with a look. Quintus just laughed.

Sib was all defiance, but rasped by the fear he had of the box and its contents. He'd wanted to bring it, but was too afraid even to bury the mule properly; it made him angry at himself and he turned it outwards.

'That mule won't be the only one of us to have to take iron. And for what? A woman and Dog's by-blow?'

'For a suck at the tits of Fortuna,' Quintus threw back, grinning like a dead fox. Sib scowled.

Ugo and Quintus handled the mules with Kag, while Manius took the rear and Sib went out ahead, just out of sight and scouting. Ugo and Drust walked at the spear tip and moved out of the cleft, onto a rolling, rock-studded plain which rose up to the distant hump of forested hills.

That night they huddled up with the mules, fireless yet again and leaching what warmth they could. They all knew it couldn't go on like this much longer, but no one voiced it. When they did, it would be far down the line of things, close to the part where they were finished and knew it.

When dawn came, Manius was missing and Drust felt a moment of panic, but they were laired up and he counted up how far they had come – enough, he thought. Sib looked at him pointedly and Drust was about to send him out to look for Manius when the man himself shimmered in.

He was breathing hard and sweating, accepted a precious lick of unwatered wine with silent thanks and, when he had drunk, told them what he had done.

'Crossed their trail. Eight men in smooth-soled boots, no heels, one has a tear on the left. No mules, one pony, unshod. One man is walking heavy, so he has a weight to carry. Where he set it down tells me it is a *scutum*. That shield is slowing them, but he won't give it up so I am figuring he is the leader and thinks it must be worth it.'

Drust sat and thought about it. Legionary shield. Looted – or were they deserters? Either of those was likely. So was Kag's voiced thought.

'You think Dog knows we are coming?'

They were two days away from Brigus, the informer. If Dog already knew that these were men sent to find him, he was waiting to see where they would go, to find the man who was betraying him. This band was watching, no more.

'If it is Dog at all,' Quintus pointed out. 'Might be just another bunch of tribals, like the ones we killed. This time the leader has a big heavy shield instead of big heavy boots to mark him as top wolf.'

Drust tried for a reassuring grin but didn't have Quintus's teeth or confidence. Truth was, we don't know, he thought. Truth was that if Dog knew, then the woman and boy might be dead already according to Julius Yahya. The only way to find out was to wait and ambush them, which was what Kag eventually voiced.

Drust told him why it was a bad idea – there were no concealing rocks, just bare hills and scrub and stones.

'There is forest,' Ugo said, pointing. Half a day away if we push it, Drust thought. He quelled a ruche of shivers; he did not like the dark forests here, the ones that sucked sound.

'This is my place,' Ugo said, grinning. 'My gods will protect us all.'

'Steel will protect us all,' Manius said and looked at Drust, smiling his soft smile; as he went to his pack, Drust felt the same unease he'd had when first they had met.

–

He walked as if he owned the earth. Came right up to Drust and nodded.

'Manius,' he said. 'Kag said to report to you.'

Drust didn't like the idea that this Manius had evaded the two men on guard, simply passed them as if they hadn't been there. He considered that they had been asleep, but one was Sib and Drust was sure of him; when he mentioned it later, Sib swore had seen and heard nothing at all.

'Kag sent you?'

'He did. I am a fighter. Like you.'

He had the mark of a slave to prove it, still raw round the knuckle for he was so new he had never been to the Ludus Ferrata in Rome;

he was one of the provincials just purchased. Might never get to Rome at all if the desert dogs besieging them had their way and worked up enough courage to rush the mud-walled compound in a shit-stained outpost called Mascula. That happened a few nights later, when the garrison commander went mad and had to be tied down, raving. That was when they lay in shrouds of dust, listening to blood-soaked howls, hearing the crack-snap of sling stones, seeing the puffs close enough to throw grit. Then the goat-fuckers, little vermin that they were, decided they'd waited long enough, had enough crude ladders and a ram for the gate.

So Drust hacked and slashed and staggered about until he found himself gasping, half on his knees staring at a dropped bow and the dead owner he had killed in a flurry of bloody blows.

'Mind if I take that?' said a voice and Manius scooped up the bow. He was loping, slightly crouched and uncaring of the chaos and fire. He looked as incongruous as an eight-legged horse. Then he was gone.

That night he was missing. All night. The mavros had pulled back over the wall and the night was quiet, as if both sides were stunned by what had happened and unsure who had won or lost. Drust thought Manius had died in the dark and he was dog-weary – they all were, having had to drag bodies up and push them out of the compound before the next day's heat started them to stink. Drust grabbed a little sleep and was woken just before dawn by Kag.

Even in the dark his eyes were red rimmed and puffed with lack of sleep. He said 'your turn' and was snoring even before his head hit the ground.

Drust took up sentry as the morning crept up, eerily silent, as if the mavros had lost their enthusiasm for those ululating howls. In the morning, despite his best efforts, Drust didn't hear Manius until the man was almost on top of him, loping out of the red dawn, dragging up one of the crude ladders to the wall and over it, kicking it off when he was at the top. He had a bow in one hand and no arrows left,

'Where have you been?' Drust wanted to know, waspish and worn and more afraid than he liked to admit. Manius smiled softly.

'Down in Dis' he answered, passing like a wraith, 'killing demons'.

-

Manius had it still, that demon-killing bow, an elegant, deadly recurve of flawless beauty and power. He drew out the arrows for it, barbed and wicked. Licked the flights, squinted down the shafts while the others watched him, silent, wordless.

That bow reminded everyone of that last night in Mascula, the *mavros* forced to silently cower in their own shelters, discovering that they no longer ruled the dark and that the Romans were not trapped by them.

They were trapped with Manius.

Chapter Five

Sib sat hunched up; he did not like Manius. Respected him but was afraid of him. 'Do not put your back to that man,' he would say, but never where Manius could hear it. Kag had laughed, but Quintus had nodded sober agreement.

'There is darkness in him,' he had said when Sib had voiced this when they were leaving Mascula. 'We must make sure he never gets out to the world.'

'There is *jnoun* in him,' Sib had added, and all the old mysteries and fears of those desert demons rolling round his blood came out in his voice then. He squatted by the fire and stared at embers as if they had some message for him.

'Why are you so afraid of him?' Drust asked, and Sib stirred the fire with a stick.

'You do not see it,' he said, 'but I am of the deep desert and I know what is in him. I was taken when older, so I went on raids until my father was killed. First time I stood watch, he told me that if a man appears out of the desert where no man should be, claiming to be one of us and asking to be allowed to the fire, I was to refuse him and run. Just that. Run.'

He stopped, dropped the stick in the flames. 'On the day my father died, our raid came on a caravan. We had been tracking it and wanted to dip our fingers in its honey, just a little, then let it go on. When we found it, there was no honey, only blood. Everything was dead.'

He broke off and looked at Drust with his big white eyes. 'I mean everything. Camels, dogs, women, children. Everything.'

He looked at the fire again. '*Jnoun*,' he said. 'There is one in that Manius.'

Drust had just thought they all trembled at old granny stories and he knew there was no one more hagged than a fighter, festooned with amulets and rigid rituals, but there had been times since when he had seen the smoky darkness in Manius's eyes.

Drust had a fire lit and then Kag slid out one way and Manius the other, leaving the others to hug the welcome, almost forgotten joy of flame. It circled them like some evil miasma in the velvet night, tendrils of heat and smoke, Drust imagined, trailing out to where someone in thick clothing and good boots and a *scutum* lifted his nose from fat moustaches to sniff the traces.

Close, Drust tried to think, though he couldn't be sure and he said nothing. No one did – if the watchers could see the fire, they could gather in whispers in the night.

The fire in the night would act as it did on all creatures; they would come to it. The foxes and owls would circle it and shun it, the insects would plunge, drunken and sizzling, into the fierce heart of it. The men would squat in the dark beyond it, see the bulked shapes hunched round against the night chill.

They were packs with hooded cloaks on and Drust was the only one who now sat at the fire; the others had slithered off to shiver in the shadows; he knew the watching men wouldn't shoot until they knew where everyone was. If they were scavs, they would not want to put holes in value – mules, wineskins and the like. They would come up, slow and quiet and, by then, Drust hoped, they would be dying.

The others crouched in the pressing dark, as if in a hole, while Drust sat like a big fat foolishness by the fire, looking as if he dozed, but moving enough to give them something to focus on, a reassurance that every shape round the flames was real. The heat was a balm, all the same, and he felt himself soak it up, sat and sweated slow rolls of moisture like rain down a window, his mind whirling back and forth on Dog, the woman, the child. How was he surviving here, in the middle of enemies? Where was he laired – had he returned to his old tribe and somehow taken them over?

Nothing, Drust thought, was easily dismissed when it came to Dog.

The clack was loud in the night; the blood raced and sluiced Drust fully awake. A hoof on a stone, a falling needle of a noise that carried too far in still, damp air and a starless night that still gave too much substance to shadows.

Perfect. Drust raised his head and peered into the dark, trying to look suspicious but idiotic while the blood shushed in his ears.

'Ho there. No evil, in the name of all gods,' he said in a whisper that he did not have to try too hard to make hoarse. 'Who are you, creeping round in the dark?'

He spoke in Local and the answer was thick with tribal gutturals and some scorn, spoken by a man who had a weapon ready and was with others doing the same.

'Me? Who in the name of all the gods of this place are you?'

'Drust. Didn't Morcant say?'

'Morcant who?'

'I don't know more. He gave us our orders and we came here.'

'From where?'

'South, where we were sent. Following them.'

'In the name of all the gods – following who?'

'Come on, you know who. Six of them, travelling north. We caught them at their stop, the rocks, and killed them all. Took their gear and Morcant said to come here. You know the rocks?'

'How do I know every rock in this country?'

'I'm trying to tell you, boss,' Drust said, knowing that everyone else was half crouched and squinting, trying to make out how many and where. He fought for the right inflections, the proper deference, and sweated like raw fat in the sun over speaking so much Local all at once. It would be worse if he came to using his birth tongue, dinned into him by his mother, who had made him speak it as soon as he could speak at all. In secret, at night and when she could smuggle herself to him; he felt the sudden sharp pang of her loss, just when he was old enough to know that she and he were slaves of Servilius Structus and exactly what that meant.

'We caught them at the rocks with the big cut in them and killed them all,' he said. 'Took all their mules, with all their riches, and Morcant said to come here with them, that you were the one to report to. Said you would find us.'

They had not expected this and confusion was sown and ripened.

'Might be,' the voice answered and now there was a shape to go with it. The voice had changed from suspicion to self-importance and Drust jigged the float a little.

'You sure Morcant is not with you? He said to bring the riches here.'

'He is not. What riches did you find on those mules?'

Now there was greed, honeyed but distinct.

'Food. Water. Weapons. Silver. Wine – a lot of wine. Those greybacks were planning on a good time somewhere. I suppose it will go to all those at the camp.'

'What camp?'

Drust finally allowed a little exasperation. 'Where we are to take these mules, boss. The ones you are supposed to guide us to.'

There was a pause. Someone mumbled incoherently and the man snapped back an answer, then turned to Drust.

'Wake your friends. I will decide what is to be done with those mules. You stay there, with your arms high.'

It was done. Drust moved forward, grumbling: 'We had to treat those mules like they were our own children all through that storm and then we got lost, to tell the truth, and it was only the grace of Scathach, blessings be, that we got out of it…'

Now Drust saw shapes against the starlit sky, one directly ahead, another skylined slightly, a short spear resting on one shoulder. Keep talking, he thought, trying not to let the dryness clog his throat or the fierce thunder of his heart drown his wits; soon they would realise none of the sleeping bundles was getting up, despite the noise. Soon he would stumble trying to speak Local, the trade tongue that let one tribe speak with another with only a strangeness of accent. Soon he would say a Roman word…

The one nearest to Drust loomed up and he caught his breath – how close did it have to be before the blessings of grime and days of travel failed and he was exposed as a greyback?

'Which mule pack has the wine?'

Two laughs came from the dark; Drust saw the skylined man jerk and there was a thump that was so soft it was lost in laughter.

'The big one there carried it,' Drust said, barely able to squeeze out the words between his teeth, hoping the man put that and his shaking down to having left the warmth. 'I think he has been sampling it on the way, for he is the laziest mule ever.'

More laughter. The leader growled disparagingly about 'mule drivers' and went to where the packs lay. Then he stopped, looking at the supposedly sleeping bundles. He kicked one and it rolled over like the loose sack it was; there was more laughter but Drust heard two more thumps, just as the leader realised the ruse. He could not see anyone but Drust and licked some wet life back into his lips as he brought up his sword and started to shout.

There was a whirr and a thump and something sprouted from the man, a sapling. The blow of the arrow staggered him back and he stared at the horror sticking in him, uncomprehending and wild-eyed. Drust brought out his *pugio*, smooth and fast, stepped forward and banged the knife in, low and to one side, feeling the heat, smelling the rank dog sweat of him.

He gave a high whine and jerked, trying to get away, but Drust held him like a brother, tasting the sharpness of something spiced and familiar though he couldn't place it. Spikenard, the hair oil legionaries loved, he suddenly remembered...

The man's last breath was a gust of terror; his beard braids trembled, the ornaments clinking. He was dead already but didn't know it, was still staggering and flailing so that Drust had to clutch him close, heard himself making soothing noises like you would with a hysterical child.

Then a black shape appeared like some death-angel rising up. There was a cough, a choking gurgle and then only Manius stood there, a bloodied barbed arrow clutched in one hand and a mad, wide grin gleaming in the dim.

'No time to dance with them,' he said savagely and there was no answer to it; Drust sank against the mule pack, found himself looking at the sprawled form pillowed in a slowly spreading lake of blackness. A pony ambled in, whuffing with disgust at the blood smell; a battered *scutum* flapped gently on its back, like a broken wing.

Manius slapped the shield and the pony shied a little. 'Well, he had poor use of that, your dancing partner,' he said. He crouched by the body, looking like some perverted demon as he cut his arrowhead free.

They were all gone, neat as snicking ears of corn. Manius had circled round in a run, in complete silence, then put four arrows in four men as swiftly as Quintus could slit the throat of a solitary man lurking bemused at the rear. Sib, Ugo and Kag prowled among the dead, disgruntled at having had nothing to do and a lot of discomfort waiting.

Five men dead in as many minutes and with less sound than the cold wind. That was good, Drust thought, even for the likes of us. Everyone was humbled to a temple hush by it for a moment, then they backtracked to where the dead men had left their own packs.

'Jupiter on a jack,' Kag swore and needed no more to make his point – these were no scavs. They had stowed ring coats, good swords, bows, arrows. If they'd had a chance to unleash that it would have been a hard fight.

Drust said nothing and everyone collected what they thought might be useful, which was mainly food, ponies to replace lost mules and skins of harsh beer so thick it needed to be strained through teeth. The ring coats were attractive, but the added weight made them no prize. The weapons were no better than the ones they had, but later, as they moved out, Kag came close enough to be heard only by Drust's ears.

'They were hunting,' he said, his breath sour with the beer, his eyes bright in the dawn. Drust nodded. If they were deliberately hunting us, he thought, it was either the tribes who were 'out' as everyone along the Northern Vallum thought. Or Dog's own men.

If it was that, then Dog had watchers. Drust suspected that Dog had men around the Wall, hunkered like beasts to sniff out strangers; it chilled him, for it meant Dog lived in fear and knew that men would come for him sooner or later. It meant the woman was probably dead now – and they might be next. It meant that Dog had gone back to his own people and had, somehow, persuaded them that he was one of them and that they should fight to protect him.

The sick rose up in Drust as he watched the others move, purposed and knowing as old hounds who had been through the dark wolf wood and staggered out the far side.

The beasts beyond the Wall were hunting. From now on it would get bloodier in Thule.

Chapter Six

More shallow graves, but Kag and Drust took the corpses with them no matter how deep they were buried; like black wolves the dead padded at their heels, haunting them with questions all through the rest of that day's journey.

Where was Dog? How many men did he have – and how were they to get the woman and child from him? In ones and pairs they had asked this at every stop, through mouthfuls of cold-soaked bread, and no one had come up with a way. Each time they failed they looked at Drust, who felt the weight of their eyes and the crushing knowledge that he had nothing to offer.

They slithered through the edges of dark woods, skipping from copse to rocks, down one bracken-strewn hill and up another as fast as they could. They came to a forest they had to pass through, creeping crouched in a dark like a temple, a dark that made them hushed as if in the presence of gods. The trees were thick with needles and the mulched ground crackled with the first frosts.

Beyond it was a land like a dragon's back, a place of slabs of rock like an abandoned game of knucklebones and a killing cold broken only by miracles of sunlight from a baleful red eye. The country rolled like a sea, slashed by steep little run-offs that wanted to be ice. The grass was sere and yellow now and the mules hoofed it mournfully at each stop; the tribal ponies, shaggy and tough, showed them how it was done, tearing and chewing with big yellowed teeth that seemed to grin derision at the mules.

'They must be your cousins,' Ugo said to Quintus and laughed into the scowls he got back. No one else joined in, nor spoke much at all save to ask the endless question – how are we to do this?

Once they came across the litter of some fight or flight or both – a lost boot, a torn baldric, curved segments of armour, the stuff that gave the legionaries the scornful name 'greybacks' from the tribes; that was also the name they gave to lice.

They came up to each stop like bird-scarers that had learned to lurch off their poles and walk. They made a fire at once, because the cold was killing them – then turned away with iron will and refused to go to it until the packs were stacked and the pack beasts picketed. The mounts gasped and blew out with the relief of being unsaddled; Quintus fed them from nosebags of grain, holding up the limp bag of it to show his concern at what was left.

Manius and Sib took a hunk of damp bread, peeling the worst mould off, took a deep slug of water then went opposite ways up to the high ground. Ugo hunched his head into his shoulders and squatted, looking up. 'I am sick of this sky,' he said.

'It's all right,' Quintus answered, smiling his big smile. 'You have forgotten the one out in the desert. It was as wide and long.'

'Don't remind me' Ugo muttered. 'It was blue, with hardly a puff of cloud and Apollo galloped in it.'

'You complained of the heat,' Quintus reminded him. 'And when you get in a dark wood your smile comes back.'

He carefully drew out two more of his little clay pots and Ugo and Drust eyed him. Quintus frowned a moment, then shrugged.

'Seems fine so far. No problems yet.'

'What problems?' Drust demanded, suspicious and alarmed. Quintus carefully lowered the pots back into their straw nest.

'Well, the cold freezes the water in its compartment. If you throw the pot, the quicklime will spill out, but without water it won't work properly. The naphtha and sulphur might also be affected.'

No one liked to be reminded of the weapon and what it could do – they certainly didn't want to know how Quintus had come by little pots of it; it was not something you found in the market.

They concentrated on getting warm and making a meal out of mouldy flatbread and dried meat strips soaked in water to make them chewable. Kag's version had been marinaded in mule sweat under the pack saddles; one reason he mourned the death of the big one was that he swore its foul humours had given the tastiest flavour.

They sat in silence afterwards. They had travelled several score miles in eight days and the pace was telling – Quintus had an ugly blister under his right toe, which Sib lanced expertly. Ugo was starting to look stringy from lack of food and when Manius came in to eat, Drust saw the etched lines of strain and weariness; it affected him as deeply as noticing the bald spot on his crown the last time he'd had a barbered haircut.

Time mauls us all, he thought – but we have got this far. Kag laughed bitterly when he said this, hoping to put some cheer out.

'So said the *tiro* fighter,' he growled. 'Look, he says – the altar to Jupiter Latista has been removed, the *pompos* parade has come and gone, with blaring trumpets and chariots pulled by tiger-horses. It's all but over.'

'Now comes the first of the main events,' he went on, 'the *venation*. The beast hunt. Guess who are the beasts?'

'Aye, aye,' Quintus said, clapping Kag on one shoulder, a friendly act that rocked Kag forward and made him frown. 'You are like a priest I knew once – you remember him, lads? Used to come down to bless our weapons in the name of Mars Ultor. Always long-faced and making miserable observations.'

'I remember Spiculus and Posta dragged him into the *harena*. My, how he screamed and beat at the door,' Kag said, brightening with the memory.

'No way back through the Gate of Life that way, they told him,' Quintus said, grinning. 'But you'll be OK – ask Dis Pater if you can pass through the other way. Mind the elephant…'

They laughed. The priest had been picked up and tossed almost out of the ring before the *venationes* had managed to hamstring and kill the great beast. Spiculus and Posta had survived unscathed, too, so the whole matter of the priest was a great joke, even when they were lashed for it.

'Are we there yet?' demanded Ugo like a sulky child on a long litter journey.

'We should be sitting in the lap of this Brigus,' Drust answered, 'if we steered true. And somewhere close by is Dog himself and the woman and child we have come to get.'

No one spoke about the pair anymore because it would air the strong possibility that they were no longer alive. Manius refused the single pull of the unwatered wine they had left; when the moon got up he uncoiled, took up his bow and nodded as if he was going down to the *taberna*. They watched him vanish into the night.

Kag scratched his beard; he wanted to go into this full bellied, warmed by wine and clean shaven, hair and beard. But who knew whether they would still need to lurk in the undergrowth of their facial hair? It annoyed him, not being able to fight like a gladiator.

Drust watched Kag scratch and methodically check weapons, Quintus with his deadly pots. He thought of Manius, hunkered like a hunting owl, sweeping the night with his magic eyes. He thought of them all, and all the times he and they had been like this, felt like this, ruche-skinned and bowel-sick, waiting in the dim. Somewhere he thought he heard the faint sound of trumpets…

–

The undercroft dim shifted with shadows, was fetid with blood and viscera; somewhere there were screams and a surgeon moved purposefully through the throng, his assistants shouldering aside the careless and slow. They were oilers and armourers, water carriers, beast handlers, all the scurrying throng in the middle of a stillness of fighters.

The screamer was a crowd-pleaser venator gored by an elephant.

'Fifty-four hunts,' his slave said bitterly. 'Fifty-four and not a scratch.'

'You go too often to the well,' Baccibus growled, 'you fall in it one day.'

They all looked at him; Baccibus was greying and scarred, reminded Kag of some old farmyard rat dog. Twenty years he had done and was still going; today he had arrived saying he was matched against Laticulus, who was a little concerned, since he and Quintus had been rehearsing moves for a week.

'Is Quintus ill?' he demanded. Their lanista, Tarquinus, who had arrived with the stolid Baccibus at his back, gave him a disgusted glare.

'He was given the rudis,' he growled and saw the astounded eyes. He shook his head; he did not want to criticise Servilius Structus but there were too many being given the wooden sword and none of them, as Tarquinus said often, deserved it. Certainly not as much, even, as Baccibus – but things were not the same as they once had been in his day.

It went as it always did, though – Drust got a missio, Kag got the win and they lurched off and out. In the dim of the undercroft they were doused with water, armour slaves hauled off their gear and they half lay, half sat, sucking in air.

A series of catcalls and boos went up and they looked at each other; the howls went on and on and a shape materialised beside them; when they focused on it, Quintus grinned back at them, though his eyes had no mirth.

'Baccibus made a poor show. Slipped or something – Laticulus had to be as inept as a tiro not to kill him. In the end it was a farce and the crowd knew it. They wanted the old boy's death but that hadn't been paid for. He got his missio.

Quintus felt bad for it but Baccibus put him right later, sitting with his scarred hands on his sand-scraped knees, knowing he had done badly, knowing Fortuna wouldn't smile on him again.

'Not your fault you got the rudis,' he said. 'Never feel sorry for grabbing that. One of the only two ways out.'

–

Drust got up with the others and they moved, slow and purposeful; Kag knew there was something and eventually Drust told him what he'd been worrying at instead of sleeping.

Kag nodded, said nothing for a bit, then: 'He found his way in the end.'

He had. That day, in the cart lurching back to the Ludus Ferrata school, old Baccibus had been nodding off – they all had, rocked and bounced by the slow ox-hauled journey home, slit-eyes glazed and blurred with lashes watching the endless tick of the spokes, lulled by the rhythmic creak of badly greased wheels. It was classed as an accident, but Drust knew better; Baccibus, scarred and limping, his knees ruined, his strength failing, his last fight a farce and his next promising no better, had let his head fall between the spokes and, before anyone knew it, the wheel had snapped his neck like a twig.

Free. The second way…

They stripped and washed down, fetched out clean, wrinkled tunics to put on because they would not die dirty this day. Their hair was grown long and they ribbon-tied it back as best they could and Ugo did the same with his beard, which grew faster than the others.

All of them longed for a decent barbering, for the whole body shave and the oils that left them slick and hard to grip. In the growing light their naked bodies were dull white, pallid as worms save where the sun had been and it cut them in lines, like fresh-broken bread. Save for Sib, of course, with his ruche-skinned blackness wriggling with the old, pale cicatrice of drag wounds and whip marks.

Kag had a long scar along one side that stood out in the strange, flat light of a winter dawn – the legacy of a knife, Drust remembered, though he couldn't recall where. Ugo had a puckered wound on the top of his left shoulder and a lump that showed where the bone had healed badly. Quintus had several vicious stripes, pocked with old suture marks, and Drust had his own marks, all of them earned at the wrong end of dangerous places.

They shivered through their ablutions, same way they had before every fight, then sat with that preternatural stillness that Drust still noticed, for all the times he had seen it.

Manius came in, took watered wine and winced at what the cold of it did to his teeth. He hunkered and took one of his knives to draw in the frosted rock like a child's slate.

'Farmstead,' he said tersely, as if he paid for the words he used. 'Low drystone walls, some fallen in. Six buildings in poor repair. Smoke from one. No sign of people. Or goats.'

'Is that how they live here?' Kag demanded. Quintus frowned and said: 'I heard it was tall stone towers.'

That was in the north, Drust said, though he was not entirely on steady ground with that. The north, the place they called Thule, the Land of Darkness, held those the southerners called Painted People because they stained themselves with blue dyes. Drust told them that, remembering the soft voice of his ma, whispering through her memories as if to hug them as hard as she hugged him. He could not recall her face…

Ugo put them all right when they crept up to a high place and peered at it, lying flat and feeling the chill soak of melting frost off the granite.

'It is a little farmstead,' he said. 'Should have a dozen people in it. And animals. But there is that smoke…'

He paused, blinked once or twice. 'I lived in one. I think. It was up on a little hill, to keep it clear of the floods…'

'How many people are there?' Drust demanded brusquely and Ugo frowned.

'I cannot see any. This man keeps goats if what we were told is true – he will bring them in at night, let them into a pen during the day.'

'Suck Jupiter's salty balls,' Kag swore. 'There might be a score of people down there. At least. Most of them holding a spear and a shield.'

'I do not think—' Ugo began and Kag snarled at him.

'No, you don't. Leave that to those with the power for it.'

Ugo saw the way of it and subsided, scowling a little. They sat for a time, feeling the seeping cold and wet. Then Drust rubbed his bearded face and groaned himself upright.

'Well, if this Brigus is in there, that's where we must go. I will go down. If I don't come back…'

'We will go down,' Kag corrected, then stared round the others. 'If we don't come back in an hour, or send a sign, have a talk among yourselves and get to the bit where you come and kick in the door as loudly as if you were a legion.'

Drust told Kag to shed weapons. 'There is no point – they will take them from us anyway and even if we get out, we will probably lose them.'

'*If* we get out?'

Drust shrugged, trying to be more casual than he felt; his heart was betraying him and he was sure everyone could hear it.

'*Malum consilium quod mutari non potest*,' Quintus said cheerfully, but no one cracked a smile at the old fighter's adage. In Drust's experience a bad plan could never be changed, mainly because if it was rotten from the start the *harena* seldom allowed time for a change. He hitched his belt and tunic and took a deep breath. Kag looked at him and they both nodded.

'Anything moving?' Drust asked the watching Ugo, a last check before they moved down. The big German shook his head and rubbed a knee that was bothering him; the wet cold was not helping. 'Once you are in there is no way we can smash through it,' he added helpfully.

'What are they?' Quintus wanted to know, meaning what tribe. He looked expectantly at Drust, who sighed with an exasperation the tension was setting alight.

'How many times do I have to say it? I am a stranger here myself. They are tribals with spears is all I know.'

He stopped, a little ashamed of his outburst, but Quintus was still grinning.

'One of them is the lad we need,' he said, and clapped Drust on one damp shoulder. 'Fight to the finger,' he added.

Drust stood up and the others closed in a half-circle, then put out their right hands, palms down, touching fingers, showing the marked knuckles, then Drust led the way down the bracken- and rock-strewn hillside, seeing the place more clearly as they moved closer. There was a fox skeleton mouldering on the tallest barmkin wall like a mantrap and old, dried-out crows were fastened, wings spread, along the wall of one building.

The wind pulled through the fox bones and all the buildings sagged like half-empty grain bags, the bracken and turf and reed thatch stuck out in clumps like a woken drunk's hair. Drust wondered how old the place was, how long people had lived here. War had come here with fire and blood, often enough for people to learn from it and flee. Yet there was smoke from one house, which was solid with drystone walls, timber and turf. It had a door that was thick enough to be out of place.

'What a shithole,' Kag hissed, then nodded at the staked crosses of the crows. 'Are they some warding curse, do you think?'

'Only if you are a crow,' he answered, hoping it was true. The house seemed empty as an upturned bowl, so that the faint bleating of goats from one of the other buildings was loud.

'If he lives here alone...' Drust muttered and left the rest unsaid, but Kag did not need the answer. If Brigus lived here alone and unmolested it was because he was feared or shunned or both.

'Magic man,' Kag whispered. Druid, Drust thought, then was ashamed at himself; there had been no Druids for several lifetimes. He laid a hand almost caressingly on the timbers of the door, ran a finger round the rim where there was clearly a shuttered grille. It was altogether too much door for such a poor place, but he took a deep breath and began to push.

The grille slammed open and Drust leaped in shock, half fell over and recovered, annoyed and angry. A soft chuckle wafted out with warm air and the voice that came with it was gentle and female and slid through his ears like poisoned honey. He had learned that language, or something like it, when his ma spoke to him, when she sneaked time to be with him, risking the lash of an overseer's tongue and worse and speaking only in their own tongue. The last time she had spoken to him at all was in this language…

'We seek Brigus,' Drust managed to answer, the words falling out like he was stumbling. He managed it in his own tongue, the one his mother had tried to teach him, and the sweat popped like apple pips on him with the effort. There was a pause, then the shutter clattered closed; the wind whined and fingered hopefully at it, then raged biting cold on the two men standing, waiting.

'Come in,' the voice said in good Latin. Drust, blinking and ruffed as a wet cat, looked at Kag, who grinned back at him.

'A witch, not a magic man,' he said, then shrugged. 'Put the ram to the gate, then.'

There were thumps and clatters, then the door groaned heavily open; a reek of savoury smoke gusted out, so thick with warmth Drust almost groaned. They fell inside, losing sight at once in the dim. Drust was vaguely aware that he was stepping downwards, that the inside had been dug out to let people stand and move upright under a roof that was low to the ground otherwise.

Drust resisted dragging out a knife, offering gifts to Jupiter, Mars Ultor and any other god that sprang to mind if they would let this end in peace; he was already regretting his decision to leave serious weapons behind.

There was a bright light that made his eyes water while he fought to adjust to the blue-reeked dim. A wraithed shadow slid into the shape of a man peering suspiciously; he was an oldster, his hair grey and straggled, his beard braids thin and a face like the hindquarters of bad luck. Beyond him, a woman stirred something in a pot over the bright fire and looked up. She was neither old nor young, her hair unbound and a colour that might have been, in the dawn light, silver or gold.

She said nothing, merely waited for them to duck under her lintel and down the three or four rough steps, with their nerves all raw and one hand at the hilt of their eating knives. The room was grey with smoke, flowered with flame from the open fire; mad shadows jigged on the walls.

'Come,' she said. 'Take the warm of the fire.'

She wore a dark green dress and seemed to have a dark beard or a thin veil – then they both realised it was no beard, but a skin mark of dots and whorls all across her lower chin.

'*Salve*,' she said, which took them aback.

'Greetings in the name of all the gods. No evil here, Mother,' Drust replied in her own tongue, which made her look and pause and then nod.

'Nicely done,' she replied in the same way. 'Do you remember more, or is that it?'

'I have more,' Drust said, though the sweat was squeezing out as he fought to recall it. 'But my friend does not.'

She nodded. 'We will speak Latin, then. I am no stranger to it.'

Drust looked at the oldster, busy wrapping himself up to go out. 'Is this Brigus?'

'It is not. He is Necthan and goes to tend our sheep – and bring yours into the fold before they freeze.'

Kag grunted. 'I will go with him.'

There was warning enough in it for the woman to agree with a nod. Ducking at the doorway, Kag half turned.

'I thought you had goats.'

She laughed, soft and cold. 'Little brown-fleeced sheep with horns. Romans think all sheep are fat and white.'

She stirred aroma out of the pot, a rich savour that made Drust's mouth salivate; he knew it was the same for Kag.

'We have few left,' the woman added bitterly, 'so the one killed for this pot is an honour you should give thanks for.'

'Who are you?' Drust demanded when they were alone.

'Verrecunda,' she said. 'Once a power in a tribe that was once a power. Now nothing at all.'

She loaded from pot to bowl, added a wooden spoon and presented it. 'Eat. Talk when you are done.'

He was all but finished when the others fell in, groaning orgasms at the warmth, falling on the hot bowls like pigs at a trough. Last to arrive was Kag, who had made sure of the mules; the old man was with him and Kag clapped him on one wet-wool shoulder.

'This Necthan,' he said, then frowned. 'If I have it right – he does not speak any tongue I know, but he knows mules.'

'He knows all livestock,' Verrecunda corrected, handing them bowls. 'Fetch the Roman drink,' she added to Necthan and Drust realised only he had understood it. Necthan went to a dim corner, raked around and came back hefting an amphora that brought surprised noises.

'Jupiter's hairy arse,' Ugo declared when a rich amber liquid was poured. 'This never saw a *taberna* counter down in Subura – it looks like my piss after a bad night.'

'Then save all your bladder and drink it down,' Kag answered. 'This is Falernum, grown to be white and aged for years until it turns to pure gold. It comes from private cellars. Can it be real wine?'

It was. The taste of it, the sheer wonder of having a wine the Palatine bathed in and Subura never saw was astounding enough without it having made an appearance in a low hut beyond the last wall to the Land of Darkness.

'If we come on dog-headed men or one-horned horses,' Quintus said, his face splitting with smile, 'it would not be a surprise after this.'

'Will we meet such things?' Drust demanded, looking at Verrecunda. 'Is Brigus as rare as any of these?'

Necthan let the woman collect the scraped-clean bowls, beaming like a mother at Ugo worrying the last of the pot. Then she squatted, knees up on either side of her chin, dress modestly between her legs and Drust revised how old the woman was; he could barely sit comfortably.

'Brigus was a trader,' she said. 'He came three, four times a year, regular as dawns. Brought good needles, spun-wool thread, those bowls you ate from. Had wool, furs, some hides, horn and the like in return.'

She paused. 'And iron. Some tin. He traded in corn.'

Drust nodded; trade in metals was seldom a private enterprise. Trading in corn was a sly term and the look they exchanged confirmed it for Drust – the *frumentarii* were supposed dealers in it, although that was also the name given to those who went out and took the pulse of Empire. The State was here in the shape of Brigus and they had been right about that one.

'Are you telling them of Brigus?' the old man interrupted in his own tongue. 'That he was like the crow who shows the wolves the way to prey?'

'Keep quiet, old man,' she answered patiently. 'The crow also warns prey to run, don't forget.'

'Ha,' the old man growled, turning away. 'You order me like a slave. Those days are done for you.'

'Yet here you still are.'

She turned back to them, aware that Drust had understood. The others looked from him to her and back. Drust shrugged.

'The old man doesn't like Romans,' he said. Kag laughed with delight.

'I like him more and more – I don't like Romans either.'

'This Roman,' Manius said, 'would like to hear why we came all this way.'

'Brigus comes,' the woman said, 'trades what he trades—'

'You get the best of wine,' Quintus interrupted. 'And salt – I tasted it in your stew.'

'You get good stuff for good stuff,' Verrecunda replied simply, and there were nods.

'Brigus came to learn more of a woman and child. A Roman woman and child, a boy,' she said. 'Brought by a man called Colm. I knew of this man, though the boy had been barely able to walk then, was carried in the arms of his mother when she was given to the soldiers from the Wall.'

'Given?'

She looked at Drust, then at them all, one by one.

'You know how it works here? Also in the lands some of you come from?'

'Works? How what works?'

She shifted a little, easing joints. 'Power. There are chiefs here, but they rule by the bloodline of women. Once I was such and Necthan here was the man I took. He was a war chief in the days when the southerners came to build their new wall.'

Everyone looked at the old man and Kag grinned and nodded. 'A fighter,' he said, beaming round everyone. 'See? I knew that. You were all blind to it, but I knew that.'

'Age conquers all,' Verrecunda said. 'I was of the Red Kites, but that tribe is no more. The Blue Faces and the River People and all the others saw to that.'

'What of Dog?' Sib asked, harsh with impatience. 'Colm.'

She looked him up and down. 'You burn without thought,' she said scornfully. 'It shows in your skin.'

He fell silent, smouldering. She took a slurp from her cup and wiped her skin-marked chin.

'Colm's mother was a woman of power with a war chief who acted at her command. The Romans took her. They took many and not all were snatched in raids.'

Her voice grew bitter. 'There were those of our own who traded honour for power.'

'They sold your queens and stepped onto their thrones,' Quintus clarified. He grinned. 'Matters here are not so different than in Rome.'

'Even less than you believe,' Verrecunda said. 'Colm's mother was handed to the Roman garrison. She took her babe with her – the Romans preferred it since it made her biddable. It was always what they did when they could. The ones who sold her like a slave preferred it, too – they did not want to kill younglings, yet they did not want kids growing up with teeth and claws.'

Drust felt a cold slithering inside of him. This had been his own mother's fate. And his…

'How did you avoid this fate?' Manius asked, and Verrecunda glanced blankly at him.

'The Red Kites were no prize for anyone by then. Also, Necthan was loyal and not foolish – those who sold Colm's mother and her son had little reward for it. The man who did it could not rule, so he was forced out and those who followed found no one would listen to them either. The old way runs deep and true, and without the line of women, no one has the right to rule. They have squabbled ever since.'

'Let me guess,' Drust said quietly. 'The Blue Faces did this. Colm's mother was queen of the Blue Faces.'

She made a gesture. 'Queen is correct, yet not all of it. But, yes, it was the Blue Faces.'

'Yet this woman, the one with the boy, is not of the Blue Faces?'

Kag was sharp and Drust watched the woman to see the lie. There was one, but he could not tell what it was.

'We are all sisters of the goddess,' she replied. 'Not by blood, but more.'

'And this woman and her child?' Drust asked. The woman nodded.

'A poor creature. A Roman fleeing silken captivity for her own reasons.'

'Touching,' Manius growled, 'but unhelpful.'

'You are harsh,' Ugo snapped and the snarl in it surprised everyone. He looked shamefacedly round the staring faces. 'This sounds like me and my old ma.'

Verrecunda squinted at him through the sudden swirl of grey-blue; the wind chugged the walls of the house, demanding entry and growing angry at refusal.

'Yes. The same happens everywhere the Empire touches. Where are you from?'

'The Germanies,' Kag said and nudged Ugo. 'I say this because otherwise he will spend long minutes telling you his line and exactly where his sorry-arsed village lay.'

She nodded. 'So it is and so it was.'

'Colm's mother died, then,' Sib said. 'And so Colm became Dog the slave. So far this explains nothing.'

'He was bringing this woman and child here,' Drust said slowly, seeing it form like a walking man in a mist. 'Coming back to his own people.'

She made a little head gesture, not looking at him.

'What?' Drust demanded. She shrugged.

'He is a long way removed from them.'

'Yet he is the son of a queen.'

Kag flung up his hands. 'Fuck Dog. Who are this woman and child?'

'I do not know.'

'What has she to do with Dog?'

'I do not know.'

'We have been led up an alley with the gleam of gold,' Kag said bitterly to Drust. 'Best we back out now before we have to take it up the arse.'

Verrecunda unfolded stiffly and went to do something with spoons and dishes; Kag leaned in closer to Drust.

'Brigus is a State informer. What is he doing here, asking this Verrecunda about a woman and child? You do not bother with that if they are just runaway slaves.'

You do if the runaways are of great value, Drust mused. Though he had to admit he could not see why a woman and boy would be of great enough value to justify the costs involved in getting them back. There was more to it, but he could not see clearly. What he did see was that the woman and boy were not prisoners; they were hiding. She is a slave, Julius Yahya had said. Do not believe anything else she tells you…

'We came as rescuers,' Kag said, frowning. 'Now it seems we are to be the thieves.'

Verrecunda came back and squatted, stared at the flames and saying nothing.

'What more is there in this?' Drust asked, and she dragged her gaze from the fire and looked at him, blood-dyed by flames.

'What more is there? A woman is here with her son, protected by Colm and all the warriors of the Blue Faces. Talk to Colm. Talk to the Blue Faces.'

'Is she a slave?' demanded Sib. 'Or a queen?'

'A slave in Rome or a queen here,' Kag interrupted softly and laughed. 'Well, there is a dilemma. Mind you, the Divine Caesar once said he would rather be first in a Gaul village than second in Rome.'

'The Divine Caesar became a god on the floor of the Forum,' Quintus reminded him. 'Assisted by the back-stabbings of all his friends. So maybe he was right.'

'No matter,' Drust said, seeing it clearly. 'Dog wants her to be here. He brought her – is the boy his?'

Verrecunda shrugged.

'You do not seem concerned,' Kag said softly. 'What does Dog… Colm… get for this if not a wife and son? Does the boy have two heads?'

Verrecunda looked sharply at him. 'The boy is perfect. Colm of the Blue Faces is as hunted as they are.'

'Have you seen this woman, then, that you know her son to be perfect?' Manius asked, silken as a strangling ribbon. She stared fiercely back at him and could not hide the truth in her face. Drust laughed softly.

'You have. You were the one who told Brigus, not the other way round,' he said, and she dropped her gaze back to the flames. 'You saw her and knew her for a foreigner. For a Roman. And more – why else would you believe Brigus would be interested?'

'Do you see how well we fare?' she asked. 'How many sheep are penned up? The Blue Faces come every now and then and take some more and will do this until we starve.'

They fell silent and she stared at the flames for a moment.

'I told Brigus about the woman and he went to them, as he usually did. Traded. Came back this way and was excited – he gave more in gifts than he had before.'

She paused. 'Brigus did not come after that. I do not think he lives – but he must have reached the Walls and spoken with the Romans within, since here you are.'

Another pause and now she stared straight into Drust's face.

'Colm Deathface knows someone will come.'

'Deathface?'

She nodded and waved to the old man. 'He is a master of the marks of power,' she said and there was pride in it. She stroked her chin. 'These are to make my words sting or sweeten as I see fit.'

'He makes skin marks,' Kag said with delight and rounded on the old man. 'Did you give Dog what he wanted? You remember, lads – the bastard always moaned about how he had missed out on the marks given for deeds done. Servilius Structus would never permit such blatant brands on the bodies of his slaves – just the discreet owner's mark on knuckles.'

'I remember,' Drust replied. 'What did Necthan do?'

'Gave him the face of power,' she said. 'The face of death. You may see it soon enough.'

'Not likely,' Sib declared flatly. 'This is too rotted to eat. We should leave.'

'Good advice,' Verrecunda added.

'Arse,' Kag said scornfully to Sib. 'Did you think this would be a little walk in the cold and wet? A bit of a shouting match and maybe a pretend fight, like Drust's contests?'

'Ho,' Drust said, annoyed, and Kag waved a hand. 'You know what I mean.'

'I know what I heard—'

'Enough,' said Manius. 'No woman, no reward. We were sent here – I would like to know who commanded it.'

The woman shrugged. 'You would know best. Who pays you when you return her?'

No one spoke because Kalutis was Servilius Structus's man and he would pass them on to Verus, who was Julius Yahya's man, and Julius Yahya was someone else's man…

'What happened to this Brigus?' Sib demanded, leaning threateningly forward; the old man growled a warning and Sib leaned back hastily. Kag grinned with delight and patted the old man as if he was a clever dog, ignoring the scowls he got for it.

Verrecunda hesitated, then shrugged. 'I will tell what I told Brigus. What sent him to the Blue Faces.'

She stopped and looked round them all. 'What got him disappeared,' she added.

'Speak on,' demanded Ugo, scowling.

'The name Julia,' she said. They waited for more. She shrugged. 'That was all of it.'

A Roman name, Drust thought. The name of her mistress perhaps.

'Or the one she was given as a slave,' Quintus pointed out when Drust asked aloud. There was no more on it and it left them with more questions than answers – but most thought of Julia Domna, the Empress.

'It is a common enough name,' Kag growled, 'even on the Palatine.'

'There are too many women in this,' Quintus declared with disgust, and Verrecunda tossed the lees of her wine to the fire and laughed.

'More than you know. Look at your lives. You are all slaves, or were. You were all taken with your mothers, no?'

They looked, one to the other, and Verrecunda saw the possibilities dawn on them. She nodded.

'Just so. Somewhere, once, each of your mothers represented the goddess in a tribe beyond whatever Wall the Romans made in that land.'

'Ha,' Kag declared, but then his scorn dribbled out to silence and the gnaw of memories. All of them fought with the lees of their lives, wanting to wave it away and sickeningly aware of the truth in it.

In the end, they were silently fighting to remember everything – anything – while the wind hurled itself to puff and bluster. In the end, they found they only had the *ludus* of Servilius Structus in common and that they all had been taken from their mothers, who had died.

In the end, most of them came down to trying to remember what their mother's face looked like.

-

The morning brought a sky which smouldered somewhere between the frontiers of grey and black. Kag did not like it after having gone to see to the mules, but Necthan merely laughed scornfully.

They chewed new bread and contributed some salt cheese and a pot of brined olives that were still fresh enough to eat. There was an awkward silence until Ugo hawked, spat in the fire and turned to Drust.

'This mothers business…'

The groans pinched him shut. Kag spat an olive stone into the embers.

'Gods above and below,' he growled. 'I have chewed on that bone all night. No more.'

'If it is true, what the woman says,' Quintus argued, grinning his big wide grin, 'then we are all kings.'

'Unlikely,' Manius grunted, gathering up cloth and fur and weapons. He nodded to Drust, then the woman and went out. She did not ask why.

'Are we kings, then, woman?' Sib demanded and Verrecunda looked up from her wool work.

'You are brothers,' she said, smiling. 'Even you, burned man. This Servilius Structus is your father, the only one you know.'

'Gods forbid,' Ugo growled. 'I am no get of those loins.'

The woman was right, of course, Drust thought. We were all taken from our mothers and ended up with him; the strangeness of it, of something that had been there and yet never been seen, ruffled him.

'If you look deeper,' Ugo said to them, 'you will find Servilius Structus and our Emperor are known one to the other.'

'They both come from Lepcis Magna,' Sib agreed.

'Perhaps Servilius Structus was his pimp when they were younger. The Palatine takes the mothers, he gets the kids. Fucker.'

'Yet you call him by his full name,' she said softly. 'Every time.'

No one had an answer that made him sound sensible, so they stayed silent and spat olive pits into the embers.

'How far to where this woman is?' Drust asked. 'Will you guide us?'

The woman shook her head. 'It is a day if the weather holds fair. I will give you good landmarks to guide you, but neither I nor Necthan will go with you.'

'Are they watching, then?' Kag asked softly. The woman shrugged.

'I do not know – I do not think so. But there is a chance they might see us if we get closer. Our life here is on an edge as it is. Besides – it is a fool's task you have been put to. There is only death in it. These Romans are under the protection of Colm Deathface – the woman has a son and no desire to return from where she came. Is that not reason enough for leaving this be?'

'Does Dog… Colm… know who we are?'

Another shrug. 'He knows folk will come. He has known that since the day he dragged himself here.'

'Does this Roman woman know people come for her?'

A pause, no more than an intake of breath, let Drust know that the next thing she said was a lie.

'No.'

'Will she be biddable and come when we ask?' demanded Ugo. 'I do not want to be struggling with an unwilling woman.'

'I have heard you in the brothel,' Quintus said. 'You are no stranger to it.'

'Ha,' Ugo said.

'Can Dog be a war chief?' Sib asked, frowning. 'I have heard you speak only of husbands.'

'They are never husbands, only men taken as partners,' she answered, but there was a brittle tension there. Aha, Drust thought, there is no queen of the Blue Faces and you have to be a bedmate to rule. There is probably some muscled leader already, unable to exert the power of kingship and needing no old queen's get turning up to add drama.

He might have said more aloud on it, but there was a rustle of black wind at the door and Manius was in their midst, bringing the chill of the outside – and worse.

'Riders.'

There was a noise like a covey of surprised birds as everyone leaped for weapons.

'How many?' demanded Drust.

'A dozen. Perhaps more. On those little ponies, but they do not fight on them.'

The woman made a grunt of disgust. 'They are come for more sheep and mischief,' she said, and her voice was tinged with fear. The oldster had a fistful of blade as ancient as he was and his beard bristled like a hog's back. Kag grinned at him.

'We could hide,' Sib suggested hopefully. 'In those other buildings.'

'If they fetch sheep they will see the mules and gear,' Drust pointed out, and everyone saw it, saw that there was no other way for it. Manius started for the door and stopped when Drust caught his sleeve.

'No one gets away,' he said. Manius nodded and flitted outside. The others followed, spilling right and left; Drust looked at Necthan and Verrecunda.

'Greet them as normal,' he told her. 'Make no sign that anything is amiss.'

He grinned at Necthan, though his top lip got stuck doing it. 'Put that sticker down,' he added in their tongue, 'or you will scare them off.'

Necthan growled and spat. 'When I am dead they can take it from my grasp – if they can.'

Drust stayed where he was, dry-mouthed in the shadows of the hut, listening to the riders come up and climb off. The voices were muted, but laughing. He heard Necthan growl and heard them spit warning noises back at him.

Then the door was blocked with darkness and a figure came in, a big man swathed in furs and cloth, peering as his eyes strained. He had nothing in his hands and came in rubbing them, looking around.

For a moment Drust wondered if he should rush him, if he could make it and kill the man before he cried out. The man turned to go; Drust tensed – then the man paused, looked down, bent and came up with a cup. He sniffed it, looked round and bent again to come up with another.

The wine cups, Drust thought. More than needed for a woman and an old man…

The man turned to leave, starting to call out as he ducked out and began to climb the three steps of beaten earth stair. Just as he reached the entrance and started to talk, he flew back inside; someone laughed, thinking he had slipped and fallen, but Drust had pulled him backwards, having registered the thump of the arrow, like a fist on a door, and did not stop or loose his grip on the man's ankle. He dragged the man down the steps in a series of skull crunches and let him go.

The dazed man rolled over, blood on his forehead and the skin scraped off, right over a blue-black mark. An ink-marked axe, Drust thought, and saw a horse on his cheek, too – the man began to get up, flapping muzzily at the strangeness sticking out of his chest, but had the last vision of a dark figure with a gleaming light in one hand, then Drust's blade slashed the sight from his eyes. A second stroke, accompanied by curses for the ineptness of the first, stole the life out of his throat.

Blood reeked and spread. Drust pattered through it, up and out into the yard, where men danced and yelled and struggled and died. The snow-bright light scarred his eyes, but he saw Ugo circling his axe in beautiful loops while Sib skipped at his back, keeping men away from the big Frisian. Necthan was blowing and swinging, showing what he must have been like in youth; a dead man at his feet proved that he still had skills.

Kag and Quintus were sword-paired and moving in fluid patterns, falling into the machine of it. Bodies sprawled in the red slush – six, Drust saw, one with an arrow. Seven down with the one I killed, he thought – not enough.

These were sometime warriors and had not been expecting trouble like this. Two more went down, carved down at the ankles and stabbed in the face. The leader was easy to spot, a big man made bulkier by furs. He had a long spear and a small square shield, but the mark of his status was all in the war hat, a beaten steel affair with silly coppered bull horns sticking from it.

He came roaring at Drust, who clutched a sword and a great deal of sweating fear. The spear came up and round in a wide sweep, but it sliced air; Drust skipped sideways, away from the shielded side.

The big warrior moved fast, but something slammed him sideways and then did it again; Drust saw two arrows in the square shield and the warrior shook them free with a curse. Drust promised Manius a gift, took his chance, darted in and slashed; the warrior howled as his leg buckled; blood flushed out into the fancy designs of his wool trousers.

He came back from it swiftly, knowing he was worse off than before – no shield, slowed to a limp. No way to win save to finish it, so he came in hard and hurled the spear.

Drust fell and rolled, came up spitting cold snow and wet with the spear bouncing and wriggling like a mad snake beyond him. He had time to glance at it before the warrior was on him, his fist full of a long, bright sword.

It came up and came down like a wall. Never block, Drust thought wildly; he heard Sophon bellow it from down the corridor of years. The bigger, stronger man will break your wrist or beat you down or break your blade even if you manage to hold him. Turn your wrist – so. Slide it sideways – so…

It was all too late. The blade came down on Drust like a wall and he heard the steel ring; he staggered and his arm seemed to have vanished, yet when he looked in panic it was there and the sword was in it – there just didn't seem to be anything he could do with it.

The warrior gave a loud grunt of delighted triumph and bored in for the kill. Drust ducked, spun and reached out his one good hand as he went sailing along the man's side. His fist closed on the horn of the helmet and he wrenched and fell and rolled.

There was a crack and a thump. He rolled over, winded and wet with slush. The warrior was down and looking back over his own shoulder. Never wear a silly hat, Drust thought. And if you must, never tie it down so that someone can wrestle you like a cow and break your silly neck.

He lay, the cold seeping into him and it seemed he was there a long time, but it was only long enough for Ugo to boot him savagely in the ribs as he moved on; Drust took the hint, rolled over to his hands and knees and got up.

Metal shrieked, wood splintered. Ugo, his hair flying round his face, whirled the axe and had no proper room for it, so that the shaft slapped a man in the upper arm – it was enough to make him yell and fly backwards.

Quintus, roaring and grinning, cut and stabbed, snapping back the head of a man who thought he had been swift and clever until he took the hilt of a second sword in what remained of his teeth. He went over on his arse, spitting blood and rolling away from Quintus, who came at him in a flurry of blows.

Drust had his own concerns – he twisted sideways to avoid a spear thrust, kept going and crashed into the owner, turned, slashed, felt the blade scoring down wood, stumbled to his knees. He saw a foot and stabbed it in the instep; the man howled and hopped until Ugo's axe crushed ribs and life.

Manius was trying to get out to where he could use the bow, but men were on him and Kag was too busy – for a moment Drust thought Manius was gone, but that curved dagger lashed and hissed. Quintus stopped his mad chopping and looked up, his face spotted with blood, then he grinned like some bloody funeral mask and leaped on one of Manius's attackers.

Drust tried to join in, found himself alongside Manius while the outnumbered attacker backed off, his face wild, his mouth open and wet; he held his blade in two hands and his hair was a tangle of wet snakes. Manius moved like silk in a breeze, there was a sharp ping of sound, like ice shifting in heat, then Drust felt something pattering on him, thought it was rain on his face until he saw the man let slip his sword and clap his hands to the bloody froth spouting from his throat like water from a burst pipe.

They were running and now it was a slaughter. A man broke from the ruck and leaped on a pony.

'Manius…' Drust yelled.

The man with the ripped throat was down, frantically trying to keep his life inside and gug-gugging while he did it. Ugo loped up and turned to where Drust stood, soaked with cold and sweat and someone else's blood.

'*Missio?*' he demanded. Kag gave him a curse and moved in, slashing, as the warriors who had thrown down their weapons yelled and tried to move away. They died on their knees and bellies, cut to bloody fret.

'I have told you before,' Drust said to Ugo, feeling sick and breathless. 'This isn't the sands.'

'There's no rule-maker with a stick,' Kag added, panting with the exertion of hacking men to pats. 'Just kill the fucks.'

Ugo casually chopped the throat-cut one, taking off most of the top of his head in a careless, uncaring strike, then leaned on his axe, pointedly wiping the clotted gore off the blade. 'You have no feeling for the way of it,' he said sadly. Drust was more concerned about the rider and couldn't see anything of him – but Manius loped up and nodded. Drust got up, feeling a rush of relief.

'Well,' Sib said, wide-eyed with it all. 'Well.'

Drust sometimes forgot that the Numidian wasn't a true fighter but a horse coper. He had handled himself well enough, though.

'Nice touch with the helmet,' Kag said to Drust, eyeing the warrior with the broken neck. 'You didn't need to let it get to that, though. Could have taken him out if you had applied yourself.'

'He hadn't rehearsed it,' Quintus said, grinning, and Drust bridled.

'I fought some real fights,' he started, but the lie in it stopped his mouth. They gave themselves a long moment of breathing and enjoying the sensation, the exultation that came with survival. Then came the sickness that always followed and Drust's was slathered with what had to be done now.

'Collect them up. Put them on their ponies and take them with us when we go,' he said. 'Bury them and all their gear some way from here.'

They saw the need and wearily got down to it. The ponies snorted and stamped at the blood smell and the old man and the woman helped lash the bodies. The woman offered a pack of dried cooked meat and filled an empty skin with Falernum. Then she stood, cradling the heavy amphora in her arms like a child.

'A day north and west,' she said to Drust and looked at the sky. 'If you get no weather you should be there as night falls. You keep towards that range of hills until you come to a river – the Smoothing Stone they call it. You won't miss it. Follow it – the Blue Face territory starts at where you find the river and they are settled midway along the length of it.'

He nodded. 'After Brigus left you told her we would be coming,' he said and, with only a slight pause, she waggled her head, that sign that could be yes and no and was always an admittance of guilt for something.

'What did she say?

'She is afraid. For the boy more than herself.'

'Will she come with us?'

'She may. It may not be possible,' she said. Even if this Roman woman had Dog the slave fucking her in her unwilling arse nightly, he thought, she will not come meekly with us. Because we represent folk who will do even worse to her.

Verrecunda seemed to sense… something. Cleared her throat and took a breath.

'Do not harm the boy,' she said vehemently. 'He is perfect.'

She moved away from him and he was disconcerted by her; he turned away and found Manius looking at him out of a dark, flat stare like the entrance to the abyss. He nodded and did not need to say more.

They moved out, and when they'd been travelling a few minutes, Manius stopped, turned his mule and loped it back.

'Where is he going?' demanded Ugo.

'Forgot an arrow,' Quintus said, knowing the truth. He was grinning his big grin, fixing it on his face like a shield against thought.

By the time they found the hollow with its skeletal trees and had started to scraping out the mulch, Manius came loping in again.

'Just in time,' Sib growled, wrestling one of the corpses off the pony. Kag, grim-faced as ever when it came to this, held the mount steady for Ugo to slam the pony's forehead with the reverse side of his axe. One by one the ponies died and were dragged into the shallow hole.

Then Ugo, wiping the gore off his hands with clean snow, squinted at the horizon where they had come from. It took him a moment to get to it, then he stared at Manius and shook his head.

'Fuck' he said bitterly. Sib's face grew hard and colder than the crusted slush when he worked it out. Kag turned away in disgust.

'I liked the old man,' he said wearily and pinched the bridge of his nose.

They gathered up the mules and plodded on into the grimming day.

Chapter Seven

It was *intempesta nox*, the dead of night when no one should be awake. This was when your soul was closest to Dis and even sentries pacing walls would sooner forget their spear than a warding amulet.

The cold was surely sent by Dis, Drust thought. It slid like mating snakes round his ankles and legs and up even to the sanctum of his fork; he would have to move soon or stiffen and die. But it was fighting with crushing weariness for possession of his body as well as his soul; he struggled against it, battled it hard with the great bell ringing blades of unanswered questions – who had sent them here? Brigus was State – yet which part of it sent the woman and her child here and which part now wanted them back? Why had Dog been involved?

It was the epitome of futility. The known world ceased to exist and there was nothing beyond the cold Land of Darkness that held any meaning. His head dropped, but he slept in fits and starts and then thought of his mother. It was all that talk from Verrecunda, he thought.

He remembered her face and was pleased that he still could, knowing that year on year it faded like a poor wall painting. Once it had been everything that was beauty, comfort, safety, love.

She came silently in the night when she could, smelled of peaches and taught him the tongue. Taught him that he was a slave and what that meant.

'How do you stop being a slave?' he had once asked her and she had kissed him, her face large, her eyes bright as stars.

'You remember. You remember the tongue. You remember me. You remember me speaking of freedom. You never forget.'

He became aware of someone settling in the dark beside him and hoped whoever it was had not heard him; he was sure he had whimpered or cried or both. It was Kag.

'You awake?'

'Now,' he said, and Kag grunted apologies.

'Cold,' he said, but that wasn't what chewed him out of sleep and Drust knew it.

'This woman,' Kag began. Drust waited.

'This woman.'

'You said that,' Drust answered, feeling the cold and the sleep and wondering, dully, if one was the other. He knew that's how true cold worked…

'He means – what about this woman?'

The new voice was rheumed but strong, with a laugh in it still. Quintus came up and squatted, so it looked as if they all sat round a fire that wasn't there.

'You are supposed to be on watch,' Kag growled, and Quintus shrugged.

'Manius went out an hour ago. Sib is watching. Only Ugo sleeps. So we speak of this woman and her kid and what we have learned and what we do not know.'

'What don't we know?' Drust asked, puzzled now. He remembering the poignancy of his mother; it was all just dreaming, he thought. That's all.

'We don't know where she is or how she is,' Quintus said. 'It seems she will scream. That makes a difference.'

'We don't know who she is, more the point,' Kag growled.

'We don't know who sent her here and who wants her back is more the point,' Drust said, and that silenced them. Kag blew out a smoke of cold sigh.

'We do not even know her name,' he muttered morosely.

'Julia,' Drust said, and Quintus, to whom the names of women meant little, blew on his hands.

'If you believe the woman at the hut,' he said.

'Why would she lie?' Kag demanded.

'We could ask her,' Quintus said in mock surprise. 'Oh no, wait – Manius saw to that.'

Kag scowled. 'I liked the old man.'

Drust lost patience. 'Enough on the old woman and man,' he snapped. 'It was necessary and Manius did it on orders.'

No one spoke and Drust was grateful for the fire that had been shoved into him, but it was already fading. He looked at the sky, felt the sword's-edge breeze and wished for the faint dim blue that marked a dawn.

'Who sent us?' Quintus demanded. 'Really. Kalutis is the man of Servilius Structus, but even he did not bother hiding the fact that he had no idea who would claim the woman and child once we'd brought them back to Eboracum. Julius Yahya works for someone else, someone high-born.'

'Julia Domna,' Kag replied firmly. 'Has to be.'

'The Empress? Why would she go to all this trouble for a slave, even a valued household one? Money and the promise of citizenship for six people – is any slave worth that, even one with a kid in tow?'

'Who else could it be?' Drust muttered, having worried at it for too long. 'The woman at the hut…'

'Verrecunda,' Quintus interrupted savagely. 'She was called Verrecunda.'

Drust paused, but ignored the stroke, partly because he did not want to provoke and partly because it was a solid blow, well delivered, and he had no reply.

'Verrecunda,' he said, 'told us this woman was a slave. One of those pampered ones taken more as hostage than slave.'

'Like our mothers,' Quintus said thoughtfully.

Kag laughed. 'Well, in point she did not say that. Just the name Julia – we have conjured everything else up like one of Ugo's shamans. And that is how this Verrecunda works, I saw. All that business about our mothers – I never knew my old ma, but I was given to know that she worked fields somewhere. Hardly pampered. Nor was she some chieftain's daughter.'

He broke off and held up both hands. 'I know, I know – we all claim we were better blood than we are. Everyone who gets *harena* between their toes swears he is a prince in his own lands. But lads – all of us, the sons of queens?'

He looked round, daring the silence. Then he shook his head.

'Quintus is a Suburan rat whose mother was a whore in the Wolf's Den and worked for Servilius Structus,' he went on savagely. 'No hostaged queen there, is there?'

'Fuck you,' Quintus replied, but he grinned all the same.

'So the woman lied?'

The bass rumble heralded Ugo, and Kag sighed. 'Now we have most of a set.'

'Yes, mountain of the Germanies,' Quintus chuckled, 'the woman lied.'

'Verrecunda,' Kag added. 'Her name was Verrecunda.'

Ugo stared from one to the other, scowling at why they were chuckling and wondering if he was the butt of another joke. He was, he knew, quite a lot of the time, and he knew he was not foolish but it irritated him that he could never quite work out if he was being cozened or not.

'If she lied about such a matter,' he said, preferring to ignore everything else, 'then what else did she lie about?'

'The very question,' Kag declared moodily. 'Brigus perhaps.'

'He is dead,' Drust said. 'He went to find this woman, presumably returned to the Wall and was never seen again.'

'We should have asked Necthan some questions about Brigus,' he added, half to himself. The old man had had a sly look about him most of the time…

'Too fucking late now,' said a voice, and a shadow loomed; Quintus made a grunt of annoyance.

'You are supposed to be on watch,' he said. Sib crouched and glared, shivering.

'Since everyone is awake, it would seem better if one of you took the watch and let those who would sleep, sleep.'

'It is your watch,' Ugo pointed out.

'Is this the Army, then?' Sib snapped back.

'If it was you would be running a line of men with cudgels and righteous annoyance,' Drust said, and Sib gave a wave of one hand, as if to apologise and acknowledge the transgression.

'I am on watch,' he said. 'So much so that I saw Manius coming in. He will be here soon.'

When he came in, the man radiated heat so that they all felt it, shifted a little closer to absorb some of it. He had been travelling hard and brought news that made everyone forget the cold.

There were fires and men sitting round them, Manius told them. No more than a long walk from here. Armed men with faces he had thought eaten by shadows or disease until he realised they were all skin-marked. Around twenty of them, all cheerful with food and flames.

'Blue Faces,' Kag said. 'Hunting us.'

Manius shook his head and told them of the others, the women bound and guarded, the driven sheep and hauled cattle. It was a raiding party, out in the depths of winter when no raiders usually moved.

'Raids are the same everywhere,' Ugo agreed. 'Winter is hard enough without what little you have being stolen and what shelter you need burned round your ears. There will be agreements on it. Understandings now broken.'

Manius nodded. 'I watched the chasers, too. Same number, perhaps a few more and not so far behind. I do not know what people they belong to, but they are vengeful for the raid and on the trail of the Blue Faces. It is my reckoning the Blue Faces will have to push to reach the shelter of their own fortress before the chasers give up.'

'We should follow these Blue Faces,' Drust said. 'Carefully and unseen. They will show us the way to this woman and her child.'

'In case the woman at the hut lied,' Ugo declared.

'Verrecunda,' said three voices, then stopped.

'It seems the woman, this Julia, if that is her name, will not come willingly,' Ugo said and shook his head. 'We are not rescuers here.'

Sib looked from one to the other, then at Manius.

'We might have brought the woman in the hut along with us, to calm or help,' he said bitterly. 'But she will hardly be of use now, eh? Her name was Verrecunda, in case you did not know.'

Manius gave him a stare like a steel wind.

'Never give a name,' he said softly, 'to something you might have to feed iron to.'

-

'What are they doing now?'

Sib was shivering, his words coming out bitten in two. They all lay at the fringe of a line of trees, some like skeletal hands clawing up from the wet mulch, most of them green with needles already clotting with snow. It had been snowing for two hours.

Below them, the scurrying pack of Blue Faces were kicking people away from them. The discards stumbled free, falling down or simply sitting where they were. Once, Drust saw a grey-haired woman dragged out by a warrior, who slashed at her legs until she fell, whimpering; there were faint cries elsewhere, too.

The pack moved on, leaving a scatter of crawling, limping bodies behind; one or two fell and stayed still.

'Those ones are slowing them down,' Manius said.

'At least they did not kill them,' Quintus said and Manius did not even spare him a look, but all the scorn was in his voice.

'Why would they? The ones coming after them are here to rescue as much as exact vengeance. They will gather them up and now they will be the ones slowed. They hamstring them.'

'Let's not wait to see,' Drust said. 'The Blue Faces in their stronghold will know an enemy is near and that will make them all look in that direction. It lets us move unseen, but we must not lose sight of the Blue Faces. They are our guides after all.'

'You will not need to hurry,' Manius said, brushing snow off his bow. 'The chasers will guide us – and they only need follow the trail of throwaways. We will stay here and try and get warm.'

'Who made you leader?' Kag demanded. Manius shrugged, looked at him and then pointedly at Drust.

'I was taken when I had sixteen seasons on me. I had already been a raider out of the desert for seven seasons before that. I know more than anyone here about what people such as these do, whether they do it on sand or snow.'

'I was also a raider at that age,' Sib hissed. 'Your people did not raid. They slaughtered. *Jnoun. Lemur...*'

'Ho, ho,' Kag protested, but Drust held up a hand and stared at Manius.

'I lead the *Procuratores*. That's always been the way of it and nothing has happened to change it. You will follow my lead?' he asked. 'If not, fare you well. We fight together here.'

'We have the same name,' Manius replied coldly, 'but that does not make us brothers. I will stay for my share – money is the mortar that has bound us all.'

He went off. Sib spat and Ugo grunted, then shook snow off his head.

'That shows he is no *harena*,' he said. 'What binds us is blood and sand, not gold.'

There were grunts of approval, but Drust doubted Ugo's ideals – on the *harena* you had no friends and the *Procuratores* had been tied by poverty and debt to Servilius Structus. Manius was the first crack in what had been coming since the day they made their mark on the contract for this – after it they would go their own ways.

Drust just did not want it to be before they had done what they came to do. He did not want it at all, for he had come to realise an uneasy truth – these, the Brothers of the Sand, were the only semblance of family he had and probably the only one he'd ever have.

When it was gone – what then? It was a matter he did not want to confront.

–

Moving out, they followed the ones following the Blue Faces. Twice they came on graves of hasty scrapes and piled stones; one was a small affair and the amulet wrapped round a stone was big enough only for a child's neck.

'They take time to tomb them up,' Manius said flatly, 'and fall further behind.'

'They keep going all the same,' Kag pointed out.

They dipped into low country where the forests frowned down on them, dripping green and gold and white; the snow drifted like goose feathers and the cold sliced them. Drust watched Sib shiver more and more and knew that they had failed to outrun the weather. Winter had come early, keen and cold.

They came on the first steading not long afterwards, stone and turf huddled low to the ground near the spill of the river they had been following – the Smoothing Stone, Drust thought. It frothed like water from a burst pipe mostly, but now and then swelled and contracted like something giving birth. This was a wide, calm stretch, the water shallow so that in summer you could see the bottom and the fish; now it was fringed with ice that would creep out, bit by bit, as winter went on.

The steading was cold, the marks of the chasers clear in the scuffed snow. The drift of flakes had stopped but the cold wet of it flushed out on their bellies as they lay on the lip of the stream's high bank. Behind, the stream slid like a black ribbon, shallow enough to already dream of being ice; it had already forgotten the men and mules who had shivered their way across it.

Drust peered through the stiff reeds, not wanting to move them because they were cold and dry and would clack like bird beaks. Beyond was the smokeless steading, a felled trunk abandoned on trestles, the adze-axe left wedged under a shaved curl of bark; beyond that was the biggest of the steading buildings, crouched to the ground like a whipped dog so that the wattle and daub and turf and stone of it seemed part of the landscape.

It was as empty as sightless eyes. Around it, the other steading buildings, for beast and fodder, were equally cold and dead; the garth was scuffed and littered with a scatter of discarded plunder, barely shrouded in the snow.

Two humps lay in the middle of it and Drust knew those shapes well enough, even if the blued feet sticking out from under the snow had not been there.

'Not hard to follow,' Kag whispered, his lips close enough to make his beard tickle Drust's ear. 'The pursuers are taking revenge on the land of the Blue Faces now – wonder is that they left the buildings unburned.'

Because some were still there; Kag hadn't considered it and it drew his mouth into a thin line as Drust went crab-walking down the line of them, hissing out this revelation.

Drust was trying hard not to think about how recently he had been in the warm, in streets that were cobbled, among houses with atriums and bathhouses and a decent inn. Seemed a long way gone, swallowed by mornings waking stiff with cold and staring into a future gaping like a pit. Staring at the rolling tawny and needle-green, the harsh crags and rocks that looked like sheep and sheep that looked like rocks.

Somewhere ahead was a new tomorrow, but while he grinned at the gold of it, his blackened past was creeping up from the cold earth and trying to steal his life.

The bodies lay in a vegetable patch, part grubbed up by the ravagers – that meant they were short enough on food to consider winter roots a prize – and when Drust and the others cat-crouched their way up, wary and watchful, they saw a man's face, then a woman's, both slack with old death. The woman's neck gaped in a savage purpled second grin, and her lined face, like a chewed-leather pouch, was clotted with tendrils of her grey-bloody hair.

There was a burst of laughter from the house, wolf-savage and sauced with a whimpering scream; Drust had an idea why some of the ravagers had stayed behind. He made signals that sent Manius and Sib on a wide circling sweep to scout out if there were others, Quintus and Ugo to find another way in and out – though he doubted there was one. Then he looked at Kag, took a breath and nodded.

Kag went in first and when Drust ducked after him, he found the usual narrow and low dugout. There was a pit fire of embers, a heavy table of split logs, a few stools and a bed. A rangy man was in the act of standing up from one of the stools; he had a worn-out look to him, a shock of red hair frosted with grey and worked up into two horns with feathers bound in.

Behind him, two men struggled with a woman who had just about given up, with no strength left to even scream. Drust thought she must have been wife to the dead man outside, for she wasn't young and her face was deep-lined enough to be used as a rack for bowls. If they hadn't been looted out and scattered along with everything else.

The man in between her spread legs had an armless sheep fleece for a coat and had undone the belt that cinched it, the better to get himself into the struggling woman. He had one leg by the ankles and the other hand on her throat, while his breeks were at his boots.

The last one was another redhead, twitchy looking and young. He had both hands on the woman's other leg, keeping her from scissoring them shut because he wanted Sheep-Fleece to get done with it and let him take over.

All of them froze as if time had stopped. The redhead with feathers stood and stared, even when Kag strode across the dim, littered floor and hammered him twice in the ribs with his *pugio*. Then he gave a whimpering yelp and scrambled backwards, hit the tripod of the pit fire and fell in the embered ashes; his foot flew up under the stool he had been sitting on and whipped it into Kag's face.

There's always that moment, that act of Fortuna that will crack your carefully rehearsed fight out from underneath you. The goddess smiles her vicious smile and makes that unarmed felon suddenly lash out and fell you to the *harena* just as the audience is baying for you to give him iron and let them see his face while you do.

Kag went down like a windblown tree. The wounded man rolled round the fire, screaming; his clothes caught alight. The twitchy youngster let go of his assigned leg and sprang away, yelping and hauling out a long knife; Drust saw all their serious weapons and armour were off and stacked – these were not the sharpest spears in the vengeful army.

The one in between the woman's legs hauled himself away from her, gawping at Drust, then at the man rolling and shrieking in the pit fire; utensils clattered and clacked and ash billowed in a choking cloud that misted everywhere.

Drust watched Kag roll over onto his knees and spit blood from where the stool had smacked him in the mouth. The two remaining men were recovering, getting lost in the ash mist, but what struck Drust was how ordinary they were. Here were the beasts beyond the Wall, three stumbling fumblers with big hair and beards – but they had stumbled and fumbled their way through this steading, crashing into the life of a couple who thought themselves inured to hard times and now the detritus of their old lives lay around her, the sole survivor with a patched dress rucked up over her sagging breasts and skinny thighs.

Drust thought of his mother, set his jaw to clench and shifted to where he had last seen the youngest of them, the one who had recoiled, trying to drag out a weapon. The ash mist stung his eyes and clogged his breathing, but he saw the shape through it and struck, felt the jar up his arm, heard the scream and whimper.

He lost the shape. Something loomed out of the mist like a charging bull and he went down on one knee, struck out with a legionary jab, one of those hard thrusts that would take a *gladius* into the guts of a shrieking warrior.

He hit nothing, but the shape hit him, gave a sharp cry and went over him; the pair of them tumbled and rolled. Drust hit his head on something that blew in white light and a shock of pain while it blew out all sense.

There was a curse, a series of scrabbles and then the redhead who had been between the woman's legs reeled out of the settling ash, his face stricken with disbelief. He maybe even tried to tell Drust how unfair it all was, but all that came out of his mouth was black blood, heart blood that meant he was a dead man standing.

Then he stopped standing; when he fell clear, Drust saw the woman, vengeful as a harpy, her face twisted with it, her dress stained and bloody and the big fish-gutting knife clotted. Drust scrabbled backwards, fearful that he might be next.

The man who had fallen over Drust was wobbling to his feet and starting to snarl when the faint light from the door, shafting in through the clearing ash, was suddenly blocked and the dark that came with it made Drust lose sight of everything.

There was a chill wind, a hissing sound, a meaty thump – the woman went sideways with no more than a little squeal. Drust got his hands and knees, then got upright; the ash drifted down like a last shroud, just in time to reveal Ugo and the young redhead, still dazed from falling over Drust. There was time to take in the frantic stare, the futile raised hand, then Ugo's axe came hissing round and slammed into the man, driving him backwards in a gout of blood and a loud cracking of tortured ribs. The axe went deep, so deep it came out the other side of him and slammed into the table edge; the young redhead hung on it, coughing and waving his arms and legs.

The last redhead had crawled out of the fire and beaten out most of the smoulder, but it did no good; Kag, spitting blood and curses, pounced on him, dragged his head back by his red hair and sawed the *pugio* through his throat. It was not a good weapon for that, having no edge to speak of – a stabbing weapon, not even used much these days and then only by officers in the Army.

As Kag had said, often: 'It was good enough for the Divine Julius to acquire several of them, so it is good enough for me.'

It reduced him to a butcher here, and when he had done there was only heavy breathing and the reek of blood and ash. Ugo started to grunt the axe out of the table, but he was having trouble with it. Drust saw the woman huddled like a pile of bloody rags in a corner of the littered hut and Ugo saw him looking.

'Sorry,' he said. 'I thought she was enemy.'

Kag levered himself to his feet. His eyes were red and teared and he spoke with a slur.

'How could you mistake that for an enemy?' he demanded savagely. Ugo tore the axe free; blood sprayed and the man fell off the table.

'Was a shape. Back to me. Fucking big knife in one hand heading for Drust.'

Kag said nothing but he spat into his hand, then held up the result.

'Tooth,' he said bitterly. 'I have lost a tooth. Juno's tits, this is a bad day.'

'Will get worse,' said a voice from outside, and when Drust and Kag ducked out, blinking, Sib looked at them grimly.

'You will want to see this.'

He led them across the rutted garth to another round building, a byre before what few kine had been here were taken by the raiders. Now new occupants huddled for heat and shelter, a dozen of them looking up with pale faces and the pinched look of those thinking 'not again'. They were the captives 'rescued' by their tribesfolk, but too far gone to keep up. The fear rose up with the fetid smell of wounds gone bad.

Kag ducked back outside and breathed in cold, clear air. Drust and Sib followed.

'They left them because they were being slowed down,' Sib said.

'Which means they will be back for them once they have run the Blue Faces to a lair they cannot assault. I am thinking they may themselves then be pursued.'

'We should move from here,' Drust said, 'without further linger.'

They went back, found Manius and Quintus already assembling mules and three ponies left by the dead men. Busy with packs and saddlery, they worked steadily for several minutes until Kag looked round.

'Where is Ugo?'

Ugo was coming out of the roundhouse when they went in search of him. He held a torch and, just as they came up, he threw it back into the entrance.

'To the Genius of the Land of Darkness, to Ricagambeda and Vradecthis,' he said, arms spread wide, head back to stare sightlessly at the sky. There was a dull hoom of sound from inside the roundhouse.

'To Mars Ultor, Minerva, Epona and Victory, Ugos Servilius of the Axe dedicates this in sorrow and begging forgiveness.'

The oil-fired flames licked briefly out the door; black greasy smoke started leaking from the roof.

'Jupiter's hairy cock,' Kag spat, staring in horror. 'What have you done, you crazed German?'

Ugo turned, his eyes miserable pools. 'I did not see her. I did not see her clearly...'

'You see nothing clearly,' Drust snarled and waved a hand at the smoke and the licking flames. 'Now you have sent a beacon that says to those who care that this place is burning. The place they left their recently freed relations, thinking them safe.'

'You have shit for thinking with,' Kag added bitterly. Ugo stood like a slaughter ox until Drust slammed a fist into his shoulder.

'Move. Our only hope is to shift away from here in a running hurry.'

Chapter Eight

They did not run so much as shuffle across a patched land of white and tawny and wet green. A mule gave a final, fretful, accusing grunt and fell over, all the pack on it rattling and crashing, splintering free.

'Keep moving,' Drust yelled and pointed. 'Make for the high ground on that ridge. The one with the woods on it. We can at least fight with advantage.'

'My pots...' Quintus yelled and Sib snarled at him to get out of the way as he tugged and cursed the mules to move faster. Quintus hesitated, dancing on the moment, but it was clear no one was stopping to unload his precious pots. In the end, he loped after the others, yelling out as he went. It was only when they were too far to turn back that they realised what he had been trying to tell them. Sib was bawling at him about how there was more of his foul brew on another mule when the true import hit him, clicking his teeth together with the shock. He sweated and shivered in equal measure and he had company in it.

'If they get their hands on it,' Quintus shouted to Drust, and did not need to say more. Everyone's face grew pinched and round and Kag yelled out that they were pelt-wearers and would probably try and drink the stuff, not throw it.

'When his head explodes,' Quintus bawled back, 'the others will know it is not just strong drink.'

Manius blew out his cheeks and hefted his bow. 'I will go,' he said. 'If I break a pot it will crack all the others.'

'You will be too close to get away from those left,' Drust answered.

'Then I had better leave none,' Manius answered, then held up a small green triangle of wrapped leaves with a flourish and gave a lopsided grin.

'This is the last,' he said. 'I was saving it for the moment we had to rescue the prize, but this seems like a good time.'

He stuck it in a corner of his jaw, nodded once and loped away, back along their scuffed trail. He spat once, leaving a bright bloody bead on the snow. Drust watched him for a long minute, then turned away and slapped the sweated arse of a mule.

'Run,' he said.

They stumbled and slipped and cursed the mules all the way up the snow-crusted slope, tearing through sere bracken and up to where the snow lay in deeper drifts. A mule floundered and they all gasped to a halt, their breath mingling with the steam from the beasts.

'Push,' Sib panted, and Kag, his shoulder to the rump of the struggling mule, his legs up to the knees in snow, gave him a glare; he had no breath for words.

Drust looked back, thought he heard a dull sound like the exhaled breath of some great bull. He made a warding sign, then lent his shoulder to the mule.

They freed it. Six steps further on, another sank to the belly and started plunging in a panic, spilling the pack.

'Juno's tits,' Kag swore, but he had no lungs left for more. Sib put up both hands to blinker his eyes, dropped them and announced he could see riders.

'Cut the fucking mules free,' Drust declared, and the others stared at him. He stared back, feeling the dull ache of the cold in his chest. If they kept running, sucking in the freezing air, it would burst them; they'd vomit blood, fall down and die.

'All our food…' Ugo said plaintively.

'My pots,' Quintus warned.

'There's a rider out in front,' Sib said and lowered his hands again to show his stricken, cold-pinched face. 'I think it might be Manius on a native pony.'

Everyone else squinted.

'Or an eager rider on a fresh mount,' Kag growled, 'new from gutting Manius with his own arrowhead.'

'Gods forgive you,' Ugo said sternly and made a swift sign, some Frisian affair of his own. Kag snarled back and turned to Drust.

'Well? Run or fight?'

The other waited while the mules wheezed and stood with their heads down; they didn't even try to hoof up the snow to get at what they thought might be underneath, which was a measure of their exhaustion. Sib saw Drust's look.

'They are too blown to go on,' he said.

'We all are,' Drust said, and Ugo unshipped his axe and blew hot life into his frozen fingers. Quintus offered a shit-eating grin from the snow-clot of his beard.

'I am tired of running. The *harena* does not teach that – after all, you only end up back where you started.'

They laughed more than it was worth, throwing their heads back with the humour of wolves. Drust waited until the echoes had died, then turned to Quintus.

'Fetch out what's left of your pots. We get to use them now.'

Quintus nodded, started to move, then hesitated and turned to face them all. 'Now look,' he said, 'you should handle these with care. Throw them to break on something – or someone – otherwise they will just plop into snow and be useless. And don't throw them close, or Minerva save us all, drop one on a stone.'

'You see any stones?' Kag demanded.

'The one that makes your head,' Quintus replied, moving off to the mules. 'The one that concerns me most is the one hidden under the snow at your feet.'

'We stand here,' Drust went on, while Kag frowned and scuffed the snow for hidden stones, ignoring Quintus and his grin. 'Let them come up through the deep snow. They don't fight on horses, which is a shame because that would make them easy to kill.'

'Manius,' Ugo said, and everyone saw the leading rider's horse stumble, recover, then stumble again and keel over; the rider rolled and got up onto his hands and knees. Behind him, the pursuers closed in, flogging their ponies hard.

'If we wait, he will die,' Ugo added pointedly.

'Call foul and send in the *summa rudis*,' Sib intoned savagely and Ugo rounded on him, snarling. Then he hefted the axe and started to slog out of the deep snow, downhill.

'Juno's tits,' Kag said wearily. 'Why does he always seem so angry?'

'He has been disappointed often,' Quintus said, returning with a wooden box which he placed carefully at their feet. 'It is likely to continue – we are all very disappointing men here.'

He prised open the box; downslope, Manius was struggling forward and the pursuers were flinging themselves off their horses, frustrated by their foundering. Ugo strode downhill like he was Colossus come to life.

'Well, are we to stand here and let him die?' demanded Kag.

'For the best,' Sib muttered. 'He is *jnoun*...'

'You have stood here long enough to change your breeches twice,' Quintus pointed out with his big grin. 'Here – take a pot or two and get ready.'

'Not something I would think on doing,' Kag growled back.

'Taking a pot?' Drust asked, bemused, and Kag looked sorrowfully at him.

'Changing your breeches.'

Sib took a pot, holding it as if it was boiling. Kag and Quintus and the others started off down the hill, loosening up weapons and getting ready.

'I truly wish that old woman in the hut had been right,' Sib said.

'Verrecunda,' Drust and Kag said together, and then laughed at it; Quintus waved a hand.

'As you say. Still – I would like to have died a prince.'

They moved on through the bracken and the half-frozen mulch-mud – no good footing here, Drust thought. Still, it's the same for them as us. Just that there are more of them than us.

At least twenty, they all saw. Ugo was starting to dodge arrows now and had stopped; he waved his arms and roared at Manius to move but the man had given up struggling forward and had his bow out. The tribesmen started howling and closing in.

Ugo spread his arms wide as if about to embrace all his enemies. '*Uri, vinciri, verberari, ferroque necari*,' he bellowed.

Sib stepped up, ran three paces and hurled his pot.

'Pull,' he screamed.

–

It wasn't true, as the others disparagingly pointed out constantly, that three of their number had been in the Flavian and survived. The implication of that included actual fighting and only Dog had done that – the others had been show fights and Sib and Manius's perambulation during the Lemurian games.

Organised by the Pontifex Maximus, which is to say the Emperor, the Lemurian were on three days when Rome appeased the spirits of its dead – the ninth, eleventh and thirteenth of May. People flooded into the amphitheatre after they had unknotted everything including their shoes, walked round in bare feet with a mouthful of black beans and spat them out, mumbling: These I cast; with these beans, I redeem me and mine.

Once you had lumbered through all that and made the 'mano fica' to ward off evil, you needed the diversion of an entertainment which did nothing more than add to the panoply of dead.

Sib and Manius had walked the perimeter of the Flavian in the lunchtime pause between the slaves clearing the condemned dead away and the start of the dwarves versus women, or the blind-helmeted pairs bashing furiously at air. Two slaves went with them, heaving big baskets filled with woven straw balls which were packed with favours.

There were sweetmeats, cakes, coin and lead-stamped ingots which could be redeemed for a cockerel, a horse, a slave or even an entire chestnut farm in Abruzzo if you were lucky.

So, while the audience stuffed their faces with hot sausage and boiled chickpeas and free bread, guzzling cheap wine to wash it down, Manius would stalk the circle while Sib took a ball from the basket and lobbed it well over the heads of the crowd. Manius would crack them open with every shot. Never missed. He had arrows with blunt tips and fat flights so that, when they fell on the crowd they did no more damage than cause a yelp and a bruise – which, if it came with a free gift, was no hardship.

The trick in it was that the balls wobbled, being packed loosely, and Sib did it from behind Manius, so he did not know where the ball came from and only saw it at the last. He had a split-second to react and shoot and never missed. Not once.

All Sib had to say was: 'Pull…'

–

Pull.

Drust heard it and knew what was about to happen, saw it with the sickening certainty of horror unborn. He was opening his mouth to scream at everyone, but what he planned to say would never be heard and later he could not even remember what that was.

The pot arced up over the heads of the warriors, struggling sweatily forward from their horses with shields and spears, lumbering in furs and bits of filched armour. Ugo was standing with his arms wide, roaring challenge to them.

The arrow flew, straight and true. There was a dull thump and a blast of heat and light that ripped the warning from Drust and threw him backwards – then the sky rained fire.

It came down in fat gobbets. Men screamed and died. A man came lumbering out of the rain with one leg on fire and beat it desperately with both hands; they went alight and melted like candle wax. Another effigy reeled in circles, his head a single flame and his arms waving wildly, his hands on fire where he had tried to beat out his own face. One or two hurled themselves into the snow, but that did no good; they burned on.

'Back, back,' yelled Kag.

'Throw,' Quintus screamed and showed them how by lobbing a pot at a burning man. It hit, broke and there was another dull whoof as flame consumed the man, all but his screams. The others threw the pots they had, as much in a desperate attempt to be rid of them as to burn their enemies; the world growled with fire and melted.

The heat drove them back, sweating and panting, to where they could turn and stand, weapons up and ready for any survivors who came crashing through.

There were none. There weren't even screams, but the snow burned and black smoke rose up in greasy plumes, each one marking a dead man or pony; there were distant squeals that grated on Kag, who knew the sound of horses in agony.

Ugo half crawled back up the slope and stood, weaving. Half his beard was gone on one side and his face looked like it had been slapped back and forth a hundred times and then drenched in soot. He turned to look back down the hill, hanging on to his axe to stay upright.

'Manius,' he said.

'Sixed,' Sib said flatly and the big German rounded savagely on him, looking like some wild troll.

'You did that on purpose,' he spat.

'There is little point in doing it any other way,' Sib answered.

'You knew he would die,' Ugo persisted.

'We all die,' Kag interrupted wearily and took the German by the arm, leading him away. Quintus slogged after them and Drust stared at Sib for a long moment. He wanted to say that he would go down and find Manius, but the truth was that he did not want to go near that burning, smouldering carnage; there was a sharp reek from it that caught his throat.

'I said we should never have let him loose on the world,' Sib said softly, so that only Drust could hear him. '*Jnoun*, I said. Now you see. He could burn the world.'

Drust turned away and followed the others up the slope. When he got to the crest, the others were standing there watching wordlessly, and Drust joined them, staring at what they saw.

There was a long spill of frost-crusted bracken and twisted trees in a patched spread. Beyond it was an irregular shadow of rampart and roofs where the smoke of cooking fires threaded a sullen sky.

In between stood a forest of spears and the grim growlers who held them.

'Fuck,' Kag said bitterly.

They waited.

'Are we supposed to fight then?' Ugo demanded, and Quintus laid a gentling hand on the big Frisian's shoulder.

'We are supposed to die, big man,' he said.

Drust saw a huddle of men detach from the pack and come towards them. Sib went into a crouch and Kag slapped him on the side of the head.

'Stop that. You will encourage them and you are no fighter at all but a cart driver.'

'Fuck you...'

Closer, the figures stopped and one stepped a little way forward. Drust thought the man was veiled with some spider-silk stuff from Parthia but it was Kag who got to it first, a second before the truth of that face sucked the air from Drust.

'Gods above and below, Dog,' Kag said loudly. 'Your face is inside out.'

Dog stepped forward and slapped them all with it, as if it had been a club. Colm Deathface they called him and it was all the truth – Necthan had been an artist in his way and had taken Dog's skull and put it on the outside. Now it grinned at them, even though Dog's lips were a tight stitch.

'No evil,' he said, spreading his hands. 'In the name of all the gods. Just lower your weapons and follow – you've been expected for some time. I would do it swiftly because the ones behind you are sorting themselves out from their scorching.'

What could they do, Drust thought?

'Lead on,' said Kag.

Chapter Nine

The village had a stockade, but round huts had spilled beyond it in some places and the entire settlement was spread out on flat land beside the river. There were no ordered streets, just rutted walkways, timbered here and there, between huts clustered like barnacles. There were people and animals and none of them looked friendly; it reeked.

On higher ground at one end was a circle of stone and turf twice the height of a man, and roofed. The palace of Talorc son of Aniel, son of Tolorg son of Mordeleg, Drust was told by Dog. Talorc was not king or warlord or anything like it, just the mouthpiece for all the warriors who thought they had a say in things. Which is what happens when there is no clear ruler and so no firm hand, he added scornfully.

Still, the grain grew and was ground, the flax got harvested, fish traps and spinning and herbs and vegetables all still appeared; people went on with their lives and would work during daylight, barter and swap and share the benefits. In summer, Drust thought – if this land had such a thing – this would be a pleasant place. Only the warlords thought warlords were needed here.

Drust learned this as they half stumbled towards the place, hemmed in by big men with big spears and big scowls. Dog spoke as if he had personally done most if not all of it.

'Who is the woman?' Drust demanded, cutting through Dog's pride. 'And the child? Why did you run to this place with them?'

They came up on the stockade gates, which screeched open; behind, Drust heard shouts and the men surrounding him looked wary and anxious.

'In good time,' Dog said and grinned, which did nothing for his face at all. Kag looked as if he would say something but the way ahead beckoned and the way behind was fenced with spears, so he kept quiet.

'Where is Manius?' Dog asked, looking round.

'Sixed,' Sib said. Dog looked at Drust, then turned wordlessly away; for a moment Drust was sure he had seen something under that death face. Not sorrow.

Relief.

They walked the length of the main, rutted, snow-patched street, fringed with a sullen hatred of faces. Kag stared defiantly back, but most, including Drust, knew better. By the time they reached the gates of the turf and stone palace, they were steaming off their fear-sweat in the cold.

Inside was shadow with smells – wood smoke, meat, fetid bodies, skins in need of airing. There was a pit fire spilling fire glow and they moved towards it, sucking greedily at the heat. Dog moved off before Drust could speak to him and other figures moved in the shadows with soft rustlings, making everyone slide closer together.

'What now, lads?' Quintus demanded, looking round warily. 'Is this the lunchtime show? Dwarves and women and crucifixions?'

There was a loud noise beyond the fire, a crashing of solid on wood. Men appeared, all iron and grim helmets – the one who led them was taller by a head and shoulders. After him came others, not armoured, but armed with sheathed blades and knives.

The tall one stood for a moment, then called out and Dog appeared, dressed in a fine shirt and leather breeks; the old Sol Invictus amulet swung on his chest and gave Drust a moment of poignancy.

'This is Talorc,' Dog said, indicating the tall man. 'He speaks for the council.'

'Council?'

Dog shrugged. 'Like the Senate. A bit. There is no war chief here, just a man who has been made mouthpiece for a time. For now it is Talorc.'

Drust remembered what Verrecunda had said about men only ruling through women here, but any thoughts he had on it were driven from him when the woman appeared. She was like a blast of light and heat and Drust heard the rustle, the sigh of indrawn breath.

She had blonde hair – true blonde, Drust was sure, not some wig of sheared hair from German slaves which was so popular in Rome. She was middling height, middling age, curved and making the most of them in a Roman dress that clung and draped; the cold must be slicing her, Drust thought, but it did things to her breasts. Behind her was a boy, swaddled in white fur that must have been a prize, even for a tribe who had such furs to spare. He was buried in them so deep Drust could not see him clearly.

'We have found Dog's bitch,' Kag said in Latin, watching Dog to judge the reaction.

'Be careful, gladiator,' the woman said in perfect Latin. 'This bitch can bite.'

Quintus laughed at Kag's discomfited face and the fact that Dog showed nothing on his at all, but since the man always seemed to be grinning it was hard to tell. That skull face was a hard matter to get round.

Talorc spoke for a time and the rest of the big room seemed to enjoy it; Drust saw that they were mostly men and all armed. The retinue, he thought, but had that thought driven from him by the sudden realisation that the woman and the boy were chained at the hands to each other. They had shackles on their ankles, too.

He tried to catch Dog's eye but failed. Then Dog told them that they were all welcome and a place would be made at the feasting table.

'Later we will talk,' he added, swiftly, as if trying to get the words out before anyone noticed.

And that was it. Women and young girls appeared and showed them benches at a table. Food was brought – meat enough to make the mouth water.

'Well,' Quintus said with his big grin, 'we landed on our feet.'

'Did you see her?' Ugo demanded.

'Of course, you arse – we all saw her,' Kag spat back. 'What of it?'

'A high-born, for sure. And that boy...'

A high-born, for sure, Drust thought. Here, in a stick and wattle hut at the uttermost reaches of the Land of Darkness. Somehow, he had imagined everything would be made clear when he saw her, but the opposite was true, it seemed.

'Nothing to do but eat and get ready,' Quintus declared.

'Get ready for what?' demanded Sib suspiciously, food halfway to his mouth and appetite suddenly gone.

'If it had been my people,' Ugo mused, 'our heads would be on poles.'

'Your people?' Kag scathed. 'You are as far removed from that as anyone here. For all you know, your people are now as decent Romans as any in Apulia.'

'I saw heads on poles,' Quintus said mildly, which stopped everyone mid-chew. He looked round them and grinned his big grin. 'On the way in. Above the main gate. Old ones. New ones, too.'

'They take heads?' Sib demanded, looking at Drust, who bridled.

'I have told you before – I know little of these people. Ask Dog.'

'Dog,' Kag said. 'What about that whoreson? That face...'

No one spoke while the noise of the hall growled round them. Drust felt like a rabbit eating clover in a grove of wolves – but he chewed and swallowed all the same. Always take food where and when you can get it was one of Kag's many sayings – if the food is good enough, folk stop complaining about the incoming arrows.

Another, he reminded them now, was checking a strange house for the exits you might need in a running hurry.

There were none they could see but the one they'd come in and a lot of hefty armed men in leather and wary looks between them and it. So they sat and ate their fill, while their conversation fell mute as the hall's roaring grew.

Not long after, some of the big men came and made it clear they were to move, herding them into the shadows where long benches curved along the wall, benches as wide as two men. There were skins that made it apparent this was where they would sleep; around them, others were settling for the night and, somewhere close by, there was the panting mewling of love in the dark. On the other side, a baby fretted and voices were raised in complaint until hushed.

'Not so different from an *insula* in Subura,' Quintus said. 'The walls in mine – you could spit barley through them.'

'The woman,' Kag said in Drust's ear, sidling close and ignoring Quintus. 'What of the woman and her child? Who the fuck is she? No slave, for sure.'

'We will find out,' Drust said, 'when Dog decides.'

'We have put ourselves in his power,' Ugo growled, close enough to hear this. 'We should have fought.'

'And died for sure,' Sib spat back. 'No *missus* here, German.'

They sank into dark silence, huddled like a herd and keyed to every sound. In the end, one voice startled them all awake into the fetid dark.

'Walk with me,' said Dog. Drust stared for a moment, then heard a rustle and saw Kag shove his face into the dim light.

'Just Drust,' Dog said quietly, and Kag scowled.

'Fuck you, Dog. You want to kill us, do it all together.'

'If I wanted you dead, you would be dead. And I am Colm now. Colm Deathface. Remember it.'

Drust laid a quieting hand on Kag's trembling arm, then slid off the bench and followed Dog out through the grunts and whimpers and snores, out beyond the pit fire and almost to the barred front doors where their breath smoked. They squatted and Drust waited, saying nothing; in the dim light, with a shaft of winter moon falling through the top of the doors, Dog's face grew luminous, eldritch. It seemed to float.

'What happened to Manius?' Dog asked eventually and Drust told him. Dog grunted.

'I saw him do that trick,' he said. 'No way to end up, melted like candle wax.'

'You never liked him,' Drust pointed out. Somewhere close, a small creature scuttered.

'He broke my fucking leg,' Dog replied sullenly and Drust shrugged.

'We all had a hand in that. Orders. Make you stop doing something stupid with a woman – was it the same one as now?'

'It was. You put her in danger, because I was supposed to flit her out of Rome quietly. When I didn't turn up she went to Gaul with just the boy, leaving a trail a blind man could follow. I got to her almost too late – didn't give enough time even for the leg to heal properly. This cold weather reminds me of that daily.'

'Who is she?' Drust demanded.

'Julia Soaemias Bassiana, first daughter of Julia Maesa and Gaius Julius Avitus Alexianus, sister of Julia Avita Mamaea, niece of Julia Domna.'

'Verrecunda said there was Julia,' Drust muttered, his mind reeling with names. 'Couple too many for me.'

'What happened to her?' Dog demanded and Drust looked at him.

'Manius,' he replied flatly. 'Necthan too. What happened to Brigus?'

Dog waved one hand. 'Spotted him right off, within days of coming here. Verrecunda was an informer – used to be a power in her day – and he was one of the State's little spies, sent out when the Army arrived.'

He stopped, shook a bitter skull at the dark. 'No one had bothered with the north before that, not for years, but old Severus was coming back so they sent out a lot of men like Brigus. He found Julia Soaemias and the boy at Verrecunda's place – they had to stay while Necthan did my face. They all knew the danger they were in, so Necthan did for him and I took his place. Everyone thinks Brigus is still out here, doing his job. He's in a hole under bracken, so lonely even foxes won't find him.'

'So who is she, this Julia? Apart from some high-born with a nice arse.'

'You noticed? She is lush, has to be said. Sol Invictus expects no less from a priestess. Work it out, Drust – you are the brains of your *Procuratores*. Her mother is sister to the Empress, so Julia Domna is her aunt. Which means?'

Drust got to it in a moment that blew light from heel to crown. She was the niece, by marriage, to the Emperor Lucius Septimius Severus.

'What are you doing with her? And the boy?'

'Rescuing her,' Dog answered. 'Her husband arranged it with our old boss, Servilius Structus, who arranged it with Julius Yahya. I suspect someone else put the husband up to it, for he was never noted for fidelity nor clever.'

'Her husband?'

'Sextus Varius Marcellus from Apamea – old Syrian nobility. He's a senator in Rome and if you saw him you'd know the boy was not his. The boy is called Varius and he is the chosen of the Sun God. He is high priest at Emesa and as such can call on a deal of support in the East if he wishes.'

'If he wishes? He is… what? Eight?'

Dog nodded. 'He is as good as an emperor there, so there are those in Rome who would not want that. Especially if old Severus dies, which is more and more likely – have you seen him?'

'Not recently,' Drust replied drily. 'The invitation must have been mislaid.'

Dog leaned his face closer and Drust resisted the impulse to draw back.

'If he does – when he does – there will be blood,' he said. 'The Hood and his brother will fight it out.'

'No contest,' Drust replied. 'The Hood will win. Geta isn't clever or ruthless enough.'

'His mother is.'

Drust blinked at that. 'She is mother to them both.'

'Favours Geta. The Hood knows it – well, who better than a mother to know the twisted flaws of her own sons, eh? Geta might be an idiot, but he's less… dark… than his brother. His father knows that, too.'

Drust waved a bewildered hand. 'What are you in all this? This is politics so high you get a nosebleed just considering it. What the fuck are you doing in it?'

Dog's hand went to the amulet. 'You remember Emesa? We went there to put on a show.'

Drust tried and failed. 'Another sand, another town.'

'It was just after…'

He stopped, but Drust knew. After Calvinus, after Dog had killed his pair-brother. Well, you were of the *harena*, the sand, and not supposed to have friends. But you did, because you were men and even Dog lost his snarl from time to time. Lost his mind, it seemed, after killing Calvinus. Drust said not one word on it, simply nodded for Dog to go on.

'Well, Julius Yahya arranged the show in Emesa and it was on behalf of the Bassianii, so I learned about them and the Temple of the Sun. Went there, saw her, saw the boy – he was barely toddling but solemnly performing all the rites as high priest. It's handed down, you see…'

'So – where does this get us?' Drust demanded. 'Apart from you finding redemption or peace and a new neck ornament.'

'You have no idea,' Dog spat back. 'That boy is Helios come to this world…'

'Well, tell him to brighten up this place. It is fucking cold and dark, Dog. Is this why you sprang to the rescue like Horatius? You made a child your god?'

Dog waved a dismissive hand. 'You believe in what you believe – which is nothing much, far as I can tell. Why do you do what you do, Drust? I never fully worked that out.'

Me neither, Drust thought – which was mostly a lie to himself. Because he had to cling to something, some little belief that there was hope in the world. He could see Dog's magic boy as the same, yet he wanted him to be wrong and savaged him for it.

'I am glad for you,' he said dismissively. 'If you laid Calvinus in the tomb, well done to you – though it seemed to all of us that you did not. Joining Bulla's band of robbers, crossing Servilius Structus…'

'Do not mention Calvinus.'

Drust flung up an exasperated hand. 'We all lost people we liked – Quintus watched Supremus die, remember? There were others – it's what we are. If you need to drown it in wine or choke it with incense, then fine – but your sun-bathing has dragged all your bunkmates to this place, Dog, so it is a little more than just washing yourself some peace of mind in holy smoke.'

Dog smiled and touched Drust's arm. 'You love them,' he said simply and laughed, not scornfully, but full of wonder. Drust pulled his arm away, scowling.

'Julius Yahya came to me when it became clear the boy and his mother had to be got out of Rome, for their own safety,' Dog said.

'Why?'

'Who knows? Perhaps Servilius Structus is at the back of it, or even the old Severan himself – they fear for Geta, the

Empress even more than him. Julia Domna wants no competition – and neither does her sister. The pair of them are hewn from the same stone, so getting rid of a son or daughter is a necessary sacrifice for whatever it is they see for Rome. A perfect, golden youth with the whole of the eastern provinces at his beck and call?'

'The Empress wants her own niece dead? The sister would join her in murdering her own daughter. And the boy, too?'

'They plan on doing away with a son and nephew and anyone else who stands to threaten Geta, apple of their eye. The Hood, of course, has plans of his own.'

He waved one hand. 'This is not nosebleed politics on the Hill. This is what they whisper in Subura. If – when – old Severus has coins on his eyes it will get bloody, and I hear you are somewhere on Caracalla's list. The word is out that The Hood seeks a *harena* fighter who kicked his balls up into his throat.'

Drust blew out his cheeks with thinking, formed the tiles of it into the mosaic and Dog waited quietly while he did.

'The husband, this senator,' Drust said, 'arranged all this with Julius Yahya, or so you say. Servilius Structus thought he was doing me – us – all a favour by sending us out of Rome. He didn't know about all this at all, I am sure of that.'

'He is the Emperor's man,' Dog said. 'Couldn't be trusted. He knew only that The Hood was taking too much of an interest and wanted to save his *Procuratores*.'

'So why is Julius Yahya now sending us to get her and the boy back?'

Dog laughed softly. 'Brigus arranged that. Sent word to fetch some picked men to come and rescue the lady from the clutches of beasts beyond the last wall before the Land of Darkness.'

Drust took a breath or two. 'You did it. You sent for us. By name.'

'*Tegisti acu*,' Dog declared admiringly. 'That nail is particularly well struck on the head. When I fled from Gaul with them – two steps ahead of some seriously armed men – I came here. Safest place, I thought. I can come home – well, sort of. Who knew the Emperor would want one last military adventure and turn his idle-buggering sons out of Rome to make men of them? Now the place is crawling with State. It is only a matter of time before they hear of a Roman woman and her son, held prisoner by savages. They may already know.'

'Your idiot plan didn't work on any level,' Drust said, seeing it. 'Got your face made into something that fell off a tomb on the Appian and turned up with two Romans only to find you weren't all that welcome with your supposed "own people". Should have gone east, back to Emesa – at least it would have been warmer there.'

Dog growled warningly. 'My idiot plan came out of necessity after you broke bones that stopped me doing the better one. I barely managed to save Julia Soaemias and her son in Gaul. Closer to here than where I had originally planned to go.'

'Back to Emesa,' Drust grunted, and was surprised when Dog shook his head vehemently.

'More danger in that – people would have seen it as... provocative. They would either be dead or rebelling by now. Besides, there are those in that part of the world who can be easily bribed to kill. I wanted to take them out of the Empire, all the way to Parthia.'

'No one likes Romans there,' Drust pointed out, and Dog nodded bitterly.

'Nor here.'

'I saw the shackles,' Drust answered. 'And we are here, whispering in secret. You are as much a prisoner as we are.'

Dog shifted and gave a grunt of acceptance. 'Partly.'

'Which part is that? The one that won't let us collect our gear and mules and walk away?'

'The part that won't let you walk south,' Dog admitted. 'We walk north instead.'

'North? We?'

'Listen closely,' Dog said, his voice hoarse and his breath like moonlit smoke. 'You know how warlords are made here?'

Drust remembered Verrecunda and nodded. Dog let out a longer, fetid breath.

'Talorc is just the current mouthpiece of all the warriors. He has no power and wants it. There is a woman who can give it, daughter of the last queen. When she comes of age, she can be wed and Talorc wants that to be him.'

'And you?' Drust scathed. 'What do you want?'

'Daughter of the last queen,' Dog repeated. 'Are you dim? Who was the last queen here?'

It smacked Drust like a douse of iced water. His mother. The last queen had been Dog's mother.

Dog saw it and nodded. 'My sister. She will have thirteen summers on her in a month. She was a scrap when my mother and I were sold – someone at least took pity on a babe.'

'So – fight this Talorc for her. You can kill him – unless all the old skills have gone.'

'And do what? Marry her?'

Drust had no answer that would not be an insult and so stayed silent.

'The problem is that the Bull People to the north have her. Taken in a raid. When she bleeds for the first time, she'll be given to the Bull on his island.'

'The Bull on his island?'

Dog growled. 'Some fucking war chief with a horned hat – but Talorc has promised them something better in exchange.'

'The woman and her son.'

'*Tegisti acu* one more time – you have won a villa in Apulia and an ox to plough it with.'

'You sent for us to rescue this woman?'

'My sister, Beatha.'

Drust waved a dismissing, angry hand. 'You never knew of her – have you even seen her? Who said she was taken in a raid – the same fuckers who did for you and your mother?'

Dog shook his head. 'Not Beatha – Talorc had designs there and still has. Perhaps he sold me and ma, but he was no more than a youth then, with no voice and little to say with it in any council – but what does it matter now? It was done. Now what matters is that, if we get… my sister… then Talorc will give us Julia Soaemias and Varius. Then we can all get out of here.'

'To where?' Drust demanded bitterly. 'You arranged for us to come here just so you could use us for this. There is no rescue – so no reward. No citizenships, no silver. How do you think that will go down with Kag? The others?'

'Julius Yahya's offer was genuine – have you any idea of the riches the Bassianii command? The Temple of the Sun in Emesa is as golden as it sounds,' Dog answered. 'The reward was promised for their safe return to Eboracum. Now there's one extra woman thrown into the mix. Besides – what alternative is there?'

Not much, Drust thought bitterly. All those who said this was too good to be true were right. *Tegisti acu.*

–

'*Imperius in imperio*,' Quintus said, then slapped one hand against the other. A power within the power. It was the first time anyone had ever seen him lose the smile. They had talked it over since Drust got back, ignoring the odd growls from the dark shadows, which meant 'shut up' in every language. Now the hall was stirring back to life and shutters were opening to spill in the wan dawn.

'*Ira furor brevis est*,' Kag answered, then gave Quintus his own grin. 'Horace. Who was an expert on anger being a brief madness.'

'Fuck Horace,' Ugo growled. 'He hasn't just been done over.'

'Up the arse,' Sib agreed mournfully.

'Well,' Kag declared, levering himself off the bench. 'We can fall no further. Death is the last boundary, as Horace said.'

'He also said, or so I hear, *omnes ad stercus*,' Drust spat back. 'It's all gone to shit. Did he write that on a latrine wall? That's where I spotted it.'

'The Bull on the island,' Ugo mused as the hall shifted to murmurs and growls and cooking smells. 'That does not have a friendly sound to it. There are tales I could tell of my own land...'

Then he brightened. 'At least we are back to rescuing women and not abducting them. And Dog's sister, too. So it's not all bad.'

Kag scowled. Sib groaned.

'Shut your fly-hole you flap-shoed *Stupidus*,' Quintus spat, then turned his anger on Drust. 'You trust Dog? A man with – what was it Kag said? Abnormal eye contact?'

'Mad as a basket of burning frogs,' Kag agreed.

'Now with a face put on inside out,' Quintus added vehemently. 'If anything gave you a clue that would be it. He organised us here, to save this sister of his – if it is his sister – and any talk of reward is just that. Where would Dog get silver enough to pay us for this? Mark me well – it is a trap to lure all those who broke him on orders once before.'

'His patron could afford it,' Kag mused. 'Those folk in Emesa are richer than gods and that part of his tale is true enough – he is a believer, it seems. Besides – if he simply wanted us all dead in the worst possible way, we would be neck deep in shit. Upside down.'

'And there's the other worrying matter,' Sib said. 'Dog and his amulet and this Sun God. I know of this one. Two lives a day that temple claims for their god – not Sol Invictus or Helios, but Elagabalus. That's not a patron you want to fool with.'

'What patron?' demanded Quintus. 'This senator husband who sent them away in the first place and now wants them back?'

Drust sighed. 'We can talk round this for hours, but Dog is right. What choice have we? If we refuse I do not think we will be escorted within range of the Wall forts and waved farewell.'

'I do not think we will be offered this woman and child once Dog's sister is rescued,' Kag said.

'A stream to jump when we reach it,' Ugo declared and beamed at Quintus. 'So says the flap-shoed *Stupidus*, who will slap Dis into you if you speak such to me again.'

There was short, mirthless laughter at Quintus's face, but it rang like a bad mint of coin.

'I wish we could be sure who we are working for,' Drust muttered to Kag as they went about sorting gear out. 'Dog says it is this woman's husband, but a senator on his own does not command the likes of Julius Yahya.'

'Dog will tell us,' Kag said grimly and did not need to add more. Drust fell silent, but he gnawed on the bone that most bothered him – who wanted to bring harm to the woman and her child? The idea that it was the Empress and her sister was astonishing, but it bothered Drust that he did not – could not – dismiss it.

Kag worked some new grease-rich fleece down into his empty scabbard, frowning at the loss of steel.

'*Omne quod non reveletur*, as the poet said.'

All was revealed the very next day.

It started with Dog, loping up to them, all tail-wag and sharp grin that put Quintus to shame. No one shared it.

'We move out tomorrow,' he said.

'Why not now?' Kag asked.

Dog made a grimace and the skull twisted in a strange rictus. 'We must chase off the last of the warriors who attacked you.'

'They were attacking you,' Drust pointed out. 'Because you attacked them – why was that? It's the middle of winter and even Romans know that's not the time to raid.'

Dog nodded soberly. 'It was decided to fetch some virgins, in case our efforts fail. Maybe the Bull People can be persuaded by quantity.'

'Virgins?' Sib scathed. 'Are there any among these skin-wearing dogs?'

Dog's look was colder than the frost leaking through the hall. 'Children are.'

Then he looked at them and jerked his skull-head. 'If you want some fresher air, come with me.'

They followed, noting the warriors who fell in around them, all big lads bulked out in fur and war gear. Dog saw their looks.

'For your protection,' he said, and smiled at the disbelief. 'Seriously. No one cares for Romans and not the ones I have described. Half the people who see you will be afraid. The other half – young warriors mainly – will want to challenge you, just to see if you live up to the tales.'

'Thanks, Dog,' Kag growled.

Outside the streets were hard with ruts and patched with dirty white; snow drifted and people moved away from them or stood and sullenly stared. Dog is not taking us for a walk, Drust thought as they followed him towards a large, round timber building, seemingly built in three tiers, each one smaller than the one it stood on.

Ugo made a sign and looked at the others. 'Temple,' he said.

A blind man could have told that, Drust thought. There was a wooden statue, blocky and rough-hewn, but clearly a warrior-god with a spear and a bird on one shoulder. There were people, all men, just inside the entrance, in the shelter of a little portico; Drust saw that some were skin-markers and some their victims; they stopped their needlework to stare, then continued on.

'Cúchulainn,' Dog explained, nodding to the statue. 'With Morrigan on his shoulder.'

'Now I know that, I know less than before,' Sib muttered.

Inside was the smell of must and old blood, cold stone and ancient wood. Torches sputtered in metal-backed holders from the wooden pillars and a pit fire glowed embers enough to throw dancing shadows. There were a lot of dancing shadows, Drust saw.

'The Senate,' Dog declared wryly.

It was the warrior elite of the tribe, wearing ring mail coats and bronzed war hats, scarred hands resting on the hilts of swords – some of them Roman, Drust saw – or long spears. Talorc stood head and shoulders above them all, but in no more command than any half his size; he wore a thin circlet of gold round his neck, smothered by a beard braided with silver wires.

He had a white tunic under a big rough-coated fur and trousers checked in blue and green. He had no sword or spear or shield, but he radiated menace just the same – yet he was one voice in the guttural spit of their talk.

None of this was what silenced Drust and the others. All of that moment belonged to the woman and boy.

The woman was as he remembered her from the last time – white-blonde with bare arms that gleamed nearly as white as her hair, and Drust knew that, for all her life in the scorch of Syria, she had taken care to keep in the shade.

She sat beyond the pit fire, in a large chair, almost like a throne, in a pillow of expensive, soft furs that she could have drawn round her against the cold had she wished it. She knew the value of a thin dress and the cold on her nipples. Drust knew her at once – Julia Soaemias, daughter of the Empress's sister and mother to the boy who sat at her feet.

He was still, like no boy his age should be, staring straight ahead with his lips moving silently. Now and then he would make a gesture, eloquently elegant. He wore the most of a bear pelt but was bareheaded, so that his golden curls waved softly in the rogue heat waves from the pit fire.

He turned and looked at them. Looked, it seemed, at Drust, straight at him, straight through him to his very soul, smiling, confident. Drust sucked in his breath, felt the stun of it all the way from crown to heel and back again, so powerful he grunted. He heard Dog's soft laugh and wrenched his eyes from the boy to him.

'Yes,' Dog said, nodding.

'Caracalla,' Drust said, and Dog nodded. It was The Hood, at the age before suspicion and venality had started to debauch the looks. At the age, Drust recalled, when he had forced Dog to kill his sword-brother in the arena.

'His boy, so they say,' Dog added softly. 'They do not say it to his face or that of his mother all the same.'

'It's his spit,' Kag muttered. 'Fuck, Dog, what have you dragged us into?'

'Riches and glory.'

Chapter Ten

There were oaks and sycamores, twisted claws clutching precarious drifts of snow. The forest floor was clotted with it, ankle deep and covering the treacherous snaking roots, gullies and ditches. The silence was cloying – the slightest crack of a hoof on a rock or a foot on a twig slammed out like a hammer on a door.

'Watch your flanks,' Drust warned. 'Try to move quietly.'

Sib, struggling with snow, turned his black, sweat-gleamed scowl on him. 'We are still in the land of Dog's folk,' he spat, and waved a hand at the big, grunting pack of warriors hauling ponies and mules behind them. 'Is there a word for "quietly" in the spit-tongue these forest dogs speak?'

Drust said nothing; Sib had a point. The warriors had been sent by Talorc to escort them to the boundary stone marking the territory between this land and that of the Bull People, although Drust was sure it had more to do with making sure they all did as they were supposed to, Dog included.

They had been given their mules and gear and a little man called Cruithne, face wizened as a walnut and stunted like some furze root. He was a great honour, according to Dog, because he was known as the Wanderer, a man who knew every stone and tree in the lands of the Bull People and here.

'Looks more like a back-knifer,' Kag growled in Drust's ear, 'sent here to make sure Dog never comes back with his sister. If I was Talorc, I'd make sure of that.'

'Dog would have to marry his own sister to take over from Talorc,' Drust told him. Even as he said it he could not be sure it was not part of Dog's plan – yet he was also sure Dog was blinded by the boy, Varius, and his equally golden mother.

One of the warriors, who had been trading growls back and forth, looked over at Sib and spat out something which didn't need translating into insult. Sib scowled back.

'What was that?' Kag demanded.

'Not something from Ovid,' Drust replied tersely.

'You never read same,' Kag scoffed.

'His epic work "*Julia Domna sucks fat cock for a denarius*" is on the wall outside the west entrance to the Flavian,' Drust fired back. Quintus laughed.

'He is called Conall,' said a voice and they turned into the wizened face of the Wanderer. His hair and beard were braided and the same colour as the snow and he spoke Latin with a thick rheum to it. 'He thinks your man there is several days dead, since he has only seen men that colour who were.'

'He wants to be polite when he says so,' Sib grunted and the Wanderer shrugged. The fact that he spoke decent Latin had not gone unnoticed.

'Conall is a little chief who wants to be bigger. He thinks Colm Deathface is dangerous because he saw him fight Oengus when he first arrived. You, on the other hand, are all just tales and he does not see greatness in you, for all Colm's strong words on your behalf.'

Drust looked at Dog, who finally forced his eyes away from pointlessly fiddling with leather.

'What?' he demanded. 'I fought someone. It was inevitable – I arrived here with two Romans and the face marks of greatness, claiming to be a member of the tribe.'

'What happened?' Ugo asked and Dog shrugged.

'I won.'

'He killed Oengus in less time than it takes to say his name three times three,' the Wanderer said flatly. 'Oengus was a better fighter than Conall.'

'Necessary,' Dog said and turned away.

'For your precious boy,' Quintus offered. 'The sun shines out of his nethers, it seems.'

They squatted in the dim of looming trees, chewing bread and hard salted cheese. In another half-day they would reach the boundary stones but Drust had already decided that they were not going there, but north, running parallel to the invisible line.

'They will have eyes on that stone,' he said and everyone saw the sense in that save Conall and the other huddle of warriors, who wanted done with escorting Romans.

Thereafter the plan was simple – reach the shores of the loch, find a small fishing village the Wanderer knew and take their skin boats across to the island, find the spot where offerings were tied up for whatever monster lurked there and hide, waiting for the arrival of men with Dog's sister.

'We have two days,' Dog said when explaining all this, 'so more than enough time. But we have to be quick and quiet.'

'What then?' Kag demanded scornfully. 'Kill this Bull-monster and the warriors?'

Dog shook his head. 'They will tether her and leave – no man wants to be around the Bull's sacrifice. We need only dart in, untie her and leave the way we came. But if we must fight, we will.'

Drust and the others looked from face to face, every man with the same thought – no man wants to be around the Bull's sacrifice.

'What is it like, this creature?' Ugo asked, frowning.

'Depends who you listen to,' Dog replied, chewing. 'South of the Wall, if they have heard of it at all, it is taller than a temple, has the teeth of a wolf and breathes fire. If you listen north of the Wall, it is a giant bull, big as the world. If you listen to Talorc and the like it is half bull, half man and walks upright carrying a whole tree as a club.'

'I have heard of such,' Ugo said thoughtfully. 'Creatures of the dark forest.'

'We are in a dark forest,' Sib reminded him mournfully and Ugo grinned happily.

'Yes, we are,' he beamed.

'What do you say, Wanderer?' demanded Drust. 'You know all of these lands, so you claim – have you seen it?'

The man's walnut face grew some more frown lines and he shook his head. 'Heard it, all the same. Bellowing. Distant, like – which is where I wanted to keep it.'

'Urus,' Kag said firmly with a slight dismissive flick of one hand. 'We've all seen urus in the *harena* – hump-backed bastards the size of a decent elephant and a spread of horn a man could lie between if he was *Stupidus* enough to try.'

No one spoke, remembering the great horned bulls hunted as part of the show – fewer these days because they were harder and harder to find.

'If the ones here have sharp teeth and breathe fire,' Quintus said, 'then we have found a seam, lads. They'd pay a fortune for one of those running in the Flavian.'

'You can throw the net,' Sib answered and the others laughed.

'A decent *venator* can six one of those big cows with a couple of arrows and a spear,' Kag declared, and Dog looked scornfully at him.

'There are no decent *venators* these days,' he growled. 'Not since Carpophorus. Just butchers of hares and burning foxes.'

'Didn't Carpophorus kill two such urus?' Ugo queried. 'At the inauguration games for the Flavian?'

'He killed one of every beast in the world if you listen to the tales,' Sib answered, but Drust saw he was watching the group of warriors and Conall. There will be trouble, he thought…

'The plan you have is bold,' Quintus said to Dog, 'but risky. I think you have been blinded by the light shining from your sun-boy's arse.'

Dog scowled back and his hackles went up. In the end, as it always did, it came back to Drust.

'What say you?' Kag demanded.

What say I? I say we cut and run from here, Drust thought. The chances of escaping and then surviving after that were about the same. Especially if they arrived back in civilisation without the woman and her child.

Yet he saw their faces, grim and badger-arse rough, waiting for him to show them the way, as he had always done because he was the one they looked to, for all Manius spat and Dog growled.

The woman had been polite at that meeting in the temple of Cúchulainn and Morrigan. There had been a huge cauldron affair, a great lump of bronze turned black and green by neglect, but you could still see the *maenad* processing round the side, naked and ecstatic. It looked to have been Greek but probably wasn't, was more likely a bad Roman copy for those with new money and no taste who decorated their dining rooms with it, then wondered why the old money sneered – and still accepted the invitation to dine.

'A little touch of home,' Drust had offered weakly, nodding to it. She'd smiled, even though the affair frothed with the scum of barley beer and not wine.

'A beautiful piece to find here, in this place. An ornament to any home.'

It was said for the benefit of all the torc-wearing growlers when the translation was rolled out, but Kag had no finer feeling of diplomacy.

'So says the one who never has to clean it.'

It had rattled out like a clatter of dull pewter on a stone floor, but Julia Soaemias had smiled blandly.

'You are slaves?'

'Freedmen,' Drust had answered.

'Double welcome then, since Crixus Servilius tells me you have to come to save us all.'

It was a long, long moment of fish-mouthed gaping before they'd all realised that Crixus Servilius was Dog. No one had known he'd had a Roman name – nor that he had chosen the most infamous gladiator after Spartacus to take as a freedman name. Kag laughed aloud, not least because Dog had never been freed.

'I believe he is called Colm Deathface here,' Drust had said and the woman had smiled. The boy stopped muttering to himself and looked up.

'Have they come to fight to the honour of Helios?' he had asked in a beautiful, fluted little voice. 'Order them to fight, Mother.'

'They have not come to fight in that way,' she had answered, softly patient. 'And you do not order free men – we have spoken of this before, Varius. Talk to Elagabalus, see if you cannot persuade the god to shine his munificence on us all.'

'The god does not like this land,' the boy had replied sulkily. 'Nor the people in it.'

'You should be polite to those for whom you are a guest. We have spoken of this before, too.'

Drust blinked back to the moment and the snow dropping from overloaded branches, the softly murmured plots of Conall and his crew, the expectant faces of his own. The woman's conversation had been stilted and the shackles were clearly on her tongue as much as her wrists and ankles, but her eyes, blue-green as gemstones, had been hot with promise and fears.

He shook her away now and dislodged snow onto his shoulders.

'Dog's plan will do,' he said, looking round, 'until someone comes up with a better one.'

They moved on, dragging their weathered mules and the ponies of the warriors, making more noise than any Bull beast, as Sib said often and loudly. Eventually, they crashed a way to the edge of the forest and Ugo sucked in a deep breath of regret, looking out at the sere tussocks and copse-dotted waves of land ahead, where a tree was a lone sentinel, twisted and bitter with branches.

Sib knelt, turning his head this way and that to use the edge of his eyes, which is where he saw most. The others waited; Conall made a throat grunt of sound and, when Drust looked at Dog, the man shrugged. Then he took out a long knife and cut a hawthorn sapling. Then another.

He walked to Sib and stretched out his handful of whip branches – one-year saplings of hawthorn with little offshoot branches stripped of leaves now; Sib looked up, took them and nodded.

'What is he doing?' Quintus hissed. Drust didn't know but the Wanderer did and he stopped worrying some dried meat from under the saddle of his pony, where it marinaded to a softness his remaining teeth could chew.

'Conall is set to wait here for us returning. It is long and cold and he may decide Romans are the enemy and not the Bull People, even if Crixus bites them a little. They fear this Crixus – now he wants them to fear everyone else.'

Sib stood up and walked a little way out into the clear, where the snow was thinner, blown like smoke by a ravaging wind. He waved one of the saplings, then the other, took out a knife and trimmed more of the offshoots and then dropped one of them. Feathered maidens, Drust thought dully. They are called feathered maidens…

'You are a goat-fucking whoreson whose mother sucked Roman cock,' he said, looking straight at Conall. 'I can beat you with a stick.'

Dog tilted his head expectantly at the Wanderer, who took the meat from his mouth and translated. Drust saw Conall blink with surprise, then his brows seemed to shutter down; the sword came out its sheath with a soft hiss.

'Oh, Juno's tits,' Ugo said and started forward, only to have Dog's arm across his chest like a log gate. He stopped uneasily.

It wasn't something they teach in a *ludus*, not used in the *harena* save in the lunchtime follies, but Sib wasn't a sand warrior. He was a cart driver, as everyone kept reminding him. You cannot, as Drust remembered being told, control a four-horse chariot with just strength – the buggers will haul you with the reins as much as the traces – yet charioteers raced them round the bends, slowed them, sped them, day in, day out, using lithe agility, the balance of weight – and the whip.

Conall looked at the men behind him, the feral pack urging him on with nods. Then he looked at Dog, who shrugged. Then he grinned and stepped forward.

It wasn't flat but a slight downward slope, layered with snow which hid the treachery of tussock and root, but Sib shrugged out of his cloak and fur wrap and danced a little. Conall saw that and thought about speed and agility – then he shrugged out of his own swallowing bearskins.

'*Omnes ad stercus*,' Kag muttered and then grinned. 'He has just shed almost all protection from Sib.'

Drust thought it more likely that Sib was dead; Conall showed some impressive wrist strength when he worked the sword back and forth to free up muscle. Then he gave a coughing grunt and stamped forward swinging.

There was a flicker and a spray of snow as Conall bulled his way downslope a little, spun and faced back up to where Sib danced lightly. Conall raised his welted free hand to a place somewhere in his beard and sucked it, scowling.

He came back up the slope more slowly, shifted sideways slightly and slashed – then he waited for the countermove. When it came, he didn't try to block or dodge, he slashed, hoping to catch Sib's stick and chop it in half.

Somehow Sib changed the direction of his flick in mid-air – the whip end caught Conall across the knuckles and he howled. They went numb at once, welted with pain; the sword tumbled to the snow.

Everyone laughed, even his own. Conall gave a pig grunt of annoyance, looked at Sib, then the sword. He knew what would happen – everyone knew what would happen – but he tried it anyway.

As soon as his fingers touched the hilt, the whipping tip of the feathered maiden struck snow close enough for him to snatch them back. And again.

Now people were shouting, urging him on, offering advice; Drust looked at Dog, not liking where this was going, but he had no eye contact. He wanted to get Sib to look at him, but Sib's face, gleaming with sweat, was focused entirely on the fight, which is why he did not miss Conall snatching a fistful of snow and throwing it, trying to make Sib react.

But whether sand or snow, that was an old trick and Sib knew it, as well as he knew the follow-up – when Conall blundered at him, trying to bull him down to the ground and beat him senseless, he slid sideways like a *venator* showing off with a bull. When Conall, off balance, stumbled past, Sib smacked him twice on his arse with the sapling.

Conall had thick wool breeks so he hardly felt it – but all of the sting was in the act itself. Now Drust saw the naked hatred and blind anger.

'Enough,' he called out sharply. 'Enough…'

Sib stepped back, but Conall tore a knife free from somewhere inside his shirt and threw it, with not much skill and a deal of anger. It wasn't even a good knife for that, tumbling over and over until the hilt smacked Sib in the breastbone, making him grunt with the pain of it.

In a savage flicker of retaliation he lashed once, twice and Conall reeled back with a sharp cry. Now there was blood and, for a moment, Drust's heart thundered – but the big warrior was on his knees, shaking his head and trying to dash the red wash from his eyes. Across his forehead was a welted cut that bled savagely.

Dog moved to the man, grabbed him by both arms and looked him in the bloody face. Then he tore the rag from round his neck and wiped the blood to smears.

'You are lucky,' he growled in Conall's tongue. 'If he had wanted to, that little burned man might have blinded you. Remember that next time you speak to him.'

Conall went off sullenly with the Wanderer, muttering and wiping his face; the crowd of warriors stayed silent, looking at Sib, who rubbed his chest where the knife had struck, then picked up the weapon. He tossed the sapling to one side and the knife to Conall's feet, then grinned and swaggered off.

'The point of this was?' Drust demanded as he passed him; Sib shrugged. 'Ask Crixus Servilius, the Dog that is. He said it would be a good thing.'

Dog overheard it. 'Talorc knew I was good because he has seen me fight. Now he knows there are more of the same. That should make him consider his treachery. And I am Colm Deathface.'

'Treachery?'

Dog shrugged. 'Almost certainly. I would...'

'If Sib had died?' Ugo growled and Dog grinned.

'He didn't. No one did. Now Talorc will hear what happened.'

'You play reckless dice.' Kag growled. 'And whatever name you choose it will always be Cunt.'

Dog looked at him, cold and hard. 'This is no game. It is no *harena* fight you are in here – stick a finger up to the ones who beat you to the floor here and they will bite it off before slitting your throat. There is no *missio* in the Land of Darkness.'

They went on down the open slope, slipping, sliding and dragging mules and ponies behind them, scarring the otherwise featureless swathe of snow. Kag kept looking back at it and muttering and Drust knew he was reciting his maxim about leaving tracks and being followed.

When Dog asked, Kag told him and had a bitter laugh in return.

'No one will follow us,' he said. 'Not here.'

The Wanderer loped off and Sib looked expectantly at Drust, who shook his head; the old warrior knew where he was going and if he planned some treachery then it was what it was. The whole affair was rotted and he said so.

'The prize is still worth it,' Quintus declared with his big wide grin.

'The size of the purse is always outweighed by the likelihood of surviving to collect it,' Kag responded. 'That's another to add to the one that says: a little trust goes a long way – the less you use, the further you go.'

He was scowling at Dog when he said this and Dog grinned back at him, shaking his nightmare face with mock sorrow.

'Do you love no one and nothing?'

It was such a strange phrase coming from the likes of Dog that it stunned everyone to silence, none more so than Drust; the words hit him like a series of face slaps – back, forward, back again… and he blurted out a name before he could stop himself.

'Cassia…'

Dog grinned; they all did, and Drust felt himself flush; it had been an old folly, when he thought he could move back into the world and the real people in it. It had ended badly and the day after he had gone to Servilius Structus and become leader of the *Procuratores* and tried to forget. Dog hadn't forgotten, and he looked and nodded while Drust fought for something to say, then was saved by Kag.

'The Wanderer is waving,' he said. 'I don't trust him.'

When they came up, the Wanderer was squatted, calm and seemingly perfectly trustworthy, his furs wrapped close and up round his ears. His eyes peered from the seamed cave of his face, bright and sharp.

'The loch is ahead and the village on its shores,' he said simply, and now Drust nodded to Sib, who slid out and away.

'Will they be friendly?' Drust asked and Dog laughed.

'Would you if you were about to steal the food from their mouths? Those boats are for fishing, and fish is about all they have. Without them they'll starve.'

'We only borrow them,' Ugo growled. 'We are coming back with them.'

'They are Bull People,' the Wanderer said and there was something in his voice, a sad, grim sort of tone, that made Drust stare.

'How many?'

The Wanderer shrugged. 'A dozen, no more. Women, bairns, oldsters and about four grown men last time I was through here, a year since.'

'Did they welcome you?' Dog asked softly and the Wanderer grinned some gum in reply.

'I did not go close enough to find out. It is best not to tempt the worst natures of suspicious people. Especially when outnumbered.'

'You sound like Kag,' Ugo grunted.

They left Ugo with the animals and went out along a draw, a frozen, reed-crusted little rill that would, in summer, gurgle and plash down to the loch. Now it was misted, as was the black, rimed lake it ran into. Kag looked at the sky.

'Getting dark,' he said. 'We should wait until morning to tackle this crossing.'

'It's barely midday,' the old man said. 'That's not time, that's weather. Good for crossing and not being seen.'

He was right, flakes were drifting down and the light was fading to a dull, dark pewter; the wind hissed snow like spume off a sea, tearing the mist to skeins. At the edge of a bend in the stream bank, they all crouched and peered out at the village. It was mainly built on stilts out onto the lake, with a low, crouching huddle of hovels which Drust took for animal shelters. Sheep, he thought. Maybe pigs and a cow or two, but even here he could not be sure; these people were the worn-down nub of poor, even in a land of miserable poverty.

'We don't need to do this,' Quintus said suddenly, and when Drust looked at him, the fabled grin was gone. No one spoke for a moment, but all of them knew what had to be done.

'We signed a contract, Quintus,' Drust said hollowly.

'It didn't include slaughter.'

'It includes what needs to be done.'

'We've done hard things, for sure. Bad things. But we always had some honour at the end of it. There is no honour in this.'

'Honour,' Kag said stiffly, 'is hard to count these days. Coin is easier. Profit can be tallied.'

'So, all the high ideals your philosophers mouth about existence are not worth a bent *as*?' Sib said.

'That is a world I would find hard to live in,' Quintus muttered, and Dog hawked and spat.

'And yet here we are. What would you rather, then? That someone with legs and tongue should run off as soon as we are rowing the boats we stole and tell the Bull People what we do? Or that no one is able to?'

Quintus managed a grin back at him. 'I should have broken your other leg. And slipped a dagger in your black heart while I was at it. Is this golden boy worth the death of a dozen?'

Dog laughed. 'You should have done something in Emesa besides drink and whoring,' he said dreamily. 'I went to the Temple of the Sun, just to see, to be diverted from… memories. There was a procession, the way strewn with flower petals. There was a pure white camel and on it a beautiful woman – older, but with a stunning look to her. There was a white horse and on it another beautiful woman, just as white, just as garlanded but younger. That was Julia Soaemias and the older woman was her mother, sister of the Empress. On an elephant sat the boy and the *mahout*. The boy wore a golden helmet and he... glowed. Like the sun.'

He stopped, looked at Drust. 'The whole of the East will follow that boy.'

'Small wonder the Empire wants him dead, then,' Kag growled.

'Which is why such a fate must be avoided,' Dog replied.

'If he is beloved of a god let him fend for himself.'

They crouched a little longer, watching the place, the slow spill of smoke from the stilt building, the quiet stillness of it. No one was out on a day like this, with the dark of a storm coming on.

'It's cold and snowing. Can we be done with this?' demanded Sib.

Drust levered himself up, stiff and wet from the cold. Nodded once. They moved out, dragging the cold fog that clung icily to them and, suddenly, he saw them as the villagers must see them – hunchback-crouched horrors with drawn swords, patched as mutton with cold, trailing bits and pieces of furs and wool and leather, and ploughing through the misted snow. We look as if we crawled out of one of their burial mounds, Drust thought. Beasts from beyond the Wall...

The first villager died with an open-mouthed stare and a fistful of moss; he had come out to take a shit but found Sib instead, a black-faced undead with a sharp blade and a snarl. He died with no more than a whimper and the scarlet skein of his throat blood had scarcely stopped spattering before the rest of the killing began.

It was as bad as Drust had imagined. Worse. They pounded onto the walkway of the stilt building, kicked in the door, delved into the smoking dim of it. Drust could not go in and lied to himself that he was guarding the door with Quintus; they looked at one another as the shrieks started, the crashes and grunts and wet chopping.

Quintus eventually gobbed too much mouth spit into the water and muttered about going to find the boats. A baby cried, a sharp wail that ended abruptly. Quintus looked at Drust, his face grim as old reef. 'No,' he said. 'No, no, no.'

Dog shambled out of the longhouse entrance, his blade smoking where the cold met the still-hot blood. Quintus stared, his mouth working. Drust wanted to ask but didn't want to know and Dog's face told him everything.

A second man was out and about – feeding kine, Drust thought when he saw him. Or fetching wood, for he had a wood axe and a desperate look. Tall, broad, bearded and long-haired – a savage from beyond the Wall who came pounding out of one of the other hovels, roaring his way up to the landing stage of the stilt longhouse.

He had the look of someone who wished he had a spear and a shield and the wall of brothers that went with all of that, but all he had was furious desperation and a wood axe and the wail of a babe in his ears. Drust had an eye-blink to decide he wouldn't attempt to block a slashing swing from an axe in the hands of a man like this, but the sheer speed and ferocity took him by surprise.

The man leaped in the air at the last, axe over his head to bring it down with crashing power. Drust barely managed to flick himself to one side and the axe came down to the wooden walkway where Mars Ultor should have buried it hard enough for it never to be freed easily.

But Mars Ultor is a fuck, as Drust knew when the man shifted his wrists and scythed it sideways at the last moment – it hurled towards Drust's shins and he screamed as he leaped, feeling the ugly wind of it on the soles of his feet.

He landed off balance and staggered back, into a portico supported by poles, backing further into it so that it was a forest against slashing. Behind the man he saw Dog lean casually against the longhouse door, smiling and watching. 'Kill him,' Quintus yelled, starting forward and the man heard it and stopped, turned and howled his frustration and rage as he lunged at Dog.

Dog took a calm step back into the longhouse as the axe whistled in and now Mars Ultor did his part; the bitt shunked into the jamb and stuck. Dog brought up his short sword and flicked it; the man screamed out and coughed blood out of the smile in his throat, then fell to his knees.

'Kill me,' he burbled through blood.

Dog bent and pulled the man's eating knife from its worn sheath, dropping it at his feet. 'Kill yourself,' he growled. 'Am I put in this world to answer your every desire? Join your babe and be done with you.'

There was a flurry that sent Dog crashing sideways out of the house to sprawl in the mess of the blood-spattered walkway. Kag poised his blade and then struck perfectly, giving the kneeling man the iron he would have done for any sand fighter. Then he looked at the glowering Dog, who sprang to his feet in a crouch.

'Go to it,' Kag said, viciously soft. 'No babe or anguished father here, Dog.'

'Enough,' Drust called out, still weak from seeing the axe come at him. 'Is there not blood enough?'

Dog stretched slowly. 'One day, Kag…'

'Any day,' Kag replied.

'You killed a babe in a cot?' Quintus demanded hotly and Dog stared coldly at him.

'Necessary,' he said, looking from Drust to Quintus and back again. 'I do what you and he are too cowardly to look on.'

Quintus started to swell with rage. Drust stopped him with a sharp bark.

'So said Saturn after eating his children. Wanderer – go find these boats and see how they are.'

'Is everyone dead?' Kag demanded.

'Everyone and his newborn,' Quintus spat, and Drust had had enough of him.

'Go back, find Ugo and bring up the mounts. We will stable them here until we come back this way.'

There was a coiled silence as men came back to the moment, to the what they had done. For Drust it was the aftermath of every fight he had ever been in, the sick elation of having survived. No one spoke or wanted to look at each other and the Wanderer loped back into the middle of it all, nodding. 'Six boats, all intact. You will be able to cross.'

'Well, get in one and show us how it is done,' Drust said and the Wanderer lost his gummed smile.

'I was to bring you here, no more,' he said. 'I would not go to that island…'

Drust took him by the front of his greasy skins, his grip so fierce that the material bunched through. The Wanderer yelped a little as he was drawn forward.

'We did not do all this here just to leave you behind to betray us,' he said. 'Get in the boat.'

The Wanderer staggered when Drust released him, but his eyes narrowed with an icy hatred and Drust knew he'd have to watch the man. For a moment he thought the wizened old tracker would haul out a knife and attack – but a noise stopped everything, even breath.

It was a brassy bellow, a low roar of sound that seemed to stir the driving snow, that seemed to come from everywhere at once, rising to a hoarse shriek. There was silence broken only by their collective intake of breath.

'What was that?' demanded Sib.

'Beasts beyond the Wall,' Dog growled, and Quintus grinned, cold and vicious, then spat into the black water that wanted to be ice.

'We are the beasts beyond the Wall.'

Chapter Eleven

The snow was a soft smothering death to warmth. This forest seemed swaddled in it, but the white drape of it, the hissing blur of driven flakes did not mask the sounds, the ones no one liked.

'I hate this,' Kag muttered. 'It creaks and cracks and whispers.'

'It is old,' Ugo said reverentially, turning in circles and staring up into the blinding blur. 'Older than any I have been in. A god of forests…'

'At least it isn't one of those god-cursed boats,' Sib muttered and no one argued. They had been withy and skin bowls that only the Wanderer knew how to steer and propel, but even watching him it had been a long, hard sail of spinning circles. No one looked forward to going back in them and Drust was worried that the enemy, if they found out their sacrifice was gone, would be able to row such affairs better and so cut them off.

'Don't worry about that,' Dog said confidently.

'Speak softly,' the Wanderer hissed, looking right to left, and Dog laughed. For a moment it seemed to Drust that they exchanged a look he did not care for, one that made him sick with unease. Then Dog pointed ahead and Drust squinted into the snow, saw the clearing and the weathered oak stump.

It was hung with old wither and Drust had to look a long time before he worked out that they were the remains of garlands, made from woven withy and worked with scraps of wool and ribbon, old bone and tarnished silver gewgaws. The patch it stood in was stained, as if the new fall of snow could not cover the dark spread of old straw and dung. Possibly worse, he thought and saw an image of teeth and fire and horns.

They were all half crouched and moving slowly when the blaring call echoed eldritch through the snow-mist. It came from everywhere, it seemed, but Dog pointed to their right, as if he knew already what it was.

'They are coming,' he said. Drust realised then that the sound came from horns – but the answer to them, that brassy, bellowing blare from the other side, came from deep in the forest. Ugo heard it and his heart seemed to thunder. He found himself, arms outstretched, axe in one hand, willing it to appear, wanting it to appear. Lord of the Forest. Ziu and Vitharr. Gna and Ing…

'Bite your lip,' Sib warned him. 'We are hiding now.'

So Drust thought. So did they all until Dog came close, so close his breath smoked on Drust's neck.

'We may have to fight,' he said and the words crushed the pips out of Drust. He stared. Dog grinned – at least, he drew his lips back from his teeth and the death face leered.

He stepped out, in full view; the sound of his blade coming out of the sheath was a hiss like the last expelled hope Drust had for truth.

'And she may not be my sister.'

-

The warriors stepped out of the swirling snow-mist, cautious and curious. Drust saw there were a lot of them – a dozen, maybe more – and no farmers with blades either. These were chosen men with ring mail and gilded helms, those square shields and decent spears – the hearthtroop of a warrior chief or a king.

Or a queen. She walked in the middle of them dressed in quality wool, bleached almost as white as the snow, with a hooded cloak of madder. She carried a garland, fresh with mistletoe, bright with berries. Some of the warriors carried sheaves of fodder, which they let slip to the ground.

Offerings. Not his sister…

Dog smiled as he faced them, a short legionary sword in each hand. The warriors saw him and came on in a war cry of murder at this violation of their sacred place, a shuffling rush of boar-bristle spears, so that there was no time for anything but fighting like wolves.

The first one was on Drust, spear out, shield up. He lunged, Drust danced, batted the head of the spear to one side, tried to dart up the shaft and get close, but the warrior was too good for that and moved back. Another came. Quintus arrived at Drust's side with a stabbing sword and a little square shield of his own – they were hardly dressed for the *harena* but fell into a pairing out of habit.

Dog was all *dimarchus*, even without the proper helm or accoutrements of that gladiator – he had the most important parts of it, two swords and a vicious skill. While Drust and Quintus bobbed and weaved, dancing with veteran spearmen, he boared in with his two tusks. Drust saw him block his way up the shaft of a spear and ram his other sword into the face of the wielder – but his own opponent almost caught him out, so he focused.

Behind, Ugo heard that brassy bellowing again, almost lost in the shouts and roars round the oak tree pillar. He let it happen behind him, waiting for the Lord of the Forest, conscious of someone shouting his name, but distantly.

‘Ugo,’ Kag yelled. ‘Ugo, you crazed fuck – the *pompus* is over, the Gate of Life open. We could use some help here.’

He would have said more, but saved his breath for fighting, slipped under an overarm spear thrust, stabbed down into the man’s instep and then, while the warrior howled and hopped, stabbed up and ripped out his throat. Blood scalded him and he cursed as it splashed in his eyes.

Drust and Quintus, panting and shouting, managed to kill two spearmen; the warriors began to realise what they faced and stopped trying to fight like old heroes; they coalesced slowly into a pack and then, to Drust’s sick lurch of fear, a shield-wall.

They drew apart – all save for Dog, who was prowling and snarling. He crouched and slashed the life out of a warrior hoarsely crying for help and Drust saw his head come up, searching for the woman, who was being hustled back into the snow-mist, towards the boats they had come on.

Drust stood on the blood-slushed snow, desperately looking for a way to break the wall ahead – there were six or seven in it, no more, but it was solid and retreating, step by step, each man hooming out the rhythm.

Behind him, he heard a crashing splinter of noise, as if some great tree had fallen. When he turned he saw Ugo, still standing with his arms out like a morning crucifixion waiting for the flames. Beyond him was… terror.

It was taller than three men at the shoulder, with a head the size of a small house and horns as thick at the base as Ugo’s waist. It was covered with a matted tangle of russet hair, a great fringe of it over the eyes – if it had any eyes. Smoke steamed out of where nostrils were and icicles had formed like fangs.

Ugo saw it. He was exultant, no longer heard anything but the rush of his own blood. The Lord of the Forest had come to him. To *him*. The Lord of the Forest had challenged and now must be answered.

Kag saw the big German bring his arms together, both hands on the axe, and he knew, with sick certainty, what Ugo intended. He roared at him to stop but might have saved his breath. Sib tried to leap forward and grab Ugo, but he slipped in the bloody slush and went to his knees.

Ugo took two steps forward and the great red Bull stood, swaying its head from side to side, blowing spumes of steaming breath; it had a withered loop of old garland round one horn and seemed to be waiting.

Ugo whirled the axe in a half-loop, raised it high, roared out his best battle cry and brought it down. He felt it crunch into the skull, heard the crack of it and then his hands were free. He stared at the splintered shaft, the end white as bone, the bitt buried in the head of the beast.

It gave an outraged bellow, a blast of sound and fetid heat that staggered Ugo backwards. It shook blood up in a massive spray, lowered its great horns and lumbered forward, crashing through the undergrowth.

Quintus saw it, the great avalanche inevitability of it and made a wild grab, snagged Ugo by the wool of his cloak and hauled him sideways; the great beast, horns lowered and spuming out snorts, crashed past in a shower of snow. One horn brushed Ugo and sent him pinwheeling, dragging Quintus with him.

Drust and the others scattered from the path of it, the shield-wall hesitated and that was too late; the Bull ploughed through them as if crashing into a bramble thicket, scattering them sideways. It bellowed and tossed its head one way, then the other; blood sprayed, scarlet slush bloomed in gobbets.

Dog followed it up, yelling at Drust and Kag to follow. Somewhere, Sib's high voice added a threnody of scream and the great beast seemed to hear that above all. It pawed and bellowed and then lumbered after it. Sib capered and ululated, that thin, eldritch sound they all knew well; the women of the desert made it as they gutted the captives taken by their warriors.

'Get the woman,' Dog yelled, pointing. 'Get to the boats.'

The woman stood on the shoreline, poised and seemingly drawn up in a haughty pose of disregard, but Drust saw the clenched tremble in her.

'No danger, in the name of gods above and below,' he said in his mother's old tongue and saw that she understood at least part of it – saw, too, by her scornful look what poor-tin noise the words made clattering out. Her men were writhing, shrieking or torn to bloody shreds. Her violated god-beast was trailing blood and rampaging in fury – but lured by Sib's cries. Her enemies were closing in, smeared with the entrails of her hearthtroop.

The Wanderer came loping up and she saw him and spat words like curses. He shrugged. Kag picked his way over the corpses, pausing to end the grating moans of one with a swift stroke; somewhere the Bull crashed and rampaged and Drust looked up in that direction.

'Sib,' he said. Kag waved one hand.

'He's fast and knows those beasts. He did some clown work in the Maximus from time to time, baiting creatures like that.'

He turned and stared at the boats by the shore behind the woman. 'Look at that. Boats with sharp ends – lend me a hand and we'll unload that fodder and get in them and away.'

Drust saw the boats were loaded with winter hay and roots and that the woman had been holding a fresh garland, now dropped. They had come, as they always did at this time of year, to make offerings to their Bull, to feed him over the winter. Small wonder he was so huge.

She was no sacrifice. The woman was a priestess or a queen – the Wanderer confirmed it warily.

'Queen of the Bull People,' he said, keeping out of range and licking his lips. Kag told him to bind the woman and then saw Drust's face.

'Not the time,' he warned, but Drust was moving, searching, his head full of Dog's thundering betrayal, latest in the long, reeking line of them. Dog was on his knees, pressing his thumbs into the eyes of a shrieking warrior too dying to be able to fend him off. The screams cut to Drust's core.

'Dog, you fuck.'

There was no response; the thumbs dug and there was a sickening wet plunge as resistance went. The man writhed a little.

'Look at me, you whoreson. You lie like a fallen tree.'

Then he did and Drust felt he had stepped into the core of a blizzard blast. Blood smeared that death face and the eyes, though open, were the most dead thing in that skull. He looked like a revenant, freshly resurrected, and he started to rise, mouth working in a snarl.

Kag laid a hand on Drust's arm and drew him aside.

'Dog,' he said quietly. 'Look at me. Look at me.'

Dog was on his feet, wobbling, his face and hands dripping; beneath him, the victim flopped and moaned, trying to clutch at his ruined face.

'Look at me.'

Dog looked at Kag, who nodded. 'Leave him. We need to get away. With the woman.'

Quintus and Ugo came staggering up and Dog swung his head, heavy as a sacrificial ox.

'He's dead,' he said and Quintus looked at the man at his feet.

'What gave it away?' he demanded scathingly. 'The gutting? The blinding? Or the fact that he has ceased to breathe?'

'Calvinus,' Dog said dully. 'He's dead.'

'Long since, you hagged fuck,' Drust spat, and Kag gave him a warning glance.

'Help unload the fodder. If that beast returns, it may be that decent pile of beets will work where Ugo's axe failed.'

'I fought the Lord of the Forest,' Ugo said, staring after the sound of bellow and crash. 'I challenged and fought. It was honourable.'

'You got sent out of the ring standing,' Quintus growled. 'Well done – now get to the boats.'

They worked swiftly and loaded the woman onto a boat with Drust and Kag. Dog plunged his head and shoulders into the iced water and sluiced the worst off. By the time they had done all that, Dog seemed to have recovered some sense, though he squatted in the boat and passed his hands over his face now and then as if clearing some veil.

'We should go,' he said.

'Not without Sib,' Kag replied.

'Longer we wait, closer the pursuers get,' Dog argued, but he was too weak to protest when Kag simply, scornfully, ignored him.

Sib arrived in a loping run, breathing hard and wild-eyed. Drust had never seen his eyes so big and white and round. He said nothing, simply came up, gasping with relief to see they were still there and hurled himself into a boat.

He said nothing while they pushed off and worked round to where they had left their mounts. Said nothing at all, but stared back at the distant blaring bellows and shivered, not all of it from the cold.

They vanished into the white mist, a dream of drifting flakes.

Drust went in one boat with Kag and the Wanderer, paddling furiously across the black water until they ran out of fear and strength. They glided for a while, sweating and breathing acrid smoke.

Behind, Dog, the woman and Quintus slid in and out of the curtain of snow and Drust turned to the Wanderer, his voice cold as the water.

'You knew of this,' he said. 'The woman. Who is she – is her name really Beatha?'

The Wanderer hunched up like a foetus, but nodded. 'She is Mother of Bulls. A queen.'

'Priestess?' Kag demanded, and the Wanderer shrugged.

'Goddess is closer,' he answered, 'but who knows with these people?'

'Not his sister,' Drust muttered bitterly and the Wanderer nodded.

'Why does he want her?' Kag demanded.

'To force the Bull People to oath with us,' the Wanderer answered. 'It means they will not attack when…'

He stopped, looked at the water. Drust's grin was wolfen.

'When you and the rest of the skin-wearing fucks rise up in the summer,' he said. Kag spat into the water.

'Fortuna attend you, then,' he said. 'The army will eat you up and spit out the broken bones.'

'What's to stop the Bull People rising up when you hand the woman back?' Drust demanded, and the Wanderer looked at him with a mixture of scorn and disbelief.

'Oaths,' he answered. 'We keep to them.'

'After stealing their goddess queen? Ugo might also have brained their big cow.'

The Wanderer shrugged. 'They will store it up. It is for another time.'

They drifted up to the silent silhouette of the stilt dwelling, where the dead ruched up with frost. Drust did not want to think about what was in the building, but Ugo and Sib fetched out the mules while Drust put his face into Dog's eyeline.

'You lied. Again.'

Dog shrugged. 'I thought you might be better disposed to help if you thought it was kin I was rescuing. Anyway – no harm done. At least to us. I would not want to be Talorc in years to come – this woman won't forget.'

He tugged at the leather leash that led to her fastened hands and she stumbled forward a few steps, looked at him with quiet sneer and said something that trilled and burned at the same time. Dog merely showed his teeth at her.

'She promises my prick will curl up and die, among other curses,' he said.

'I promise your prick will curl up and die,' Drust answered quietly. 'As far from your broken carcass as I can throw it if you lead us into another danger. On Jupiter's balls I swear it, Dog.'

'On your best day,' Dog replied, 'you could not.'

'I could,' Kag said softly. 'We could. All of us could. We did before and should have ended you then instead of just breaking bits…'

'Enough,' Quintus said, then offered his white grin, 'good fun though it is to think on. Warming on a day like this – but we have to move. What's the next part of this, Dog?'

The tension uncoiled slowly. 'We send the Wanderer, and Julia Soaemias and her son are brought. We make the exchange…'

'They will be on us like a pack of wolves directly afterwards,' Drust said. 'Best we let her loose when we are within sight of Roman walls.'

'They might not agree to that,' the Wanderer said uncomfortably, and Drust scoured him with a look.

'Make them. What do we need some cow-feeding tribal Druid for?'

'Druids are all men,' Ugo pointed out, lumbering up with the mules. 'In fact, they are—'

'Move out,' Kag said, slapping him on an arm. The big German scowled and started lashing the mule packs tighter; Drust saw him wince.

Dog blew out his cheeks and tugged the leash. 'Now comes the hard part.'

'The dark is coming,' Sib said. 'We should wait for light.'

'They will be on us before that,' Kag answered, but Sib was right and everyone knew it. The day was sliding into black with lowering cloud; the white was changing to grey, but the snow still whirled and blew off mounds in spumes.

'I will not stay here, in this place,' Ugo said, his face etched with pain and old terrors. The wind moaned agreement.

'We won't get far in this, at night,' Quintus said, but Drust looked at Dog.

'We won't have to. Dog has picked a place and it cannot be far from here.'

Dog nodded and Kag squinted at Drust. 'They will be on us, those Bull People. We have stolen their queen and all but killed their god-beast – why would they not? We can't stay here.'

Drust thought about it. No one had survived, either here or back where they had taken the queen, so the Bull People would not react until it became clear something was wrong and it could be well dark by then – with luck this blizzard would still be on, too. Warriors would go out in it, but it would not be a happy experience; Drust was sure there were spare boats at the far landing stage and they'd go fearfully to the island, find the bodies – the dark and snow would confuse the signs and the beast-crushed bodies would make them wonder. Maybe the creature was still rampaging and bellowing in pain.

'They may work out that their queen is not among the dead,' he told them. 'I do not think anyone will want to stay on that island for long at night, so they will come back to this side, maybe start working their way up the banks. They will come here because this is a place they know and, besides, the poor sods sent out to search will look for an excuse to get in the warm.'

'So? All the more reason for moving,' Dog growled. 'The place I have in mind is half a day from here.'

Drust shook his head. 'Too far in this and in the dark. We could wander in a half-circle, like we did once in the desert when a storm hid the stars. We need shelter and warmth at least for a time and we need daylight to see at least a patch of sky where your Sun God might be. We can light fires here, too, because those who come will expect it.'

'I will not stay in that stilt house,' Quintus muttered. No one disagreed with him, but it wasn't necessary. All they had to do was hunker down in outbuildings and make it look as if the place had warmth and light, food and shelter; the ones stumbling out of the dark would die half frozen and dull with cold.

'When we can see,' Drust added, 'we will move quickly.'

The woman spat something at Dog, who grinned and translated.

'She says we are all dead unless we set her free. There is more, but mostly the same.'

'She may be right,' Ugo grunted and moved off, tugging the mules back into shelter. He would keep them packed, though, for a swift move in the morning.

Quintus sidled up to Drust's ear. 'He's hurt, the big man. Bad. He won't admit it but something is broken in him – that horn hit him hard, I heard it. He spits blood when he thinks no one is looking.'

Drust looked at Dog, who had overheard.

'I hope this,' he said, indicating the woman with a scornful flap of one hand, 'is worth it.'

'She is worth not one *as* to me,' Dog answered, 'but Talorc values her, and so I will get what I want.'

'The Sun Goddess and her boy,' Quintus growled. 'What then, Dog? What do you do then?'

'We,' Dog said, stressing the word, 'take them to Eboracum and claim reward.'

'Who wants them, Dog?' Drust demanded. 'Who wants them dead and who wants them saved?'

Dog shrugged. 'I want them saved. That's all you need to know.'

He moved off into shelter and the rest followed, though Kag paused and caught Drust's arm.

'He will betray us in Eboracum, I think. He needs us now to get his charges there. *Omnes ad stercus*. Drust. What does the likes of Dog have to do with a Roman priestess of the sun and a boy in the mould of The Hood? And to do that to your face for it? Is he mad?'

'You have to ask?'

They leaned into the snow and sought shelter and fire. The heat was a blossom of bliss from the gods above and below and Sib started a pot, loading it with savoury and pinches of spices from shadowed areas of his clothing, where his body heat kept them dry.

They spooned it up in the flickering dim, where the animals shifted and ate fodder that would condemn the other beasts to death once they had gone. Now and then Quintus would cock his head and look out into the shadows, out to where the stilt house mouldered in frozen blood; Drust knew he was hearing a baby cry, for he thought he heard it himself.

The woman sat impassive and refused food and Dog shrugged at the sight. 'She won't be with us long enough to starve to death,' he said. 'Afterwards is Talorc's problem.'

The Wanderer stood watch with Kag while Ugo got prone and leaned on one elbow because lying down seemed to cause him pain and discomfort. He waved it off as well as his sudden long silences.

'I mourn,' he said, 'for my axe.'

No one was fooled, not even the woman; when the Wanderer came back she spoke to him in flat tones, cold as Drust's back.

'She says the big one will die,' the Wanderer translated. 'She says the Father of the Forest has claimed him.'

'If I were her,' Drust answered savagely, 'I would worry about the Father of the Forest, who has the bitt of a great axe sticking out of his head.'

He had the satisfaction of seeing the woman flinch, but it felt cheap as old pewter in the next second. She said something else and then folded her hands in her lap and stared off into the dark. The Wanderer stroked his beard braids and translated.

'You will never find Mag Mell. You are condemned to wander in eternity.'

Mag Mell was a name that hurt. His mother had told him of it in those stolen moments in the soft dark and Drust had not realised then that she was preparing him for her passing. 'Mag Mell,' she would whisper. 'The Plain of Delight.' There were other names, too – the Land of Apples, The Silver-Cloud Plain, the Place of Youth – but it all meant the same. Escape from slavery.

Drust looked at the woman and saw something of what he remembered of his mother there, felt the pain of old loss.

'Gag her,' he told the Wanderer, 'lest she call out when others come.'

He went back to the fire, where his front toasted and his back chilled. Kag and Dog were there and Kag asked what the woman had said, so Drust told him. Kag grunted.

'Stopping her mouth was a good thought.'

They sat and stared at pictures in the flames. 'Do you think there is such a thing?'

'What thing?'

'Eternity. I mean – when does Cronos claim you, as opposed to Dis Pater or Pluto?'

Dog growled out something like a laugh. 'You can ask this? This proves you are now uncoupled from being a *harena* warrior and that you never were a true one to start with.'

'Fuck you, Dog,' Kag spat back. 'You think because you had a fight to the death once makes you special? Everyone who stepped on the sand put their life on the line, every time.'

'What do your philosophers say?' Drust demanded, not wanting a fight at this good fire. Kag subsided slowly and thought.

'No man ever steps in the same river twice, for it's not the same river and he's not the same man,' he said eventually. 'Thus said Heraclitus.'

'Greek,' Dog declared dismissively.

'Most of the good ones are – but here's Cicero for you. The life of the dead is set in the memory of the living.'

'So there is no such thing as eternity? And I am to accept this from someone calling himself Chickpea?'

Kag shrugged. 'Are you so hagged by that skin-wearing queen's words, then?'

'I have seen people be born and seen them live for a time, then die,' Dog said, staring at the flames and so astonishing the others that they gawped. 'That is a constant experience I can see for myself. No one has ever come back from beyond the curtain of death, but I know that curtain is a thin veil. It can be torn in an eye-blink by death, which can come in an instant – one moment here, next moment... somewhere else.'

They stared at him while the flames dyed his death face bloody. He raised it and looked at them.

'All we have is our faith in the gods, and faith is not knowledge. Who can say they know the truth if the truth never lets itself be known?'

'Yet you believe in that golden boy,' Kag managed hoarsely. 'All this for him. Does he hold the secret of eternity for you, then?'

Dog broke his eyes from them and stared blindly at the fire.

'He might. And if prayers teach you anything it is this – nothing ever comes if nothing is ever offered.'

In an hour they offered what the gods appear to like best, no matter on which side of the Wall they dwell.

Blood.

–

They came when it was light enough to see at least something, but they were numbed and stumbling, six men swathed with wool and fur, hands chapped red and not able to even feel the shafts of spears or the shield-grip.

Gwynn Ap Nudd, Drust thought. He remembered the god's name from when his mother had taught him it and others, trying to keep the flame of his heritage alive. Poor ma, he thought sadly. My heritage was not in the blood but in the upbringing. It is less in knowing Gwynn Ap Nudd, God of the Dark than in knowing which areas of Rome are watered by the truly foul Alsietinian aqueduct which usually serves the fullers and waters gardens. Or every street in Cispius and Fagutal and Oppian and how to get from the slums at the bottom of the Esquiline to the purples at the top without being seen by the Watch.

It did not matter, then, that he knew the god fears of these six, who had preferred to shiver than move in the night. It mattered only that they were dead men walking, even as they moved like moths to the light and the fire.

There was a flurry, a swift moment of snarls and wet, sick sounds. Someone managed a sharp despairing cry, but that was all. Dog came up to where Drust stood, breathing hard and wiping his blade on a greasy fur cap.

'Where were you?' he demanded.

'Watching the woman,' he said. 'She can't speak, but you did not fasten her ankles.'

Dog was embarrassed at the oversight, so he merely growled while the iron stink of blood washed briefly out, then moved to the woman and tore the gag free. She worked wet into her mouth and spat on him. Drust laughed.

The reek went quickly because the cold seeped away the heat from the new blood. They moved off, leaving six more ragged, sad little corpses. Sib looked back now and then as they plodded out, wondering if their *jnoun* wafted like invisible smoke, bewildered at where they were and angry. He shivered and it was not all cold.

He looked at Dog, who had done most of the killing, swift and frenzied as a desert fox. He did not like Dog's face now, with its skin markings, the *jedwel.* Such markings were known to him – most woman of his tribe had them, the *siyala* on the chin, the *ghemazza* between the eyes which, when extended to the forehead, becomes *el-ayach.* They were all *khamsa*, protection from the evil spirits, the *jnoun*, and placed at vulnerable entrances to the body: eyes, nose, mouth, navel and vagina.

But Dog's face markings were the opposite. They attracted *jnoun*, and Sib feared that more than one was in him now. Manius had been bad enough, with no *jedwel* protection at all – but he was dead and gone and Dog was not.

The snow had stopped falling, but lay thickly, frozen to a crust that cracked open and dropped man and beast to the fetlock. Bracken spears snapped and Kag turned once or twice to look back; Drust knew that he was thinking about the long, beaten trail of scarred snow. If you leave tracks…

It took them most of the rest of that short day to reach Dog's hideaway and they only recognised it by the strange copse of sharpened trees angling up. It took all of them – save Dog – a few moments to realise they were the remains of old stakes. Then came the ditch, which they had to slog round to find a way through – if they'd tried to cross it otherwise, they'd have floundered in deep snow and suffered the agonies of lily-pit stakes.

'A fort,' Kag muttered between smoking breaths. 'An Army fort? This is your hideout?'

'Good defences,' Dog said, 'and close enough that Talorc can reach it before the Bull People get here.'

It was thirty paces long and twenty-five paces wide – a cohort-sized detachment had built it and the inscription revealed all when Ugo rubbed the snow off the burned wood.

'You can read,' he growled to Drust. 'What's it say?'

> mp L. S. Severus Aug
>
> p p vex leg
>
> VI V fec p
>
> For the Emperor Lucius Septimius Severus Augustus, father of his country, a detachment of the Sixth Legion Victrix built this

'A newish one, then,' Quintus said, grinning. 'A year old. Or two. Perhaps the oven is still workable and we can make bread.'

Despite himself, Drust's tart reply got lost in a rush of saliva at the idea of fresh bread; he saw the others were similarly entranced.

'Two years ago,' Dog agreed. 'Marching camp. Or maybe just one of those outposts to shout out that the Army was back.'

'Before the skin-wearing beasts got brave,' Kag grunted. 'There's nothing here but ruin and fresh snow.'

Dog shrugged, then flapped a hand at the Wanderer, who nodded and went out, moving fast.

'Light a fire with what we have, thaw out some timbers for firewood,' Drust said, and Kag went to it. Ugo, holding himself on one side, took Sib and saw to the mules and eventually Quintus came back, wide grin still in place.

'The oven is there, cracked a bit but useable. No buildings, of course – they tented it and they are all gone, but they made a couple of withy shelters for mules and we can use them.'

'We need to make sure we have at least three mules alive,' Dog said. 'We will take the Bull queen with us when we go and won't let her go until we see the smoke from Wall fires.'

'Even then,' Quintus said pointedly.

'Then we run.'

Drust looked at the woman, who sat on a mule-pack saddle violet-eyed and pinched. She was trying to hold herself together but it had been a long, hard time of refused food and defiance and the cracks were showing. Her bottom lip trembled now and then and she bit it so it wouldn't show.

'How long before Talorc gets here with the Roman woman and her son?' Drust demanded, and Dog stopped sorting out his pack to look up, squinting with thought.

'A day, no more. He will move on horses and he does not have many of those. He will have twenty, perhaps thirty, with him and they will all be chosen men and the chiefs they serve, for none of those will let him do this on his own.'

'Some of us may be dead in a day,' Drust answered, looking pointedly at the woman. Dog straightened, wiping his hands down his front.

'I am sure Ugo will be first. I will give you good odds.'

Drust stared into those dark pits set in the skull and only knew Dog's eyes were open by the feral gleam in them. Abnormal eye contact, he remembered Kag saying.

He turned away and tried not to shiver.

Chapter Twelve

The snow stopped falling, but the wind was a sibilant sneer that sifted what lay into drifts, then moved it on for no other reason than cold spite. In the old fort, the men huddled round a fire made from old abandoned stakes and stayed silent, as if even opening their mouths let too much freeze in.

Drust found Quintus, who spat the words out in quick, smoking bursts. The fodder was almost gone. The food was almost gone. The water was all gone and they were melting snow because mules were too foolish to eat it to quench their thirst. The mules were almost gone.

'Keep them alive,' Drust said. 'We will need them for the woman and the boy.'

He moved on to Ugo, who was sitting lopsided by the fire, looking like a half-empty bag of grain.

'How goes it?' Drust asked, and was startled at the etched lines on the face that looked back at him; even under the tangle of beard and the brow braids you could see how it was.

'I defeated the god of the woods,' Ugo said and held up the splintered haft. Then he sighed. 'I fear it has sixed me though.'

Drust felt his insides lurch at this admission, for he knew it wasn't lightly given. He clapped the big man's shoulder. He saw the woman look at them and she said something, slow and awkward – it took Drust a moment to work out that she laboured her way in the Local tongue, the trade tongue.

'He may die. I fix.'

Dog tugged the leash, jerking the woman towards him and away from Drust. 'What's this? She speaks to you now?'

'It would seem so,' Drust answered levelly. 'Badly, but good enough to say she can do something to help Ugo.'

'What?'

'I have ways,' the woman said, and went to the belt round her middle – Dog jerked her leashed hands away, scowling with suspicion.

'Let her,' Drust said sharply, then looked Dog in his skull eyes. 'You searched her for weapons, did you not?'

Dog had but was starting to wonder. Drust reached, unlooped and unfastened the belt, noting that the body he touched now and then was firm and ripe underneath. He tried not to think of it, squinting at the belt in the firelight.

It was the width of three fingers, set cunningly with little pouches and narrow sockets. At first Drust thought they were for needles of some sort but when he plucked out what was in one, it seemed to be no more than a sliver of wood.

'In my land she would be called wood-wife,' Ugo said. 'The splinters are all sacred to some gods somewhere. If she touches them she can make a ward against evil.'

Drust carefully put the sliver back. The first pouch he opened had some dried plant in it, desiccated almost to dust. It smelled musty and sweet at the same time and he did not dare touch it to his tongue.

'I make,' the woman said and mimed drinking with her bound hands.

'She will poison him,' Dog growled, and Ugo laughed blood onto his lips.

'I am dead already,' he said.

'Untie her,' Drust said to Dog, and could almost feel him swell but he did not look.

'Who are you to order? This woman is mine.'

Now Drust looked. 'This woman was taken by all of us. Untie her. If she can do good for Ugo, I want her to.'

Dog winked on the brim of it for a moment and the knife came out of the sheath with a sibilant hiss. The moment hovered and coiled – then he reached and slit the cord between her wrists.

'Leader,' he said scornfully. 'Father of us all, is it? A little Servilius Structus…'

The woman massaged her wrists, then rooted for a pot and snow to melt. She refastened her belt and bent by the pot, muttering while the flames danced on her face. Sib made signs against evil.

'Why?' Drust asked her as she worked, and she looked up.

'The God Bull let him live. That means something.'

Only because the God Bull had a splitting headache and a great many other targets, Drust thought, but he did not argue – everyone was gods-hagged here.

Drust drew apart a little, to where Dog glowered. Quintus sat on the other side, nonchalantly honing the blade of his *gladius*, grinning at the rasp. It was clear he had drawn it at the same time Dog had whipped out his knife.

'How is that German *Stupidus*?' Dog demanded.

'If he was a mule,' Quintus said through his smile, 'I would slit his throat, for the mercy in it.'

'We will make it back and Ugo will be with us,' Drust said, trying to make himself believe it. 'He probably broke a rib – you know how that is.'

They had all cracked one at some time or other, usually in the practice ground with those heavy wooden swords. It taught you to be better, for all that was done for you was tight-lashed bindings and a drop to light training at the Sweating Post.

The woman made her potion and let it cool. Then she fed it to Ugo, who drank and grimaced. There was a sheen on him now; he looked grey and the sweat had popped on his forehead like fat apple pips. Drust almost envied him the heat.

'Well, brothers,' he declared. 'If I am bound for the Dark Land, it has been an honour. And I fought the god of the forest and won.'

'You deserve the hero's portion, for sure,' Drust said, remembering the whispered tales of his youth.

'We are already in the Dark Land,' Kag answered bitterly.

It grew darker, then into a sky of iron and milk as the day crawled up onto the horizon and shivered. They spent all of it waiting. Ugo growled and fought the god beast in fevered dreams while the water lashed off him and they tried to keep him covered each time he threw them off, for fear the cold would eat him where the fever-heat did not.

Towards what Drust worked out was the next dawn appearing, Dog leashed the woman again.

'They are hours late,' he said, 'which means Talorc is thinking to be clever. He has sent men out to move fast and get ahead of us, to the south, between us and the Wall.'

Drust had expected it but hearing it did nothing to shift the cold settling haar of it in his belly. Then Sib called out that men were coming and Dog rose up as if his knees creaked. They probably did.

'He took horses,' he said, 'He does not have many horses.'

He had enough, Drust thought, to mount twenty or so men and they were not so chewed by cold that they could not climb off them, form up and fight. In the middle he saw the swaddled bundles of fine wool and fur that marked the woman and the boy.

Dog tugged the Bull queen up and she stumbled towards him, then fell. 'Now we watch closely,' he said, then nodded to Drust. 'You go and talk. Fetch the Domina and her son. Tell that whoreson Talorc that he will get the Bull woman when we are within sight of Roman walls.'

'And where will you be?' Kag demanded sarcastically. Dog's look was cold and silent for a moment, then he grinned rictus onto his ink face.

'This is what a leader does,' he said. When Drust moved out across the snowfield to where Talorc and his men waited, feeling like a bug on a silver salver, he looked back once and saw Dog standing where he could be seen, the woman leashed to him and on her knees, a spear resting lightly on her neck.

Talorc saw it too and spoke to the Wanderer, who squinted at Drust, then past him to Dog.

'Will he kill her, then?'

'If you make a move to try and take her,' Drust said. He saw the Roman woman, Julia, sitting on a small horse beside her son, seemingly unconcerned, but he also saw that she missed nothing.

'Talorc thinks you will try and take them all,' the Wanderer said.

'What use is the Bull queen woman to us?' Drust countered.

'Talorc thinks Colm Deathface wants her. Maybe make himself king there.'

'Deathface will not be coming back over the Wall to visit you.'

Drust had no idea whether that was true, but he felt it. Dog would go wherever Julia Soaemias and her son would go, he thought. He looked at the boy, that perfect face, that Caracalla smile.

Talorc spoke briefly, a short guttural spit that the Wanderer took in with a nod and then passed on.

'Talorc will follow you to the Wall,' he said. 'When you are close to it and only then will he hand over the Roman woman and the boy.'

Drust knew it was the best that could be achieved here, so he nodded and crossed back to Dog and the others, feeling the itch of all the Blue Face warriors on his neck and refusing to turn and look.

He told them. Dog nodded; it was clear he had expected it. Somewhere up ahead would be Talorc's blocking force, stopping them before they got close enough for the Wall garrisons to be a refuge. The woman gave a little soft moan and cut it off with a clench of lip; Drust almost felt sorry for her; whatever happened she was faced with captivity.

'Pack up and move,' he said. 'Hollow square, animals and the woman in the middle, like the army do. Watch your sides like we do – Kag, you are the tail man in this.'

Then he jerked his rasping chin to the east. 'We go that way, run along the line of the Wall and then turn south. With luck we will avoid the closing trap.'

Dog nodded thoughtfully. 'That way takes us to the farm of Verrecunda.'

Heads came up; no one wanted to go back there, but it seemed to Drust as if the gods were throwing dice, the winner pushing them in different directions. When he muttered it, Quintus offered his tireless grin.

'Well, the answer there is simple. It's how he got the name, after all – always put your stake on the dog.'

–

Hollow square was a jest for what they had – a loose ring of men with Ugo on a mule, lolling and barely conscious and the woman on another. They were all aware of the trailing warriors, but they kept their distance; Kag reported that a horseman had gone flogging out through the snow, heading south to take a message to the force there.

'We should turn south soon,' Sib called out, but that was only because he did not want to go to the house of Verrecunda and everyone knew it and ignored it.

It had been a good plan but Drust realised just how he had underestimated the cunning of Talorc when he saw the line of warriors in the spindrifting snow. Behind them huddled the buildings, but it was clear Talorc had sent men east.

'Probably west, too,' Kag agreed. 'He needs to stop us going anywhere. The cold will do the rest.'

'How far behind is Talorc?' Drust demanded, and Kag squinted.

'Out of sight. Could be a good walk. Might be further.'

'Then we need to rush these and end them,' Drust declared. Dog nodded. Sib laughed aloud.

'Us? Now? As we are?'

'Shut up, cart driver,' Ugo rumbled amiably, and levered himself painfully off the mule. 'I will take the mules. The rest of you hit them hard – there are only six or seven.'

More like a dozen, Drust thought – but he was cheered by Ugo's face, which looked better than it had. He saw the woman looking at him and nodded his thanks; Dog handed the leash to Ugo and scowled.

'Make sure you don't lose her, else this is all for nothing and we are sixed for sure.'

Drust felt his bowels melt – an old, familiar and unwanted feeling. No matter how rehearsed, no matter that no deaths had been paid for, every *harena* performance had made him sick like this. He knew Dog knew it, too, and could not look at the sneer in that skull face as they gripped weapons and started to lope at the men. He flexed his frozen fingers on the grip of the silly little square shield, gripped the hilt of the *gladius* more firmly and followed on.

There was one who was clearly leader, a big one too. He stepped forward of the rest and flung his arms wide, shouting as Drust and the others came up. Dog loped to a halt and stood, hipshot. Uncertainly, Drust glanced at him, saw him grinning his death grin.

'He challenges the chief of us,' Dog said. 'He believes it to be me.'

His grin was carved from old stone and then he stood back and spread his arms mockingly. 'Here it is,' he said to Drust, his skull mouth twisted. 'Here is the truth of it, of *uri, vinciri, verberari, ferroque necari* – I will endure, to be burned, to be bound, to be beaten, and to be killed by the sword.'

His face shoved at Drust like a weapon, savage and feral. 'See what it feels to be a first-rank fighter, Drust. No rehearsal…'

The warrior strutted back and forth. He had a face marked with scars and fierce blue signs of power and boast, seemed as large as the Wall itself. He had a ringed coat under his bear pelt and the tarnished remnants of some centurion's *phalerae* hung about his massive chest.

'I am Lann, son of Aindreas, son of Adhamh,' he bellowed in Local, waving his weapons in the air, then said it in his own tongue so that his folk growled and roared back at him.

'I am the greatest warrior in this land,' he roared in Local. 'I make mountains of dead enemies. I fought the Rock Tribe's chosen and wiped them out in one battle and took four arrows – one here.'

Drust stood dry-mouthed, involuntarily glanced once at Dog and saw the grin. He saw Kag start to move and warned him with his eyes, the sick dread welling up. It had to be him. He had slipped and slid through contest after contest, a good actor who learned the moves and made it look real, even with a mediocre partner for an opponent.

But here was the truth of it, as Dog had said. No rehearsals, no assured let-off in this *harena.* Snow or sand, it was all the same… the gods never let you miss your destiny, he thought.

Yet some elements from those old rehearsed fights still mattered here. Flyting he knew well enough for they had worked on that many times when the fights were in *harena* small and intimate enough for all the audience to hear the jests and smile. He almost smiled himself when Lann indicated a vicious lash of scar beside his nose.

'I got this when I fought Lorcan, champion of the Bull People and killer of forty-two men. He broke my arm with a mighty blow, but I carved him to pieces anyway. I took this coat from a lord of the Short Hairs and killed him and all his twenty-four little Romans – see this hole? It was made by my spear, even though his own went through my side.'

At each feat, his shook his spear and sword at his men, though they barely understood Local; they had heard it all before and roared and howled. Drust worked spit into his mouth.

'You should think about ducking now and then,' he managed. 'Or a shield. Save all those wounds.'

'I will take yours when you are dead,' Lann declared.

'Since nothing you have fits me,' Drust answered, trying not to let his lip stick to his teeth, 'I will content myself with wearing your life for the rest of mine.'

Lann was done with talk. He fell into a crouch, which did not make him much smaller, and started to circle. Drust felt his legs wobble and hoped no one noticed. He affected nonchalance while trembling and occupied the centre ground, following Lann's wolfen circling in little shuffles, like a man at a crossroads wondering which road to take.

Lann moved swiftly – blindingly swift for a man of his size – and everyone thought it was the end, for a giant who moved like a flung *pilum* was a victory waiting to happen. The spear blurred, the curved sword flashed and Drust reeled away, half turned and stumbled.

He had nothing but old training, rigorous and daily, and the trick he and Menophilus had worked out one afternoon, a real crowd-pleaser. Drust spun back with sword hissing, a bar of silver that splintered sunlight. Lann, in the act of following up, sure that he had knocked Drust off balance, suddenly had to hurl himself away.

They paused, looking at each other while the warriors howled and the snow hissed off the tops of drifts. Drust managed a grin and a prayer to Menophilus for forcing them both through that afternoon until it was perfect. Menophilus, who had died of the sweats the next year, wasting to a yellowed husk, his life-water bleeding off him into stained straw.

Lann moved again, the spear darting, an adder tongue that slammed once, twice, three times against Drust's shield; the blows rocked and staggered him and he heard the wood splinter. Then, suddenly, Lann whipped in with the curved sword, Drust met it with his own and the high, thin clang of blades was loud as a bell. There was a moment when Drust was sure his arm was gone entirely, but he saw it flapping and numbed useless.

The shrieks grew wilder when folk saw the sword flying, beaten from Drust's grasp by the sheer, brute strength of the warrior. Lann bellowed and slashed, seeing his advantage, then gave a sharp yelp and a curse when Drust desperately brought the shield rim down on his wrist and the curved half-moon spun out of his own nerveless fingers.

I am good after all – let Dog eat this, he thought in a sudden spasm of anger.

Yet he was blowing and unsteady, had lost his sword and now stood against a man with a face like a bag of painted blood and armed with a spear, whose point he whipped in solid bangs on Drust's shield. Drust backed off. Lann did a swift reverse and scythed the butt round to whack the shield. Each blow was like a hammer that sent Drust stumbling; the warriors howled and, briefly, Drust caught sight of the anxious faces round Dog; Kag was clenched, ready to spring forward at the last. Dog was impassive as a tomb carving.

Drust, barely covering himself, backed off a little and stopped, breathing hard, his face streaked with sweat.

Lann flourished the spear in the air and grinned – then he threw it. Drust blocked and knew the mistake the moment he did it. Should have dodged… the blow sent him sprawling and he scrambled up wearily, only to find that the spear was through the shield and had almost hit him. He flung the skewered shield away and stood, empty hands by his side, while Lann raised his equally empty fists to the sky in triumph.

Kag started to draw his sword but felt something grip his wrist in an iron clamp. When he looked, Dog stared back.

'Easy,' Dog said. 'Stay your hand.'

Kag struggled and wrenched himself free, glaring. 'Fuck you in the arse, Dog – if he dies I will kill you myself.'

'Only the gods know the answer to that,' he said. 'Helios, hear these words…'

He prayed, to Kag's astonishment. Quintus picked up on it, spread his arms and offered chants to Nemesis and Fortuna.

Drust heard the chants even through the howls of Lann's exultant men, felt the deities swirl around him like the spin of drifting snow. Gods of the *harena* fighters…

Minerva.

Pluto.

Mars Ultor.

I am a grain of sand, the sparkle of sunlight on water. *Uri, vinciri, verberari, ferroque necari…*

The warriors' howls trailed off. They were uneasy about this clear sign of spell-making and called out to their own gods for help; Drust's own skin was gooseflesh as he heard the names, one by one, each one louder than the last.

Lann heard it and frowned, wondered if the Bull woman had something to do with it and vowed vengeance there when Talorc was done with her – then he growled, shook the sweat and blood from him and closed for the kill.

Drust dodged, spun and whacked the giant in the mouth, so that blood flew, but Lann shook his head, spat, grinned and sprang again.

Drust was no more than a core in a blossom of scarlet pain. He staggered sideways with a last, desperate burst of foot skill and avoided another rush, whacked the passing Lann high on the arm and bellowed with anger and pain at what the arm ring did to his knuckles.

Might as well slap a cliff…

Lann advanced, steady and relentless as an avalanche; Drust ducked but made a hash of it and an elbow caught him in the ribs, the pain blasting him with white light. He went off his feet entirely, flew back and landed in a sliding heap of snow. The crowd of warriors roared and stamped up more snow, beating their weapons together.

Lann moved slowly across to where Drust lay, face down and barely aware. Lann dragged him up and threw him flying to thump and roll in a blizzard of snow; he walked forward and slammed a kick that shifted Drust in a rut, then turned and raised his fists in triumph, so that the crowd bellowed even more loudly.

'Fuck you, Dog,' Kag said and sprang forward. As if he had let go of some tether, the others rushed and the warriors howled. Steel clashed, shouts went up.

Lann ignored them, bent at the waist and grunted with the effort, but he hauled Drust up, tearing off the man's helmet as he did so. He grinned into the lolling face. Drust saw it, the eyes cold and red, the scar beside the nose, the blue skin marks. There was blood in the tangled beard and Drust thought – I did that. I drew blood. If he bleeds, he dies…

He felt the man's massive hands clamp on either side of his head, then the wrenching pain of being lifted up – his neck felt as if it was stretching out and he could not feel the ground with his feet.

Kag saw what Lann intended and tried to get to it, but two warriors were in the way and Quintus was struggling with one of them while Dog weaved and slipped and stabbed. There were howls and clatters, shrieks and bellows like a slaughter yard.

Something smacked Kag's cheek – blood, flesh, snow, he did not know. Quintus felt his face in a rictus of grin but his mind was full of light and his hands full of steel – crack, smack. Die, die, you rat-fuck… a spear came in at him, the face behind it ink-marked with whorls which no doubt meant power or glory. Quintus let the spear slide over one shoulder and then ruined the face with a back slash and a howl, cut off when the man's blood splashed in his mouth.

Kag tottered and reeled, stabbed a man in the groin and then found himself on his knees in the wet, bloody slush, stabbed a man in the foot, rolled, slashed ankles and knew it was all going badly. Once you were down, you seldom got up in a fight…

Ugo had nothing but hands and the last of his strength. He let the mules loose, shouldered an enemy warrior to one side with a thump that racked white pain through him, then grabbed Kag by the scruff and hauled him up, ignoring the flowers of agony that caused.

'Stay up, keep going forward…'

Sib was dancing and shrieking, his head buzzed with his own noise, his whole being vibrant with fear while he blocked and slashed, whimpering with the utter terror of knowing that it was inevitable, at some point sharp metal was going to enter him like rape.

Lann looked round and laughed at the shape of it, the screams, the clashing metal, then shook Drust like a dog with a rat while men slavered and roared and bled around him. He started to squeeze, wanting to feel it, the moment when his enemy's skull splintered to ruin under his massive palms.

Drust was barely aware of it, but in the roaring tide that threatened to swamp him he heard a faint, distant cry.

'Drust…'

This last bellow by Kag drowned out the crunch and the high, thin whine that came from Lann when the arrow went into the nape of his neck, through his tongue and out of his mouth. Drust saw it as a spurt of blackness that spat in his face and a vague shape that wavered as Lann stopped like one of the Flavian machines when the gears jammed.

Drust dropped from his numbed fists into a heap on the ground and the giant weaved, coughed blood from his mouth and nose and then toppled like a falling oak. There was a pause, an intake of breath, no longer than it took the snow of the giant's collapse to puff into the air – then the warriors broke and ran.

There was a moment of whirling dark and light, then another when Drust felt like a great weight had lifted from him – the burden of living, he thought, with the one tiny part of himself that remained.

Then the light burst open like a great flower and he seemed to rise up into the face of Kag, streaked and etched and strained. Kag grinned and hefted the body of Lann to one side; behind him, Death loomed bloodily and grinned and spoke.

'You got a *missus*,' Dog said.

Chapter Thirteen

'I heard your prayers,' Drust said hoarsely, 'though I don't know which god to thank.'

'Start smaller,' Dog advised with a slanted grin and that left Drust squinting in bewilderment. Behind Kag, he saw Quintus holding up the tarnished, battered rig of *phalerae*, stripped from Lann's body with the ring mail.

He gave an appreciative whistle and turned the harness this way and that. 'Look at this. Awards up the *cloaca* – poor bastard, it didn't save him, whoever he was. Nor that Lann.'

'I wouldn't weep too hard,' Dog said. 'A man this garlanded is a centurion of the 1st – whenever did one of those wear this rig on campaign? It was looted from some baggage and he is back in Eboracum, arguing with clerks to get them replaced so he can look regulation on pay parade.'

'Weep for the cart driver who carried it,' Sib added mournfully and folk laughed. It was a good sound.

'What did you mean, start smaller?' Drust demanded. He felt like a cart had driven over him, but he wanted up if nothing was broken and struggled to rise. Then he saw a familiar face that soused him with iced water.

She came forward and squatted beside him, offered him a beaker with something bitter in it.

'Verrecunda,' he said, and she looked blankly at him.

'Who did you expect? You are in my house.'

Not dead, then. Drust looked at the beaker, then up into Verrecunda's eyes, which mocked him.

'You think I am poisoning you?'

He swallowed another mouthful. 'I sent Manius to kill you and Necthan.'

She nodded. 'He came. He warned us and then he left.'

The other woman said something sharp and Verrecunda ignored her. 'That one is called Eithne and she is the Horned Queen of the Bull People – but you knew that. She is also the one whose folk drove mine to ruin, but she was a child then. She promises dire revenge for my part in her capture.'

'You had no part in it,' Drust managed weakly.

Verrecunda nodded. 'She does not know that. I am Roman to her now.'

'You had better flee, then,' Drust said. He felt a warm glow through him and the aches and pains seemed to have faded. 'Dog… Colm… will trade her to the Blue Faces, who will only release her for oath-sworn promises of peace or alliance.'

Verrecunda snorted. 'She will never get free. Talorc will keep her close and bind the Bull People with her. He needs something because this has cost the Blue Faces dearly – too many prime men have been killed.'

Drust felt good enough to move upright and realised Verrecunda was right. They had gone through Blue Face warriors like shit through a goose – he almost laughed.

'I fed you a potion which will dull the pain and break the fever. Eithne did the same for your big friend and I will give you more of it for when it wears off. He is worse off than you – something broke inside him and if it leaks more he will die. But he is strong – Eithne fears him because of what he did to the Father of the Woods. Did he really split its skull with an axe?'

'Almost,' Drust answered. The little room seemed busy with people and he saw Necthan waving his arms at Kag. Verrecunda followed his gaze and translated. 'He is telling your man to leave off stripping the dead. Talorc is coming and will want the gear back; best not to make matters worse by robbing the dead.'

Drust told Kag, who set the *phalerae* rig down reluctantly. 'This is Roman,' he muttered.

'It's a tarnished pile of shite,' Quintus corrected, grinning fiercely. 'Even if the old owner could see it he wouldn't want it back – he'll get shiny new.'

The skin across the door parted, letting in a blast of icy light blotted by a shadow which moved down the steps and into the fire glow.

'Men are coming. Fifteen, perhaps twenty. There are a deal of big war hats among them.'

Drust's mouth went dry.

Manius.

His head reeled and he barely managed to get the name out. He remembered the arrow coming out of Lann's mouth. Manius turned at the sound of his name and Drust saw that he was clean-shaven and wore a linen cap stained yellow; under it, he was sure, was also shaved. There were strange, shiny snakes along his jaw – half-healed scorching, Drust saw.

'Our Manius can't be burned,' Dog announced. 'Now all he needs is to defeat being bound, beaten, and killed by the sword.'

'He can be burned,' Verrecunda corrected. 'I treated him for it.'

'My hair went on fire,' Manius explained matter-of-factly. 'Beard too. Went into the snow and smothered it. Stayed there until everyone moved on.'

'Thought you were dead.'

The voice was a sibilant whisper from Sib and Manius turned to him.

'Fire came down between us. Good trick, that, little man. I should have waited until it was further out before I shot, though.'

Sib felt the roaring of demons, wondered if Manius was truly unaware of what he had tried to do or was waiting, taunting… that would all be part of a vengeful *jnoun* like him. In the end, all he knew, when he saw Dog's skull grinning mockingly at him, was that now there were two.

'You did not kill them,' Drust blurted, and Manius stared levelly back at him.

'I did not. I made sure no one else was sent.'

Drust held out a hand. 'Get me up. I will be on my feet when Talorc comes.'

'You will be on your knees more like,' Dog offered. 'And no good to anyone. I will speak to him, standing on two good legs and looking like a warrior.'

Drust's snarl was sharper than anyone had seen before and Dog's eyed widened a little. 'As you pointed out before that fight, I lead here, not you. And with Lann at my feet I look more warrior now than you.'

Dog stepped back, spreading his arms, but no one missed the narrowing of his eyes. Leaning on Manius, Drust hirpled up the stair and out into the scarred snow of the garth.

Ugo was there, trying to look like a dangerous mountain, but he grinned when Drust limped up and straightened painfully.

'Well, we might make one good man if they take the best bits.'

'We need to stop taking on the worst beasts beyond the Wall,' Drust agreed, and Kag shifted up beside him. Nearby, Necthan looked up from stripping the furs off a dead warrior.

'Told you before,' Kag growled. 'We are the beasts beyond the Wall.'

The warriors rode up through the kicked spray of snow and Talorc was not hard to find in the midst of them. He looked at the dead with a face patched as old mutton; behind him, other heads turned and muttered, not keeping it from him either, for Drust saw him flinch now and then at what was said.

Behind he saw Julia Soaemias and the boy, swathed in furs and impassive; the boy looked at everything the way a curious unafraid bird does, cocking his head slightly. His mother simply looked haughty and straight ahead.

The Wanderer came forward, all pinched face and ferret. 'It has been decided,' he said, 'to do the trade here and now. After it, we will go home.'

'Who decided?' Drust demanded. 'Talorc? If so, tell him piss comes out his mouth and so it is best to avoid getting his words anywhere near my shoes.'

The Wanderer did it and Talorc's face suffused – but he stayed silent and Drust knew then how the situation had changed. The Wanderer confirmed it.

'You have won, Roman. Too many good men have died for Talorc's plots and now the other war chiefs have forced him to accept this. They will hold to it.'

Dog tugged the leash and the woman stumbled forward. He grinned and indicated for them to bring mother and son to the fore.

They were dismounted and walked, slightly unsteadily, through the snow. When they got level, the woman turned and nodded to Drust.

'Well done. To you all.'

Dog scowled at not being the sole beneficiary of the praise, but he threw the leash to the Wanderer and, with one last scornful scathing curse of eyes, the bound queen strode into the middle of the pack and was hoisted onto a horse.

The Wanderer grinned thoughtfully and nodded once to Dog. 'You had best keep to your side of the Wall from now. We will look for you. Warriors will line up to test you.'

'Not you, though,' Dog answered scathingly, and then grinned that weapon of a face at the little man. The Wanderer seemed unaffected by the insult, simply offering a wan smile, one more crease in a face of ridges and troughs.

'There are other ways,' he said, and turned to spring onto a pony with an agility that made Drust wonder at how old he really was.

'Come to the warm,' Quintus said to Julia Soaemias and the boy. She looked at him, smiled sweetly and said: 'Domina. Or Domina Julia. You may address my son as Varius or Sextus Varius. Or Heliogabalus, for he is the personification of the risen god.'

'Sol Invictus,' Dog said reverently.

'Just so. Shall we go?'

They watched Quintus escort the woman and boy down into the mean hut and the warm.

'Go where?' Kag demanded.

'Eboracum. Find this Kalutis, hand over the woman and boy, get the reward,' Dog said. 'Quiet and swift, for not all our enemies are on this side of the Walls.'

'Who are our enemies?' Drust demanded, and Dog frowned, then shrugged.

'Anyone who comes with a sharp blade and a bad attitude. Same as always.'

'Not good enough,' Kag hissed. 'You must know who you work for and who you work against, Dog.'

'No more than you. Kalutis may tell more if you are interested, but he is a *ptolemy* and you can't trust any of them. All that matters is that you have that letter and seal somewhere about you. Without it, we will not get anywhere.'

That, too, had been part of his plan, Drust realised. Dog was cunning, no doubt of it. And they were riding his luck, which was a bad thing – his name was not Dog because of what gamblers shouted – always put your stake on the dog. The dog was a dice gamer's fantasy – two ones, thrown twice for a fabulous pot. Losing gamblers always went for it, that one great stroke to make Fortuna love them. More often than not, though, it betrayed them at the end.

That was how Dog had got his name.

-

Down in the red warmth of the fire-glowed hovel, Drust found a seat opposite Julia Soaemias and stared at her for a long moment, until she raised her eyes from watching her son laughing at the flames.

'I am used to amorous looks but you are merely rude. Keep it up and I shall have much to explain to my husband.'

'I would think you had more than enough there already,' Drust retorted drily. 'Such as where you have been for half a year.'

'You are impertinent,' she replied. Her eyes were green, he saw, and even with the frets of age at the corners, augmented by wood smoke and poor washing, she was stunning. She had endured what few Palatine woman could endure and he must remember that.

'Lady,' he began again, and she withered him with a cool look.

'Domina,' she corrected, and he bridled.

'We are a long way from the Lupercal. Nor are we slaves to be reminded of our place. In case you need reminding of yours, we are the ones wading in blood to get you free.'

She drew the furs round her – expensive, he noted, and no doubt given by Talorc, who had not taken them back as he had the ponies they'd ridden on.

'I have been weeks in hovels such as this, in the dark, without perfumes, face paints or even a decent wash in water anything better than tepid. I have daily been subjected to the barking of dogs as conversation and the sure knowledge that one or more of those savages would violate me. Or worse, my son.'

She broke off, then added: 'Do not speak to me of sacrifice.'

Drust sucked in a calming breath or two and began again. 'Forgive my clumsiness. The idea of speaking with a high-born such as yourself in a place such as this is strange. For us both, I think. Nevertheless, we have bled for you.'

'The lot of the *harena* fighter, I'd have thought. You have bled for reward.'

'Believe it or not… Domina… we have the highest respect here.'

Her eyes widened and grew amused. 'I am relieved to hear it. I thought perhaps my slovenly condition and frightened demeanour had persuaded you I was some slave wench, easily cozened. Being unattractive is foreign to me.'

'No doubt,' Drust answered drily. 'Hopefully we will have you back in a warm lake of perfumes before long. If we circumvent our enemies.'

'You have shown considerable resourcefulness thus far,' she answered, and reached out a delicate hand, clean and white for all her arguments to the contrary, laying it gently on her son's forearm. 'Do not stir the embers so. You cause sparks.'

'I was trying to see if Helios was there.'

'Fire is fire and Helios is Helios. It is not the same. We have talked of this.'

'We talk of many matters, Mother,' he answered. 'I cannot be expected to remember them all.' There was a tart steeliness beneath the blandness that made Drust look a little harder. When the boy became aware of it, he smiled sweetly.

Drust took Julia Soaemias's arm and drew her forcibly to one side. She looked astonished and outraged, then recovered herself when he spoke.

'Listen, lady. I need to know who wants you dead and I need to know who wants you safe. Dog – Crixus, as you know him – claims ignorance. If we are to return you safely and all of us with you we need to know.'

She adjusted her furs. 'You need to know only that Kalutis will reward you. As to who to avoid – everyone who is not him.'

Drust scrubbed his harsh stubble with frustration and grew desperate.

'The boy…' he began.

'Varius,' she interrupted.

'Varius. It occurs that he is the image of Caracalla. Is there something in that?'

It hung and coiled in the air. She drew herself up haughtily. 'Now you are beyond impertinent…'

He gripped her wrists in both his calloused, cold-split hands and saw her wince. 'Listen closely, Domina. I do not care if you fuck your cousin all over the Hill and all his street-rat friends with him – there are Suburan whores who can claim the same and some of them are friends of mine. I need to know if that is The Hood's son and whether he is the one seeking him out.'

She removed herself from his grip, firmly and gently.

'I am married. My husband is governor of Numidia. My son is High Priest of the Temple of the Sun in Emesa. My mother is sister to the Empress. It would be best if this was not pursued, and for the service you are doing me I will be gracious and forget you spoke.'

'Time we were moving.'

Drust looked up and had to focus out of his anger to see Kag, his look one of warning. He became aware that others had been watching and stood up.

'Get them on the mules,' he rasped. 'Manius – move ahead and make sure of the land in front. Sib – watch our rear.'

At the door, he turned and looked at Verrecunda; behind her, Necthan watched from the shadows.

'Fortuna smile on you,' he said, and managed one of his own. 'I shall send no one back.'

'Thank you for the blessings of your gods,' she answered, 'though I have my own and better ones. Even if you change your mind and send someone back, you will not find us here. It is a foolish prey who waits to be eaten.'

He felt her eyes on his back a long way off from the squatting hut and even when nothing could be seen behind them save the trail they left, he felt her stare.

It was not warming.

–

No one knew how he did it, but everyone agreed he did something. He stood like a small statue, arms outstretched, while his doting mother looked on and everyone fretted about the delay. Kag, as usual, was convinced they were being followed because they were leaving tracks. Ugo was just grateful for the rest, Sib at least knew where Dog and Manius were – both were watching the woman and boy.

Drust had no idea what the boy said, even when he got close enough to hear the high, thin flute of his voice. It wasn't Latin, nor even Syrian, for he had enough knowledge of it to know that. Older, he thought and wanted to shiver, but fought it, for it would do no good for folk to see him tremble at some boy invoking a god in a strange tongue.

It was cold to be standing on white-patched heather and bracken which rolled away in ridges like a frozen ocean. The only sound apart from the boy was the guttural harshness of birds, black crosses against the pewter sky. Rooks or ravens, Drust thought, neither of whom are good omens.

He saw a hare, too, darting into the tangled brown, heading for a rill that gurgled over stones, exultant at having been freed from ice.

They had smashed their way up and over this land for a day and a half and there was still no sign of the Northern Wall, which they should have reached. But the land dipped and swelled, so you could lose all Rome in its folds, Drust thought, until you were pushing your face against the gate.

The boy finished. His mother praised him and he beamed. Manius stamped his feet and glared; he did not like the sun worshippers, Drust saw.

'Can we go?'

Kag came loping up and Drust saw his face and sighed, knowing what he would say.

'We are being followed.'

'Of course.'

'No, really. On our arse, right now – about twenty on foot but running hard.'

Drust felt his bowels melt. Talorc had found a way to persuade the other chiefs into one last throw of the dice. He said the name aloud, but Kag shook his head.

'Not them. The others. The ones they raided for slaves – we fell over their trail, remember? Killed some who were raping.'

He shrugged and frowned. 'Or another tribe who watch the Wall.'

'Fuck all their mothers,' Sib spat. 'Why is Rome even here? Leave these snarling rats to eat one another.'

'They will stop fighting each other for one reason only – to fight Romans. We are Romans, so move,' Drust advised. 'Fast. Or be eaten.'

They whipped and kicked the mules and stumbled over the clutching bracken and heather as fast as they could, until their breath rasped. There were more hidden tarns and sudden dips in this part than the rest of both Britannias, Drust spat out, picking himself out of a sodden patch and cursing because now he had wet feet to add to everything else.

They were jogging now, but it was more stagger than run. Then, in a miracle the boy acknowledged with a high, thin shout and a clap of his hands, the sun broke through like a great golden coin and everyone stopped long enough to stare their astonishment to the sky.

'That boy,' Kag said on his way back to the rear to spy on their pursuers, 'is gods-struck after all. Perhaps we should follow Dog's lead.'

Privately, looking at Dog's raptured face, Drust thought the man too hagged to be sensible when it came to this woman and boy. Yet he had seen him gouging out the eyes of a man in the name of the dead Calvinus, and if worship of Helios kept that at bay, more power to the shiny god.

The sky started to lighten and, by the time the heat was sweating smoke off them, it was blue, with the wheeling, raucous birds like sharp black crosses.

'Ravens,' Quintus said, pulling on the halter of the woman's mule. 'They are not happy birds.'

'Rooks,' Ugo said, lumbering heavily and trying to keep up. 'They are rooks.'

They had to stop, drooling and heads bent, hands on knees. A mule keeled over and Quintus went to it, started unlashing the pack.

'Leave all that,' Drust ordered. 'We cannot carry it.'

'Last of our gear,' Quintus pointed out, but then grinned his grin, shrugged and did as he was told. He was soothing the mule before giving it iron when Manius came loping in, so silent and sudden that Sib failed to see him and recoiled with a yelp.

Manius spared him a single look, then went to Drust. 'Wall fort up ahead. Little one. A long run will take us there.'

'Then let us run long,' Drust said and started forward, smacking the rump of the boy's mule. The boy sat it like a bag of spilled grain, staring at the sky and smiling.

It was closer than that and Drust felt a swell of freshness that banished fatigue. We will make this after all, he thought exultantly. We will make this…

Then he made the mistake of looking back to see Kag sprinting, hurdling tussocks of bracken as if he was in a foot race.

'They are coming,' he bawled. 'The fuckers are coming at us.'

No one argued; everyone simply tried to outrun Kag, kicking and beating the mules in a frenzy, lurching and staggering until they hit the rutted trail that led up to the Wall fort. It was a little signal tower, no more and the turf rampart stretched out on either side of it, twice the height of a man and made taller by a wooden stockade. There was a deep ditch thick with snow, where the last weathered ends of stakes stuck out like bristles on a frozen chin.

There was not a single man to be seen.

Manius was calling out as they came up, looking behind them constantly now. 'Ho, there,' he called. 'Romans here. Open the gate.'

Everyone joined in, roaring and bawling. The mules picked up on it and started braying and, at last, a helmeted head appeared at the top of the tower, truculent as a routed pig.

'Ho yourself – what's all the noise? This is Compitalia – have respect for the *lares* if not my head.'

'Never mind celebrating your wine-soaked household gods – open the gate, you flap-sandalled, rat-fuck Army shit,' yelled Kag. The helmet leaned arms on the stone tower crenellations and scowled.

'Says who?' he demanded, and Kag took a breath but was forestalled by the firm, clear voice of the woman.

'Domina Julia Soaemias Bassianus, wife of the governor of Numidia, niece to the Emperor Lucius Septimius Severus Augustus. Open the gate at once or suffer the consequences.'

The helmeted face stiffened, then squinted. He has seen the warriors coming up, Drust thought, and that means they are far too close.

'Form,' he said. 'Pair brothers.'

They formed, fell into their familiar fighting pairs and braced as the warriors came up, breathing hard after a long run but with shields and spears and drool from feral snarls. Behind Drust, there was a series of dull thuds and a grating scrape as the gates opened.

'Get in, get in,' yelled a voice and everyone crowded for the entrance. Quintus started ragging the stubborn mules to move, but the woman and boy had slid off them and were hurrying through.

'Leave those, you arse,' Drust shouted, and Quintus looked at the nearest of the stumbling warriors, then gave a curse, threw the halter away and slid through the narrowing gate. It crashed shut and two men, helmets askew, manhandled the bar on it, then turned to where Drust and the others stood, hands on knees, sucking in breath in whoops. There was an echo of pounding on wood that somehow managed to convey frustrated fury.

Somewhere, a commanding voice was shouting for a messenger. He would send one to the nearest large fort and warn them that some fool tribesmen were milling round the Wall, Drust realised. Then he heard him command the signal fires lit and that brought his head up.

'We made it,' Sib declared joyously. 'We made it.'

Drust was aware, suddenly, of Julia Soaemias standing in front of him and stopped to look back at her.

'Well done, Drusus, and thank you.'

'We are not out of it yet,' he replied grimly. 'The *optio* is lighting signal fires.'

The woman did not know but everyone else did and had it confirmed when they went up to the top of the tower and looked out cautiously. The brackened plain to the north was stiff with men, two hundred and more – their pursuers had been mere scouts and they were prowling and howling insults.

'Who the fuck are you lot?'

The *optio* was called Caius Rogatus and he and his men were part of the 20th Valeria Victrix – 500 paces to the west was another signal tower, 500 paces to the east one similar. Beyond that was a bigger fort with a cohort in it, which was where the messenger had gone.

Which left Rogatus with seven men to defend this entire length of the Northern Vallum.

'But no one expects that, Domina,' he said, in reverence now that he knew who she was and had inspected the creased, dirty but still inviolably sealed document plucked from Drust's tunic. 'We have lit signal fires and shall simply close ourselves up here in the tower.'

'They will get in the ditch and scale the earthworks and stockade,' the boy said and the *optio* smiled benevolently on him.

'Clever lad. Yes they shall. Nothing we can do about that, and it's because most of the Army is off in the north, waiting for spring. But these beasts won't get far. The lads will round them up and then you can carry on. With an escort once things are clear, I am certain of it. My centurion will insist on it, I am sure…'

There was a sudden series of sharp bangs on the northern door and everyone leaped at it. Rogatus snarled out some orders and four men went to the top of the tower, to make sure it was defended.

'If they get on it,' Kag muttered, 'they can prise the hatch cover off…'

'Have no fear, Domina,' Rogatus enthused, 'we are snug as lice… er… bugs here. And the rest of the lads will up before morning.'

He had a man lead the boy and his mother to a corner of the tower, where no doubt his own bed was. Outside, a mule died with a series of braying screams and Quintus scowled.

'I liked those mules. Survivors, like us. Deserved to make it to safety.'

'Wouldn't, though,' Ugo said from where had slumped, grey-faced with pain. 'So they aren't survivors. Mules is like that. Dumb as greybacks in the Army.'

A soldier scowled at him, not liking the greyback reference.

Rogatus came back, wiping sweat from his face and listening to the thumps on the door. He did not look happy.

'Good door, is it?' demanded Dog and Rogatus looked from him to Drust and wiped away more sweat.

'The door is. The jamb less so. We are supposed to be rebuilding in stone, so the lintel was due for replacement and...'

He stopped. And you didn't think it worth the effort to repair round the door, Drust thought bitterly. Just as no one thought it worth it to man this Wall properly, since the army was wintering to the north after spending all summer burning and killing.

'The Army is up at the naval storehouses,' the *optio* confirmed. 'Twenty thousand and more – you'd think they could spare a couple for here, eh?'

The naval storehouse – Horrea Classis – was where The Hood was squatting, brooding in the mess halls of the 2nd Augusta and a mob of detachments from every legion in the Empire, plotting what he and all the men under his command would have to do when the campaign season started. Same as last year and the year before, which had not won anything close to a victory, just a series of truces none of the tribals had any intention of prolonging.

Now Severus himself was too ill to do the job, the *optio* confirmed, so young Antoninus was doing it for him. Geta was in Eboracum with his mother, the illustrious Julia Domna.

The *optio* was effusive in telling Julia Soaemias this, worried about keeping the boy soothed from the howls and bangs outside – when the southern gate boomed like a drum, he expected squeals, but the boy simply nodded and said: 'The beasts are over the Wall, *Optio*.'

Rogatus was the one unnerved and moved away, ostensibly to organise matters, though there was nothing left to do but endure.

'Not normal, that boy,' Quintus pointed out to him, his grin bright in the darkness. The *optio* sweated and agreed.

Drust went up to the tower roof, warned by one of the soldiers to keep low when he did it.

'They have slings,' he explained, at the foot of the ladder. 'Turds want to drive us off the roof so they can climb up.'

Up top was a moaning soldier with a dent in his helmet and blood coming out of his eyes. Two others were trying to manhandle him back down the trapdoor without straightening above waist height, so Kag and Drust helped and then crept to the edge of the crenellations. They could hear the smack of stones, see chips fly. Dominating the centre of the tower was a tripod brazier whose contents flared; there was a lot more smoke than flame.

Drust risked a look to the south and saw the swarm of them, over the ditch, up the Wall and rampart and now spilled out beyond; the huddle of two or three buildings nearby smouldered. It was not good and Drust said so, but Kag shrugged.

'The *optio* is right. Hunker down and keep them out until reinforcements arrive. They won't be long because Domina Julia and her son are here. They'll come sprinting up, mark me. All we have to do is keep the fuckers from getting in.'

They both heard the pant and scrabble at the same time and looked up as a face came over the lip of the crenellations. It was sweat-gleamed and skin-marked where braided hair didn't hide it. Kag struck like an adder's fang, drove the *gladius* hard into one eye and listened to the falling shriek.

'Cheeky bugger,' he said amiably.

Dog came up and Drust took the opportunity to go down; he was sure the attackers would think twice about scaling the walls in ones and twos now and that their confidence in not seeing anyone did not mean their sling stones had driven them off.

Below, the dark was fetid with fear and blood; two men were down and only one was moving and making a deal of noise about having been smacked on the elbow. The other, Drust saw, was the one with the dented helmet.

The woman was kneeling by him and the *optio* hastened to her.

'Now, Domina, that's no place for you…'

'I am more used to treating abrasions on the knees of my son, but I can at least offer comfort,' she replied, then smiled wanly. 'I am not unused to blood. I am a priestess of Helios and the temple needs at least a chalice of it every day when I am there.'

The *optio* hesitated, then gave up trying not to look grateful and hurried off, glancing at Drust as he did. There was a loud, rhythmic booming from the north door. The woman laughed wryly.

'Here I am in Roman territory,' she said, 'and I am no further from a noisome dark with no bath than before.'

'It will never be as you dream it now,' Quintus declared, bustling past with a hammer and a length of timber. 'Like women, baths are fickle.'

'An object in possession seldom retains the same charm that it had in pursuit,' agreed Kag, coming up with another timber balk. 'As old Pliny once said.'

'Young Pliny,' Julia Soaemias declared, then frowned. 'What has happened? Why the timber?'

Kag's eyebrows knotted. 'Young? Are you sure? The timber is for the northern door. The lintel won't hold.'

'Young. The old one thought honey fell from the air and snakes leaped at you from trees – have they a ram then?'

'They have, Domina,' Quintus said, still grinning. 'We will shore it up all the same.'

They hurried off and Drust started to follow them but felt his sleeve tugged. He looked down into the hard stare and marvelled at how the eyes were cold as emeralds now.

'If they break in, you must promise me they will not take my son or myself back with them.'

Drust realised what she meant and blinked, his mouth dry, but he nodded. She let him go and he went off, relieved to be away and wondering whether he could do it if it came to the bit. Wondered, too, at the determination of the tribals to get in. He wasn't the only one.

'They have come for her,' Dog said fiercely. 'And the boy. Perhaps someone has told them how Talorc prized them and they seek revenge.'

'Who knows?' Sib said, just eyes and teeth in the dark. The boom of the door drowned them out, then everyone was bracing timbers and hammering back in turn. The *optio* danced with frustration.

'That will only let them know the door is weak,' he wailed.

'They will know soon enough,' Kag spat back, wrestling with a timber, 'when the whole rotten fuck of a thing caves in.'

There was a clatter as Manius half fell down the ladder from the trapdoor. He stood and blew out his cheeks, then shook his head.

'Can't get a shot off – too many stones. They will take the roof.'

'Batten the trapdoor,' Drust ordered and turned to the *optio*. 'How is the lintel on that?'

Rogatus nodded to one of his men, who helped him uncouple the wooden ladder. 'No one likes rain leaking in,' he said. 'It is solid.'

They put the ladder along a dark wall while the tower boomed and the north gate shuddered. Then the south gate was struck a hefty blow and everyone looked at each other. Rogatus licked dry lips and answered Drust's unspoken question.

'It will hold,' he said. 'Longer than the other, for sure.'

'I am guessing sometime around dawn,' Dog declared, his face a sweat-gleamed nightmare in the guttering dim. 'Then we'll have to fight them in the doorway.'

Rogatus shook his head. 'Not there – a few steps back.'

'You will let them in?' Sib declared anxiously, and Rogatus looked scathingly at him.

'Trust me, *mavro*, I know how to fight skin-wearing arse-fuckers – apologies, Domina.'

'We are gladiators,' Quintus pointed out, 'and we know a bit.'

'Not about this,' Rogatus said, 'though you will be useful, trust me. This is the Army here and we have been doing this for some time. I have four men left with me – Shambles and Mule, you will stand with me in the front. Ditch the *pilae* and *spatha*, use your *pugio* dagger which is best for close work like this. Keep it low. Stick and block as you have been trained, four paces back from the door. Falco, you are second rank, and if a couple of you gladiators could grab the shields off Lentulus and Caius, you can join him.'

He looked at Drust and Dog. 'Pick your two best men – you'll find some decent shields in a corner and they'll serve you better than those silly square tribal affairs. You never heard me say this but I envy you the old *gladius* you have – nice and short and sharp for in here. You will take up the corners, on either side of the door.'

Drust saw what the *optio* intended – the warriors would cram in, no more than two abreast at best, then have to fight front and flank. The *spatha* was longer than the *gladius* and that was an advantage for front men in a ranked wall – but not in this tight space. Here, the little sword was emperor.

'Good plan,' he said, and Rogatus offered a wan smile.

'Told you. We have done this before. I know you lot like to leap and twirl and have a referee to prevent serious damage, but you'll have to do it Army style here.'

Dog laughed mirthlessly. 'You did not go on the death days, then. Else you'd have seen how men fight for their lives.'

Rogatus looked at him. 'I never saw a fight but once, on leave in Eboracum. I would truly like to see one in the Flavian.'

Kag clapped his shoulder and laughed. 'I can get you tickets to the good seats.'

'I will borrow a sword from this man,' said Julia Soaemias, indicating the lolling figure whose helmet was now off; it had made little different to the dent, which was now in his skull.

'Well, Lentulus won't need it, for sure,' Rogatus said, 'but I am not sure about giving it to… a Domina.'

'I will take it,' the boy said, tilting his chin back. His mother put a hand on his cheek.

'Very brave and correct – but I know how to use it and you do not.'

The boy frowned. 'I will summon Helios to burn them up,' he said.

'Good work,' Drust agreed. Rogatus looked at Drust and back to the lady, then thought better of anything he had to say and went off to help with the timber shoring. Drust took the legionary's sword and handed it to her, saying nothing. She was not fooled.

'You want to know how I can use a sword such as this,' she said and Drust gave in and squatted beside her. She laid the blade aside with a soft tink and instructed her son to soak another cloth, which she laid on Lentulus's head. Drust did not think the effort was worth it; if he had been in the *harena* they'd have sixed him with the hammer of Dis Pater by now.

'I know many things it is not considered ladylike to know,' she said. 'But that is the nature of life in Rome.'

'Down our end, perhaps,' Drust said. 'You learn blade work at the breast down below the Palatine.'

She smiled. 'How do you think matters are ordered on the Hill? Want to prevent the election of an *aedile*? Embarrass him with some clapped-out whore paid to complain about him in public all over the City. You can find one in the Basilica with all the rich crooks – or go to the Tuscan quarter and do a proper job with a male prostitute. If you want a perjurer, try the Comitium or head for the Lacus Curtius and find a whole flock of spite willing to spread nasty rumours for money.'

Drust whistled his amazed admiration. 'You know as much about my world as I do. I know nothing of yours.'

'Know only that I am no naïf,' she answered, and laid a hand on his cheek. It was cool and yet sent a thrill straight through him. Her eyes as she spoke seemed to burn him with green fire.

'You are a handsome one,' she said, and lust ripped through him; she saw it and laughed huskily, then patted the cheek. There is nothing so stimulating to a woman as seeing how her beauty works, Drust thought.

'Listen to me,' she said, coming closer to him so that he smelled the unwashed sweat of her and was aroused by it as by no other perfume. 'I am in no danger of death from those who seek me and my son. You need not fret about that. No one wishes me physical harm in this.'

Drust, bewildered, scrubbed the tangle of his beard, aware of his own stink suddenly.

'Then what was all this about? The running and hiding. Dog—'

'Power,' she said. 'That is what it is always about.'

Drust knew there was something there but not what. Power he had seen, down in the Wolf's Den where folk scrabbled and lied, cheated and fought and the most cunning – like Servilius Structus – claimed a corner and defended it. He had never considered that the Hill folk lived the same way.

He was distracted by a clattering from above that froze everyone just as the boom of the ram on the door stopped. Everyone stared at the hatch, waiting, sweating… but there were only more clatters and once a loud yelp. Rogatus got to it first and went to the gate, placing his palm on it.

'They took the signal fire timbers off and piled them at the gate. Trying to burn it down.'

'Is that possible?'

Rogatus thought a bit, then shook his head. 'They might char it a bit, weaken it even more for the ram. The signal fire's been alight for a while now, so most of it will have been burned through. No spare timber for it that won't have to be unfrozen before it can be burned. Most of the pyre wood is green anyway.'

'Green?'

'Makes smoke,' said the legionary called Mule. 'So it can be seen during the day. At night we stick a bucket of that on it.'

He waved to the corner where they had dumped the ladder and Dog took a look, then a closer one.

'Makes the flame bright and hot,' Mule added helpfully.

'Powder for pouring stone,' Dog said. 'Burned limestone. Mix it with water and you get slaked lime – add a little sand or rubble and you get pouring stone.'

'We were rebuilding the Northern Wall in stone,' Rogatus said. 'Had lots of it outside, but they took it away to the north. Keep some in here for the signal fire.'

'Quicklime,' Quintus said, and smiled his big shit-eating grin. 'Have to work carefully with that stuff – ask the *harena* slaves.'

Drust did not need to ask, for he remembered all too well.

–

The fifth visit to the underbelly of the Flavian – or perhaps the sixth. No matter, it is fetid and dim as it always is, thick with air so foul it is like breathing through wool.

Gennadios is showing the boy, yet again, where the heart in the throat is when Charon looms out of the shadows like a bad omen.

'Make way – stand clear!'

His slaves follow him, wearing leather gauntlets halfway up their arms, faces veiled with wraps that go all the way round their heads. They carry one of their own, who writhes and screams.

'Can you fix him?' Charon asks from under his mask. Gennadios looks. Drust looks. The writhing man has a face that seems to bubble and his eyes weep onto his cheeks – or what had been his eyes and what had been his cheeks.

'Lime?' demands Gennadios. Charon nods.

'Bugger slipped and went face first into it.'

'Nothing I can do. Gods could not fix him. Eyes is burned from his head. Probably got in his chest, too, by the way he is frothing blood out.'

'Ah well,' Charon says sorrowfully. Up goes the hammer, down it comes. Crunch. The writhing man stops weeping and screaming.

'Lime?' the boy manages to ask and Charon's blank mask turns to him.

'For the corpses, lad. How else do you think you get rid of a dead elephant and the like down here?'

He goes off laughing, leaves Drust to watch him and his slaves drag one of their own back to the pit he fell in.

-

'Are you thinking what I am thinking?' Quintus asked, and Drust shook himself back to the now. Not likely, he thought – but he knew what Quintus had worked out.

'We need to take back the roof,' he said, and Ugo struggled up.

'I will go. I can do it.'

'Unlikely,' the woman said, and looked at Drust, who nodded. 'You can gather the lime, though. Be careful with it.'

Ugo nodded meekly and did as he was bid. Drust and Kag fetched out the ladder and Dog huffed and puffed his cheeks out a few times, then went up it, unlatched the hatch, paused and threw it up, hurling himself out. Like a dark flash, Manius leaped up the ladder after him.

Drust helped pass up three covered wooden kits, then took the last one up himself, in time to see Manius duck behind the stone rampart, leaning his back to it and blowing out his cheeks; stones rattled and zipped.

'Bastards is laying down some fire,' Dog declared, near prone in the scattered ashes of the ravaged pyre. He beat out a smoulder on his tunic and took up a charred length of timber, using it to lever away a ladder. They were made from a frozen timber with short crosspieces lashed to them and Drust marvelled at how determined you'd have to be to risk climbing on that.

Not all, he revised when he went to the south rampart and looked out at where the legionary buildings and what had passed as a mean little *vicus* burned. There were warriors milling in no order at all and Drust knew these were the ones who had not grasped what the war chief wanted or did not care; they were out for plunder and a handful had found legionary pack mules which they would use to gallop off in pursuit of more.

Those that stayed, Drust had no doubt, had worked out that if you wanted to get your stolen beef, ale kegs, bales and boxes back to the hold you couldn't manhandle mules over the Wall and back down the ditch. They were willing to capture the tower and free the gate.

Only a handful knew what the war chief really wanted. They were the ones standing in a group directing others, the ones Manius was trying to aim at, rising swiftly and shooting in a fluid movement that let him duck before the stones showered.

'Too far,' he said, and Drust saw him count arrows and frown.

'Save them,' Drust advised, 'for when they decide to try their luck with the ladders again. Keep them off the roof.'

From below, Drust heard the voice of the legionary Falco telling them that was all the lime buckets they had.

'There's a ladle about somewhere,' added Shambles helpfully, and Falco snorted derision.

'They ain't going to spoon it down on them, you arse.'

Shambles finally got it and went to sit sullenly against a far wall as Drust and Dog clattered back down the ladder, almost into the arms of Julia Soaemias. She looked at Dog and smiled.

'Now you look almost acceptable. Filthy, but acceptable.'

Drust realised Dog's face was covered in charcoal where he had wiped his sweat with a blackened hand; his death face was veiled under it. Not the nature behind it all the same, he thought. Not that.

There was water in a butt, rain run-off from the roof. There was a foul bucket in a corner which Rogatus, half embarrassed, offered to curtain 'for the Domina's needs'. She merely smiled and said she had used worse – and the boy revelled in trying to emulate Shambles and hit it from a distance until Rogatus, inflamed, told Shambles to put his cock away in front of the Domina.

They ate bread and hard, salted cheese while the warriors growled and prowled. Now and then one would hammer on the southern gate and the crowd he was with would laugh. It grew dark and Rogatus had torches lit; the air became even thicker.

'Taking their time, these lads of yours,' Sib muttered, and Rogatus glanced scathingly at him.

'Coming in force, *mavro*, which takes time to organise properly. On foot, too. Heavies, not your silly little dog-riders with their little throwing sticks and spotted pelts. They will get here and then these skin-wearing sheep fucks are dead.'

'Let's hope they get here before the gate goes rather than after,' Quintus answered.

'Hist on that,' Rogatus said, 'don't alarm the Domina.'

Drust doubted the Domina could be alarmed by a closing circle of wolves, but he said nothing and they sat, listening to the torches fight them for the air; the shadows caused by their guttering danced madly on the walls and if the roof hatch had not been open, they'd have suffocated.

Towards dawn, Drust and Dog went back to the roof, revelling in the crisp coldness. The air seemed pure and precious with every suck, heady as wine.

The boy had been busy, too, as Dog pointed out. He had, at one point during the night, suddenly declared that Helios had had enough of this Land of Darkness. Soon it would bow to him, but it had refused and now he would turn his divine back on the denizens of this place until such time as they bowed to the Unconquered Sun. Drust had wanted to ask what the god meant by 'denizens' and if it included unwilling visitors, but he saw Dog's raptured face and stayed silent.

Now Dog looked at the puling sky, face upturned to a mirr of rain.

'Helios has turned his back,' he said. 'Now these fuckers will feel the coldness of his wrath.'

Drust thought this land had been feeling the wrath of coldness for long enough not be bothered by a little more, but the rain was fine by him; it would dampen the fire at the gate. Another idea occurred to him and he took the lid off one of the wooden kits. The others saw it at once and all the lids came off. Manius went to the hatch and called to Shambles for the ladle.

'See!' the legionary declared triumphantly, handing it up. Drust stirred the grue that was forming and warned the others to keep clear, bind their nose and mouth and not to let the fumes near their eyes. It helped that a cold rain wind swept icily over now and then.

In the end it looked disturbingly like most of the stuff they'd eaten as gladiators being fattened for the fight; if he squinted, Drust could almost swear he saw leeks.

'Will it work like this?' Manius asked, peering cautiously.

'Slaked lime,' said Dog, licking satisfied lips as if he was about to spoon it up. 'Ask Manius. It was part of what was in those fire pots we had.'

Manius had taken off his head square and bound it round his nose and mouth and Drust now saw the still-weeping burn sores from Quintus's fire pots. He did not say anything.

The warriors worked out what rain would do to their fire and sent out the ram to hasten the collapse of the gate; Manius saw them coming, loping over the dark bracken, flitting like shadows over the revealing trampled snow.

'Well,' said Dog, 'we have had the dancing dogs and the drumming bears – now comes the scheduled matches.'

He grinned out of a horror of a black, streaked skull face. '*Uri, vinciri, verberari, ferroque necari.*'

Chapter Fourteen

They came two on two with the ram and one or two looked up, raised shields and expected arrows, for they had seen the archer. The slingers let loose and volleys of stones rattled and cracked against the ramparts to keep heads down. It worked.

'Watch your hats,' Dog advised, as Drust and Manius took one of the wooden kits; Drust swore he could hear it hiss and sizzle but that might have been the rain. He was more worried about his hands and face and eyes than his skull.

They got it on the edge and tipped it, just as the ram hit the door with the sound of a dull bell – the white paste poured down and there was a moment just after the splashing stopped when there were only shouts of outrage at having the stuff emptied on them.

Then they started screaming and running. Drust risked a look, saw warriors hopping and sprinting everywhere, running half-circles, running full circles and slamming one into the other, shaking their heads, waving their arms, rubbing their melting eyes out of their sockets.

The war chief shouted and waved; more ran up and the second kit went over. More men screamed and died, blood pouring out of seared mouths, eyes blinded and burning.

'Now they will come for the tower again,' Drust said, keeping low. No one doubted it, and when the first of the pole ladders clattered between the crenellations, the last kit went out and down and sent the climbers falling and writhing and shrieking.

There were other ladders, though. Dog forced one off with his timber balk. Manius shot the first man up another one, taking him in the throat and sending him backwards with his arms spread wide as if he could fly. He couldn't, and two more below him helped him fall.

'Time,' Drust called and Manius nodded, then slithered down the ladder into the shelter of the tower. Drust followed, half dragging Dog by the hem of his stained tunic, because he couldn't be sure the man would leave the roof.

They slammed the hatchway shut and dogged it, then took down the ladder and flung it in a corner. For a moment there was no sound but their own ragged breathing – then the boom of the ram on the door started up and, from above, another on the hatchway.

'They will prise it up in the end,' Rogatus said dully, but Quintus slapped his armoured back.

'Look on the bright side,' he said with his big wide, white grin. 'The door will have been put in by then so it won't matter.'

Rogatus favoured him with a sullen scowl, then lifted his big shield. 'Form!' he bawled out, so loud that it rang the ears. In a moment there was a short little line drawn up across the doorway, two or three steps back. Drust pushed himself into one corner beyond it, Kag into the other; they nodded at each other across the divide.

'Brace!' Rogatus called out. 'Shields up – use the point. Stick them in the feet, in the neck, anywhere you can. Big man – you get in the back and make sure we aren't forced back by numbers.'

Ugo nodded and lumbered up. He grinned over at Drust, though his face was still wan. In the torch-dyed dim they waited, listening to the thunder of the ram and the answer of their own hearts; breathing was ragged, mouths went dry.

In the end, the gate didn't burst open in splinters. The jamb buckled, as Rogatus had known it would, and the warriors outside dropped their timber balk and started worrying at the gap with axes, levering it with spears and, finally, Drust saw hands curl round and start pulling and tugging.

Eventually, the gate was torn off its hinges, straight out of the jamb. As soon as a gap appeared, showing the snarling, feral faces of men who wanted to kill them, Manius started shooting.

'Don't move,' he advised Rogatus once, who had to wait and feel the snick of the flight passing his ear. In the end, though, the warriors came on, shields up, big slashing swords and axes ready. Under battered war hats and tangled, greasy braids, their eyes were desperate and howling.

Drust stabbed at the first one to hurl himself in the gateway, heading for the shields, but the man was moving too fast. He saw the flicker from his left, though, and shied away from it, stumbling sideways to Rogatus and the others. There was a swift movement and he screamed and went down.

Others crowded in, colliding with the locked shields, the pressure from behind crushing those in front. They tried to spill out but Drust and Kag were there. They had no room to wield their big swinging axes or slashing swords and so were reduced to howls and shrieks, shoving and stabbing.

They died swiftly at the front, the legionaries stabbing in short, controlled movements that the warriors could do nothing about. In what seemed a long day of it, Drust found himself in a reeking charnel house of blood and entrails, foul onion gasps, the high, thin smell of fear.

He was pressed up against the Wall, unable to move, barely able to shift the big shield up and down, but no blade could reach him though several tried. Those that did had no swing, just blunted points banging on the shield like some frantic late-night caller on a door. Once a long, notched blade slid over the top of the shield, missed Drust's ear by a whisker and rasped the stone of the Wall. For a long, long time he and the warrior stared at one another across the width of his shield, until he knew every whorl of the skin marks, every louse that crawled in the red beard, every pore, pock and nick of the man's face. He had green eyes that reminded Drust of the Domina Julia, but they blazed with an impotent fury and he struggled to get his big sword raised.

When he did he could not bring it down again and Drust flicked his own into the exposed armpit, feeling the flesh and cloth part like a cheese rind. The man gave a whimper and tried to reel away, but those behind stopped him. In desperation, he slithered to the ground and Drust, panicking at what he might do there, brought the shield up and down like a broken cullis until the man's head was bloody pulp.

They were like two big Greek wrestlers in a tiny box, unable to do their moves, unable to beat the other with sheer strength, unable to do anything but strain back and forth. In the end even the shouting stopped, reduced to a frantic panting for air, for life.

Then the spear came through the gateway. Someone outside did it and was either an expert or did not care who it hit, Drust thought. It came past him, flexing, so slowed he could see the ripple along its length, the way it spun on its own axis. It could easily have taken one of the warriors in the nape of the neck, or even the ear of those who were half turned, looking for a way to step back, get out, get some air, get away from the crush.

Instead it whirred like a bird through them all and took Rogatus in the eye. He made no sound, just jerked his head as if to avoid it – too late – and Drust saw the bloody tip of it come out the back of his skull with a spume of blood: his helmet wanted to fly off but was tied, so it tilted down over his good eye, but it did not matter, for both were already dark.

Breach.

The warriors saw the hole his falling made and started to rush it before someone from behind could step in. The howls went up, so loud they buzzed through Drust's head and he had the thought, dull as pewter, that now they were finished.

Then, above the wolfen wails, he heard a louder roar, half ironic, half fearful, and he knew the voice of Quintus, could almost see him grin his big grin.

'*Cave canem*.'

Dog had stripped to no more than a loincloth, the *subligaculum* of a true *dimarchaerus*, and he had a shining *gladius* in either hand. His face was a grinning rictus of wickedness, a night horror from every one of the enemy's dreams. He launched through the gap and death came with him.

Even if they had wanted to fight him they couldn't, but most tried to reel away, panicked and screaming at this apparition. The swords worked in a flurry, like the Persian chariots Drust had seen once or twice in the Circus, a novelty item to make blood for the crowds between proper races.

He stepped lithely over the tangled, writhing bodies while warriors slipped and stumbled, half fell and scrabbled away, back out the door, over the carpet of dead and dying. No one was fighting him with any skill or desire; they were all flailing wildly to get away.

He went past Drust, out under the gate, and Kag gave a loud groan. He and Drust looked at each other, then Kag said 'Fuck' and followed him. Drust pumped in some foul air, blew it out and went after them both – somewhere, as if in a dream, he heard horns blow, as if the *harena* marked the next entertainment.

Outside, the warriors had scattered and Dog had stopped, his chest heaving, dripping with gore from the shoulders to the waist and beyond, as if he wore a scarlet cloak with a ragged hem. He turned his face, a crimson skull with blank, dark sockets where the eyes were supposed to be; Drust stepped back a little. Dog stepped up to where a groaning warrior crawled weakly back towards his war chief. He buried both swords in the man's lower back and squatted to twist them, pull them out, work them in again; the warrior howled and more blood flew up, spattering everywhere.

Beyond, the war chief was yelling and waving his arms, but Drust couldn't hear what he was saying and did not look for long. All he saw was a sea of warriors, waiting to surge forward. Kag said 'Fuck' again, clearly and with no tremor.

'Back to back,' Drust said and wondered if Dog had understood, then saw the man was grinning under the skull face's permanent smile. He got up, blew a mist of someone else's blood from his inked teeth and laughed.

'They are going,' he said and Drust looked. It was true. Left and right, warriors were scrabbling down through the stakes into the ditch, clawing their way up the far side. In front of them, they were starting to move back, quick but still ordered.

'Ha,' said Kag, and waved his sword as if he had personally caused it all. Then he heard the horns as Drust did, as Dog already had, and looked embarrassed.

The Army had arrived.

–

Titus Floridus Natalis, Quartis Pilus Prior announced himself with the air of a man reporting to the Emperor and confident in his role as senior centurion of a 4th Cohort. He stood with his helmet tucked under one arm and his regulation vinestaff tucked under the other, looking Drust and the others up and down.

He blinked once or twice at the Domina Julia, streaked with dirt, her dress stained. His eyes widened slightly at the sight of the boy, smiling beneficently.

When Falco stepped up, bloody and filthy but giving a firm regulation salute, Titus could not hide the relief of something familiar. Falco, now in charge, gave his report in quick, succinct tones and Titus nodded once or twice.

'I am sorry to hear of Rogatus. Good man. You have other casualties, I understand.'

'Two, yer honour. Caius has a broken arm, Lentulus has a broken head. If it wasn't for these here gladiators, we'd have been worm food, for sure.'

Now Titus had to look at them and they saw his disgust at the sight of them. Knew it from old.

'Gladiators,' Titus said slowly and then stopped at the sight of Dog, the blood on him drying to a dark rust, his face even more a nightmare. Titus had seen a lot of horrors in his career but even he blanched at this one.

'Gladiators,' he repeated slowly, 'is fat poncified slaves dancing about like Greek girls. They do not save the Army.'

'You would do well to revise that opinion,' said a light voice, and the centurion turned, stiffened slightly and bowed from the neck.

'Domina. I merely state what I know to be true.'

'Then you are an idiot.'

Titus's face seemed to writhe as if snakes wriggled beneath the skin. He recovered, breathed deep and turned back to Falco.

'Gather up your dead and wounded, load them on that cart. You are relieved. I will leave a vexillation here to tidy up and repair. Domina – you and your son will proceed south to the Wall of Adrianus. Sorry, but only there will you find proper transport, cart or litter.'

'My escort?'

Titus looked blank for a moment, then realised she meant the gladiators and wondered what a woman of the Hill was doing with a pack of them. He'd heard rumours of course of what went on – now and then you got salacious gossip about some high-born tart running off with a favourite of the *harena*...

'Horses,' she said, 'for all of us. I wish to be quit of this pestilential country as quickly as possible.'

Titus gave in, forced a smile, tried to be equable and mend what was clearly a broken fence.

'Yes,' he said knowledgeably. 'I have noticed how the Empire places its frontiers in the worst possible spots.'

'Never a problem in Trajan's day,' Kag said sweetly.

–

Dog doused himself in water and let himself be scrubbed with cloths until he was pink and the ground around him snaked with scarlet runnels. They hunkered in the shelter of one of the destroyed outbuildings and ate legionary porridge from borrowed bowls – it was hot and wonderful and they watched other men struggle from the tower with body after body.

'We sixed a few,' Ugo said. He actually looked better, Drust thought. War suits him.

Falco came up, Shambles and Mule and the wounded Caius with him. They stood in front of the gladiators and eventually Falco cleared his throat.

'Thanks.'

Drust nodded. Kag waved one hand, Ugo grunted, Sib simply scowled and Quintus grinned his big grin. Manius looked up once and studied them, then went back to eating. Dog never looked up at all.

When they had gone, though, he scooped bread round his bowl and paused before sticking it in his mouth.

'That was nice of them,' he said. 'Never get that from Tight-Arse the centurion.'

'Don't want anything,' Sib muttered, 'save a good horse and a road south.'

What they got was a long ride in the rain, travelling at the pace of the poor sod Heavies who made up the escort and trudged down the middle of a decent, recently repaired road while the horses and baggage carts sensibly took to the verge. It saved hooves and wheels, but nothing prevented the soaking rain.

'The thaw is here,' Dog noted, his hood up and a scarf bound round his face so that only the eyes showed. He looked at his least confrontational but still the trudging legionaries squinted suspiciously at him over their burden yokes. They spent more time laughing and pointing at Ugo, who had a swayback mare that let his feet almost drag on the ground. They called out 'dog rider' to him when they thought no one in authority could hear.

'The Hood will be on the march soon,' Kag declared at one rest halt, a *mansione* which had been refurbished and smelled of new wood and cooking. It was luxury, and Ugo sat at the open-shuttered window, gloating while he pilled bread and threw it at the luckless legionaries who squatted under hastily erected tented hangars.

'He will wait a while yet,' said the *optio* commanding the escort. 'Until the ground has dried. That could take to high summer and even then it will rain.'

The Army *medicus* who had attended to their various cuts and bruises on the instructions of Domina Julia had confirmed that more men were falling from chest infections and coughing sickness than swords and axes.

'Your big German there is healing,' he said, nodding at Ugo. 'Cracked a rib and nicked a lung, I think. Keep him warm and dry if you can – such an infection will be fatal.'

Warm and dry was what they had in small measure only in a military rest stop which was so new, Sib swore, squirrels were still nesting in the timbers. That hadn't prevented the first whores from moving in and, in time, the place would become like all the others, even the ones for the army – shabby, infested with fleas, whores and thieves.

It would take two days to reach the big Army fort at Luguvallium, another three, perhaps even four, to get to Eboracum – the *optio* wasn't marching hard because he was escorting a high-born Roman lady and her son. He was, however, happy about the rain.

'Keeps those tribal lice in their foul huts,' he growled, wiping wine off his moustaches. 'Biggest fear round here is that they break the truce between the Walls and come out fighting while the Emperor is off in the north.'

They were handed over like packages in Luguvallium – Drust and the others were taken off to be stuck in an empty barrack block and he saw how many there were. All the troops were in the north, beyond the new Wall they were now calling 'Severan', waiting for the chance to conquer what remained of the country.

There were dry, proper beds, decent food and a chance to braid themselves back, sort out equipment and start thinking about how they might just have pulled this trick off after all.

'I mean,' Sib said, 'two days, maybe a bit more and we are home and dry, friends. We get our copper citizen plaques and our cash.'

'What will you do then?' Manius asked, touching his head to feel for the healing scabs. The *medicus* had given him some green ointment to smear on it, which added nothing to his look.

Run a Roman mile from you, was what Sib thought. And when I get to the end of it, run another and keep going. But he smiled. 'I may go back to my people.'

'Who are they?' Manius asked interestedly. 'I am a mongrel from El Kef, which the Romans call Sicca Veneria, but everyone assumes we are brothers.'

No brother of mine, you desert demon, Sib thought, but he managed a smile. 'I am Toubou,' he said. 'Go south of Lepcis Magna until you come to the land of those you know as Garamantes. Go south still and there are the Toubou.'

'A long way. Too far and in too many lands of bandits to be hauling all that cash, brother. I will make for the City and consider myself Fortuna's favoured if I get there unwounded and rich,' Kag said, then accepted the agreeing nods of Ugo and Quintus like a senator who had made a good point from the floor.

'Who would dare attack a citizen?' Quintus added, grinning. They all laughed wryly.

Drust had not thought about what would happen when they succeeded, mainly because he had never quite believed they would. In the rare moments he had, it had been a poignant realisation that, one day, they would all go their different ways, like leaves fluttering from an autumn tree.

He did not want to admit to anyone, not even himself, but he dreaded the day and was aware that he had invested too much in them. They were not brothers, even if they called themselves such. He was not the head of a family, just a battered second-rater from the *harena*.

Dog, peculiarly, seemed to have some insight into it, but it was never said, simply revealed in a hard-palmed hand on Drust's shoulder in the quiet dark.

'Before we all go our ways,' he said quietly to Drust, 'there is the problem of getting the Domina Julia and her marvellous boy into the hands of Kalutis. This escort will march us up and into the fort at Eboracum. Right into the imperial apartments and the hands of her enemies.'

'Who are her enemies?' Drust demanded with a frustrated wave of one hand. 'Her mother? Her aunt? Any one of three emperors – or all of them? Even she will not say.'

Dog frowned. 'I know no more than you, but when I set this in motion it was through Kalutis, who is Servilius Structus's man in the north. It was the Domina Julia herself who sent me to him, so the only safe thing to do is to take her and the boy there.'

There was silence while they chewed on it. Drust was sure the only way they would see any reward was through Kalutis, and he had not known the Domina herself had recommended the man. She must know what was best…

'We must speak to her,' he said eventually, and Dog, who had reached the same conclusion, simply nodded.

They waited until the last *mansione* on the road to Eboracum before going to her. If they needed to make a break, they'd have to do it from here and have a long, hard ride through the night, hopefully leaving the foot-sloggers far behind.

They found her in a small room, her son dutifully beside her. She looked radiant, wrapped in a soldier's cloak against the damp chill and, though a bath had been beyond the amenities, she had washed in hot water and borrowed some of the less garish face paints from whores on the way. She looked regal, sitting on a cushioned bench with one leg tucked up, painting a toenail, with her tongue stuck out slightly between her teeth.

The sight struck Drust with a bewilderment of feelings. He wanted to put his head in her lap and have her stroke his hair – his mother had done that. He wanted to fuck her up against the damp plaster wall.

When Dog had finished telling her what he thought was what, she stopped attending to her toe and sighed.

'I usually have a slave who can do this. I never get it right, and in this poor light I am likely to have it everywhere. The colour is called, I am assured by the raddled sow who sold me it for far too much, Syrian Sunset, but by the time I am done with it my toe will simply look as if some horse stepped on it.'

The boy laughed. 'You should have got me to do it, Mother. We have talked about this before.'

'Ha,' she replied with sour admiration and then looked at Dog. 'He is right, all the same. He does it beautifully.'

'Domina…' Drust said, and she stopped him with another look.

'Aha, it speaks. I thought you were going to stand and gawp at my naked feet all night.'

Drust lost all ability to think or talk, felt his face burn, but she took pity on him and sighed, waving one hand dismissively.

'I have told you both before, I am in no danger of harm. I am more at risk from falling off a horse on a wild night ride than I am from anyone in Eboracum.'

She fanned the toe to hasten it drying, then gave in and stretched out a white arm with the brush in it, waving impatiently at her son. He smiled, took it and knelt at her feet.

'My mother, my sister, my aunt the Empress – they are all there in Eboracum, and this poor excuse for a town at the edge of Ultima Thule is the imperial court until the emperors decide otherwise. All Rome is ruled from Eboracum, and has been for two years and more. It will not be when old Severus goes to his ancestors, but whisper on that.'

She shifted slightly and frowned at her toes. 'Kalutis was to get my son and myself back to Emesa, where my mother was until recently. That was to avoid entanglement with anyone else – my aunt, any one of three emperors or all of them.'

She looked at them both. 'I tried not to let my son become a counter in their games of *latrones*. Did you know the name for that in Emesa translates as "the game of brigands"? Never was anything better named for the way they play in the imperial court. And the court is here. Everyone who is anyone is here – the Palatine is emptied and they have brought all their plots and venality with the baggage.'

'All the more reason for getting you away from it,' Drust answered, and she smiled, then jerked her foot with a sudden giggle, followed by a scowl. Her son smiled.

'Don't tickle, you fiend. You know I can't stand it.'

She made herself comfortable again while the boy expertly washed toe after toe with paint.

'It is of no consequence to me now,' she went on, 'that I am here and will go to the imperial apartments. There will be some polite stab-work as to which of the residences I end up in, but we are four women against some poor men, so that will work in my favour.'

She had a moment of bliss, it seemed, when her son blew on her toes to dry them and Drust wished it was him putting the expression on her face, then forced himself to stop thinking it.

'You,' she said suddenly, opening her eyes, 'would be well advised to ride off into the night, mind. They will imprison you otherwise. It will not seem like it, but that's what it will be, and you are no longer of any use or consequence, so are in considerably more danger than me.'

Drust and Dog exchanged glances while the Domina exchanged feet.

'Go to Kalutis. If I am right, he already knows of all this. I will make sure word is sent to him to bestow the reward as promised. Then I would get out of Eboracum and Britannia. Out of the Empire entirely if you have sense.'

Dog looked stricken. 'I hoped to serve you, lady.'

She pouted. 'Fascinating though that is, I don't see quite how.'

'I want them all,' the boy said, smiling. 'They are so fierce – and they saved us, Mother. Did you see how Dog fought in that tower? Slice, slice, slice…'

She frowned at him, then brightened. 'Well, if you and your companions can make your way to Emesa, I will find shelter for you all. I doubt you will make it, all the same.'

None of the others disagreed with that when it was put to them, but all of them were sure the lady was right. If they didn't gallop for it, they'd be sixed, for sure.

So they got together what they could and went to the stables, where the half-dozing guard leaped up guiltily and then blew out his cheeks with relief when he saw them.

'Thank all the gods above and below it's only you lot.'

Then he frowned. 'Why are you all here anyway? You are to stay where you are.'

'Well,' said Kag, 'it isn't to stop you being stone-ground by your mates for falling asleep on sentry.'

'Ho, now lads, I was just resting my eyes…'

'Rest them a little more,' said Quintus, nodding to Ugo, who looked desperately round in time to see a massive hand come round his mouth, choking off his cry. Another pulled his helmet off, snapping the leather thong and leaving a rasp round his throat.

The man struggled, wild-eyed and gagging, but Ugo hefted the helmet and whacked it down with a sound like a cracked dinner gong. The man sank to the stable straw.

'Is he alive?' demanded Drust.

'What do you care?' Dog demanded, saddling a horse. Drust sighed with exasperation.

'Because killing someone in the fucking Army will get you back in the *harena* – part of the morning crucifixions.'

'They'll never give over on hunting us down,' Quintus agreed, and Dog finally got to it. He knelt, put two fingers against the man's neck, then held the dull metal of the helmet close to his mouth.

'Alive,' he said finally, and there was relief in his voice. Now Ugo looked annoyed, for he had hit him as hard as he was able, and to find that it hadn't cracked him to death only underlined how weakened he still was.

They resisted the temptation to run madly away in a flurry of hooves and flying mud. Instead, they walked as slowly and quietly as they could out of the *mansione* compound and onto the road. They'd have to ride on the road because the shining wet of it was all they could see, risking a cracked hoof or a strained fetlock.

So they ambled until they could trot and then kept that up until the daylight started, wan and pale. It began to rain again. Drust thought that their disappearance would be noted by now and the miserable sentry would be nursing a headache and the wrath of the *optio*. At some point, they would form up and start marching the Domina into Eboracum and, if there was a horse left to be had, a messenger would be striking out now, when it was light enough to ride hard along the verge.

'We could wait and ambush him?' Sib offered, but Drust did not want to risk it.

'Push on into the *vicus*, get to Kalutis and sort this all out.'

'We might have to wait and hide,' Dog said, 'until the Domina sends him word to pay us.'

'Or turn him upside down and shake him until our rewards fall out,' Ugo said, and Quintus clapped him on one wet, meaty shoulder.

'I like how you think, big man.'

'Do I really want to be a citizen this badly?' Manius demanded sourly. 'I am thinking I was happier before.'

'No one was happier than before,' Kag spat back. 'But the money is good – and living is better still, so ride.'

–

The road up to Eboracum was cold and wet and swollen as a bad-toothed jaw with too many people, most of whom were army. In the daylight, grey as the segmented iron on their backs, the legionaries trudged in step, rank on rank, straight up the middle of the road. Carts lurched and trundled alongside, horns blew, vexillation flags fluttered and, in the middle of it all, a big panoplied litter swung in the strong arms of soaked naked slaves.

'Gods above and below,' Kag hissed as he came up on the rear of it all. 'These are Praetorian. What the fuck—'

'Just drop back and keep behind them,' Drust warned. 'Don't try to push through. Some Big Crest is moving here and we'll only attract unwanted attention.'

They attracted attention anyway, from the rear ranks of the marchers. A horseman swung round and trotted back to them until they could see that it was a fully armoured centurion of the Praetorian, the guards of the Emperor.

They might just as easily be escorting figs in ice, or some fabulously expensive and inventive whore for a high-born, Drust thought. Doesn't have to be an emperor. Not at all…

But it was. The centurion removed his ornate helmet and cocked his head expectantly. Drust bobbed a bow from the neck.

'*Procuratores*, your honour. Gladiators and others, bound for the *harena* here, at the pleasure of the Emperor.'

The man was burly, dark-skinned, olive-eyed and with a full beard whose black was streaked with grey and artfully teased into fashionable curls.

'Macrinus,' he said. 'Centurion of the 1st. I will inform the Emperor, perhaps it will cheer him. The weather certainly does not.'

He laughed. Drust laughed and then had to force himself to stop because it was becoming manic. Macrinus reined round and trotted back down the ranks, which dutifully halted to let him cut in to the panoplied litter. Drust was sure he could hear the thoughts of the greybacks who waited in the drizzle, soaked through and wanting out of it.

'Is it?' Quintus asked, half afraid, half in awe. 'Himself?'

'The old Severus,' Kag confirmed, scrubbing his beard, and then turned to Dog. 'Hide that face… that gilded fool is coming back.'

'He is a *jnoun*,' Sib said suddenly. 'I hear it in his voice. He is a *jnoun*.'

'You think everyone is a desert demon,' Manius said, and offered up a wicked smile that withered Sib. 'Perhaps he has some chewing leaf on him.'

'Keep silent on that,' hissed Drust in a panic. The centurion was turning back to them when the head of the column reached the gates and horns blared. Lights sparked – the lanterns of the gate guards, trying to look efficient and alert.

People stood on either side of the road, carts and horses too, for this was a Roman town and they'd arrived too late to be let in. They would have to wait all the rest of the day in the rain now and the sullen faces gave away how they felt.

The centurion was heading for an old woman, a crab-handed affair of dark wrappings and a hood which fell away to reveal snake tendrils of grey hair. Drust spat a swift prayer to Jupiter to keep her spells away, but she just seemed to be waving a wreath of flowers and leaves.

'Witch,' Ugo muttered, and Quintus waved his hands and made 'ooooh' sounds to mock him.

'It is the festival of Sementivae, I wager,' Kag said, and Quintus snorted derision.

'How could you possible know that?

'We fought in it once. This time of year.'

Drust could not remember and did not know why a festival to Ceres, goddess of dirt-grubbing farmers, and Tellus, the Mother Earth they fingered, needed gladiator fights. Blood, of course, he decided. Every deity needed blood.

The old witch seemed to have hers up, for she was screeching and did not stop until Macrinus signalled two men out of the serried ranks to pick her up and carry her off, away from the road. They dumped her, none too lightly, beside a pack of watchers, who all ebbed from her as if she had the plague.

A cloaked and hooded man, festooned with cross-belted satchels, hurried up to the litter which had been set down – a *medicus*, Quintus said. For sure.

The centurion trotted back to them, frowning and dripping. 'There will be a delay. If you want to push on, you can leave your horses at the gate and go on foot. Or stay here all night in the wet. I would not see some decent fighters felled by snot and fevers.'

'Thank you, your honour.'

They bobbed and smiled and rode their horses as fast as they dared, right down the whole waiting ranks of dripping men, past the grounded litter and the gleaming, dog-patient slaves. The *medicus*, only his arse visible, was talking animatedly to whoever was inside the litter and Drust tried hard not to look.

The ostler wanted to haggle, but Drust paid what he asked, though it took all they had and a silver ring out of Ugo's beard braids; he was scowling and promising dire revenge for it when Drust started to hurry them to the gate.

The guards looked them over, but they had seen the centurion wave them through and weren't going to argue with that – anyway, they had more to concern them when fresh horns blew and the ranks stamped to attention in a rippling crash. Then they started forward, the litter was picked up and wavered along to the gate.

'Jupiter's hairy balls,' Sib whimpered.

'Keep moving, keep moving.'

Drust muttered it out like a long prayer, but he knew it would do no good – they were sidling along the wall, pressed close to the cold, damp stone when the lead ranks tramped through, their nailed boots echoing in the arch of the gate.

Then, like a bad dream, a horror jest from some vengeful god somewhere, the litter moved up alongside, so close Drust could see the sweat and rain on the slaves and the bulge of muscles trying to hold the litter level, hold it up, stop it from swaying.

They stopped and gawped. They shouldn't have, but it wasn't every day you got so close to an emperor. Drust smacked Ugo back into movement, was starting to heave in breaths of relief when they reached the far end of the gate's arch and started to spill out to one side, clearing the way, dipping for shadows.

Then a slave slipped and the litter banged the curve of the archway. There was a querulous, annoyed shout and the curtains twitched, a face poked out angrily. They all stared. Dog stared. He looked at the Emperor Lucius Septimius Severus Augustus and saw a ravaged hawk of a face with the remains of a beard straggling over dark-skinned withered cheeks and a scowl that screamed hot-iron punishments.

The Emperor Lucius Septimius Severus Augustus stared back. Dog smiled weakly. The Emperor saw death grinning at him, surrounded by giants and black demons from his homeland.

He screamed and fell backwards into the litter.

Chapter Fifteen

He was still a centurion of the 1st even when he wore a narrow-stripe tunic and toga, though the *gravitas* was, for Drust at least, somewhat ruined by the thick wool socks Macrinus wore under his sandals.

The Praetorian centurion was not fazed by it at all, though he seemed ruffled at something. In the polished-wood Principia room, where braziers fought the damp, he sweated more than he should.

More than us, Drust thought, looking round, who had good reason to. Yet they had been in places such as this before and what was happening now was no worse than waiting for the Gate of Life to open and spill them out into the *harena* and the blare of people wanting blood.

'Gladiators,' Macrinus said, walking round to the desk and sitting closer to the bell-mouthed brazier. 'I suppose you might have been once. I never saw the like of you.'

'As your honour suggests,' Drust offered, 'we were not of the first.'

Dog cleared his throat and Drust cursed him. 'Beg pardon,' he added, teeth clenched, 'save for Do— Crixus here. He was better ranked than the rest of us. And Sib here was a cart driv—a charioteer.'

Macrinus looked them over again and shook his head.

'Crixus,' he repeated slowly. 'I never heard the name since tales of Spartacus – and that face. Gods above and below, you'd be remembered if you'd fought in Rome with that face.'

They were alone with him in what was the headquarters of the legion detachments currently lolling all over Eboracum – they were mainly, Drust had worked out, the Praetorian. Guarding the imperials, who were all in their disparate apartments wishing they were back in Rome; they had been wishing that for three years and looked no closer to uprooting the centre of Empire from here.

The room was small, with a tiled floor, neat desks and tally sticks, racks with slates and all the panoply clerks would need. Macrinus had one such slate in his hand and studied it, frowning.

'I have had instructions regarding you people,' Macrinus said. 'Only found them when I reached here. Men, gladiators including some northern barbarian and *mavro* from Lepcis Magna or some such place. To be detained and held, especially the leader, one Drust.'

He frowned and studied Dog. 'No mention of a man with his head on inside out, mind, but since the instructions came from the Emperor Antoninus himself there is no argument – he is galloping south from the naval storehouse camp even as we speak. The Prefect is with him.'

He seemed to be speaking more to himself than them and it was clear to all that they were a puzzle. He had instructions to lock them up, Drust was certain of it, and no reason given as to why.

'You accompanied the Domina Julia,' he said, and they nodded and shuffled.

'Saved her from tribals, your honour,' Kag answered politely. 'Scooped her and her son out of their clutches and fought our way back to here.'

Macrinus stroked his oiled beard and looked at them with his slight, popped eyes, glaucous as a fish.

'You have influence there?' he asked, and no one answered because no one was sure what he meant. Drust thought he was being sly, trying to establish if they were some sort of stud stable for a lecherous high-born with more money than sense or morals.

'Influence, your honour? In what way?'

'Is she obligated to you for your service? Likely to grant favours?'

'Possibly,' Dog answered carefully. 'She is a priestess of the temple in Emesa. To Heliogabalus – who is Sol Invictus under another name. So is her son. Preserving the life of such a pair would, perhaps, gain a favour or two. Depending.'

'Depending on what it was,' Macrinus finished, then sighed. 'What have you done to that face? And why? And why were the Domina Julia and her son far beyond the Walls in the first place?'

He clearly expected no answer and flapped a frustrated hand. 'Look – I had instructions regarding the Domina Julia and her son. Take them to the imperial apartments of her illustrious cousin, the Emperor Marcus Aurelius Antoninus. But when she gets here, I find she has been whisked off to the residence of the Empress and her sister and others of that family. A whole flock of Julias.'

Drust could sympathise – there would now be Julia Soaemias, her mother Julia Maesa, her sister Julia Mamaea and her aunt, the Empress Julia. What do you call them all, he wondered? A flock sounded too benign. A jewel of Julias? Poetic but lacking some sharpness. A javelin of Julias, perhaps…

Macrinus got up and paced, stirring the vexillation standards; the fluttering made shadows leap madly on the walls of the *sacellum*. Drust suspected they were in this sacred place because it was small and secure – it was where the standards were kept and venerated and in the centre of the room was a sunken pit which had a great bound chest in it, all the cash of every legionary in the Army. The money was kept here to deter thieves who would be committing sacrilege if they stole from the shrine; the standard bearers acted as treasurers of these funds, keeping track of what money was paid in and out.

'Here's the thing,' Macrinus said companionably, clutching the drape of his toga like he was about to address the senate. 'I do not know what happened to Severus Augustus earlier, or whether you had something to do with it, even though every statement taken seems to imply you did nothing at all but stare.'

Drust tried hard not to look at Dog. 'How is the Emperor, your honour?'

'Becoming a god I suspect,' Macrinus answered drily. 'He was not far from it when we started for here and that witch at the gate did not help. He seemed to believe she was cursing him but I have it that she was simply offering him a wreath of Ceres and the blessing of the goddess.'

'It unnerved him,' Ugo declared solemnly. 'Gods do that. My old uncle was convinced a black dog stalked him and kept seeing it everywhere. No one else did.'

'Fascinating,' Macrinus said insincerely. 'However – I am hoping you might use what favours you have with the Domina Julia to persuade her to move to the residence of Antoninus. So she will at least be there for him arriving.'

Drust saw that Macrinus could not order her to move and was afraid of The Hood. Well, there was good reason for that, and Caracalla had clearly gone to a lot of trouble to track her down and try and take her from her rescuers. But Drust was sure Domina Julia would come to no harm and that The Hood was simply trying to isolate her from the protective javelin of Julias.

Not us, though – Drust's mouth went dry at the thought of what The Hood might do when he had no good reason for holding back his hand.

'That may be beyond us,' he answered carefully, then saw the frown and added hastily: 'we will, of course, make every effort.'

'Good,' Macrinus said levelly. 'Otherwise I will squeeze you all into the smallest, tightest prison space I can find.'

'Really?' said a voice that was soft and silken and still made everyone leap with the effect of it, none more than Macrinus, who dropped the slate and started to work his mouth like a landed fish. No one had heard anyone come in, yet the room was suddenly full of women who seemed to glide over the tiled floor.

'Is that wise, Macrinus? These are citizens of Rome, and you have already noted that there is no reason for them to be imprisoned.'

'The Emperor...' Macrinus offered desperately and the woman smiled wryly.

'My husband is dying,' she said. 'In his absence it falls to me and my son, Geta. Who has granted these heroes citizenship, as reward for saving our beloved Julia Soaemias and her son.'

She wore blue and gold with a creamy-white *stola* and her hair was dressed as if for a banquet, gilded to replace the gold that had once been there. Her sisters stood like a coterie of identical statues behind her, all blonde, all white arms and ivory complexions – save for Julia Maesa, who had not kept the sun from her darker skin and now looked like the cracked remains of a dry watercourse. She held the hand of her grandson, the golden copy of Caracalla.

They wore teal-egg blue and the same over-robes, their hair dressed to fit them like caps and netted in fine gold to land on their bare shoulders. Round all their necks were identical gold collars, loose pearl belts; sun-shaped earrings danced along the line of their jaws. It was at once beautiful and sinister, as if a coterie of goddesses had descended from Olympos.

'You will come with us,' the Empress said to Drust and the others. 'Domina Julia Soaemias will guide you to quarters best suited to heroes of Rome. These are your awards of citizenship.'

She gestured to a slave, who produced a basket of metal plaques and handed it to Drust; his fingers were so nerveless that he almost dropped it and he could find no words that would track across the desert of his mouth out onto his lips. To his astonishment there was a sound like mice running on the polished floor and he realised all the Julias were softly applauding with little hand pats. The moment was surreal, but Dog was unimpressed and cocked one eyebrow.

'There was coin promised also.'

'Be silent,' Macrinus said, finding his voice and making it a stern one. 'You are destined for a cell, the lot of you…'

The air was thick with coiled tension, then the boy tore free from his grandmother's hand and darted forward, his beautiful face truculent.

'Leave my gladiators alone. I wish them to come with us.'

'Be silent, child,' the Empress said in a voice like whetted steel and, to everyone's astonishment, the boy did so. The Empress patted his head and cooed.

'Beautiful boy,' she said and then turned as someone else entered, bringing a blast of cold rain-wet air and a deal of noise, as if someone had sparked up a lighthouse and shone it on all of them. He was plump and curly haired and in a bad mood.

'What's all this about, Mother?' he demanded, and the Empress turned soothingly to him.

'Only a little misunderstanding,' she said sweetly. 'Centurion Macrinus here seems to think your brother orders here and not you.'

'Domina,' Macrinus began desperately. 'Empress—'

'Really?' demanded the plump newcomer – Drust now knew it was Geta, The Hood's brother and an emperor in his own right. There was little love between them.

'My brother has the Army. I have the imperial residence. Do as you are commanded.'

There was so much purple in the room that Drust was getting dizzy with it. Macrinus gave up because he had no choice and had to watch Drust and the others trail after the delighted boy and his calm, regal mother. Like a rank of legionaries, the other Julias closed in on her back and started to glide away.

'Is that it?' Geta demanded and his mother patted his arm. He flung up his hands in frustration.

'My brother is always forgetting his place,' he said firmly to Macrinus. 'We share duties. Perhaps you can remind him.'

Macrinus had recovered and regrouped; this was an old battle, much fought and refought. He picked up the dropped tablet and adjusted his tunic.

'He will be here soon, *sacratissime imperator.* I am sure he will speak to you on the subject.'

Drust didn't hear more, passing out into the Principia courtyard, where slaves with rain shelters hurried to protect the delicacy of Julias; the boy happily strolled alongside his gladiators, heedless of the drizzle, and the duty guards looked on impassively.

They ended up in a *cucina*, all red brick and tiled floors, where slaves moved and called out to one another while they sweated over stove and oven. They were seated at a benched wooden table and served up chicken and fish, olives and bread.

'Fortuna's tits,' Quintus declared, licking his fingers and waving them for the *garum*. The cook passed it over with the sour expression of a man who does not want to see his delicate creation drenched in fish sauce.

'Good point, well made,' Sib echoed. 'We fell on our feet here, lads – and look at this. I am a citizen of the Empire now.'

He waved the copper plate *diploma* until the light bounced brilliance off it, then tucked it back inside his filthy tunic, while the cook and his slaves tried not to pass judgement on these, the new favourites of the Empress. By the time the unwatered wine had gone round again, eyes were drooping. It was mid-morning and they were stretching and yawning; Ugo slept with his head pillowed on his arms and Drust saw that the kitchen staff wanted rid of them but did not dare say so.

'What now?' Kag demanded, sidling along the bench to talk quietly with Dog and Drust. 'We have part of the prize, but when The Hood arrives I am thinking we will be back in the grip of that Macrinus turd. I don't imagine he will be offering applause as the Julias did – did you hear that, lads? I have been called a Roman hero by an empress. By all the gods above and below, that's something to tell the grandchildren.'

'If you live to have some,' Dog muttered. 'And where is the better part of what was promised – the *denarii*?'

'Dog,' Drust said wearily, 'I will be happy to get out of this alive. So will you. Be happy with a burnished *diploma*. Get some sleep – I am sure one of those Julia creatures will be around soon enough, for we are now only counters in this game.'

Dog shrugged and studied the copper inscription, turning it upside down and sideways because he couldn't read it.

'Does this mean I am no longer a slave?' he asked; everyone save the sleeping Ugo stared, astonished.

'What do you mean?' demanded Manius. Dog shrugged.

'Servilius Structus never manumitted me – I fucked him over, remember? So I am a runaway – that Crixus name was a fake, but if I am a citizen, am I pardoned all that? That might be useful.'

'Jupiter's salty balls,' Kag said with breathless admiration, and that seemed about as much as anyone could add to it, so Drust fell asleep thinking about Domina Julia and her son and how they were no better than nubs in the game, too. He dreamed of his mother, the first time he had done that in a long time. When he woke it was because someone was shoving him roughly by the shoulder.

'Wake up. Follow this slave. Leave your companions to sleep.'

The cook indicated the young man waiting, patient as a chair, to be acknowledged. Dog was also up, but Kag snored. Drust looked at Dog, shrugged and rose up, wiping his bleary eyes until he noticed the lit lanterns. Outside it was dark; they had slept all day.

They followed the slave through corridors and never once stepped out into the dark, though once they passed round the portico of a peristyle, where lanterns swung in the wind and rain dripped softly from the eaves.

There was a low moaning, too, that Drust could not place, but they saw no one else, which was also strange. Not one slave, nor a guard. This was, for the moment and the foreseeable future, the heart of the Empire, the Palatine Hill transported to the wilds of the north – and it seemed empty.

In the end they were ushered into a room whose torchlight showed blue and gold walls and latticed windows, a painted ceiling with fruit and Ceres, a floor mosaic in geometric patterns made from black and white marbled *tesserae* which gave a dizzying, unnerving perspective.

There were cushioned couches, ivory tables inlaid with gold leaf and a couple of wide braziers; Drust smelled cedar wood.

There was also Julia Soaemias, quite alone and unattended, wearing a simple ankle-length blue dress and a white *stola* carelessly wrapped round her as she sat. Her hair was undressed, but she wore a splendour of jewels: moon-crescent earrings, large pearl and ruby and emerald finger rings and a necklet made of many lappets of gold holding a sun symbol big as Drust's palm. She was also artfully made up, with kohled eyes and painted lips.

'Domina,' Drust said, offering a formal obeisance. Dog went to one knee and bowed his head, which was a bit too Syrian for Drust's taste, but the Domina seemed to like it and smiled. It seemed wan and strained to Drust all the same and his stomach started to churn.

'You found the baths, then, Domina,' Dog said, and that made her smile warm a little.

'I did. Tell your friend – Kag, is it? Tell him he was right. It was not as good as I had imagined it to be and finding my face paints simply makes me now feel as if I am wearing a mask in some rustic play.'

She reached beside her and fetched a small wooden box and opened it. There was no wine to be seen, no slaves; it was clear this was clandestine and hurried.

'I will be brief,' she said, taking something from the box. 'The Emperor died an hour ago, which makes Geta and Antoninus joint rulers of the Empire. Antoninus will arrive soon and when he does, sparks will fly. Geta and my aunt will have no authority.'

'The Empress has no authority?' Drust blurted, astounded, and then looked embarrassed at the outburst. 'From what happened before, I did not think she lacked it.'

Julia Soaemias nodded. 'That was then. When Antoninus arrives, he will demand my presence in his own apartments.'

'You do not need to go to him,' Dog declared vehemently. 'Even in this place there must be… rules.'

She favoured him with a cool look. 'There will be no impropriety. It is not me he wants, it is my son. He will take him whether I go with him or not, so I will go and be a barrier, as always.'

'Why?'

She gave Drust a warmer look than the one Dog had received, but it still gave nothing away. 'Antoninus will also want to visit wrath on those who tried to help me escape his… influence. He cannot harm anyone but you and Kalutis – at least as long as he is here. I suspect it will not be long before the soldiers are removed from the north and everyone returns to Rome. There he will find the time to root out his enemies, now that he has power to do so.'

'Is not Geta on your side?' Drust asked, and she smiled.

'Geta is a year younger than his brother and might well be a child before a monstrous wolf. He was raised to the title of Augustus only a few months ago, a last desperate effort by his father to make him the equal of his brother. It will not save his life.'

It was flat and matter-of-fact and that was more chilling still – she had seen what everyone had seen but Drust and the others, that there would be no joint rule, at least not for long. It said much that she spoke of it aloud. Drust swallowed thickly but Dog was on it. 'What do we do, Domina?'

'You run,' she said, and handed him the contents of the box, a handful of small brass tokens. 'These will get you out of the imperial residences, out of the fort and out of Eboracum. Beyond that, I can do nothing. Kalutis has been informed – he has the money you will need to make your way and can be trusted only so far. He will run, too, of course, so you should reach him before he does.'

Drust's head reeled and Dog got up and stood, head bowed for a moment. Then he nodded.

'You take a great risk. The Hood may work out that it was you who helped us.'

'Or the Empress. Or my mother, my sister – there are many Julias,' she answered and the smile was suddenly candied-sweet. 'We look after our own – even against our own.'

She clapped her hands and the same young slave appeared. 'Now go. Follow Zahid to your friends, pack swiftly and leave at once.'

'Domina,' Drust said, neck-bowing. He turned to go, the brass tokens burning in his fist. She stopped him at the door by calling his name; it was the first time he had heard it from her mouth and for some reason he felt his heart leap.

'Find your way to Emesa one day. Gods willing, we will all meet again.'

–

'Can you trust her?' demanded Quintus. 'Women are not noted for it.'

'The ones you know,' Kag answered sharply. 'We have no choice but to grab our gear and run. You say these will get us out of the camp and across the bridge to the *vicus*?'

Drust nodded. 'Beyond the walls of that place, too. After that we are on our own.'

'Horses,' Sib said pointedly. 'Otherwise they will run us down in hours.'

'We left some at those stables,' Ugo reminded everyone and Drust nodded. The Emperor was dead – long live the emperors. Drust realised that they had some time in hand, because Geta was the only one who had been on hand when it happened and he'd have been the one to perform the *conclamato*, the formal calling of the Emperor's name in the hope of bringing him back to life.

'There's a lot of this stuff, then?' Sib demanded; he had no experience of the Roman way since all the people he'd seen die were simply flung in a pit with the horses who had failed them.

There was. The eyes of the dead were closed, limbs straightened, the body washed – because it was an emperor, a wax effigy of his face would be made. He'd be formally dressed and laid out on a funeral couch, surrounded by flowers and incense. The door to the room would be surrounded by branches of pine or cypress to warn those that the house was polluted by death.

Then there would be the pomp and ceremony of making the dead Emperor a god. While all of that was going on and the entire world held its breath before letting it out in mourning wails, a band of men could slip easily and quietly away.

'The Hood has missed all this part,' Kag added, 'so he will be anxious to stamp his own authority on the affair. They will burn the dead Emperor here and take his ashes back to Rome.'

'More to the point, The Hood will start carving out his own throne,' Dog said. 'He will prowl and bribe and promise – and he has the legions, so it won't take long.'

'Long enough,' Drust said. 'If we move.'

They moved. They had nothing much to take other than weapons and some coin, and tried to look as if they belonged on the bridge as they reached the camp gates. The sentries were not fooled, but everything was in uproar and, besides, they had the imperial tokens.

It was the same at the far end and they found themselves in a wet paved street curling into the curfewed dark.

'Where is this Kalutis?' demanded Ugo, frowning.

'A house near the meat market,' Dog said. 'You were there more recently – can you remember it?'

Drust thought he could, but there was another problem; they'd need to get back the horses they'd left in the stables.

'If not, we are on foot and won't get far. Even with all he has to do, The Hood will find time to send pursuit, so we need to move fast.'

'They are outside the northern wall,' Dog reminded him. 'We'd have to ride the length of the *vicus* to get out the south gate.'

'We won't,' Drust said, working it out as he said it. 'You go and secure the horses and we will meet Kalutis, fetch the money and meet you there. Then we can ride north and east, maybe trade the horses for a ship passage south. Throw them off.'

Dog scowled suspiciously. 'I am supposed to believe you will turn up with all that coin?'

'There speaks one who knows only himself,' Kag spat back; they glowered at one another.

'We need the horses,' Manius pointed out. Then he fished in his tunic and pulled out the *diploma*; even in the dark it seemed to glow.

'Look,' he said. 'Take all our proofs of citizenship until we reclaim them. Surely that is surety enough, even for you.'

'Fuck your mother, whoever she was,' Dog growled. 'I get a pile of copper and you get all the gold?'

'Then I will fetch the fucking horses,' Quintus said exasperatedly. Dog's scowl deepened, crumpling the skull tattoo into a parody, but he nodded reluctantly.

'Mark me well,' he said, turning into the shadows, 'if you fail me I will track you down. What happens then will not be pleasant.'

'I will not be hard to find,' Kag snarled back. Drust dragged him away and they watched Dog vanish into the dark.

'We should six him,' Sib said fearfully, and Manius looked at him, then followed Drust deeper into the streets and houses.

Eboracum had been small and badly built at the start, an unplanned riot of alleys and bad streets. In the three years that the entire Empire had been ruled from it, it had swelled like a sick toad and there had been even less planning to that.

It took Drust an hour before he finally was convinced they were on the right street and most of that was smell – the meat market stank of old blood and rotten entrails, mingling with the wood smoke of cooking fires. Faint flickering lights behind ill-fitting shutters, or simple cloth coverings revealed that this was not the fashionable end of the *vicus*.

'That one there,' Ugo said suddenly, pointing to a two-storey affair of peeling plaster and leaning walls. The roof tiles gleamed in the wet but that was the only light; the place seemed dark and cold. They huddled together on a corner across the way while the drizzle sifted down on them; the streets in every direction were deserted and the only sound was the rain and a distant, mournful dog.

'Perhaps Kalutis has already legged it,' Quintus offered, and Sib spat.

'Never trust your *ptolemy*,' he intoned bitterly, 'they are worse than Greeks.'

Drust licked his lips and thought hard. Then he told Manius to stay and watch and led the others across the street in a low-crouched run into the dark lee of the building. He tried the door, found it open – to his surprise – and showed that to Kag.

'Too convenient,' he said. 'Only *Stupidus* would enter.'

'If *Stupidus* does and makes it…' Quintus hissed back.

'He is still *Stupidus* but has fucked Fortuna in her arse. Next time…'

'Just get in,' Drust growled, and let them follow him or not.

Inside was darker still and he waited until his eyes adjusted, eventually making out a stairwell leading up and a room off to the right. There was a smell, one he knew well.

'Blood,' he whispered, and Kag nodded. Sib raised his head and worked his nose, frowning.

'Oil?' he said. 'The sort you clean armour with.'

The sparks were large as cartwheels, a brilliance of orange that revealed the presence of shadows. Kag went into a fighting crouch and growled – then a torch burst into a sun that scorched their eyes to tears. Through the blur they could make out the shades of big armoured men – and a red cross on a wall.

'Stand where you are and drop your weapons,' said a familiar voice, and Drust's belly dropped to his knees. He had wiped the tears from his eyes and the red cross had leaped into a horror of splayed blood and nails – Kalutis was crucified to the wall. He had been slashed with a steel-tipped whip and whatever he had told them had kept all the Heavies of the Praetorian waiting here in the dark for them.

They were Danube men, too, the ones old Severus had replaced the original guard with when he assumed the throne. They were loyal to him and his sons and Drust knew it was all up the moment he'd heard the voice. He'd only heard it once before, when it had said, laughing: 'Just a bit of fun…'

That was a moment before he had kicked the boy who'd owned it in the groin. Drust was sure the man who shouldered his way into the light of the torch had not forgotten or forgiven.

He was still as handsome as his father had been, dark olive face made darker still by the lighting which mercifully hid the frets and eye rings of venality and debauchery. He had close-cropped hair and a curled fringe of beard round his jawline and across his lip, while his eyes were dark, cold pools under a terror of knit brows.

This is what that golden boy will look like in a few years at court, Drust thought. Who could not fail to see that little Helios, the tiny Sun God, was the offspring of this man?

'You dance well,' Caracalla growled. 'With some partners you should not even be looking at, let alone guiding in false steps.'

'Fuck you,' Kag said.

'Sorry about your father,' Quintus offered, his smile wavering. The Emperor looked at them all, one by one, and shook his head. Then he looked at Drust with eyes that promised chains and beatings, pain and death.

'It has taken a long time,' he said, 'but be assured of how the *Parcae* work – everything turns on the wheel and all life is a circle, like the moon. The Goddess Selene promised me revenge and here it is.'

He leaned back and exhaled, like a man who had just savoured a good wine. 'You are bound for the sands, little man, you and your friends, back where you came from. There you will find out what it means to injure an emperor.'

He turned and left, replaced by another figure Drust knew well, this time in the full panoply of his centurion office.

'Macrinus,' Drust said, and the centurion smiled; he nodded to the Heavies, who closed in and started huckling them out into the rain – Drust saw Manius on the wet cobbles, pinned by a hobnailed foot.

'All this because Drust kicked him once?' Kag spat out. 'Served the little bugger well for running round in the dark clubbing people.'

Macrinus stared for a moment, then laughed and shook his head. 'I cannot fathom how you can have come so far and still live with the level of ignorance you possess. There are stones with more sense – and corpses that look and smell better.'

'Fuck you, too, Roman,' Ugo muttered, but Macrinus seemed more amused than ever and leaned forward to where Drust was now kneeling, feeling the wet seep up the hem of his tunic.

'The Hood,' he said in a soft, sibilant whisper, 'is a bugger for the women. He would fuck a knot-holed floor in a barber's if there was a lick of hair on it.'

The delivery shocked everyone to silence. Macrinus stroked his beard and shook his head once again with mock awe.

'In all that time, with all those women, what is the single lack in it?'

He waited. Nothing came. Ugo was frowning so hard Drust could hear his brows squeak – then, like a flash of bright white light, it came to him.

'No by-blows,' he said, and Macrinus slapped his hands together with genuine joy.

'There it is – you throw the dog at the last,' he said and leaned closer still. 'He is a mule. Someone kicked all the children out of him on a hot night on the floor of a cheap Roman eatery.'

Drust felt the world was roaring at him, that all the blood in his body was drained away. Everything became clear and he felt sick – the boy, the little Sun God, was from before that. He was the only son The Hood would ever have.

I did that, Drust thought. Oh, gods above and below – I did that…

Macrinus straightened and was no longer smiling as he indicated to nearby men to drag them away.

'There was a deal of pain for a long time after – and then the knowledge that all the seeds had been crushed from him. No man forgets such a thing, particularly a man charged with preserving a dynasty. I would not expect to come out of the *harena* through the Gate of Life this time.'

Chapter Sixteen

Rome, the following year

In the consulship of Hedius Lollianus Terentius Gentianus and Pomponius Bassus

It was the second hour of the night, and the third day of the Romani games was winding to a close, mainly because the light was too bad for the audience to properly see. The fighters couldn't see properly either but no one cared about that.

Sophon wandered up to them, as he had done on the previous days, and nodded, grinning out of a mouth made lopsided by an old wound. Even if a sword hadn't done it, Drust thought, he'd have a permanent sneer.

'*Missus*,' he said, as he had said for the last three days, and jerked his thumb. 'Move it.'

They got up and moved through the sweating, fetid throng under the Flavian, where the noise was a shrieking horror of ungreased machinery, men being sewn up by a squinting *medicus*, and the fighters who had walked through the Gate of Life and were loud and proud about it.

Some of them Drust and the others knew, but any who met their eyes averted them; most studiously found something else to be doing until the band passed into the reeking shadows, following Sophon and sliding between sweat-gleamed slaves and fighters.

They went into the tunnel that led to the Ludus Magnus and in the beating heat of Mensis September the arched roof dripped with sweat as if it rained.

No one spoke on the way out in the scarring light of the Magnus, where the oval *harena* was a miniature of the Flavian. It was surrounded on all sides by three-floored buildings housing barracks, messes, armouries, offices – 3,000 people worked here.

The State kept and trained its own gladiators, but other owners could use the Magnus too, especially on important game days – there were no more important ones than those of the Ludi Romani. Fifteen days of blood and howling from the time of Tarquinius until now. Once they had been held exclusively in the Circus, but when the Flavian was built, that was the preferred spot and the Circus ended up as a great egg-shaped market stall for those days because no one could be bothered with chariot racing.

Fifteen days and every one a torture of waiting. Drust knew The Hood would eke it out, bringing them every day as if they were due to fight, and sitting them in the heat and blood reek of the Flavian underbelly, listening to the catcalls of the fighters, the bellowing of slave-masters, the shudder of elephants dying above. They sat and waited and waited and waited for the call to go out and die.

Which would not come until The Hood was finished twisting his knife of fear in them. He had buried his father and deified him, withdrawn the Army from Britannia and come back to Rome, dragging the entire court with him. Since then he had worked to undermine his brother and all his supporters – Drust wondered how the javelin of Julias fared now.

Most of the fighters here belonged to the State, mainly the Emperor, though several senators had their own, calling them 'family'. They were organised into *decuriae* of ten and there were a lot of them – at important games permission was given to some favoured outsiders to use the facilities of the Ludus Magnus and Servilius Structus – supplier of Circus horses, grain, fighters and special sand for the Flavian – was one of those. Drust and the others knew the place well from their days in the Ludus Ferrata.

It was no great trial, then, for them to be shoved back into the cramped single-person cell rather than the wider rooms that held groups of fighters – all of the same fighting class, because no gladiator ever fought one of his own style, so some small measure of friendships might safely be formed.

Still Drust and the others had been awarded the *rudis*, the wooden sword releasing them from slavery, so it grated on them almost as much as it did the other fighters – and the *lanistae* – who knew them. None of them wanted to see such folk forced back to the sand to die.

Except Sophon, their old *lanista*. He had volunteered for this – though the coin he had from the State helped him eke out a life after Servilius Structus had decided he was too harsh to keep as a trainer.

'They might let us train a bit,' Ugo said ruefully, studying his biceps one by one. 'Even lift some weights. Get used to armour – it's been weeks.'

'No one will get armour,' Kag explained patiently as they filed into the only communal room they were allowed in, the mess. 'Or weapons. We are not expected to fight, just to die.'

There were several messes, usually dominated by one family or another, but the visitors all mingled in where they could; this time, whether by accident or design, Drust saw they had been ushered into one where he recognised men from the Ludus

Ferrata. He half expected to see Servilius Structus, but he did see a couple he knew.

For all that, they were placed at their own bench-table, apart from everyone else. Sophon, his duty done, swaggered off to find folk he knew and would tolerate him, while Drust and the others collected up wooden bowls and spoons, to be served up barley porridge and fava beans, standard fare. It produced a layer of fat which most fighters thought beneficial if they were cut – though some preferred to stay lean and fast, depending on how they fought. You could always tell the barley men – they were the ones who farted everywhere they went.

They filed back, sat, ate silently and drank water from wooden cups. Then Kag said: 'Isn't that the new kid, the one from Gaul? What was his name again?'

Drust looked up. Lupus Gallicus, he remembered. Ridiculous name no self-respecting fighter adopted, but the Gaul had been a swaggering *novicus*, still under six months' training and not allowed to fight a real bout when they'd known him in the Ferrata.

He was now a *thraex*, one of the most popular of styles, all flash and fancy hat, and it showed in his own appearance – he had a lithe, muscular, olive-tinted body which he managed to show off even under a wool tunic. He had dark curled hair and a smile which rivalled that of Quintus.

'Ho, I remember you lot,' he said cheerfully, leaning on their table. 'You used to be good entertainment once. Well rehearsed.'

'You used to be a snot-nose,' Kag said blandly. 'An arse calling himself Wolf? Only thing worse than that is a lion-fighter calling himself Androculus.'

Lupus's olive skin darkened a little round the face and his smile grew twisted and ugly.

'Well, I am no *novicus* now. Nor *tiro*. I have twelve wins under my belt, have gone up in the world and will go higher still. You, on the other hand, are on a nosedive, that's clear.'

'Twelve wins in the provinces,' Drust said, and though it had been a guess, he saw by the man's face that he was right. 'Your footwork was always poor,' he went on, studying him. 'If it is still the same I would not bet on you past tomorrow – there are too many real battlers in these games.'

Lupus had a retort somewhere in him and given a week might have brought it up, but he was saved the effort by the arrival of an older man that Drust and the others also knew – Curtius Martialus, who had been with Servilius Structus when Drust was a lad. He was slab-faced and silvered where he wasn't bald, with a bad limp and rheumy eyes which he laid on all at the table.

He had three others with him, a greybeard like himself and two younger ones, all in stained tunics and carrying shovels and picks. The old man was hunched and small, his sons straighter but no taller.

'Drust, Kag – I would say it was good to see you, but it isn't,' Curtius said. 'Not under these circumstances. Still, maybe I can lighten your burden – Lupus, you stumbling fuck, piss off out of it and leave decent fighters alone, but only after you attend to these people. They seem to want to talk to you.'

He nodded to Drust and the others, scowled into Lupus's face and went off with a bandy-legged limp.

'Gods above and below,' Sib said, 'how old is he? I remember him taking me on my first overseas.'

'Me too,' Quintus mused, then looked round. 'All of us, I expect. Those were the days.'

When we were young, glad to be out of the *harena* for a time and not expecting imminent death, Drust thought to himself, but was saved from more mawkishness by the greybeard.

'Beg pardon, your honour,' the old man said, looking at Lupus. 'I am Gaius Plancus. These are my sons Caius and Marcus.'

'I make my mark on wooden swords and the like later, down in Chio's. See me there,' Lupus said, and then flushed when Drust and the others laughed; Chio's was a notorious dive in the middle of the Wolf's Den in Subura.

'No, beg pardon,' the old man said. 'I am here about the sewers.'

'Do I look like I am the Procurator of the Ludus?' Lupus spat back, and had more which was wrenched from him by Sophon. No one had heard the man come up and Drust marked that; he could move quietly when he chose, could Sophon.

'You don't look anything like the Procurator of the Ludus,' Sophon said to the flustered Lupus. 'You look like a sack of shit that needs clearing out of the sewers. Perhaps you could do old Plancus here a favour by flushing off.'

Lupus hesitated a moment, thought better and went. Plancus, bemused and uneasy, looked from Sophon to Drust and the others; his sons smirked behind his back.

'Come for the sewers you say,' Sophon declared, and Plancus recovered himself, nodding.

'As I said. Blockage somewhere in the system. Me and my lads are here to clear it out but we need some help. A few slaves for the heavy work. I was told to look for Sophon – sorry, I mistook that young fella for him – is it you?'

'Flattery will get you on,' Kag interrupted, laughing, and Sophon's eyes narrowed.

'It will, as much as your mouth will lead you down a blocked alley. Yes, I am Sophon and here are your helpers, Plancus, all neatly gathered together and waiting.'

Plancus looked delighted; he had clearly been expecting no more than two and now he had a pack.

'Well, don't hang about,' Sophon said to Drust and the others, his grin straking back to show teeth on one side. 'Take up the tools. Get digging.'

They followed Plancus and his sons, who had clearly been here before and knew the way.

'Always choking up,' Marcus explained as they went. He was like his dad must have been when young – pale, sanded and plump, he looked like a happy ginger pig and his brother was much the same.

'Made the pipe work too narrow,' Plancus added as they descended stairs into a fetid darkness, pausing only to get six or seven torches. They lit three after Plancus had spent an age sniffing.

'Fumes,' he explained. 'They can collect, and if you smell rotten eggs, don't light up or else – boom.'

'Gods above and below,' Ugo muttered, looking round. 'This is a fearful place.'

'This is Dis,' Sib answered, rolling his eyes.

'Does it go a long way, this sewer system? Kag asked innocently, and Plancus stopped, turned and eyed him up and down, then shook his head.

'You think you are being clever. Don't blame you, mind – I see that you are condemned, for Sophon would never have sent real fighters on a task like this.'

'Fuck you, too,' Manius said flatly and Drust saw the two boys get better grips on the hafts of their picks. Plancus raised a placating hand.

'Mean nothing by it but the truth,' he said. 'So I don't blame you for thinking you can escape down here.'

Kag scrubbed his beard, which he did when he had been fairly caught or was bewildered at what to say or do next.

'Not much chance of it,' Plancus went on, shuffling ahead into the dark. 'I mean, there are all sort of *tabernae* tales about it – I enjoy them meself after a few. Hero has to escape prison, gets into the sewers, battles giant rats and emerges with laurels to claim the lady.'

He sighed. 'Bollocks, of course. I mean – this lad manages to negotiate his way in the dark, while the truth is you need these…'

He paused and waved the torch so that Kag had to step back in case his hair caught. Plancus laughed.

'You need lots of 'em, for if you don't have light you are well fucked. Not that it matters, because our hero lad also manages to get through without getting much of his feet wet. Somehow, all his sewers are built wide and arched, with walkways along one or both sides.'

He stopped, held up the torch so that the brick arches were clearly seen. There was a final flight of stairs leading down to a round, black hole they'd have to crouch to get in and would be ankle deep in a filth of scummy water.

'There's the truth of it,' Plancus said. 'Why the fuck would you bother making a fucking great basilica just to carry shit? No, you have this – a hole you have to go through bent. If our hero had to do that, he'd never be able to make the beast with two backs afterwards. He wouldn't have one back to do it with.'

He laughed, coughed and spat into the water.

'But he won't have to. He will have to transform himself into a rat-sized rat, for this is just the entrance pipe. A few hundred paces on you get to ones only a rat can go down or up – and somewhere in there is a great backed-up pile of shit preventing the outflow from dropping. That's what we have to bucket out.'

Kag looked sick and Quintus laughed at his face.

'There's no strolling out of the Maxima smelling of heroics – fucking Cloaca Maxima is a drain, not a sewer. There's a difference. No, your hero lad will come out crippled, tiny and smelling like a turd,' Plancus finished. 'Find me the woman who will want that.'

'Your fucking wife,' Ugo growled, and even as their hackles came up, the sight of the big man kept Plancus and sons from doing something foolish.

They started down the steps, then Drust stopped, held his torch up and squinted at the opposite wall.

'Drains,' Caius said helpfully. 'Old ones.'

'Why block them off?' Drust asked, seeing the brickwork was a different colour even under a patina of scum.

'Dunno,' Plancus said, and there was something about the way he said it that made Drust look again at him. He saw nothing.

'Not sewers, mind,' Plancus went on, slowly and deliberately. 'Drainage. Got blocked off years back. Found a better way, no doubt – but should have used it, I say. Drains is always bigger and wider than sewers.'

He led the way, crouching into the dark hole. Marcus sidled up to Drust and whispered.

'Da knows everything about sewers and drains,' he said. 'That bricked-up bit is where the drainage was for the *naumachae*.'

The *naumachae*, the naval displays, had been a feature of the Flavian for a while. The sands were drowned in water, ships launched and battles fought – then the whole affair was drained off, fresh sand put down and the fighters brought back for the evening. Domitian had ordered the network of rooms and machinery and cages under the amphitheatre which made it more useful for gladiators of all sorts – and the builders used the drainage tunnels where they could. The ones not of use had been blocked off. No more *naumachae* in the Flavian.

It was said they could fill and drain the Flavian in an hour or less, Drust remembered, and Marcus nodded enthusiastically.

'Knowed how to do it in them days. Pumps and pipes, that's what it takes. Forty-two inlet pipes, four big outflows – Da told me that. He knows it well.'

'Come on, boy, don't dawdle.'

Marcus leaped to obey and Drust followed thoughtfully.

–

Later, in the fetid dark, feral with hidden scutterings, Drust and Kag talked from their separate cells. They had done it before and, as Kag said when it was easier to speak, they had Polybius to thank for it.

'Jupiter's hairy balls,' Quintus had moaned, 'not you and your girl Greeks again. Boring lot, looking down their noses and droning about their… ideas. We gave them an idea – it was called fighting, and they didn't care for it.'

'Dogs' Heads,' Manius had added, referring to the battle which ended the glories of Alexander at the place of that name – the Cynoscephalae hills.

Polybius did not fight. He played games with numbers and letters and, though no one knew that when they'd learned it, Drust and the others played it nightly, taught it by others who had been taught it before. Tap-tapping, soft as mice feet, they spoke where no speaking was allowed.

'Thinks there's a way out?' Kag asked. Tap-tap, tap-tap.

'Yes. Need to find out more. Water drains. Flavian.'

There was a long pause, for it took a deal of tapping just to spell 'water' – five taps, pause, two taps. Then one-one, four-four, one-five, four-two.

In the end, Drust heard: four-one, four-three, two-two, shut his eyes and visualised the board.

Dog.

It was the ever-present thought in everyone's mind, voiced only at this, the last hour of the night, like a prayer – some whispered sacrament to the one who had got away.

Dog.

Drust tapped it back, heard the faint echoes of it passing up and down the line of them. Privately, he thought Dog was long gone but could not – still – believe that he was dead.

But unless they found a way and soon, he and the rest of them would be.

–

'Drusus,' he said, and the boy looked at him and smiled. He liked the big man, even if he was the master and his mother had always told him to watch him, be polite and do what he was told round him. Call him 'your honour' or 'master' but not his name – Servilius Structus was not something for the mouths of slaves.

'Master?

'I have bad news,' Servilius said, and to the astonishment of everyone, not least the boy, he levered himself painfully down on one knee, to be closer to the boy's level.

'Your ma is no longer with us.'

The boy blinked. His mother had said this might happen and not to worry because she would find a way to see him, no matter what. But slaves were sold all the time and the boy knew that already.

'Yes, Master,' he said. Servilius Structus looked relieved and then had to wave to Curtius to help him up. He nodded to the boy, patted him on the head and turned to Curtius.

'Put him with Gennadios, for the learning in it. Let him take the boy under the Flavian and teach him the basics. When you are ready to go, take him with you this trip. Show him the way of it. Bring him back safe.'

Curtius knew better than to argue. Servilius Structus waddled off into the dark and Curtius turned and looked down at the boy.

'Drust, ain't it?'

'Yes, Master.'

'Curtius will do. How old are you?'

The boy didn't know, but Curtius went and fished out a tablet from one of the many slots.

'Nine summers. You'd best come with me now, kid, and stick close. We are off to a far land, across the sea. That will be an adventure, with some sweetmeats and then home. How does that sound?'

'Will I see my mother then?' the boy asked. Curtius frowned, then saw the way of it and shook his head, eyes sorrowful as a whipped hound.

'Boy, you ma ain't sold on. She's dead. Died trying to bring a sister into the world for you. Babe died too.'

The boy heard the words tumbling like spilled bricks. They seemed to clatter after him for a long time until they hit him, one by one, after Curtius had shown him to a straw pallet and blown out the lamp.

Then the pain ripped him and squeezed up his face until tears popped like pips from a crushed apple.

-

It was seeing Curtius again that had brought this, a strange gift from Morpheus. The revelation in it as he woke to his cell, weeping, was that Servilius Structus had probably fathered the child who had killed his mother, and he had always avoided the memory, shoving it deep in the sewer at the back of his head.

Not that any of it mattered, not now. If there were gods above and below then perhaps, if they saw fit to favour him, he'd be able to ask her in a day or two. Yet he wondered at Curtius, who was still the tool of Servilius Structus.

Sophon came for them, as usual, unlocked the cells and looked them over. He wore the same tunic as he had the day before and the day before that, but if there was a fresh stain anywhere on it, it was hard to find among the older ones; he smelled of fava bean farts and stale wine.

'Come on, then. There's bread if you want it.'

They all ate, though when they'd been fighting they never did until evening; lots of fighters thought a full belly meant death if you got sliced there. Most fighters knew a slit stomach meant death whether it was full or not.

The day was warm, the sun hazed and, as they filed through the riot of the *ludus*, they saw the sailors arriving, a new batch looking all round and gaping. They were the ones who would work the Flavian awnings when the crowd needed some shade, scampering up and down the ratlines as if they were aboard their ships.

Drust saw men of the Ludus Ferrata just as they came out of the tunnel into the undercroft; above was the blare and pomp of that day's opening ceremony and the early risers had claimed their seats for the first of the day's sport – the crucifixions.

Sophon saw their faces and grinned his ruined grin. 'Not that for you lot, not today. Now I have to sit with you sorry fucks all through the rest of the day…'

The last of his words was driven from him in an explosion of lost breath; Drust saw Curtius standing while a big *hoplomachus*, all fat and lazy amble, massaged the elbow which had driven into Sophon's side.

'You should watch where you walk here,' Curtius said. 'And talk.'

Sophon wanted to explode at them so badly Drust could even taste it; the man was a *lanista*, after all, but he had nothing to do with the Ferrata or any other school now, and all of those gladiators were moving past him with stone stares, oiled muscles and old grievances.

They sat in the undercroft all the morning, listening to the beasts die; the blood and heat rose until, suddenly, there was the faint scent of roses where slaves had started damping the *harena* with perfumed water, pumping out sprays of it.

They sat all through lunch and had only water while men wearing the skins of wild beasts raped young girls; the children of *noxii* who had not been put to the beasts in the morning show were hung from poles by their legs. The crowd made bets on which wild dog could jump highest to drag down a meal while they munched chickpeas and bread.

Then, just after the start of the afternoon's real entertainments, they all saw a crowd of fighters, sweated and gleaming, coming up through the crowded dark, carrying one of their own.

Drust didn't see it at first because the body was splatted with gore and crusted with sand, but Curtius wiped the face clean while others shrieked for the *medicus*; a masked Charon and his slaves came rolling up, the Charon hauling off the mask.

'You should have left him to me, you slave fucks. To *me*.'

They wanted to save him, but it was way too late and everyone knew it. He was young, barely out of *tiro* and lay writhing and clutching the sides of a vicious belly wound as if squeezing would somehow make it whole again.

–

'Sniff his belly,' Gennadios orders, and the boy blinks a bit and hesitates.

'Get to it. Tell me what you smell.'

The man is a venator caught by a frightened, enraged leopard and raked by the back claws. He gasps and moves his head and whimpers, but his eyes are glazed, halfway into the Other while the sweat and blood rolls off him like a sluice. He is bandaged and strapped, but the blood seeps through; the boy grits his teeth and bends to it, sniffing.

There is the iron stink of blood, the smell of shit where the man has shamed himself, the warm hot fetid smell where he has just staled. And onions and garlic.

He tells this to Gennadios, who sighs. 'Soup wound,' he says, and signals to a slave to call for someone who can give the man the release of iron.

'Fed him onion and garlic soup an hour ago,' Gennadios says. 'Now it has seeped out of the bowel. So he is dead – we cannot repair that organ and it will fester if left. Best he dies now than a few days from now, stinking and in pain.'

The boy watches the medicus watching the man while an assistant finds the heart in the throat which pulses like a trapped bird until the thin, steel blade releases it in a weak gush of blood. Gennadios watches and watches intently, but in the end, as always, what he seeks at the man's moment of death eludes him again.

–

Drust shook the memory away, feeling shivered and strange, like some beast on the point of running.

'They have paid for a lot of deaths,' Sib said, and Kag slapped him, a loud wet sound that made Sib scowl and rub his shoulder.

'Do not speak of deaths,' he said and made a warding sign with his fingers.

'No matter,' Curtius said, coming up and sitting. He had the eyes of a dead fish and the air of a man unable to walk a single step more – and he had not been fighting. He had been watching friends die.

'Four so far these games,' he said and shook his head. 'I had thought the Ferrata would get off lightly today, but those bastards out there are taking their lead from the fucker in the good seat. No one gets a *missio* granted today.'

He levered himself slowly up and took a step, then stopped, shook his head and looked at Drust. Behind him, they all saw Sophon lumbering up and their hearts stuttered.

'Forgot,' Curtius said. 'Had a message from Servilius Structus. Says to tell you to hold fast and bet on the dog.'

Sophon wanted to make it seem that he had come for them, wanted to twist the knife, but thought better of it when he saw Curtius. Instead, he waved a hand as if to flap Curtius out of the way, then stood with his hands on his hips.

'You won't be dying today,' he said, and then indicated a group of sweat-patched men behind him, mostly slaves with picks and shovels, their faces and heads wrapped as protection for where they had been. Lime, Drust thought.

One was Plancus, both sons on either shoulder. He waved at them and Sophon smirked his straked grin.

'Make yourself useful, the *aedile* says – so you lads can grab some tools and follow old Plancus here. There's work for you. Make sure you wash before you come back near me.'

He stood aside, chuckling. Plancus spread his hands apologetically.

'Sorry, but it's going to need a lot of men. The flow isn't clearing out the stuff they are throwing down the pit. It's a fucking mess down there and getting worse.'

He led them far into the deep recesses of the undercroft, but Drust knew where they were going, had been here before and felt his belly clench. When Marcus handed out long poles with hooks he suspected the worst, and when he handed them squares of cloth, he knew it.

'Bind your heads and faces with this,' Marcus said. 'Watch out for your eyes.'

'*Omnes ad stercus*,' Quintus declared viciously. 'The lime pits.'

'Better in the *harena* than this,' Ugo muttered.

'You lot – with me,' said a voice, and they followed the man, his face swathed in cloth-backed leather; Drust saw that this one had dark glass lenses set in a leather rig that let him fasten them round his face, protecting his eyes.

'Any more of those?' Kag asked hopefully, but had no reply. They started to smell the choke of it, the reeking stench of old meat and blood and acrid lime. The man led them down to where the water turned milky and Drust balked.

'Fuck that,' Manius agreed. 'It will burn my feet to stumps.'

The man didn't answer, but hopped in with a splash and then, bewilderingly, turned away from the worst of the reek, where they could hear others cursing and struggling, the splash of them disgorging lumps of blockage.

Kag and Drust shared a look, then they all looked at one another. Ugo shrugged and stepped in the water while the man with the dark lenses turned and waved them on. No one had any idea why they were moving away from the worst of the work but didn't argue with the ethos of it.

When they reached a low pipe, the man crouched and crab-walked into it. With only a slight hesitation, Drust followed and the rest filed after. The pipe was short, then opened up into a shaft which left them blinking at a distant, faint light and sunlight fell in small spears through a metalled grille. There was the sound of the *harena*.

The man with the lenses looked up, then down at the nearby wall, spat on his hands and swung his pick at the bricks. The others stared in confusion.

'That's one of the beast entrances,' Ugo said, turning this way and that, dappling himself with the light as if he was standing under a spray of water. He dropped his face when grit sifted down and the place went dark; the slaves had sanded the area where the beasts entered the amphitheatre and they heard the scrabble and coughing roar of lions.

'Can they get down?' Sid demanded, crouching and looking up.

'No,' said the man with the lenses, 'nor can we get up. Only way out is this way.'

He pointed his pick at the patched brick wall and peeled off lenses and veil and head wrap in one smooth motion. They stared at death while it grinned back at them.

'Dog,' said Drust with awe and wonder.

'Fuck me with a trident,' Kag echoed.

Chapter Seventeen

Dog had taken two horses and ridden a third, leaving the others behind in the stables. He'd headed north as if back towards the Wall but veered west before long and come down the road from Isurium Brigantium, across the river to Calcaria.

It was a staging post with a *mansio* and some workings for lime; he sold two of the horses there for half of what they were worth and then rode on. No one had yet heard of the death of the Emperor there, but the ripples of it spread. By the time he reached Lindum, the news had beat him to the place. By the time he got to where he could cross to Gaul, using the last of the horse money, everywhere was in mourning.

He'd had a long, hard trip through Gaul and Italia, thieving and hiding. In Rome he had gone to Servilius Structus.

'I looked to scare out where you lot had gone before I slit through all his chins to the heart in the throat,' he told them, 'but he wasn't afraid at all, just seemed relieved that I was not dead. Then he told me what had happened to you lot and how we could get you out. So I gave him a *missus*. For now.'

He told them this while he picked apart the brickwork and eventually stood back, panting.

'Servilius Structus arranged this?' Drust said, voicing the wonder of them all. Dog grinned from his sweat-gleaming face, hawked up enough spit to clear the dust from his mouth and gobbed it on the litter of broken bricks.

'Naturally – Jupiter's cock, Drust, sometimes you amaze me. Why d'you think you were handed the *rudis* so early? Why did he make you leader of his *Procuratores*?'

Drust blinked, trying to think. Kag made an exasperated sound. 'He bought you and your ma because he liked your ma. He took her to his bed and she warmed it right up until she died. It was his babe in her at the time. You are the nearest that fat old fuck has to a son.'

Drust stared from Dog to Kag and round them all. Dog shrugged. 'Maybe that's why he knew what The Hood would do,' he said, then laughed sourly.

Kag flapped his hands and shrugged. 'Everyone fucking knew this but you, it seems.'

'Work on that later,' Manius growled, and pointed with his long, hooked stick. 'Work on this now – you have dug through to more brick, Dog.'

Dog grinned and slapped the wall. It wasn't brick but large blocks of pale stone.

'The Divine Domitian had this plugged and all the others along the way. Beyond are the old channels for the *naumachae*, and it would have taken too much work to block the lot of them off. So he made sure they wouldn't leak into his precious Flavian machinery and cages.'

'Get to work prising out those stones,' he said, 'before you are reported missing.'

The realisation of that raked them into action and they all started scrabbling at the stones until Drust got some order; he had some of the longer implements hacked short enough to be useful – they were poles with a blade for slicing the clogged flesh and shit, a hook for pulling the gristled lumps free. Now, cut down, they were used to rake at the crumbling mortar of the stone blocks.

There wasn't enough room for everyone, which was good as far as Dog was concerned – he had Sib go back to the pipe entrance and keep watch. Then he and Drust squatted in as dry a corner as could be found and looked at one another.

'What brought you back?' Drust asked. 'You were free and clear. You could just have kept going.'

'Where?' Dog countered.

'East. Your Sol temple.'

'The boy and his mother are still here. The Hood won't let them out of his sight, none of them, not his mother and certainly not his brother. Once his brother is gone, they are in more danger than ever. Old Servilius Structus knew this, planned for it. He was always a supporter of Geta – The Hood knew that. That's why he attacked the litter that night.'

He scrubbed his deathly face, made mad with a beard. 'The Hood was ever the problem, the reason she had to flee – well, that's what you get for giving in to the boy in the first place, though I am thinking she did not have much say in it. I am thinking it was her mother, or the Empress or all the Julias who got me to take her beyond the Empire. They got desperate and called in Servilius Structus. He called in me.'

'He got us to beat you up,' Drust pointed out, and Dog nodded, rubbing his leg.

'I owe him for that – and you lot. The cold makes it ache.'

'Why did he do that?' Drust asked. 'It all but ruined your plans.'

'Not really. I didn't have any and I didn't want to be involved with that fat old fuck's plans. I tried to get out of it by running off, which is the last resort of any slave other than sticking your head through the spokes of the wheel.'

They both shared that distant tragedy, but Drust's look made Dog scowl.

He spread his hands. 'What? I didn't want any mad journey to the far north, the Land of Darkness beyond the Wall – I took a chance and joined up with Bulla. Second Spartacus, I thought. Well, we all saw what came of that – when it went to shit and you lot came at me, I tried to tell you I'd do what Servilius Structus wanted. I didn't know you had no idea what was going on.'

He glanced sideways at Drust. 'To be honest, you never know much of what's going on, and old Servilius Structus was too afraid of The Hood to share it with many.'

Drust bridled a little, but it was true enough. 'Gives me nosebleed looking up at the Hill and all its plotting.'

Dog nodded. 'I am with you there, brother. And who's to say you are *Stupidus*. I am *Stupidus*. We are all *Stupidus* – I mean, I took the Domina as far north as you could go. The gods laughed at that trick – I am working hard at keeping us all safe from emperors when three fucking emperors turn up on a frontier no one had considered for years. As if I did not have enough with Talorc.'

'Fuck Fortuna up the arse,' Drust said.

'Then a *frumentarius* turns up and finds out about a high-born Roman and her son squatting in a mud hut with the beasts beyond the Wall,' Dog went on. 'Starts sticking his long nose in.'

Dog's eyes were hooded. 'Brigus was a brief problem, easily solved, and he became a help – I used his name to get a message back to Kalutis, asking for trusted men. Asking for you lot. No one questioned the word of a good informer, but I killed the scribe who worked the wax.'

'You asked for us,' Drust said dully. Somewhere distant, the crowd erupted in a great roar, muted to a sound like surf on a shore. 'I am guessing we should be flattered.'

'Could have done without it,' Manius growled, wiping his streaming face; he had come up silently, as ever, and stood over them. He had lost his bandana and the flesh on one side of his head and the pocks on his face were a twisted cicatrice, smooth and pale as milky glass. 'Same as we could do with some help now.'

Dog took the proffered pole and Manius's place. Manius sat heavily and cocked his head to look up, as if he could see through the stones, through the sour slickness, the tunnels, the sand, out onto the blaze of the amphitheatre.

'The crowd is thirsty. There will be blood,' he said, then looked at Drust and round at the others and shook his head wearily. 'My ma taught me that if Romans come to you, fear them even if they bring gifts. What were we thinking? Citizens? With piles of coin?'

'Publius Vergilis Maro,' Kag said, stepping away from the hard work. His tunic was dark with sweat, and dust crusted it and his face as he handed the pole pointedly to Drust. Then he grinned at Manius.

'He first said what your ma told you, but it was Greeks he feared.'

'Never saw Greeks out our way,' Manius replied. 'Saw too many fucking Romans though.'

'Go and relieve Sib,' Drust said, and shouldered his way into the crowd raking lumps round a stone.

It took another torch to do it and Drust was glad Dog had thought to bring a bundle, but if it all took this long they'd be out of light before they even broke through to the dark beyond. The longer sticks became invaluable when it came to levering the block out, the hooks scraping for purchase like talons; eventually the stone crashed out with a noise that made everyone freeze. The torchlight guttered their shadows in a mad dance and they all fought against the panic.

'The next will be easier,' Dog said. 'We need three out to get through.'

'Two,' said Sib, eying the hole, and Manius clapped him hard enough on his back to make him stagger.

'For you, maybe, little man,' he growled and Sib glanced guiltily at big Ugo, his elbows working furiously as he straked mortar from a block.

They had a second out and were working on a third, watching the torches gutter and smoke in the poor air, gasping and streaming with sweat. Then, suddenly, Sib came scuttering back from where he was watching the end of the pipe.

'Someone is coming,' he hissed. 'Jupiter Optimus Maximus… someone is coming.'

'Shut up,' Dog spat in a hoarse whisper, and smothered the torch in brick dust. They crouched, trying to control the rasp of their breathing, and Drust listened to his own heart, like a galloping horse. If they were all like that, he thought, whoever was arriving couldn't fail to hear…

'Ho,' demanded a voice in a low growl. 'Are you there? That Sophon is looking for you, so if you want to avoid a beating, I'd get back.'

'Plancus,' Drust mouthed, and Manius nodded, then started to slide silently towards the sound of the man's voice; Dog caught his sleeve.

'Don't,' he said, and then called out to Plancus.

'Ha, fuck – there you are,' the voice said. 'Gave me a right scare. Look, my lads and I have done all we could but we'll be in trouble if Sophon has to search. He's starting to ask about you.'

He came ducking into the pipe, smiling in the torchlight, and when he saw Drust he fumbled inside his stained tunic.

'Old Servilius Structus gave me this for you,' he said, and handed over a small pouch; it chinked softly with coin and Plancus nodded.

'Few *sestercii* to help you lads on your way – and this,' he went on, handing over a small amulet on a thong. Drust's heart stumbled a few beats; it was one his mother had worn, a bronze oval of some face made of leaves, a forest spirit from her own time and place. It was worn shiny here and there by her fingers.

'You have kept your bargain,' Dog agreed, and Plancus smiled amiably.

'Well, that old bastard and me go back a long way, so I am glad to help. Besides – getting condemned folk out of this black pit is my pleasure. Remember – go left. There were forty-two run-ins and four big drains to take the *naumachae* flow in and out. Go left and you will come to the place where the boats were launched into the *harena* and after that you'll be walking double for some of the time.'

He broke off and winked. 'Like that lad in the tale.'

'I remember what you told me,' Dog said patiently, and broke off as another great muffled roar drifted down. Plancus frowned.

'I think the favourite got sixed,' he said. 'That won't make the Emperor any happier.'

'Go,' Drust said, slipping the amulet over his head. 'And thanks.'

Plancus flapped one hand, then stabbed a grimy finger in Dog's chest. 'After the place of boats, keep going, follow the curve of the highest arch. You will come to a crossover and must not miss it – there is an inscription to the Divine Trajan marking it. Cross to the next canal – that's the inflow. The outflow will spill you into the Tiber, but the inflow will set you climbing to where Trajan's aqueduct crosses the river on stone columns. You will then be in the open, high up on the aqueduct itself, and if you follow it on, will be over the City walls, where you can get down.'

He saluted them with a wave. 'I hope you make it – and remember the time, Dog.'

They watched him go and Drust held the amulet as if it was itself a prayer. Dog stood for a moment and Quintus laughed softly, which made him scowl as he shouldered away. Quintus winked at Drust and then threw his cut-down pole at Sib.

'My turn to sit and take my ease,' he said, and went off down to the pipe end.

They were manhandling the last stone, gasping and cursing in muted, sweating struggles when a voice echoed, loud and careless and angry. No one needed to ask who it was and Quintus didn't have to duck back to tell them.

Sophon had found out they were missing.

'*Faex*,' Kag growled. Dog moved swiftly and indicated to the others that they should pick up the pole-blades. He crab-walked back out the pipe and stood upright as Sophon came barrelling down, his face bloody as a bad pudding.

'You bastards. I have been too lax, it seems. Get yourselves out of there and back to your cells. You can wish for a meal…'

Then he saw Dog's bared face and stopped. Drust came out and Kag behind him. Sophon stood, hands on hips, still triumphant in his power and seeing only slaves, even if one was disfigured. Dog sauntered towards him with the pole on his shoulder, every inch of him arrogant disdain, and Sophon's face grew dark. He opened his mouth to start yelling as Dog swung the pole-blade in a perfectly timed arc, off his shoulder and curving towards Sophon's neck.

The *lanista* had a moment to realise just how bad things were for him, then he felt a tugging and reeled back. He wanted to yell out but all that emerged was a horrifying spray of blood...

Drust watched him dispassionately as he gug-gugged, clutching his opened throat and sinking slowly to the ground, gasping for air and speech. Then one of the Charons, mask in one hand and irritation making a new one all over his face, turned down into the tunnel, saw the terror of it all and stopped, his mouth working.

'Oh, Juno's twat,' Kag said sullenly, and Dog sprang forward. The Charon fled, screaming, and Dog pulled up short and turned back.

'Time for us to be gone,' he said.

Drust knew he was right; it wasn't that the Charon was screaming, it was what he was screaming, the one thing guaranteed to get the Urbans clattering down in a running hurry, in full gear and wielding blades, not cudgels.

'Spartacus. Spartacus.'

It bounced and echoed round the walls, was picked up by other throats and roared out until it drowned the noise of the animals and men and even the crowd outside.

Spartacus.

-

They scrambled through the hole they had made, dropped a man-height into ankle-deep water in the dark and stumbled left up the tunnel a little way. It was cold and smelled musty; Drust felt a slight chill breeze on his face.

Then Dog came up with a torch and holding a bundle under his arm. 'We have twelve,' he growled. 'When they run out we will be in the dark.'

Sib muttered to himself until Ugo slapped his shoulder. 'Ease yourself, little man – you should not fear the dark. If those whoresons come for us, you are the one they will miss.'

He threw back his head and laughed delightedly at his own joke, but the sound belled and thundered; Manius told him not to do it again.

'Will they follow?' asked Manius, and no one answered. Drust knew they would, all the same – they would follow regardless, follow until they tracked down and killed gladiators who had dared kill a *lanista* and raise the spectre of Spartacus.

It was why the Urban Cohorts were in the Flavian in the first place – the Vigiles dealt with crowd control, but the Urbans, dressed and equipped like legionaries, were there to guard against packs of armed slaves, should they decide to emulate the Spartacus of old. From time to time, Drust knew, there circulated a rumour of a 'second Spartacus', though few believed it; most, like Drust, thought the fighters did it simply to watch the owners and *lanistae* and others squirm.

The other side of that *as* was when anything that smelled of revolt was sniffed out; then the Urbans went in, tooth and claw. No wooden cudgels either – spears and shields and sharp blades.

'They will want us double when The Hood finds out we have made a run for it,' Drust told them, but they needed no spur. They moved as fast as they dared up an arched passage as wide as Ugo and only slightly taller, only stopping when Dog's torch sputtered down to a gasping rat's eye glare.

Then they stopped and fed another to the embers until it flared into life. Sib said he saw light ahead in the moment when the torches were exchanging lives.

'Up ahead,' he said. 'It was lighter, for sure.'

Back was only darkness, but Kag studied it while Manius tasted the air of it with his upraised face.

'They are following. They are in the tunnel.'

They went on, stumbling a little because there was enough fetid water round their feet to slosh and catch. It came to Drust, sudden as a stab, that there should be no water in these old tunnels if they'd been blocked off and he said so, looking at Dog.

'No, no – they blocked off the access to the Flavian undercroft. This is still attached to the aqueduct that feeds it, the big one, Trajan's one. It flushes out the sewers of the Flavian when the day is done there.'

Drust heard Plancus's last hissed warning – remember the time. Dog shrugged.

'They open the same sluices that served to flood the Flavian in the old days. Lot of pressure on narrow sewage pipes according to old Plancus, so they have to divert the flow, slacken it a little.'

'In here?' Sib shouted, and everyone winced as his voice shrieked round the stones like nails on slate.

'Now and then,' Dog admitted, but the reactions to that were shredded by a yelp from Quintus; he had gone ahead and come out into a wide circle of stone, broken into large canals. When the others came up, he pointed to what had made him cry out.

It was the timbers of a ship, lying half in the silt like a dead beast with all its ribs showing. All round it was a litter of spars and ropes, a fallen mast.

'It's a two-decker,' Kag said, staring in wonder. 'A two-decker – down here?'

'It's not a real one – look at the bottom,' Ugo declared. 'It is flat. Not enough water in the Flavian for keel.'

He was right. It was one of the ancient *naumachae* ships, flat-bottomed replicas of warships, and this was where they had lain, waiting for the crews to come from above and then sailing out. They stared round at the ramshackle litter of walkways and half-fallen timbers that marked where the sailors would come down; the grilled entrances spilled in the faint light Sib had spotted.

The wide archways where the boats had sailed into the flooded *harena* were blocked off by the same carefully laid stone blocks, no doubt brick-finished on the far side. Higher up, above where the water would flow, had been left alone. It meant…

'They are coming through from up there,' Quintus said as the first grindings began. The old grilles were being forced open and, behind, they could hear the echoes of men arriving up the tunnel.

'Gods above and below,' Sib moaned. 'We are trapped.'

'Shut up,' Dog snarled. 'Save your breath for running.'

'Get to the far tunnel – it is narrow. We can fight better there.'

They obeyed and Drust led them, leaping old timbers and sloshing through shallow water. Behind, he heard the blare of a *cornicen*, a great echoing blast; Ugo stopped and turned, his face etched with frown. Drust slapped him hard on the arm as he ran past.

'Move. That's not your big Bull, Ugo. That's a lot of little ones.'

Above, they all heard the grille open with a screech, then it suddenly flew down at them, wrenched out and flung away to spiral into the silt with a dull thud.

The Urbans spilled out and balked; no one had been here in a long, wood-rotting time and they realised that as soon as the walkway sagged, then started to sway and splinter. One panicked, tried to get back and threw another off; he fell with a long, mournful wail, hit the wet ground with the sound of a pile of tin kettles thrown in mud.

'Jupiter's salty balls,' Kag gasped, 'the gods are hurling enemies at us now.'

They almost made it without a fight, lumbering up in a lung-searing gasp to where the tunnel entrance they needed loomed like a welcoming mouth.

Then the first of the Urbans dropped off the walkway and came at them, forcing them to turn and fight.

Drust and Kag went left, Quintus and Dog went right. Sib kept running for the tunnel and Ugo and Manius ran with him a little way then turned. No one other than Dog had anything but a pole with a blade and a hook on it, so the Urbans came up hard and fast; somewhere up on the walkway a frantic *optio* was yelling for them to form.

He knows, Drust thought, his mind suddenly cold and slowed. Formed shield to shield they can take us. One on one – we can kill them. It is what we do...

The Urbans rushed in, shouting to bolster their courage, shields up, swords ready to stab. They had the *gladius*, Drust saw, because it would be better in the narrow passages in and around the Flavian and the streets outside...

The Urban who came at Drust was a young lad, eyes wide, jaw dropped and crouching behind his shield, trying to shrink even smaller because now he saw what he had run at. Like a dog chasing a galloping horse, he had gripped it by one fetlock and, in the moment before it reacted, knew just how badly he had fucked up.

He skidded to a halt rather than crash forward, even though he saw a man with a long pole in one hand and a torch in the other. No shield, no armour – but he had been told Spartacus was here, and what if this was him? Or the one next to him, the one armed with a pick…

Dog slammed his shield with the butt, swung the pick hard and wood splintered – then Dog had another to face and Drust stepped in, his pole-blade cut down by half and swung overarm.

The whole of it slammed into the lad's young, frightened face, framed by helmet and half hidden by shield. Flesh burst apart and blood flew, pit-patting into Drust's cheeks. The lad howled and Drust wrenched the pole-blade free, for the impact had driven the hook in to snag the boy's mouth like a gaffed fish.

He made unearthly noises when his jaw was torn off and his tongue flapped. He was still making them when he fell and another man stepped into his place, lunging out with an inexpert stab. Drust twisted sideways, collided with another Urban attempting to flank him – the impact rocked the soldier on to his arse and flung Drust backwards, staggering.

He saw Dog, skull-snarling at an Urban as his pickaxe slashed once, twice. Then he dropped it, dived for the ground and the fallen *gladius* that lay there, rolled in a flurry of wet silt and came up like the risen dead, howling.

Drust had other worries, with enemies closing in on his right and front; he shied away from a flicker behind his right shoulder, almost took a sword from the front, which raked along the side of his head – he felt it pink his ear.

The flicker was Kag; the Urbans washed away from him like ripples from a stone in a pool. Drust heard Ugo bellowing: 'Fall back, fall back.'

He risked a quick glance, saw Ugo and Manius ready, the big man with what seemed to be part of a ship's mast, the other with a pole-blade in one hand and a torch in the other.

'Back,' he yelled, ducking sideways to avoid a stab, and lashed out with the gore-spraying pole-blade. When his opponent leaped back, he took the chance and dropped the shaft, scooping up Dog's discarded pick. The feel of it in his hand made him snarl, his teeth clenched hard enough it seemed they would break.

He backed off a few steps, making sure Kag and Dog were with him. They backed off a few more and the *optio* was down at ground level now, screaming for his men to form up, form up. Calling them whoresons. *Stupidus*. Every curse he could find.

They realised their mistake and started to do it; the attacks slackened and Drust ended the last of it by shoving his torch in a face. He did not stay to watch the hair flare up, nor hear the shrieks from a man with hot embers up his nose, in his mouth and eyes.

He ran back, past Ugo and Quintus into the tunnel mouth. Then he turned, panting, and yelled at that pair to leave off and move.

Quintus, grinning madly, trotted easily back. Ugo, roaring out challenges, finally heaved the timber up above his head with both hands and hurled it; the forming wall of shields broke apart with loud shouts and yelps of pain.

Then he lumbered back to where Drust waited; the rest were already moving into the shadows of the tunnel.

'There is a palace rat among them,' he growled as he shouldered Drust to one side to get up the tunnel. 'I saw him. The one from Eboracum who wanted us fucked up the arse.'

Drust paused and stared back to where the lights flickered mad dancers on the high arches and distant walls bounced shrieks of fear and pain.

A Praetorian. The one who called himself Macrinus, who was The Hood's man.

Chapter Eighteen

They moved fast and hard for a long way until the tunnel opened up into yet another wide circle of vaulted barrel arches. Cautiously, they crept out, looking round in the bloody light of torches. No grilles or daylight-spewing holes here, Drust thought. Nothing but shadows and blocked-off entrances. Good…

They sank down to check one another over; Drust knew he bled and that there was a lot of it, but Kag took a look, soaked a neck cloth in some scummy water from a puddle and wiped hard enough to make Drust wince.

'Notched an ear is all,' he said. He had a slice along one arm, Dog had one on his forearm.

'We will live, then,' Quintus declared cheerfully. 'I could do with a drink to celebrate.'

It was ironic; there was water and the threat of it but nothing anyone would swallow who had sense. Besides, as Sib declared fearfully, there were beasts living in it.

'What beasts?' demanded Ugo, and Sib glanced up round.

'I heard splashings. And there are tales of monsters down here.'

'Giant rats,' Drust offered wryly, and those who remembered Plancus's tale laughed.

'No, no,' Ugo said seriously. 'I heard this. Sometimes they put beasts into the *naumachae* – river lizards from Aegyptus and those big sea cows. A few went missing when it was drained. Some say they are down here still.'

'Living on what?' Dog scorned. 'Giant rats?'

He cocked his head, listening, then shook it. 'We have to move.'

'Why?' Kag asked. 'What are you hoping to hear?'

'Hoping not to hear men coming up behind,' Manius declared softly, but Dog shook his head.

'Hoping not to hear the horns of the closing ceremony,' he said. 'When the Flavian is empty, they will open the sluices to scour the sewers free of the day's shit. And the overspill goes here.'

'Fuck me with Neptune's sacred fork, Dog,' Kag declared wearily. 'You are too miserly with vital information.'

'Would you not have come if you had known?'

There was no answer to it and Drust ended the squabble over it. 'Move,' he said. 'Look for a marker to the Divine Trajan.'

They filtered on up the tunnel, following the swaying rat-eye of the torch Drust held up, with Kag in the rear, turning now and then to listen, then hurrying on to catch up with the bobbing, fading light. Shadows danced wildly on the walls.

They came to two more areas where the tunnel splayed out into an oval channel around a central block of stone with no seeming purpose, though everyone had a thought on it. In the end, it was simply attributed to the *aquarii*, those endless wandering gangs who patrolled, inspected and cleaned. Drust had no worries about meeting any here; this part, the outflow from the Flavian, had been closed off long since.

In the third area, Sib had taken the lead and came scuttling back, his torch waving wildly and dangerously as he spoke, and turned to look fearfully over his shoulder at the same time.

'There's someone up ahead,' he hissed. 'A woman.'

Quintus gave a soft laugh but everyone else looked to their weapons and Kag growled: 'I would not unfetter your cock just yet – have you thought what sort of a woman inhabits the dark of a pit like this?'

Everyone had, and Quintus lost his grin. They crept forward, Drust taking the torch because Sib was trembling so much he risked setting hair on fire, not necessarily his own.

'The *mavro* was right,' Manius breathed, peering out, and Sib glared at him.

'My eyes are as good as yours,' he spat back. 'Go speak to her – she is probably closer to your kin that anyone else here. *Jnoun*...'

'You will call me demon once too often,' Manius said flatly. 'Then you may find the truth.'

'Shut up,' Drust said, and walked out into the oval area, torch held high. Everyone else crouched and held their breath, watching the clear figure of a small woman in a *stola*. She watched them, holding one hand high in the air, as if about to hurl some spell.

Drust walked casually up to her, right up, climbed the plinth and leaned casually against her, one elbow on her head.

'Make your honours to Venus Cloacina,' he said, loud enough to boom his voice round the space and make them wince. Shamefaced, they trooped out.

'I knew all the time,' Ugo lied, but everyone was prowling round to examine the object, a balustrade of rusted iron circling the statue. Up close, the statue was worn and the nose was missing, the upraised hand held something that might have been flowers and there was a thin stone pillar with a time-worn bird caught in flight on it.

'Flowers and birds,' Quintus noted, 'all symbols of Venus. Never seen any shrine to Cloacina before, though.'

'Not much worshipped these days,' Kag admitted, 'but she is the symbol of purity and filth, so where better to raise her up than here.'

'Raised by the engineers,' Dog said, signalling to Drust to bring the torch. He pointed to a plaque near a grille in the right-hand wall and they squinted at it. It was streaked with green stains and the inscription was mostly lost, save for the words *Aqua Traiana*. Even Dog could work that out.

'This is us,' Dog said, and studied the grille. Peering beyond it, he saw only the faint outline of more brick, another arched tunnel. The grille itself was buried deep in silt, but Dog pointed out the way the bars of it vanished into a slit at the top.

'It raises up,' he said. 'Probably to allow the engineer gangs in and out. Ugo...'

Ugo tried. They all tried, but the grille stayed stubbornly shut and half buried. They struck it hard a few times and found the rust on it was only a veneer – underneath, the iron seemed solid. The noise of it, though, the great bell clangs that echoed up and down and around, made them all determined not to do it again.

'We will summon them to us,' Sib said, as if no one had worked that out.

'We will have to dig it out,' Ugo said, and everyone looked at one another. Drust handed the torch to Dog and hefted the pick.

'Just as well I did not leave this behind, then,' he said and handed it to Ugo. 'You first, giant of the Germanies.'

Ugo spat on his hands and got down to it, the thunk of the tool and the odd accidental slam on the iron making everyone clench until the rhythm of it eased on the nerves.

'Thank fuck for Trajan,' Kag said, sitting on the plinth and wiping the sweat from his face with a rag. Quintus scratched his beard, dug out the itching culprit and cracked it between the broken nails of finger and thumb.

'Hardly fair on the Divine Domitian,' he said, leaning on the goddess. 'I mean, it was him who started it so the Flavian would get finished. It was only blessed and official during the time of Trajan.'

'Always someone trying to steal Jove's thunder,' Kag agreed. 'And take your hand off the arse of Cloacina – it does not surprise me that you would feel up a goddess, even a stone one, but I don't want your whoreson behaviour to get me sixed. If we get out of here at all, stay clear of me lest I get smacked by the thunderbolt meant for you.'

'When,' Quintus said, stressing the word, 'we get out of here, I will take myself to a part of the City where the women are not stone and don't object to being felt up.'

'Then you will die soon after,' Manius said, 'since that means old haunts and they will find you, double quick.'

Quintus scrubbed his beard, not liking the truth of it and yet forced to throw his plans in a discarded heap.

'Where will we go?' Sib asked. 'We have no coin – what happened to those manumissions, Dog?'

'The copper? I rolled them up and sold them to a smith for melting.'

'Fuck you,' Kag declared miserably. 'That was all we got out of this mess and now you have thrown it away for a *sestertius*.'

'Several, as it happens,' Dog admitted cheerfully. 'Helped fund my way through Gaul and Apulia and everywhere else so I could get to you lot and free you. Thank me later.'

'Besides,' Drust offered, 'those copper squares were just the ones you get for framing on the wall. The truth is registered on the Hill; we are citizens and freedmen.'

He hefted out the pouch Plancus had handed to him. 'And our old boss hasn't forgotten us.'

When he opened it, even he was surprised by the gleam of gold; everyone crowded to look, fixed by the shine of it.

'Three apiece,' Drust noted, 'and from the time of the Divine Vespasianus, not those clunkers of old Severus.'

'Unclipped,' Ugo noted, with a practised eye. 'The boss is generous, right enough. Lot of good drink in three gold pieces.'

'Well, hand mine over, then,' Quintus said, sticking out a hand and hopping down from Cloacina.

'Not so fast,' Drust said, picking out a stone among the golden eggs and holding it up. Everyone squinted at it, puzzled. It was a stamped pewter token.

'It's a token,' Drust said, 'one of those giving access to the boss's grain stores.'

'He only has one such,' Sib pointed out. 'In Lepcis Magna...'

His voice trailed off and everyone groaned. Kag spat sideways. Drust scooped the coins and token back into the pouch and the light seemed to dim a little.

'Servilius Structus wants us to go to Lepcis Magna?' Ugo asked. 'Why?'

Drust did not know, nor care overly much. It was a direction and with the stipend for it, same as they had been handed before every enterprise, and he said as much.

'We are the *Procuratores*,' he added, looking round them all. 'Did you have better places to go?'

'Away from all this,' Quintus muttered. 'I plan to head for the Den. No one can get you in the Den.'

'You think that?' Drust declared, 'If so, Fortuna walk with you.'

'Fortuna will cut your balls off,' Dog said. 'Staying in Rome? You might as well hurl yourself into Father Tiber and drown.

I favour Emesa and will go there – but Lepcis Magna is a fair stepping stone to the right part of the world, so I will take the bounty of Servilius Structus and be grateful for strength in numbers.'

'Me also,' Ugo declared, slapping his chest. Drust fixed him with a jaundiced eye.

'Then why have you stopped digging us out?'

Ugo went back to it with even more frantic viciousness than before and Drust went with him, to provide the light. He was happier than he had been for a long time and all of it was from knowing that they would be together for a little longer. Dog saw it and laughed.

'This is the only *familia* you have. All those years as a slave in the *harena* have left you with nothing else.'

'You have a mother and brother, of course,' Drust snapped back. 'A wife waiting with something tasty in the kitchen and tastier in the bedroom. Friends who are not dead.'

He felt ashamed of it as soon as the words were out, but Dog shrugged.

'I have a mother and a son,' he said, and Drust did not need to ask who they were. He nodded. We are the same, he thought, Dog and me. Of all of us, though, he will be the first to leave...

'This is the way of it,' Dog said, squatting in the bloody pool of flickering light, drawing in the silt with the point of his *gladius*. 'Through that grille and to the left a little way is a set of steps. It used to be the way the engineers came after inspecting the top of the aqueduct, but this part has been closed for some years. According to Plancus, the aqueduct comes into the City up on the Janiculum...'

'Jupiter's cock, that's high,' Kag noted. 'Will we have to climb up that? And how do we get across the Father?'

'The aqueduct leaps the river on four stone columns according to Plancus. High above the Tiber. Engineer gangs climb up and walk it all the time, looking for leaks,' Dog said. 'Once we are over the City walls on the Janiculum, we can come down, pretending to be one of the water gangs. Then we head out along the Portuensis to old Claudius's port – we all knew it well enough, for we have sailed in and out many times.'

'I know people there,' Drust said. 'We can get away from there.'

'It's not far,' Kag said, seeing it. 'We could make this yet…'

'We may have to hurry a little,' Manius said, loping back from where he had been watching and listening to the shadows. 'They have caught up with us.'

Everyone froze at that and, in the silence, they heard the shouts and the rattle of armoured men. Drust turned and found Ugo, standing with his mouth open and the pick in one hand.

'Dig,' he yelled.

Dog ran to where the tunnel mouth gawped and Kag joined him, then Quintus and Sib and Manius. They would defend here, choking the Urbans in the tunnel – if they spilled out, then numbers will do for us, Drust thought.

He went to where Ugo flurried up silt with the pick, which he threw down with a sudden gesture, bent and gripped the exposed bottom of the grille; Drust saw the muscles on his shoulders bunch as if something struggled to be free.

He added his own strength, puny though it was in comparison. The grille creaked and cracked, flaking off rust, and Drust saw that the slit above was choked. He took his sword and raked it with the point, careless of what he did to the blade – more rust showered down.

Ugo heaved and strained and the grille started to creak upwards, while Drust risked a glance at the others.

They were dancing, it seemed to him, until he realised they were skipping out of the way of thrown javelins. When he saw the first spear points waver out of the tunnel entrance, his heart tried to hammer a way out of his ribcage.

Pilae and spears. This was not the Urban Cohorts, but the Praetorians and those, for all folk sneered at them as peacocks, were Danube legion veterans. Old Severus had replaced the previous Praetorians with these and they were loyal to him – and his sons.

They were also experts.

Drust gripped and hauled even harder, roaring it out while Ugo did the same until their ears buzzed. When he had to stop, gasping and tear-eyed, he saw Kag with blood all over his face, Dog batting spear points aside and trying to stab a soldier with quick strikes, Quintus laughing, smashing the metal rim of a stolen shield into someone unseen.

He heard it, too, the crunch and smash of it. The die-you-fucker of it. He saw Manius reeling out the pack, cursing and flinging one hand up, trailing blood from the cut.

Ugo bent and growled and heaved. The grille cracked and screeched up while Drust gawped at the sight, then sprang to help. It rose two thirds of the way, then there was a loud, thin crack of sound and Ugo grunted as the grille sank.

Something had broken. A counterweight, Drust thought, which made lifting the great heavy thing easy, but now that was gone and the grille hung in Ugo's massive fists, with just enough room for a man to squeeze under.

'Back,' he yelled, then saw Quintus throw the stolen shield to one side in favour of a dropped spear. He ran to where the sweat and screeches and grunts seemed to swamp him, snatched up the shield and ran back.

He rammed it sideways and Ugo gratefully let the grille sink until it ground onto the metal rim. The shield bowed a little, then held while Ugo ground himself under it and slid down a few feet into water.

'Back,' Drust yelled, and watched Quintus and Kag turn and spring back, launching into a sliding skid that took them under the grille and out to the passage beyond, a drop that made them yelp as they splashed into unseen water.

'Sib,' Drust yelled. He saw Sib start to move and the errant spear that flew through the entrance, missing him with the point and smacking him in the face with the shaft as he ran into it. He went down in a flurry of waving arms like an upturned beetle, then crawled weakly to his hands and knees.

Manius turned, dragged him up and threw him at the grille. Then he and Dog stood shoulder to shoulder and backed off slowly, while men with big shields and spears spilled out.

Drust slid under and stood uneasily balanced, trying to reach up and snag some part of Sib's clothing; he heard Ugo and the others splashing away.

'Go, Dog,' he heard Manius say as Sib started to crawl weakly under the grille. Drust grabbed him and hauled him through, throwing him into the water beyond, where he splashed and yelled.

Dog gave a final, fearful snarl at the men and spun away, sprinting and sliding as he went, showering Drust with damp grit and sand. Manius danced. He seemed like smoke and oil and Drust heard a voice yelling for him to be brought down.

'He will not make it,' Dog declared and, as if he had heard him, Manius turned once and Drust's breath stopped, for he swore the eyes that stared at them were black. He nodded at them, stepping sideways to avoid a thrust he could not even see.

Dog kicked the shield once, twice and it grated sideways, then collapsed. The grille slammed down like a knell.

'Move,' Dog said, clapping Drust on one shoulder.

–

Drust dropped into water that seemed slick, but it was ankle deep and he sloshed after Dog, hearing the ring of steel on steel, the shouts. He felt sick all the way up what seemed a long tunnel of dark, for he had no torch.

Then they were shapes and looming faces. 'Here. Over here. Anyone got a torch?'

And then – 'Where's Manius?'

'Sixed,' Dog said tersely, and looked up the steps, testing the rusting balustrade; it swung and creaked.

'Manius? Gone?' Kag said.

'For sure?' Ugo growled mournfully.

'Possibly,' Sib declared darkly. 'You do not kill *jnoun* so easily.'

The words fell on Drust like searing brands.

'Fuck you, you goat-fucking sand louse,' he spat back. 'He saved you. He saved you and you still think he is some demon from Dis…'

Kag laid one gentling hand on Drust's forearm as people milled and waited at the foot of the steps.

'Ease,' he said. 'You always knew you would not get us all away.'

It was exactly what chewed Drust and he did not want to be soothed – but Quintus slammed a door on it by announcing he could hear the grille screeching. When they fell silent to listen, they all heard it; the Praetorians were opening it.

'Juno's tits,' Kag growled. 'Just leave us alone…'

'There's a door here.'

Dog's voice was a faint echo from what seemed a long way up. 'It's closed. Ugo, I need you...'

'In the name of all the gods above and below,' Kag spat. 'Fuck their mothers. Are we never to get out of this place?'

'I hear a monster ahead,' Sib yelped fearfully. 'I hear it splashing...'

'Palace rats behind, giant rats in front... well, I will take the giant rats,' Quintus said, his grin wide and mad.

'You can't go that way,' Drust said dully. 'It's the outflow. It gets too narrow, Dog says. You'd have to not be a giant rat to get out.'

'If one of them sea cows can get up,' Quintus argued, 'then I can.'

'There isn't a sea cow,' Drust spat back, exasperated.

'Listen, lads,' Kag said, 'can we start thinking about the bastards coming up the tunnel? They will get to us before any sea cow.'

'Splashing is getting louder,' Sib exclaimed. 'It's coming down on us...'

There was a sudden blast of cold air, a chill that blew away the sweat and all the veiled mists in Drust's head. His stomach lurched.

'Get up the steps. Up the steps. That's no sea cow. The games are done for the day...'

They scrabbled for the steps, throwing themselves up just as men with shields and spears came sloshing up. Drust, the last man, turned to see the one in the lead, a big man in full armour, his torch dyeing his face with bloody light as he pointed a sword and yelled for his men to go on.

Then Macrinus saw the wall of water thrashing down the tunnel, spilled from the sluice and galloping like mad, white-maned horses to relieve the pressure on the too-small pipes of the Flavian sewers.

He gave a bellow and lost the shield, springing for the steps and the rusted balustrade. The wall of water hit him and his men. They vanished into the spray with brief shrieks, but Drust turned as he reached the pack above, struggling with the door.

Macrinus hung on grimly with one hand; he would not let go of the sword in the other.

Ugo and Dog were slamming the door in rhythm with their shoulders. Kag turned and looked at Drust.

'What was that?' he demanded. 'Sib says sea monsters came down the tunnel.'

'Just washing some turds out,' Drust said as cheerfully as he could manage. 'Can we hurry?'

The door burst open with a shattering bang and Ugo fell through. There was a blast of rain-wet air, cold and sweet, and then, suddenly, they were out onto a walkway, looking at rat eyes in the darkness.

'Ho,' said Kag, crouching. Then everyone realised, as the wind soughed clouds from the moon, that they were on the aqueduct above the Tiber and the rat eyes were the distant pinprick waver of lights from the torches and fires of Rome.

'Fuck,' Ugo said sombrely. 'We have made it.'

'That way,' Dog said, pointing to the gleam of ribbon-black water and the walkways on either side, 'leads to the Janiculum. And freedom…'

'Halt.'

The voice shattered the night, the reverent silence and their dreams, making them all spin to face it.

Macrinus hauled himself out of the door, soaked and panting, sword in one fist.

'Come quietly, in the name of all the gods. Or I will set my men on you.'

'Move,' Drust said over his shoulder. Dog laughed, soft and admiring, then trotted off. Sib followed and Ugo, reluctantly, lumbered after. Quintus paused for a moment, but Kag slapped his arm and he went off.

'You too, Kag,' Drust said. Kag grunted and moved.

Macrinus stepped out. 'You're an annoying little sod,' he said, shaking water off him like a hound from a river. 'You really think you can stand against the Praetorian.'

'I am not. There is you – all the rest of your men are drowned or almost so. No one is coming up those steps behind you. I sent the others away because you will die here if you try and fight us all.'

'And now you believe you can do this on your own?'

'I am pointing out that you can live,' Drust said, feeling his bowels slide queasily. He hoped his voice sounded less trembled to Macrinus than it did to him. 'You can turn and go back down those steps and, when the surge stops, find your way back.'

'I was sent to take you. You in particular if I could get no one else. I have one and soon I will have the rest of you. The Hood will suffer nothing less.'

Drust shook his head. 'It will not happen. Take what is offered. Turn and go.'

'You arrogant fuck,' Macrinus spat. 'You were never any good in the *harena* – you think you can stand against me? I have fought more than you have eaten. My first baby shit was harder than you.'

Drust waggled his head from side to side. Each moment bought the others time and his heart was thundering with the news that Manius was not dead. It made him smile; Macrinus saw it as a sneer and his anger tipped over the brim.

Drust should have been thinking about what he would do when that happened. About feint and thrust and footwork on this high, awkward, narrow place – but all he could think about was his mother's face. Kag had always said he was a sentimental arse-brain and that had no place in the *harena;* it seemed now he was right.

Macrinus darted forward, lashing out with an underhand stroke designed to take the point of the *gladius* at Drust's throat. He was so surprised by it that he barely managed to lurch back a pace, found himself with a heel over the walkway and took a short drop into the water.

He floundered, found his footing in the waist-deep flow and backed off while Macrinus prowled, unable to reach Drust; he could only watch impotently as Drust clawed himself up the far side and stood, shivering and dripping.

Macrinus pointed his sword. 'You think that was clever? You think you have escaped?'

Honestly, yes, Drust thought. He almost said it, then saw Macrinus take several short quick steps along the walkway and hurl himself into the air. He watched with sick admiration and fear as the man landed lightly on the other walkway – lightly, by all the gods, and he wore polished body armour with the outline of muscles which were probably no lie to what lay beneath.

Macrinus advanced on him and Drust parried, blocked, backed off and wished, prayed, dreamed of an opening he could use to strike back. The bell rings were whipped away in the night wind on top of the aqueduct; all Rome seemed to be waiting for the inevitable outcome.

Macrinus stamped and flicked with flourishes – left himself open, just for a moment, an eye-blink of arrogant warrior.

Drust poised for it, started to strike, and then saw it was a feint and couldn't stop himself.

He felt the sword spin out of his hand as if something had wrenched it. Heard it tinkle and splash into the water of the canal, then tried to spring back as Macrinus rushed close. He saw the bearded snarl, the dark, raging eyes and, too late, the sword pommel that smacked him in the breastbone, driving all the air out.

He collapsed, gasping and wheezing, while Macrinus took two steps back, flourishing the sword in easy circles.

'Well, I hope you play dice better than you fight,' he said, 'because this gamble has failed. Get up.'

Why? Drust would have asked it aloud if he had breath, but he had even less when Macrinus slammed a boot into him and skittered him almost off the walkway; he scrabbled frantically to stop hitting the small lip that was all the barrier between him and a long drop to the Tiber.

'I was told to bring you alive,' Macrinus went on bitterly. 'Pained, but alive. I was told I could do one particular thing to you and I will do it now. Then I will drag you back down those steps by your ankle.'

He stepped forward and Drust tried to rise up but each limb felt it weighed far too much.

'I shall cut your balls off,' Macrinus said, 'and drag you away from here to find a torch to cauterise the wound. I would not want you to die before The Hood has his full measure.'

He kicked Drust's numbed legs apart, splaying them like a spatchcocked chicken and poised the sword. Even in the dark, Drust thought numbly, this bastard will not miss…

'You threw for the dog,' Macrinus said, raising the blade, 'and failed at the last.'

'You always have to throw the dog to win,' said a voice, and Macrinus jerked, too late, as the whirling *gladius* came out of the dark.

It wasn't balanced for throwing and smacked Macrinus flatly on his armour, the pommel striking his face, making him curse and reel back. Drust looked weakly up, in time to see Dog step over him, but his hands were empty. Macrinus shook blood from his nose and snarled.

'Well, well – now I get two...'

'Three,' said Kag.

'Four,' echoed Ugo.

'I am Five,' said Quintus, grinning wide as the Tiber. 'Which is apt, don't you think?'

Macrinus backed off a little, but no one seemed to have a weapon and he started to grin. 'Come to your senses, eh.'

'Six,' said a spluttering voice at his feet and he looked down, in time to see the wet black glisten of Sib's face emerging from where he had swum, underwater and silently, to come up at Macrinus's ankles.

Which he grabbed and pulled.

Macrinus gave a hoarse cry and clattered to the walkway and suddenly everyone was moving, it seemed to Drust. There were shouts and clangs and then Macrinus was up on his feet, held in the bear grip of Ugo, struggling and red faced. Kag had his sword and tickled his throat with it.

Drust wanted to tell them that the man was a senior centurion of the Praetorian, an *aedile* who wore a toga with narrow russet-red stripes on it. A man of substance...

But he knew Kag would probably cut Macrinus's throat – so he was surprised when Dog thrust his death face up close and stared Macrinus in the eye.

'Can you swim?' he asked.

If there was answer, it vanished in a descending rush of scream as Ugo heaved the man over the aqueduct lip to spiral in a whirl of arms and legs down into the river.

'Father Tiber take you,' he intoned piously.

'Bet the bastard can swim,' Kag answered bitterly. There was a dull, distant splash, then hands hauled Drust up and held him while he wobbled. Kag grinned. Dog added his terrible parody to it.

'Leave you to fight like a gladiator?' he said wryly. 'Didn't think we were actually going to go along with that, did you? Then he thrust out his hand, palm down, fingers splayed. One by one the others closed in and formed the circle, with one space left.

Drust filled it with his own hand and spoke hoarsely, while the wind beckoned them to freedom.

'*Uri, vinciri, verberari, ferroque necari.*'

Later…

Matemas

Somewhere in Africa, south of the Imperium

Gorlades was late, but he had been late the year before and the one before that. Since the people he visited were going nowhere, he wasn't concerned – but he knew they wanted what he brought, be it fish sauce, decent wine, the smell of Rome – and news.

He came to fetch the animals these people trapped, filling in requests for the exotic from Servilius Structus, who had them from the curator of the Flavian, or the Faleria, or the Capua or a score of other venues. Last year it had been cameleopards. This year it was river lizard. Did not matter much, since they all ended up dead.

He was greeted and looked at, as he did with them – they looked leaner, darker and more feral than ever but there were a handful of them and they had somehow made the surrounding tribals work for them. Gorlades knew the surrounding tribals as naked ebonies wearing beads, most of them sweat. They ate one another…

He settled himself, they dealt with the ladings and the payments and then fell on the olives he brought, moaning with ecstasy. Finally, he told them that this might well be the last trip he made.

The heads came up; the olives lost their attraction.

'Servilius Structus has gone to his gods. Peacefully.'

'He was old,' Kag admitted bleakly. 'Still…'

'So we have to leave here?' Drust demanded, more harshly than he had intended. It seemed inconceivable that Servilius Structus had died, just like an ordinary man. He felt cheated and bereft at the same time – he'd had questions he had always wanted to put to him and now never would.

Gorlades indicated it was true with a delicate wave of one thin-wristed hand. His long spider fingers plucked another olive. 'His business affairs are being wound up. I do not know who owns what now – but beasts for the *harena* is not an enterprise that is profitable.'

They sat in silence, working the news around, each trying to feel something more than a wonder at what happened now. He'd been their master and patron, a facet of their lives for so long – they'd been relatively safe, relatively comfortable here because he had cared enough to work at making it so.

Yet no one could mourn him like a lost father, even though they had his name.

'Of course,' Gorlades said suddenly. 'I leave the juiciest news until last – there is a new Emperor.'

'Again? There was a new one when last we met,' Quintus said, and Gorlades acknowledged it. The name of that one had astounded them at the time, Drust recalled – Macrinus. Kag had looked at them all and said slyly: 'I win my bet – he could swim after all.'

'Alas, yes,' Gorlades explained, 'Macrinus has succumbed to the disease of all Roman emperors, it appears – he has become a god.'

'Dead?'

'Fled from a battle with the forces of the new Emperor. Made it as far as Chalcedon, I am hearing, before he was killed. His son is also dead.'

'Fuck him up the arse, then,' Ugo declared. 'Fortuna shows some style for that one. The Hood was a rancid cunny but he didn't deserve to be sixed by that treacherous bastard while taking a piss in the desert. That was a bad death.'

'There are few good ones,' Kag growled back.

'New Emperor?' Drust interrupted.

'Yes,' Gorlades said, 'Marcus Aurelius Antoninus Augustus. They say he is the risen image. The son.'

'Of Marcus Aurelius?' Drust demanded, bewildered. Gorlades laughed.

'No, no. Of the late Divinity Antoninus, known better as Marcus Aurelius Severus Antoninus. Better known as…'

'The Hood,' Kag finished. 'What son? Drust kicked…'

Quintus saw it and laughed, cutting Kag off and making him scowl.

'The boy,' Quintus explained. 'The golden boy? Dog's little Sun God is now an emperor. Gods above and below – he really was The Hood's son after all.'

'You think Dog is now a senator?' Sib asked, and they laughed; Dog had left for Emesa long since but he could just as easily be dead as a senator. Yet the thought of that skull face swinging round all the old serious pomposities on the floor of the chamber, lecturing them on this or that – well, it reduced Quintus to a ruin of laughing and his infection spread to the others.

'I have not heard of one with a face you described,' Gorlades said, and then waved his flywhisk at Sib. 'Nor the *mavro* with smoke in his eyes, Sib – I must say you fellows are as colourful as ever…'

'Well,' Quintus said when he had recovered, his grin as wide as the Tiber. 'You know what this means, lads?'

They stopped laughing and stared at him as he spread his hands into their dullness.

'We can go back to Rome. It's safe now.'

'We can claim favour,' Sib said, seeing it suddenly. 'That boy loved us, remember?'

Drust saw men struggling with the cameleopard, others loading a lion in a cage onto a two-wheeled cart. We can go home with this last load, he thought, and eventually said it aloud. It was Kag who found the truth of it, his grin a twist of bitterness.

'Just one more pack of beasts from beyond the Wall.'

Notes

This novel is based on certain historical events. In AD 208, the Emperor Severus had ruled the Empire for fifteen years. He was now advanced in years, but had two sons, Antoninus and Geta. Antoninus was the elder and had been made co-emperor when he was young, which only added to his general level of brat. The teenage Antoninus ran the streets with a crowd of his peers, beating up anyone they met and wearing masks or cloaks with hoods – he had his nickname, Caracalla, after the same hooded cloak, though few if any used it to his face.

In a last attempt at glory – and to instil some discipline and cooperation in his sons – Severus decided to bring all of Britannia into the Empire. In 208 he moved massive Roman forces and the entire imperial court to Eboracum (York), where it remained for three years. In a last-ditch attempt to force his sons to cooperate, he made Geta a co-emperor, which only split them into two rival camps of plot and counter-plot.

Part of this festering court were the 'Julias': the Empress Julia, her sister Julia Maesa and Julia Maesa's daughter, Julia Soaemias, as well as Julia Soaemias's son, Sextus Varius. While Severus was North African and frequently trumpeted as the 'first black emperor of Rome', the actual impact of his skin colour probably had less to do with his strangeness to Romans than the fact that he came from outside the European heartland of Empire. His wife and all her relatives, who were essentially

Syrian and priestesses of a strange Eastern cult of the Sun, only added to the unease.

In AD 211, with Severus failing in health and Caracalla fretting that his father wasn't failing half fast enough, the imperial court at Eboracum was ripe with plots and counter-plots, with brother against brother and followers of both in between.

That year, Severus returned from an attempt to take command of the army which proved too much for his health. There is an account of him being made anxious by some encounter on the road into Eboracum and subsequently dying, possibly of a heart attack or a stroke, the same evening.

Thereafter, the two brothers jointly ruled the Empire – until Caracalla, in front of his mother, knifed Geta to death and assumed sole control in AD 212. By AD 217 Caracalla was attempting a military victory against Parthia and was in Edessa when he stopped for a 'rest break'. It was there that he was stabbed, possibly not by Macrinus, by then the Praetorian Prefect – though he quickly took advantage of it and made himself Emperor.

Not long afterwards, the legions, whipped up by the formidable Julia Maesa and her relatives, were persuaded that young Varius, the image of Caracalla, was that dead Emperor's son. Since Macrinus was making a mess of things, they quickly announced their support for the boy and, not long afterwards, Macrinus fled from a losing battle, was run down and killed.

The boy-Emperor then decided on the title of Heliogabalus, or Elagabalus. He subsequently became one of the worst emperors Rome had – Gibbon, for example, writes that Elagabalus 'abandoned himself to the grossest pleasures and ungoverned fury'. Much of his bad reputation, apart from the usual debauchery you might expect from an ungoverned, overprivileged youth, was his disregard for Roman religious traditions and sexual taboos.

Five years after his formidable grandmother, Julia Maesa, installed him as emperor she devised his assassination and replacement by his cousin, Severus Alexander.

This, then, is the background. The foreground belongs to Hadrian and Antonine – the Walls of Britannia. There is, of course, no historical record of Julia Soaemias or her son being north of the Antonine Wall – or, indeed, being in Britain at all. However, since the Empire was ruled from York for almost three years, the court was there and anyone who was anyone in the imperial family would have been there, too.

The 'heroes' of this tale are a band of amphitheatre performers, sometime gladiators, horse handlers and charioteers. These are not the sort of crowd pleasers who ended up on commemorative cups or had their names slathered all over Rome's walls, and are far removed from Maximus or Spartacus. They are seedy, slightly desperate men out to try and raise themselves from the stigma of being former slaves and socially disgusting gladiators. Worse still, in their own eyes, they are dirt poor. Nor are these fighters the heroic legionaries who have made modern Roman tales so popular. Their stories are far removed from the works which climb inside the heads of Nero, or Trajan, or Marcus Aurelius, or any of the other emperors with a bit of documented history to them.

They once blazed bright colours under a hot Roman sky – and should be remembered for it.

Acknowledgements

The people without whom…

Kate, my long-suffering wife, the bedrock, lodestar and frequently abandoned woman who puts up with me living in some strange century with stranger people for protracted periods.

Jim Gill of United Agents, a loyal and determined friend who has been instrumental in getting what I write to the right people for more years than I care to remember.

The good and professional people at Canelo – Kit, Michael and others. You know who you are.

The loyal fans of my writing out there. More power to you and I hope you enjoy this new direction.

Glossary

Auctoratio

Most gladiators were slaves but some were volunteers. The *auctoratio* was the swearing of a legal agreement by free men who joined a school for whatever reason and for a contracted period, by which they handed themselves over as slaves to their master and trainer, agreeing to submit to beating, burning, and death by the sword if they did not perform as required. Gladiators were expected to accept death. The familiar 'we who are about to die salute you' was used once only by gladiators forced to fight in a naval battle on a lake in armour and who expected that even if they won they'd drown. It was shouted as an ironic protest to Emperor Claudius, whose less well-known response was simply: 'or not, as the case may be'.

Dis Manibus

A standard phrase of dedication to the 'Manes', the spirits of the dead. Effectively they are being warned that there's another one on the way. In the gladiatorial amphitheatre it was an actual person, also known as Charun, the Roman form of Charon, the Greek demi-god who ferried the dead across ther Styx. Pluto, the Roman fgod of the underworld was also used. A man traditionally masked as someone from the underworld, accompanied by other masked helpers would stab the fallen to make sure they were dead and, if not, use a traditional hammer to make sure of it. Then others would hook the body by the heels and drag if off through the Gate of Death. Those who had survived left they way they had entered, through the Gate of Life.

The Morning Shows

Starting early, the arena served as a place of dramatic public execution, including *damnatio ad bestias* or *obiectio feris* (throwing people to the beasts). The victims were *noxii*, criminals, deserters, rebels, traitors, runaway slaves, and those guilty of various sorts of antisocial behaviour. In the 3rd century, few if any Christians were persecuted in Rome itself – but the provinces threw them to the lions in droves.

The Ludi

Games in general, and festivals involving games. Games could be private, public, or extraordinary – since gladiators were so expensive to train and keep they fought three or four times a year and, unless the giver of the games – the *editor* – paid for it, there was no fight to the death. Contests were, in fact, one-on-one and regulated by a referee, usually a former gladiator. Criminals and prisoners could be damned to fight in the arena, with the hope of a reprieve if they survived a certain number of years. These men were trained in a specialized form of combat. Others, untrained, were expected to die within a short time. There were also volunteer gladiators, ones who either enlisted voluntarily as free or freed men, or who reenlisted after winning their freedom. Even *equites* and, more rarely, senators sometimes enlisted. The word 'gladiator' simply means 'swordsman'.

Ludus

The gladiator 'school'. It's estimated that there were more than 100 gladiator schools throughout the empire. New gladiators were formed into troupes called *familia gladiatorium* which were under the overall control of a manager (*lanista*) who recruited, arranged for training and made the decisions of where and when the gladiators fought... There were gladiator schools near all the major cities around Rome and one of the ones which has stayed in history is that of Batiatus in Capua where Spartacus was trained. But the most famous gladiator schools of all were those in Rome: The Great Gladiatorial Training School (*Ludus Magnus*), which was actually connected to the Flavian Ampitheatre by a tunnel, The Bestiaries School (*Ludus matutinus*) which specialised in training those who fought, handled and trained the exotic wild beasts, The Gallic School (*Ludus Gallicus*), smallest of the schools which specialised in training heavily-armoured fighters and The Dacian School (Ludus Dacicus), which trained lightly-armoured fighters in the use of the sicari sword, a short curved weapon about 16 inches long.

Ludum venatorium (venatio)

The animal hunts - *venatores* were skilled men usually pitted against carnivorous beasts; *bestiarii* were animal-handlers and killers of less skill and finesse. Literary accounts and inscriptions often stress the numbers of animals killed. As in gladiatorial combat, men condemned to fight or perform in such games could sometimes win their freedom. By now, the 3rd century, the games had degenerated into vicious spectacle, with such crowd-pleasers as children hung up by the heels to see which of the starving dogs could leap high enough to get a bite, foxes let loose with their tails on fire and worse.

Flavian

Now better known as the Coliseum, it was, originally known as the Flavian Amphitheatre because of the Flavian family of emperors involved in it. Commisioned in AD 72 by Emperor Vespasian, completed by his son, Titus, in AD80, with later improvements by Domitian. Located just east of the Forum, it was built to a practical design, with its 80 arched entrances allowing easy access to 55,000 spectators, who were seated according to rank. The Coliseum is huge, an ellipse 188m long and 156 wide. Originally 240 masts were attached to stone corbels on the 4th level to provide shade on hot days. It was called the Coliseum because of a massive statue of Nero which stood nearby – later remodeled into the god Helios or Sol and sometimes the heads of succeeding emperors.

Harena

Literally – 'sand'. Possibly Etruscan, which was believed to be the origin of gladiatorial contests.

Missio

A gladiator who acknowledged defeat could request the *munerarius* to stop the fight and send him alive (*missus*) from the arena. If he had not fallen he could be 'sent away standing' (*stans missus*). The editor took the crowd's response into consideration in deciding whether to let the loser live or order the victor to kill him.

Munus (pl. munera)

The show (the term has a connotation of 'duty'). It usually lasted for three or more days and, under special circumstances, for weeks or months. Provincial games rarely lasted more than two days, but Titus's games in Rome for the inauguration of the completed Flavian in.AD80 lasted 100 days. The classic Italian *munus plena* included *venations* in the morning, various noontime activities (*meridiani*), and gladiatorial duels in the afternoon.

Munerarius (Editor)

The giver of the games. It could be a member of the nobler orders of Rome who put on the show privately (a rarity post-Republic) or in his official capacity as a magistrate or priest, or it was more likely the State, putting on Games whose dates and functions were set in the Roman calendar. Outside Rome, *munerarii* were generally municipal and provincial priests of the imperial cult, or local governors.

Omnes ad stercus

Not strictly a gladiatorial term, but certainly used by them and liberally scrawled on walls all over Rome. Best translation is: 'it's all shit', but 'we're in the shit' can also be used depending on context. It is not, as internet translations coyly have it 'get lost' or 'go to hell'.

Pompa

The parade that signaled the start of a gladiatorial *munus*; it included the *munerarius*, usually in some outlandish costume and carriage, the gladiators, musicians, a palm-bearer, and various other officials and personnel, such as a sign-bearer whose placard gave the crowd information about events, participants, and other matters, including the emperor's response to petitions.

Pollice verso

'With thumb turned.' Much debated signal, though most assume the thumb is turned down if a gladiator is to die. There are accounts of it being passed across the throat, turned to the heart etc etc.

Pugnare ad digitum

'To fight to the finger.' Combat took place until the referee stopped the fight or the defeated gladiator raised his finger (or his hand or whole arm) to signal the *munerarius* to stop the fight.

Recipere ferrum

To receive the iron. A defeated gladiator who was refused *missio* was expected to kneel and courageously accept death. His victorious opponent would stab him or cut his throat. The referee made sure it was done properly and swiftly.

Signum pugnae

The signal given by the *munerarius* for combat to begin. It is not always clear what form this took, and it may have varied.

Sine missione

'Without *missio*:' a fight with no possibility of a reprieve for the loser. Rare.

Six

Number tagged against a fighter's name in the Ludus he was part of when he had died. Origin unknown – but to be 'sixed' means you are a dead man.

Stantes missi

A draw, with both 'sent away standing'. Both gladiators walked away neither having won or lost.

Spectacula

Spectacles are the seats as well as the events viewed in the arena. *Harena* or *arena*, the sand sprinkled on the field of combat to absorb blood, can also signify the place of combat.

Eques

A gladiator who fought on horseback, like a Roman knight, against other mounted fighters. An *eques* carried a spear, but also used a sword, so he could dismount to duel with an opponent. His helmet often displayed two feathers on either side of the dome (with no crest).

Essedarius

A chariot-fighter who probably dismounted to fight hand to hand.

Familia gladiatorium

A troop of gladiators who lived and trained under one *lanista.*

Gallus

A Gaul, a type of heavily armed fighter named after the Romans' tribal enemy. The original *Galli* were probably war captives. This type of fighter died out in the Empire.

Hoplomachus

This gladiator was distinguished by his short, curved sword. Like a *Thrax*, he wore high leg guards.

Lanista

An owner, recruiter, trainer, and speculator in gladiators who sold or rented men to *munerarii.* In the Empire this job came under the jurisdiction of the emperor.

Liberatio

The freeing of a gladiator who had served his time (a period of years varying according to when and how he was inducted).

Manica

Arm padding of wrapped cloth and leather.

Murmillo

A fighter apparently named after a Greek word for fish. He wore a crested helmet and carried a tall shield.

Retiarius

This was the most distinctive-looking gladiator, a bareheaded, unshielded fighter whose main protection was padding and a shoulder guard on his left arm. He used a net to ensnare his opponent and a long trident to impale him.

Rudiarius

A gladiator who had received a *rudis* – the wooden sword that marked him a retired and no longer a slave - was therefore an experienced volunteer, especially worth watching. There was a hierarchy of experienced *rudiarii* within a *familia* of gladiators, and *rudiarii* could become trainers, helpers, and arbiters of fights, the referees. The most elite of the retired gladiators were dubbed *summa rudis*. The *summa rudis* officials wore white tunics with purple borders and served as technical experts to ensure that the gladiators fought bravely, skillfully, and according to the rules. They carried batons and whips with which they pointed out illegal movements. Ultimately the *summa rudis* officials could stop a game if a gladiator was going to be too seriously wounded, compel gladiators to fight on, or defer the decision to the editor. Retired gladiators who became *summa rudis* evidently achieved fame and wealth in their second careers as officials of the combats.

Samnis

Like the *Gallus*, the *Samnis* (Samnite) was originally an enemy of the Romans from Campania in the south. Captives taken in battle in the Republic undoubtedly provided the model for this type of heavily armed fighter.

Secutor

The 'follower' was paired with a *retiarius*. His armor was distinguished by a helmet with small eyeholes that would presumably impede the trident's prongs.

Thrax

The 'Thracian' was another type of fighter equipped like a former enemy soldier (from Thrace in northern Greece). He fought with a small, rectangular shield and his helmet bore a griffin crest.

Tiro

A gladiator fighting in his very first public combat.

Venator

Venatores were skilled spearmen, usually pitted against carnivorous beasts.

Veteranus

A veteran of one or more combats.

The Gear

Fascia

Protective band of material, skin, or leather that protected the leg below the knee and provided padding below a greave.

Fascina (or tridens)

The long, three-pronged metal trident that was the hallmark of a *retiarius*.

Galea

The helmet worn by all gladiators except the *retiarius*. These were domed and often featured decorative crests and visors pierced with eyeholes.

Galerus

The distinctive metal shoulder-guard of a *retiarius*. It curved up strongly from the shoulder, away from the neck, so that neck and head were protected but the fighter's head movements were not restricted.

Gladius

This was the long, straight sword of the gladiator after which he was named.

Ocrea

A metal leg guard that ran from the knee (or above) to the shin and protected mainly the front of the leg.

Parma

A round or square shield that was smaller and lighter than a *scutum*.

Pugio

A dagger, weapon of last resort of a *retiarius*.

Rudis

The wooden sword or staff symbolizing a gladiator's *liberatio*.

Scutum

A large rectangular shield (curving inward so that it formed part of a cylinder) of the sort carried by a *murmillo*.

Sica

A short, curved sword of the sort carried by a *Thrax*.

Subligaculum

A traditional loincloth worn by gladiators (the chest was almost always bare).

Brothers Of The Sands

Beasts Beyond The Wall

The Red Serpent

Beasts From The Dark